Approaches to Teaching Chaucer's *Canterbury Tales*

Second Edition

Approaches to Teaching
World Literature

For a complete listing of titles,
see the last pages of this book

Approaches to Teaching Chaucer's *Canterbury Tales*

Second Edition

Edited by

Peter W. Travis

and

Frank Grady

The Modern Language Association of America
New York   2014

MLA and the MODERN LANGUAGE ASSOCIATION are trademarks owned
by the Modern Language Association of America. For information about
obtaining permission to reprint material from MLA book publications, send your
request by mail (see address below) or e-mail (permissions@mla.org).

Library of Congress Cataloging-in-Publication Data

Approaches to Teaching Chaucer's Canterbury Tales / edited by
Peter W. Travis and Frank Grady. — Second edition.
pages cm. — (Approaches to Teaching World Literature ; 131)
Includes bibliographical references and index.
ISBN 978-1-60329-140-8 (cloth : alk. paper) —
ISBN 978-1-60329-141-5 (pbk. : alk. paper) —
ISBN 978-1-60329-196-5 (Kindle)
ISBN 978-1-60329-195-8 (EPUB)
1. Chaucer, Geoffrey, -1400. Canterbury tales.   2. Chaucer, Geoffrey, -1400—Study
and teaching.   3. Christian pilgrims and pilgrimages in literature.   4. Narrative poetry,
English—Study and teaching.   5. Tales, Medieval—Study and teaching.   I. Travis,
Peter W., editor of compilation   II. Grady, Frank, editor of compilation
PR1874.A67 2014
821'.1—dc23   2013042289

Approaches to Teaching World Literature 131
ISSN 1059-1133

Cover illustration for the paperback and electronic editions:
Ezra Winter, details of a mural illustrating characters in
The Canterbury Tales, Carol M. Highsmith Archive, Library of Congress.

Published by The Modern Language Association of America
26 Broadway, New York, NY 10004-1789
www.mla.org

CONTENTS

Strategies for Teaching

Theory in the Classroom

PREFACE

Approaches to Teaching Chaucer's Canterbury Tales was the first volume of the MLA Approaches to Teaching Masterpieces of World Literature series. Conceptualized and edited by Joseph Gibaldi, this inaugural work, published in 1980, established a standard that subsequent volumes in the series (now approaching over 130 in number) have sought to equal. A staple text in the personal libraries of Chaucerians, medievalists, and nonmedievalists alike, its fifteen essays on different ways of teaching *The Canterbury Tales* have had a long-lasting influence in thousands of classrooms. However, more than thirty years have passed since the appearance of *Approaches to Teaching Chaucer's* Canterbury Tales; in that time Chaucer scholarship has evolved in directions the authors of those essays could hardly have imagined, American pedagogical styles have changed dramatically, and new technologies have provided extraordinary opportunities to teach *The Canterbury Tales* in innovative ways. For these reasons and others, the Publications Committee of the MLA, at the recommendation of Joseph Gibaldi, determined that a second edition of *Approaches to Teaching Chaucer's* Canterbury Tales was in order. This edition is not intended to be a replacement of the first: the earlier essays are as useful now as they were then. Rather, arranged on the same model as the first, the second edition is a twenty-first-century update: a go-to handbook of scholarly information, pedagogical counsel, and teacher testimonials, whose primary purpose is to be immediately useful in the classroom. There is presently an overwhelming abundance of theoretical studies of Chaucer and of *The Canterbury Tales*—as our review of monographs, companions, and critical collections in the "Materials" section illustrates. By contrast, the hallmark of this volume is its focus on praxis: in ways large and small, how might we improve as teachers as we engage our students in the study of one of the great masterpieces of English literature?

This volume has been a collective effort from the start, beginning with questionnaires mailed to all members of the MLA who identified Chaucer as one of their teaching interests. The response was remarkable not only in the number of respondents (see "Survey Respondents") but in the care with which they answered the individual questions. Of all the messages conveyed, the most consistent and moving is how passionately Chaucerians love Chaucer's poetry and how intent they are in sharing that passion with their students. Some of us fear that Chaucer may be losing ground in the hearts and minds of the academy. Yet if these testimonies are at all representative, the study of Chaucer, and especially of *The Canterbury Tales*, would appear to be alive and well in the American undergraduate curriculum. Just as striking is how strongly our respondents feel about teaching the *Tales* in the original: with only one or two exceptions, respondents are persuaded that their students must become comfortable with Chaucer's Middle English and must make a major effort at mastering the sounds and rhythms of his verse. Impressed as we are by the wide variety of ideas and testimonials in these responses, we attempt to do them justice in "Survey Responses: A Selected Census," an appendix to the "Materials" section. Whereas the first edition of *Approaches to Teaching Chaucer's* Canterbury Tales featured fifteen essays, here we include thirty-six. We feel this increase in number reflects the variety of situations in which *The Canterbury Tales* is now being taught—not just traditional university and college settings but also two-year colleges, technical institutes, and high schools. It also reflects the expanding range of classroom needs and teaching styles that bespeaks an increasing emphasis in American undergraduate institutions on interactive learning within a diversified student body. Comparing the two volumes once again, we note that while the contributors to the first edition viewed the lecture as the keystone to their classes, the contributors to this edition view themselves as collaborative interrogators with their students, providing information, guidance, and creative criticism at appropriate moments of intervention.

One further impression inspired by some elements in the survey responses is that Chaucerians generally do not foreground theory in their classes, despite their own interests in theoretical issues. When asked in the questionnaire, "What kinds of critical approaches or methodologies have you found most helpful in teaching *The Canterbury Tales*? What approaches or methodologies do your students find most helpful?," the majority allow that with so many other challenges—historical, cultural, linguistic, and literary—going much beyond a New Critical or reader-response approach is something most students would find overly demanding. Yet one section of essays in this volume, "Theory in the Classroom," illustrates how theoretical concerns can be used imaginatively to shape one's teaching of *The Canterbury Tales*. And the remaining essays (especially when compared with the essays in the 1980 *Approaches to Teaching Chaucer's* Canterbury Tales) are clearly influenced by modes of theoretical interrogation distinctive to the twenty-first century. A number of questionnaire respondents initially assert that they do not emphasize theory in their *Canterbury Tales* class but then allow that they incorporate such approaches as feminism, psychoanalysis, Marxism, postcolonial theory, queer theory, structuralism, Robertsonianism, and postmodern theories of textuality into class discussions—but only intermittently and at strategic moments. Accordingly, this volume focuses on the practice of teaching *The Canterbury Tales* and not on critical theory as it might be applied; nevertheless, the essays that follow illustrate in their entirety how teaching Chaucer entails both enterprises of theory and practice moving along a Möbius-strip continuum.

The final questions on the questionnaire ask, "What sorts of information would you like to see in this second edition of *Approaches to Teaching Chaucer's* Canterbury Tales? What issues would you like to see addressed?" Among the many issues highlighted, a number of respondents asked about opportunities provided by the radically changing domain of information technology: What electronic, visual, and audiovisual materials are presently being used to teach

Chaucer? In what ways are these experiments working? How can digitalization empower the teaching of hybrid courses on *The Canterbury Tales*? How can long-distance students reading Chaucer in different places be provided a unified experience? Five essayists in the last section of this volume, *"The Canterbury Tales* in the Digital Age,"* address these and related matters, describing in some detail how they have designed Web-based courses, all the while acknowledging that new technologies will necessitate innovations every year.

We want to recognize the founding role of Susan Schibanoff in the early stages of this effort. A contributor to the first edition of *Approaches to Teaching Chaucer's* Canterbury Tales, she eloquently articulated the need for a second edition and assisted with its initial development. We also want to recognize the extraordinary help provided by our Dartmouth Presidential Scholars: Sarah White, Rachel Siegel, and Torrey Barrett. As research assistants, they reviewed with sophistication and insight the many early drafts that eventually evolved into the following essays. Finally, we wish to thank the following: Joseph Gibaldi, for initiating this second edition; James Hatch, acquisitions editor of the MLA office of scholarly communication, for overseeing its development; and Angela Gibson, associate managing editor of book publications, for her patience and diligence in bringing it to completion.

PWT and FG

Part One

MATERIALS

Editions

Middle English Editions

Chaucer's Complete Works

Chaucerians will not be surprised that the editors of this volume have selected *The Riverside Chaucer* as the standard for all citations. The work of a team of scholars under the general editorship of Larry Benson, *The Riverside Chaucer* (1987) has assumed the place of preeminence earlier enjoyed by its magisterial predecessor, F. N. Robinson's *Poetical Works of Chaucer* (1933; rev. 1957). Improving on the revised Robinson edition in innumerable ways—with larger print, the addition of marginal glosses, a much-expanded glossary, capacious explanatory notes and textual notes—*The Riverside Chaucer* was seen at the time of its publication as "virtually assured [of its] continuation as the standard scholarly edition" (Brosnahan 645). Yet because its bulk and cost were problematic, the Oxford University Press published a paperback *Riverside Chaucer* in 1988, reprinting the same text in 2000 with an added foreword by Christopher Cannon. The paperback *Riverside* is smaller and lighter, yet its reduced font size is not that easy on the eyes, its paper quality is rather poor, and its cost has remained only slightly below that of its hardcover sibling. Nevertheless, *The Riverside Chaucer*, hardbound or paperback, has no viable competitors at present. To most readers except editing and archival specialists interested in stemmatic manuscript studies, *Riverside* is likely to remain the definitive edition of the complete works of Chaucer for the near future.

The Canterbury Tales: Complete

Since it is *The Canterbury Tales* to the exclusion of Chaucer's other works that is most often the staple fare of undergraduate Chaucer courses, a number of inexpensive and reliable editions of the complete *Canterbury Tales* are, unsurprisingly, now in print. Larry Benson's Riverside edition The Canterbury Tales: *Complete* (2000) embraces all the virtues and strengths of *The Riverside Chaucer*; however, its cost—only slightly less than the hardbound *Riverside Chaucer*—is a major disincentive. Jill Mann's *The Canterbury Tales* (Penguin, 2005) has responded impressively to this problem. The work of one of our major medievalists, this quite sizable (1,254 pages) yet easy-to-read paperback is amplified by an impressive scholarly apparatus: a fifty-page interpretative introduction, bottom-of-the-page glossarial notes, 317 pages of explanatory endnotes, and a 142-page glossary.

Robert Boenig and Andrew Taylor's *The Canterbury Tales* (2012) is the most recent edition of the complete *Canterbury Tales*. Foregoing a self-standing glossary, explanatory notes, and textual notes, Boenig and Taylor provide marginal glosses and explanatory notes on each page. Their introduction is masterful, including sections titled "Chaucer's Life and Times," "The Construction of the *Canterbury Tales*," "Chaucer's English," "Chaucer's Versification," "Editorial Principles" and a thirty-page survey, "The Reception of Chaucer's Poetry," in which the editors lucidly trace *The Canterbury Tales*'s critical reception from the eighteenth to the twenty-first century. Another individuating feature are the book's background documents: a forty-two-page section of primary materials by medieval authors ranging from Saint Jerome and Boethius to William Langland and Jean Froissart and textual excerpts relating to historical matters such as the black death, the Peasants' Revolt, and the Jewish blood libel. Five hundred and two pages long, with attractive facsimiles from the Ellesmere manuscript, the Broadview *Canterbury Tales* is likely to give the Riverside and Penguin editions challenging competition in the marketplace of Chaucer classroom texts.

The Canterbury Tales: Selections

Since most undergraduate Chaucer classes study a limited number of tales, pared-down editions are becoming increasingly popular. These editions focus on a selection of tales and are enhanced with useful background materials. Now in its second edition, V. A. Kolve and Glending Olson's Norton Critical Edition, The Canterbury Tales: *Fifteen Tales and the General Prologue* (2005), includes fifteen of the twenty-four tales (always with their accompanying prologues).[1] The edition's second section, "Sources and Backgrounds," provides a useful array of primary texts that pertain directly to the tales: for example, fabliau analogues, for the Miller's and the Reeve's Tales; selections from the writings of Jean de Meun, Saint Jerome, Walter Map, Saint Paul, and John Gower, for The Wife of Bath's Prologue and Tale; Boccaccio's *Decameron*, day 10, novella 10, along with Petrarch's Griselda story, Petrarch's two letters to Boccaccio, and a snippet of *Le ménagier de Paris* for the Clerk's Tale; and "The Story of the *Alma Redemptoris Mater*," "A Miracle of Our Lady," *Alma Redemptoris Mater*, and a selection from Pope Gregory's "On Christian Mistreatment of Jews," for the Prioress's Tale. In the final section, "Criticism," Kolve and Olson include a selection of time-honored critical essays by F. R. H. Du Boulay, Arthur W. Hoffman, E. Talbot Donaldson, Barbara Nolan, George Lyman Kittredge, Lee Patterson, Paul Strohm, and Carolyn Dinshaw.

Boenig and Taylor's The Canterbury Tales: *A Selection* (second ed., 2013) includes fourteen tales (with their prologues).[2] The same excellent apparatus provided in Boenig and Taylor's complete *Canterbury Tales* is also found here: introductory materials, background materials, and facsimile pages from Ellesmere. Focusing in its closing section on primary texts rather than interpretive essays, this attractive and inexpensive 450-page paperback is positioned to give Kolve and Olson's Norton Critical Edition a run for its money.

Translations

Translations of *The Canterbury Tales* are ever abundant. They are used unreluctantly in some introductory and survey classes, and in many Chaucer classes they are used heuristically. (A useful assignment might focus on the language and verse of Chaucer's original and the success and limitations of modern adaptations.) From an earlier generation, Vincent F. Hopper's *Chaucer's* Canterbury Tales *(Selected): An Interlinear Translation* (1948) remains popular, as does Nevill Coghill's verse translation (1951). More recent translations include David Wright's *The Canterbury Tales* (2011) and Joseph Glaser's The Canterbury Tales *in Modern Verse* (2005). Both are attractive verse translations, although Glaser's dominant verse form is rhymed iambic tetrameter couplets. Burton Raffel's *The Canterbury Tales* (2008) is a lively rendering by one of the most accomplished translators of medieval texts, even if Raffel occasionally strays unaccountably from the original, as in "these twenty men / And women" for "nyne and twenty in a compaignye" (Raffel 4; GP, line 24). This translation is also available on CD-ROM, read by Raffel with strong "opinioun." The Parson's Tale, for example, is scornfully voiced with vitriolic ironies. Another recent verse translation of a majority of the tales is Sheila Fisher's *The Selected Canterbury Tales* (2011).

Anthologies

Oftentimes serving as core textbooks for undergraduate survey courses, several major anthologies of medieval and early modern literature include a significant number of the tales (and prologues), as well as selections of Chaucer's other poems. One notable anthology is Joseph Black's *The Broadview Anthology of British Literature: The Medieval Period* (2009). In addition to ten tales and the Retraction, this volume includes "To Rosemounde," *Parliament of Fowles*, "To His Scribe Adam," "Complaint of Chaucer to His Purse," "Lenvoy de Chaucer," and, from *Troilus and Criseyde*, "Troilus' Song."[3]

Christopher Baswell and Anne Howland Schotter's *Longman Anthology of British Literature: The Middle Ages* (2010) includes the General Prologue with a facing-page modern translation by David Wright, four full tales, selections from the Parson's Tale (introduction, remedy for the sin of lechery), and the Retraction.[4] Also included are "To His Scribe Adam," "Complaint to His Purse," and *The Parliament of Fowls* (Web ed.).

Stephen Greenblatt's *The Norton Anthology of English Literature: The Middle Ages through the Restoration and the Eighteenth Century* (2012) includes the General Prologue, a summary of the Knight's Tale, the Miller's Tale, the Man of Law's epilogue, the Wife of Bath's Tale, the Pardoner's Tale, the Nun's Priest's Tale, an excerpt from the Parson's Tale, and the Retraction. Also included are "Troilus' Song," "Truth," "To His Scribe Adam," and "Complaint to His Purse."

The freely accessible Norton *Archive*, available online, includes tales and selections that once appeared in the Norton edition but have been eliminated from subsequent editions, the Franklin's Tale and the Merchant's Tale among them. Greenblatt's single-volume *Norton Anthology of English Literature: The Major Authors* (2013) includes the tales.

The Oxford Anthology of English Literature, volume 1: *Medieval English Literature* (2002), edited by J. B. Trapp, Douglas Gray, and Julia Boffey, intercalates a few medieval texts that relate to individual tales: the Nun's Priest's Tale includes bestiary depictions of the fox and the cock and an excerpt from Caxton's *History of Reynard the Fox*, and the Wife of Bath's Tale includes "Of Hanging" and "Application," from the *Gesta Romanorum*.[5]

Derek Pearsall's *Chaucer to Spenser: An Anthology of Writings in English, 1375–1575* (1998) includes the General Prologue and the Miller's Tale, the Wife of Bath's Tale, the Franklin's Tale, and the Pardoner's Tale. Also included are "Adam Scriveyn," "Truth," "The Envoy to Scogan," "The Complaint of Chaucer to His Purse," *The Parliament of Fowls*, and, from *Troilus and Criseyde*, "The Wooing of Criseyde," "The Winning of Criseyde," "The Loss of Criseyde," and the epilogue.

Recommended Reading for Undergraduates

While the ideal student may read widely among the master texts of the past, a much more realistic scenario is one where Chaucer instructors provide a quite limited list of all-important texts for their students to consult. Minimally, such a list is likely to include the Vulgate Bible, Augustine's *Confessions*, Vergil's *Aeneid*, Ovid's *Metamorphoses*, Boethius's *Consolation of Philosophy*, Macrobius's *Commentary on the Dream of Scipio*, Dante's *Divine Comedy*, Boccaccio's *Decameron*, Andreas Capellanus's *Art of Courtly Love*, Jacobus de Voragine's *Golden Legend*, Guillaume de Lorris and Jean de Meun's *Roman de la Rose*, Chrétien de Troyes's romances, Marie de France's *Lais*, and a collection of Old French fabliaux.

For historical and cultural contextualization, the following studies are among many that are pertinent to reading *The Canterbury Tales*: William R. Cook and Ronald B. Herzman's *The Medieval World View: An Introduction* (1983), C. S. Lewis's *The Discarded Image: An Introduction to Medieval and Renaissance Literature* (1964), Lillian Bisson's *Chaucer and the Late Medieval World* (1998), E. Edson and E. Savage-Smith's *Medieval View of the Cosmos: Picturing the Universe in the Christian and Islamic Middle Ages* (2004), Norman Cantor's *In the Wake of the Plague: The Black Death and the World It Made* (2001), Eamon Duffy's *The Stripping of the Altars* (1992), Barbara Hanawalt's *Chaucer's England: Literature in Historical Context* (1992), Linda Olson and

Kathryn Kerby-Fulton's *Voices in Dialogue: Reading Women in the Middle Ages* (2005), Dennis H. Green's *Women Readers in the Middle Ages* (2007), and Ardis Butterfield's *The Familiar Enemy: Chaucer, Language, and Nation in the Hundred Years War* (2009).

To avoid setting Chaucer entirely apart from his peers, teachers might wish to offer one of the many scholarly works on late medieval English literary production, including Christopher Cannon's *Middle English Literature: A Cultural History* (2008), Douglas Gray's *Later Medieval English Literature* (2008), James Simpson's *1350–1547: Reform and Cultural Revolution* (2007), Paul Strohm's *Middle English* (2007), Jocelyn Wogan-Browne and others' *Language and Culture in Medieval Britain: The French of England c. 1100–c. 1500* (2009), Andrew Galloway's *Medieval Literature and Culture* (2006), and Larry Scanlon's *The Cambridge Companion to Medieval English Literature, 1100–1500* (2009).

Excellent collections of primary materials useful to designing Chaucer class syllabi are now available. Matthew Boyd Goldie's anthology *Middle English Literature: A Historical Sourcebook* (2003) fulfills the promise of its title, providing succinct essays and a capacious array of primary texts organized under such general themes as conventions and institutions; force and order; gender, sexuality, and difference; images; labor and capital; style and spectacle; and textualities. Laurel Amtower and Jacqueline Vanhoutte's *A Companion to Chaucer and His Contemporaries: Texts and Contexts* (2009) hosts an array of introductory surveys complemented by a rich selection of primary texts. The volume is divided into eight chapters: "Politics and Ideology in the Fourteenth Century," "The Structure of Society," "Daily Life in Medieval England," "Religious Life, Ritual, and Prayer," "War, Pageantry, and the Knighthood," "Reading, Literacy, and Education," "Science, Medicine, Psychology, and Alchemy," and "International Influences and Exchanges." Informative, varied, and student-friendly, this is the kind of volume instructors eager to situate *The Canterbury Tales* inside the realia of Chaucer's world might be eager to include in their syllabi.

Carolyn P. Collette and Harold Garrett-Goodyear's *The Later Middle Ages: A Sourcebook* (2011) is an equally rich compendium of primary materials immediately useful for Chaucer instructors. Intent on recovering "some of the varied modes of thinking and registers of expression that English people used during the later Middle Ages" (1), the volume's scope is ambitious. Even so, the organizing themes of its seven chapters are all immediately relevant to teaching and studying Chaucer: "The English Languages," "Spiritual Affirmations, Aspiration, and Anxieties," "Violence and the Work of Chivalry," "Scientia: Knowledge, Practical, Theoretical, and Historical," "Book Production: The World of Manuscripts, Patrons, and Readers," "Producing and Exchanging: Work in Manors and Town," "Polity and Governance, Unity and Disunity."

Robert P. Miller's *Chaucer: Sources and Backgrounds* (1977) remains a durable anthology. A collection of primary texts (and parts thereof), it arranges its materials under a variety of rubrics that segue readily into a study of *The*

Canterbury Tales: "Creation and Fall," "Medieval Literary Theory," "Selected Narrative Sources," "The Three Estates," "Antifraternal Texts," "Modes of Love," "Marriage and the Good Woman," "The Antifeminist Tradition," "End of the World and Last Judgment."

Ancillary texts often used in Chaucer courses include literary-critical primers that directly engage the student in the challenge of interpreting each of the tales. Among these, two are outstanding. Helen Cooper's *Oxford Guides to Chaucer*: The Canterbury Tales (1989) focuses on the date, genre, sources and analogues, structure, themes, literary context, and style of every tale and remains the most highly regarded and informative guide among Chaucerians. Helen Phillips's *An Introduction to* The Canterbury Tales: *Reading, Fiction, Context* (2000) provides an equally sophisticated and practicable assessment of each of the tales (even though a sustained reflection on the Retraction is conspicuously absent).

The Chaucer publishing industry in the past three decades has witnessed a parallel explosion of Chaucer companions and critical essay collections, both of which are designed to provide interesting primary texts and interpretative guidance for students and teachers alike. The preeminent collocations are listed below.

Gillian Rudd's *The Complete Critical Guide to Geoffrey Chaucer* (2001) is a compact, reliable, and extremely informative guide to Chaucer's life and works and is of equal value to students and teachers. Piero Boitani and Jill Mann's *The Cambridge Companion to Chaucer* (2002) includes seventeen original essays by major scholars on issues pertaining to all Chaucer's works. Peter Brown's *A Companion to Chaucer* (2002) organizes twenty-seven topical essays by major scholars writing about their fields of specialization, progressing alphabetically from "Afterlife," "Authority," and "Bodies" to "Translating," "Visualizing," and "Women." This is a thoughtful and theoretically inflected cluster of studies.

Seth Lerer's *The Yale Companion to Chaucer* (2006) contains essays by ten eminent scholars. Christopher Cannon's "The Lives of Geoffrey Chaucer," James Simpson's "Chaucer as a European Writer," D. Vance Smith's "Chaucer as an English Writer," and Rita Copeland's "Chaucer and Rhetoric" provide an overview and critique of their subject matters. Seth Lerer's "*The Canterbury Tales*" undertakes a compressed reading of all the tales, while Stephanie Trigg's "Chaucer's Influence and Reception" and Ethan Knapp's "Chaucer Criticism and Its Legacies" survey Chaucer's literary afterlife and the evolution of Chaucer criticism. With its three other essays addressing Chaucer's dream visions, his shorter poems, and *Troilus and Criseyde*, this is a volume that Chaucerians should have near to hand.

Kathleen A. Bishop's The Canterbury Tales *Revisited: Twenty-First-Century Interpretations* (2008) is an equally commendable text. Prompted by a session of the 2006 International Medieval Congress at the University of Leeds, this is a collection of eighteen spirited essays that "revisit" a large number of the tales. Steve Ellis's *Chaucer: The Canterbury Tales* (1998) gathers together twelve essays written in the preceding decade by major scholars. Ellis's *Chaucer: An Oxford Guide* (2005) is a capacious (646 pages) compendium of thirty-seven essays by various scholars arranged under five rubrics: "Historical Contexts," including essays on Chaucer's life, politics, science, and marriage; "Literary Contexts," which addresses theoretical interpretations; "Afterlife," covering topics from editing Chaucer to his reception and performance; and "Study Resources." This volume should be on every Chaucerian's bookshelf; many of its individual essays might well serve as critical primers for class discussion and as surveys of major areas of study. And, more recently, Lee Patterson's *Geoffrey Chaucer's* The Canterbury Tales: *A Casebook* (2007) provides a selection of previously published articles written by a range of notable scholars.

Aids to Teaching

Web Sites

Trying to capture the state of the constantly evolving World Wide Web in printed form is inevitably a quixotic exercise. Webmasters move or retire, sites change servers, and every Web page is susceptible to link rot. At the same time, the Web does live up to its name—find your way to one of the sites described below, and you will encounter links to many of the others.

Georgetown University's *The Labyrinth: Resources for Medieval Studies* (http://labyrinth.georgetown.edu/) and the *ORB: On-line Reference Book for Medieval Studies* (www.the-orb.net/index.html) are perhaps the most venerable of the general medieval studies sites. *The Labyrinth* is one of the most extensive aggregator sites, collecting links to various kinds of medieval studies materials in over forty categories, from "Archaeology" and "Architecture" to "Welsh" and "Women." The *ORB* includes the *Internet Medieval Sourcebook* (www.fordham.edu/halsall/sbook.html), which is focused on primary texts—literary, legal, historical, documentary, theological, and ecclesiastical—in Latin, multiple medieval vernaculars, and, typically, in English translation. Other full-text sites include the *Online Medieval and Classical Library* (http://omacl.org/) and the site formerly known as the *Electronic Text Center* at the University of Virginia. The latter Web page, one of the first substantial digital humanities sites of use to medievalists, is no longer maintained in its original form (though most of the texts have migrated and can still be accessed through the university's main library catalog at http://search.lib.virginia.edu/). The resources of the *Middle English Dictionary* are fully available online in the form of the "Middle English Compendium" (http://quod.lib.umich.edu/m/mec/).

Sites specific to Chaucer have been growing in number and breadth. The home page of the New Chaucer Society (http://newchaucersociety.org) maintains a lightly annotated but substantial list of links to texts, Web pages, multimedia sites, other medieval studies sites, reference materials, images, texts, journals, and organizations. The *Chaucer MetaPage* (www.unc.edu/depts/chaucer/index.html) has now been around for more than a dozen years; it offers a somewhat shorter list but fuller accounts of the resources described, and it contains annotated links to individual instructors' Chaucer pages, including such well-built link-aggregating sites as Anniina Jokinen's *Luminarium* Chaucer pages (http://www.luminarium.org/medlit/chaucer.htm), Dan Kline's *Geoffrey Chaucer Online: The Electronic* Canterbury Tales (www.kankedort.net/), and David Wilson-Okamura's *Geoffreychaucer.org* (http://geoffreychaucer.org/). *The Geoffrey Chaucer Page* (or "Harvard Chaucer Page": http://www.courses .fas.harvard.edu/~chaucer/) is possibly the most extensive (and most linked-to) resource for teachers of *The Canterbury Tales*—mainly because it provides full interlinear translations of every tale (except the Parson's, which is offered in modern English only) and generous supplementary materials on language, literature, and historical and cultural topics. Side-by-side Middle English and modern English texts of *The Canterbury Tales* can also be found at the *Librarius* Web site (http://www.librarius.com/cantales.htm).

Bibliographies also proliferate, and the sites just described supply many links. Three of the most substantial annotated online bibliographies are Mark Allen and John Fisher's *Essential Chaucer Bibliography* (http://colfa.utsa.edu/chaucer), which offers a selection of over nine hundred items (more than four hundred of which are specific to *The Canterbury Tales*) and spans from 1900 to 1984 in an extensively cross-referenced and well-indexed but not searchable format; the fully searchable *Chaucer Bibliography Online* (http://uchaucer .utsa.edu), which includes material from 1975 to the present, much of it drawn from the annual bibliographies published in *Studies in the Age of Chaucer* since 1979; and *The Chaucer Review: An Indexed Bibliography* (vols. 1–30) (http:// library.northwestu.edu/chaucer/), which permits keyword searches and contains a browsable subject index to the nearly eight hundred articles published in the journal through 1995. *The Chaucer Review* is available through *Project Muse* (from 2000 on) and *JSTOR* (all issues), and articles in *Studies in the Age of Chaucer* from 2008 and after are available on *Project Muse*.

Video and Audio Materials

Many of the sites listed in the previous section include links to audio resources for the study of Chaucer's language. *The Chaucer Metapage*, for example, features *The Criyng and the Soun* (www.vmi.edu/english/audio/audio_index .html), a collection of brief Middle English selections from *The Canterbury Tales*, *Troilus*, and shorter works, while the *Geoffrey Chaucer Page* offers a pronunciation guide and a "Teach Yourself Chaucer" series of lessons that include some audio files. A newer Harvard site is *METRO* ("Middle English Teaching Resources Online"; http://metro.fas.harvard.edu/icb/icb.do), a "virtual classroom" providing "guided, interactive instruction on the linguistic, stylistic, and editorial features of some of late medieval England's greatest texts" (by Chaucer, the *Gawain* poet, and the Wakefield master). The multiple levels (or "platforms," in keeping with the transit metaphor) move deliberately from shorter to longer passages with careful exposition of sound, meter, grammar, syntax, and style and provide plenty of opportunities for self-testing. The site also includes a basic illustrated introduction to the editing of medieval texts.

More substantial recordings of *The Canterbury Tales* are the province of *The Chaucer Studio* (http://creativeworks.byu.edu/chaucer/), a joint project at Brigham Young University and the University of Adelaide, founded in 1986. Here one can purchase audio recordings in Middle English of most of the tales and the early poems, available on CD-ROM for around ten dollars and downloadable for half price.

Between 1998 and 2000 the BBC produced Emmy- and BAFTA-award winning animated adaptations of some of *The Canterbury Tales*, which are available on VHS and DVD; each thirty-minute episode tells three (or four) tales, preserves some of the frame narrative (in Claymation), and offers both modern English and Middle English soundtracks (Antrobus). The programs are rated "grade 9 and up" and include the Nun's Priest's Tale, the Knight's Tale, and the Wife of Bath's Tale; the Merchant's Tale, the Pardoner's Tale and the Franklin's Tale; and the Squire's Tale (much altered), the "Canon's Servant's Tale," the Miller's Tale, and the Reeve's Tale.

Several short educational films that offer introductions to *The Canterbury Tales* or to Chaucer's life and language are still available, albeit not inexpensively, from Films for the Humanities and Social Sciences (http://ffh.films .com/); these include *A Prologue to Chaucer*, *Early English Aloud and Alive*, and *Geoffrey Chaucer:* The Canterbury Tales.

Electronic and Multimedia Resources

The Internet has made images of medieval life and culture widely available, and most of the sites noted above contain links of interest to instructors who would like to supplement their teaching of *The Canterbury Tales* with references to contemporary illuminations, maps, relevant locations, and the material traces of life in Chaucer's era. In addition, research sites, museums, and libraries can supply images of the manuscripts of *The Canterbury Tales*. The *Digital Scriptorium* (www.scriptorium.columbia.edu/) hosts images of a half dozen such manuscripts, including several pages from Ellesmere, while the whole of Corpus Christi College Oxford MS 198, an early fifteenth-century manuscript of *The Canterbury Tales*, can be found at *Early Manuscripts at Oxford University* (http://image.ox.ac.uk/). *Geoffrey Chaucer:* The Canterbury Tales, *the Classic Text: Traditions and Interpretations* (www4.uwm.edu/libraries/special/

exhibits/clastext/clspg073.cfm) offers a tour through medieval manuscripts and both early and later printed editions of *The Canterbury Tales*. The British Library online exhibit *Treasures in Full: Caxton's Chaucer* (www.bl.uk/treasures/caxton/homepage.html) contains complete image sets of William Caxton's two editions of *The Canterbury Tales*, from 1476 and 1483. And still available is *The World of Chaucer: Medieval Books and Manuscripts* (http://special.lib.gla.ac.uk/exhibns/chaucer/index.html), an online exhibit prepared by the library at the University of Glasgow to coincide with the 2004 New Chaucer Society Congress there. The Canterbury Tales *Project* (http://www.canterburytalesproject.org/), currently at the University of Birmingham, is in the process of producing CD-ROM and online digital facsimiles and transcriptions of pre-1500 manuscripts of *The Canterbury Tales*, which are suitable for research purposes; some samples are available online.

Chaucernet has long been the most active electronic discussion list for Chaucer studies. It is a forum that includes "professors, graduate students, undergraduates, and others from all over the world who either specialize in—or are merely interested in—Chaucer, his works, and related topics." It is free to join (http://pages.towson.edu/duncan/subchau.html), archived back to 1995, and frequently touches on pedagogical issues. The MLA Division on Chaucer also sponsors an online forum for MLA members.

The Instructor's Library

Background Studies

While acknowledging that the distinctions between background studies, critical works, and reference works are often more heuristic than absolute—texts in the first category frequently propose a critical argument, while those in the last often presume one—this final section seeks to offer a suggestive overview rather than an exhaustive account. And because it focuses largely on monographs (and on *The Canterbury Tales*), it necessarily excludes the rich harvest of Chaucer scholarship to be found in journals, essay collections, and anthologies. In our defense, we can only suggest that "[t]he remenant of the tale is long ynough" (KnT 888).

Sources, Analogues, and Literary Relations

To appreciate the immediate literary context of each of the tales, the most thoroughgoing resource is Robert M. Correale and Mary Hamel's *Sources and Analogues of* The Canterbury Tales (2002–05). Robert P. Miller's *Chaucer: Sources and Backgrounds* (1977), described above, also supplies a handful of narrative sources. The General Prologue is best contextualized by Jill Mann's venerable

Chaucer and Medieval Estates Satire (1973). Alcuin Blamires's *Woman Defamed and Woman Defended* (1992) collects pro- and antifeminist texts from the classical to the (medieval) contemporary that contributed to the medieval representation of women.

Chaucer's biblical inheritance is discussed by Lawrence Besserman's *Chaucer and the Bible* (1988) and *Chaucer's Biblical Poetics* (1998), David Lyle Jeffrey's *Chaucer and Scriptural Tradition* (1984), and of course D. W. Robertson's magisterial book *A Preface to Chaucer* (1962). On the classical side, the importance of Ovid is taken up by John Fyler in *Chaucer and Ovid* (1979) and Michael Calabrese in *Chaucer's Ovidian Arts of Love* (1994). The influence of Statius governs David Anderson's study *Before the Knight's Tale* (1988), while the role of classical satire is the subject of F. Anne Payne's *Chaucer and Menippean Satire* (1981). The broad influence of the *Aeneid* is the focus of Christopher Baswell's *Virgil in Medieval England: Figuring the* Aeneid *from the Twelfth Century to Chaucer* (1995).

The indispensable text concerning Chaucer's relation to French narrative poetry is Charles Muscatine's *Chaucer and the French Tradition* (1957). Broader in its focus is William Calin's *The French Tradition and the Literature of Medieval England* (1994), while Barbara Nolan's *Chaucer and the Tradition of the Roman Antique* (1992) focuses on Chaucer's borrowings from the continental versions of classical epics (*Roman de Troie, Roman de Thebes, Roman d'Eneas*). John Hines's *The Fabliaux in English* (1993) traces the genre from its French origins through its Middle English translations and adaptations.

Chaucer's debt to the work of Dante and Boccaccio has been extensively studied. The influence of the latter is the focus of David Wallace's *Chaucer and the Early Writings of Boccaccio* (1985), Leonard Michael Koff and Brenda Deen Schildgen's *The* Decameron *and* The Canterbury Tales*: New Essays on an Old Question* (2000), and Robert R. Edwards's *Chaucer and Boccaccio* (2002). Dante's role is explored by Karla Taylor in *Chaucer Reads the* Divine Comedy (1989) and Richard Neuse in *Chaucer's Dante: Allegory and Epic Theatre in* The Canterbury Tales (1991). The essays in Piero Boitano's *Chaucer and the Italian Trecento* (1983) and the work of Warren Ginsberg in *Chaucer's Italian Tradition* (2002) widen the scope to include Petrarch's place as well. Finally, Chaucer's relation to his English contemporaries, increasingly a topic of interest, is surveyed in the essays collected in R. F. Yeager's *Chaucer and Gower: Difference, Mutuality, Exchange* (1991) and by John Bowers in *Chaucer and Langland: The Antagonistic Tradition* (2007).

Chaucer's Language

For those intent on having their students learn to appreciate *The Canterbury Tales* as both language and verse, an invaluable teacher's guide is *Essays on the Art of Chaucer's Verse* (2001), a collection of studies chronologically arranged and edited by Alan T. Gaylord, whose "Scanning the Prosodists: An Essay in

Metacriticism" serves as the collection's keystone essay. An overview of contemporary issues in the study of Chaucer's language is provided by the group of essays collected in *Studies in the Age of Chaucer* (vol. 24, 2002), in a colloquium called "Chaucer and the Future of Language Study." Other recent studies are Simon Horobin's *Chaucer's Language* (2007) and Christopher Cannon's *The Making of Chaucer's English: A Study of Words* (1998). Out of print though still available used (and of course in the library) is David Burnley's *A Guide to Chaucer's Language* (1983). Betsy Bowden's *Chaucer Aloud: The Varieties of Textual Interpretation* (1987), now difficult to access, was accompanied by an audiocassette, an emphasis on hearing Chaucer pronounced and performed aloud (often by different voices) that has been dramatically realized more recently in the many CD-ROMs produced by the Chaucer Studio (see "Video and Audio Materials" above).

Chaucer's Life

A reliable biography that successfully integrates Chaucer's works with his career is Derek Pearsall's *The Life of Geoffrey Chaucer: A Critical Biography* (1992). Donald Howard's *Chaucer: His Life, His Work, His World* (1987; published in the United Kingdom as *Chaucer and the Medieval World*) continues to be relevant, while a more recent and controversial account is David Carlson's *Chaucer's Jobs* (2004). A succinct and richly informative vita is Christopher Cannon's "The Lives of Geoffrey Chaucer" in *The Yale Companion to Chaucer* (2006). Martin M. Crow and Clair C. Olson's *Chaucer Life Records* (1966) remains indispensable.

Reference Works

The definitive language resources for Chaucer are of course the *Middle English Dictionary* and the *Oxford English Dictionary*. A compact option is Norman Davis's serviceable *A Chaucer Glossary* (1979), which remains in print, while Helge Kökeritz's short pamphlet, *A Guide to Chaucer's Pronunciation* (1961), remains available through the Medieval Academy Reprints for Teaching (MART) series. A more thorough account of Middle English can be found in N. F. Blake's *The Cambridge History of the English Language, 1066–1476* (1992). The most usable concordance to *The Canterbury Tales* is Larry D. Benson's *A Glossarial Concordance to the* Riverside Chaucer (1993), which corresponds to a text that is still in print. However, at 1,384 pages over two volumes, it is obviously more of a library-use item than a desktop reference.

The history of Chaucerian reception can be tracked in the three volumes of Caroline F. E. Spurgeon's *Five Hundred Years of Chaucer Criticism and Allusion, 1357–1900* (1925), which has been supplemented and updated by Jackson Campbell Boswell and Sylvia Wallace Holton's *Chaucer's Fame in England: STC Chauceriana, 1475–1640* (2004). More selective is Derek Brewer's *Chaucer: The Critical Heritage* (1978).

An absolutely essential editorial, textual, and critical authority for the individual tales is the Chaucer Variorum, published by the University of Oklahoma Press. At present, nine volumes dealing with *The Canterbury Tales* have appeared, covering the General Prologue, the Miller's Tale, the Summoner's Tale, the Physician's Tale, the Squire's Tale, the Prioress's Tale, the Nun's Priest's Tale, and the Manciple's Tale. The fate of the Variorum series in the electronic age and its relation to the Web- and CD-based *Canterbury Tales* project (http://www.canterburytalesproject.org) are unclear. A related series associated with the University of Oklahoma Press features facsimiles of important Chaucer manuscripts, including Hengwrt (Ruggiers) and *Cambridge Library MS GG.4.27* (ed. Parkes and Beadle [1981]). For descriptions of the manuscripts, one can turn John Matthews Manly and Edith Rickert's exhaustive edition of 1940 or the somewhat more wieldy survey by M. C. Seymour, *A Catalogue of Chaucer Manuscripts:* The Canterbury Tales (1997).

While the Chaucer companion volumes described in the "Recommended Reading for Undergraduates" section tend to take a discursive approach, there is also a growing body of encyclopedias that seek to be fructuous in a different way. At the head of this list is the single-volume *Oxford Companion to Chaucer*, edited by Douglas Gray (2003), which covers Chaucer's life and his contemporaries and the sources, contexts, and themes of his works in over two thousand entries, arranged alphabetically, carefully cross-listed, and bibliographically supplemented. Malcolm Andrew's *The Palgrave Literary Dictionary of Chaucer* (2006) is another recent entry into this field; it supplies over seven hundred entries. Rosalyn Rossignol's *Critical Companion to Chaucer: A Literary Reference to His Life and Work* (2007), also a one-volume work, revises and expands her 1999 *Chaucer A to Z: The Essential Reference to His Life and Works*, replacing the original alphabetical arrangement of topics with a four-part scheme (life; works; people, places, and topics; and chronology, maps, and bibliography). Shannon L. Rogers's *All Things Chaucer: An Encyclopedia of Chaucer's World* (2007) does not have separate entries for individual works but includes them in an introduction that is printed in both volumes. More narrowly focused texts include Edward E. Foster and David H. Carey's *Chaucer's Church: A Dictionary of Religious Terms in Chaucer* (2002) and A. F. Scott's *Who's Who in Chaucer* (1974), a glossary of names in Chaucer's work.

Print bibliographies remain useful, particularly for finding earlier material. Indeed, one could trace the history of Chaucer criticism back to the late nineteenth century through the succession of such volumes, namely: Bege K. Bowers and Mark Allen's *Annotated Chaucer Bibliography, 1986–1996* (2002), John Leyerle's *Chaucer: A Bibliographical Introduction* (1986), Lorrayne Y. Baird-Lange's *A Bibliography of Chaucer, 1974–1985* (1988), Lorrayne Y. Baird's *A Bibliography of Chaucer, 1964–1973* (1977), William R. Crawford's *Bibliography of Chaucer, 1954–63* (1967), Dudley David Griffith's *Bibliography of Chaucer, 1908–1953* (1955), and Eleanor Prescott Hammond's *Chaucer: A Bibliographical Manual* (1908).

Critical Works

Providing an evenhanded survey of *Canterbury Tales* criticism published since the first edition of *Approaches to Teaching Chaucer's* Canterbury Tales in 1980 may well be an *impossibilium*. One way of measuring the annual output of recent Chaucer scholarship is simply to scan the annotated Chaucer bibliography in *Studies in the Age of Chaucer*: in length, over the past ten years this bibliography has averaged ninety pages. Since nearly ninety percent of these studies take the form of articles rather than books, it follows that much of the cutting-edge work in the field is to be found in essays published in journals such as *Chaucer Review, Studies in the Age of Chaucer, Exemplaria, Viator, Review of English Studies, PMLA, JEGP, Postmedieval*, and so on. Yet because of spatial restrictions we cannot—with very few exceptions—recognize these achievements. Rather, in the following pages we offer a discrete selection of book-length studies that have been influential in defining the direction of Chaucer criticism over the past thirty-some years. While these monographs are not likely to serve as primary readings for undergraduates, they instantiate various critical perspectives that teachers of *The Canterbury Tales* may choose to integrate into their lectures and classroom discussions.

Fredric Jameson's celebrated challenge "always historicize!" has been honored by Chaucerians in several ways. Representative of the "old historicism" of mid-twentieth-century scholarship are studies such as G. G. Coulton's *Chaucer and His England* (1930), D. W. Robertson's *Chaucer's London* (1968), and A. R. Myers's *London in the Age of Chaucer* (1972). Our most recent generation of historicists, influenced by the ideologies and methodologies of Marxist and cultural studies, have much more aggressively and self-consciously interrogated the political inflections, materialist foundations, and evidentiary problematics of the relations between literature and history in the late fourteenth century in England. By century's end, these interrogations produced an impressive run of revisionist historicist studies, notably David Aers's *Chaucer* (1986), Paul Strohm's *Social Chaucer* (1989), Lee Patterson's *Chaucer and the Subject of History* (1991), and David Wallace's *Chaucerian Polity: Absolutist Lineages and Associational Forms in England and Italy* (1997). It is inevitable, perhaps, that the theoretical substrate of the historicisms of the 1990s would be retheorized in turn, as evidenced by Elizabeth Scala and Sylvia Federico's *The Posthistorical Middle Ages* (2009), a collection that includes essays with titles such as "Time Out of Memory," "Naked Chaucer," "The Gender of Historicism," and "Historicism after Historicism." As an integral part of recent reformulations of Chaucer's world, the critical foci of orientalism, Jewish studies, and postcolonialism have also effected valuable reassessments of Chaucer's poetics and cultural politics: Brenda D. Schildgen's *Pagans, Tartars, Moslems, and Jews in Chaucer's* Canterbury Tales (2001), Sheila Delany's *Chaucer and the Jews: Sources, Contexts, Meaning* (2002), and Kathryn L. Lynch's *Chaucer's Cultural Geography: Basic Readings in Chaucer and His Time* (2002).

Studies of the religious valence of Chaucer's poetry have been morphing, as have historicist and cultural studies, into a new and "revisionist" body of work. A once preeminent way of interpreting *The Canterbury Tales*, especially in the third quarter of the twentieth century, was to adopt the allegorizing strategies of a Christian hermeneutics (preeminently Augustinian). Notable examples of this approach—often called Robertsonianism—are D. W. Robertson's *A Preface to Chaucer: Studies in Medieval Perspectives* (1962), Bernard Huppé's *Fruyt and Chaf: Studies in Chaucer's Allegories* (1963), and Robert Kaske's *Medieval Christian Literary Imagery: A Guide to Interpretation* (1988). In recognition of the continuing significance of the religious dimensions of Chaucer, even while eschewing many of Robertson's hermeneutical techniques, are essays collected in a festschrift honoring John Fleming, one of Robertson's most articulate acolytes, in: Robert Epstein and William Robins's *Sacred and Profane in Chaucer and Late Medieval Literature: Essays in Honour of John V. Fleming* (2010).

The explosion of medieval books and essays concentrating on "new" and "excentric" religious matters—personages, texts, performances, sects, and philosophers all given short shrift a generation ago—has directed scholars not only toward reinterpreting Chaucer within the context of a contentious environment of beliefs, practices, and disputes but also toward appreciating his voice as but one voice, and oftentimes a minor voice, among many others. Exemplary of this tendency toward reading Chaucer as part of a much larger religious zeitgeist is Jim Rhodes's *Poetry Does Theology: Chaucer, Grosseteste, and the Pearl-Poet* (2001), Rita Copeland's *Pedagogy, Intellectuals, and Dissent in the Later Middle Ages: Lollardy and the Ideas of Learning* (2001), and Andrew Cole's *Literature and Heresy in the Age of Chaucer* (2008). It perhaps needs to be noted that the "Whiggish," humanist, and anti-Robertsonian proclivities of a late twentieth century bent on secularizing and de-catholicizing Chaucer have been trenchantly addressed by these studies of a newly conceptualized religious Chaucer. Helen Phillips's *Chaucer and Religion* (2010) is salutary in this light, not only in the critical focus it places on the Christian inflections of Chaucer's verse but also in its immediate pedagogical applicability, concluding as it does with essays arranged under the rubric "Teaching Chaucer Today."

Few would take exception to the assertion that feminism is the most significant school of Chaucer criticism to have emerged in the past thirty or forty years. Since Susan Schibanoff's hallmark review of medieval feminist studies in *Approaches to Teaching Chaucer's* Canterbury Tales ("Crooked Rib" [1980]), feminist readings of Chaucer—be they first, second, or third wave in their theories and practice—have outnumbered all other kinds of critical interrogation. The presuppositions and politics they embrace have dramatically influenced the ways teachers and students are prepared to think about Chaucer. While most of these influential studies were published in the form of essays, we nevertheless can point to a few magisterial monographs as having significantly changed (and sometimes confirmed) our ways of thinking about gender in Chaucer, notably Carolyn Dinshaw's *Chaucer's Sexual Poetics* (1989), Jill Mann's *Geoffrey Chau-*

cer (1991) (a new edition was published under the title *Feminizing Chaucer* in 2002), Elaine Tuttle Hansen's *Chaucer and the Fictions of Gender* (1992), Susan Crane's *Gender and Romance in Chaucer's* Canterbury Tales (1994), Anne Laskaya's *Chaucer's Approach to Gender in* The Canterbury Tales (1995), and Catherine S. Cox's *Gender and Language in Chaucer* (1997). If presently there appear to be fewer Chaucer studies that now straightforwardly identify themselves as feminist, this is scarcely a sign of feminism's diminishing appeal; rather, it bespeaks the nearly universal integration of feminist belief, theory, and practice throughout the domains of Chaucer scholarship and teaching.

The new direction of feminism is also symptomatic of the expansion of gender studies generally, a movement whose liberating social, theoretical, and legal dimensions are powerfully embodied in the domain of queer theory. Robert Sturges's *Chaucer's Pardoner and Gender Theory: Bodies of Discourse* (2000), Glenn Burger's *Chaucer's Queer Nation* (2003), and Tison Pugh's *Sexuality and Its Queer Discontents in Middle English Literature* (2008) all deploy the tenets of queer studies in their critiques of Chaucer. Perhaps the most influential of queer Chaucer studies is a now-reprinted essay, Steven Kruger's "Claiming the Pardoner: Toward a Gay Reading of Chaucer's Pardoner's Tale," the only "applied" theoretical study in the "Gender and Queer Theory" section of David Richter's anthology, *The Critical Tradition: Classic Texts and Contemporary Trends* (2007). Theorizations of masculinity are gaining a belated foothold in Chaucer gender studies as well, most notably in Peter Beidler's *Masculinities in Chaucer: Approaches to Maleness in* The Canterbury Tales *and* Troilus and Criseyde (1998), Alcuin Blamires's *Chaucer, Ethics, and Gender* (2006), and Holly Crocker's *Chaucer's Vision of Manhood* (2007).

Some critics have seen a continuum from gender studies to psychoanalytic studies. For several decades, scholars have productively uncovered the psyche and the subconscious of Chaucer's most powerful tale-telling pilgrims—most notably the Pardoner (Dinshaw) and the Wife of Bath (Leicester, *Disenchanted Self*). But the one study elevating all matters psychoanalytic—and especially Lacanian—to another theoretical level is L. O. Aranye Fradenburg's *Sacrifice Your Love: Psychoanalysis, Historicism, Chaucer* (2002). While George Edmondson's *The Neighboring Text: Chaucer, Boccaccio, Henryson* (2011) offers an equally sophisticated Lacanian reading focusing on *Troilus and Criseyde*, since 2002 no psychoanalytic reading of *The Canterbury Tales* has appeared to rival Fradenburg's. Instead, excellent studies influenced to a degree by psychoanalysis but more attentive to medieval faculty psychology have recently been written: Carolyn P. Collette's *Species, Phantasms, and Images: Vision and Medieval Psychology in* The Canterbury Tales (2001) and Sarah Stanbury's *The Visual Object of Desire in Late Medieval England* (2008). It should also be remarked that resistance to psychoanalytic literary criticism persists among Chaucerians, two of the most articulate examples being A. C. Spearing's *Textual Subjectivity: The Encoding of Subjectivity in Medieval Narratives and Lyrics* (2005) and Lee Patterson's "Chaucer's Pardoner on the Couch: Psyche and Clio in Medieval Literary Studies" (2001).

Although Chaucer, unlike Dante, chooses not to advertise his learning in every line of verse, many scholars have explored the extraordinary range of his erudition. Recent book-length studies of Chaucer's learnedness in matters scientific, psychological, theological, and philosophical include John North's *Chaucer's Universe* (1990), Robert Myles's *Chaucerian Realism* (1994), Norman Klassen's *Chaucer on Love, Knowledge, and Sight* (1995), Ann Astell's *Chaucer and the Universe of Learning* (1996), J. Stephen Russell's *Chaucer and the Trivium: The Mindsong of* The Canterbury Tales (1998), Marijane Osborn's *Time and the Astrolabe in* The Canterbury Tales (2002), Suzanne Akbari's *Seeing through the Veil: Optical Theory and Medieval Allegory* (2004), Mark Miller's *Philosophical Chaucer: Love, Sex, and Agency in* The Canterbury Tales (2004), and Alastair J. Minnis's *Fallible Authors: Chaucer's Pardoner and Wife of Bath* (2008).

One of the most celebrated narratives in Chaucer scholarship is the production history and eventual publication of Manly and Rickert's magisterial collaborative effort, *The Text of* The Canterbury Tales: *Studied on the Basis of All Known Manuscripts* (1940). Empirical and interpretative studies of Chaucer manuscripts, however, were scarcely brought to a halt with Manly and Rickert's efforts; in fact, since midcentury, new modes of archival analysis have generated a dramatic surge in the field. The labors of Charles Owen in *The Manuscripts of* The Canterbury Tales (1991) and of Martin Stevens and Daniel Woodward in *The Ellesmere Chaucer: Essays in Interpretation* (1997) are complemented by the interpretive methods employed by Thomas Prendergast and Barbara Kline in *Rewriting Chaucer: Culture, Authority, and the Idea of the Authentic Text, 1400–1602* (1999) and Kathryn Kerby-Fulton and Maidie Hilmo, *The Medieval Professional Reader at Work: Evidence from the Manuscripts of Chaucer, Langland, Kempe, and Gower* (2001). Digitization has given new energy to Ellesmere studies alone, as evidenced in Herbert Schulz's electronically produced *The Ellesmere Manuscript of Chaucer's* Canterbury Tales (1999). And studies such as Elizabeth Scala's *Absent Narratives, Manuscript Textuality, and Literary Structure in Late Medieval England* (2002) illustrate how materials analysis, social and economic contextualization, and literary interpretation are mutually informing practices.

Many Chaucerians have been inspired to write about the challenges involved in teaching Chaucer to undergraduates (since 1980 the *PMLA* bibliography lists 108 studies focused under the categories "Teaching" and "Chaucer"), and these studies are obviously addressed to other Chaucerians intent on honing their classroom skills. *Exemplaria* gathered together six essays on teaching Chaucer in its fall 1996 issue; Gail Ashton and Louise Sylvester's excellent *Teaching Chaucer* (2007) offers nine more essays, most composed by teachers in the United Kingdom. Tison Pugh and Angela Jane Weisl's *Approaches to Teaching Chaucer's* Troilus and Criseyde *and the Shorter Poems* (2007) provides a total of twenty-nine new essays focused on ways of teaching Chaucer's works excluding *The Canterbury Tales*. And this present volume is of course intended to provide further practical aid in the ways one might teach *The Canterbury Tales*.

One more productive way of approaching Chaucer instruction is through his "afterlife"—that is, tracing Chaucer's influences on future poets and artists, his interpretations by his future readers and critics, and his re-presentations in different media all the way to the present. A selective list of these varied enterprises includes Seth Lerer's *Chaucer and His Readers: Imagining the Author in Late Medieval England* (1994), Steve Ellis's *Chaucer at Large: The Poet in the Modern Imagination* (2000), Thomas Prendergast's *Chaucer's Dead Body: From Corpse to Corpus* (2003), Joseph A. Dane's *Who Is Buried in Chaucer's Tomb? Studies in the Reception of Chaucer's Book* (1998), Stephanie Trigg's *Congenial Souls: Reading Chaucer from Medieval to Postmodern* (2002), and Candace Barrington's *American Chaucers* (2007), a study of America's "rampant modernizing and bowdlerizing [of Chaucer], freely transposing his life and poetry into popular media" (Barrington 3).

Among the many other monographs that have appeared since 1980, the following might be considered most instructive in preparation for teaching *The Canterbury Tales*: Helen Cooper's *The Structure of* The Canterbury Tales (1983), V. A. Kolve's *Chaucer and the Imagery of Narrative: The First Five Canterbury Tales* (1984), Derek Pearsall's *The Canterbury Tales* (1985), Paul Olson's *The Canterbury Tales and the Good Society* (1986), Stephen Knight's *Geoffrey Chaucer* (1986), C. David Benson's *Chaucer's Drama of Style: Poetic Variety and Contrast in* The Canterbury Tales (1986), Carl Lindahl's *Earnest Games: Folkloric Patterns in* The Canterbury Tales (1987), Laura Kendrick's *Chaucerian Play: Comedy and Control in* The Canterbury Tales (1988), Leonard Koff's *Chaucer and the Art of Storytelling* (1988), John Ganim's *Chaucerian Theatricality* (1990), Peggy Knapp's *Chaucer and the Social Contest* (1990) and *Chaucerian Aesthetics* (2008), John M. Hill's *Chaucerian Belief: The Poetics of Reverence and Delight* (1991), Peter Beidler's *The Wife of Bath: Geoffrey Chaucer* (1996), R. Allen Shoaf's *Chaucer's Body: The Anxiety of Circulation in* The Canterbury Tales (2001), J. Allan Mitchell's *Ethics and Exemplary Narrative in Chaucer and Gower* (2004), Lee Patterson's *Temporal Circumstances: Form and History in* The Canterbury Tales (2006), Marilynn Desmond's *Ovid's Art and the Wife of Bath: The Ethics of Erotic Violence* (2006), John Fyler's *Language and the Declining World in Chaucer, Dante, and Jean de Meun* (2007), V. A. Kolve's *Telling Images: Chaucer and the Imagery of Narrative II* (2009), Geoffrey W. Gust's *Constructing Chaucer: Author and Autofiction in the Critical Tradition* (2009), Peter W. Travis's *Disseminal Chaucer: Rereading the Nun's Priest's Tale* (2010), and A. C. Spearing's *Medieval Autographies: The "I" of the Text* (2012).

As a counterweight to this "presentist" review of Chaucer scholarship, we direct readers back to the "Materials" section of the 1980 *Approaches to Teaching Chaucer's* Canterbury Tales, where Joseph Gibaldi reviews the major achievement of Chaucerians in the first three quarters of the twentieth century. Here we conclude by saluting just a few influential studies written in earlier times, some of which we have already recognized: George Lyman Kittredge's *Chaucer and His Poetry* (1915), Charles Muscatine's *Chaucer and the French Tradition: A Study in Style and Meaning* (1957), D. W. Robertson's *A Preface to Chaucer: Studies in Medieval Perspectives* (1962), E. Talbot Donaldson's *Speaking of Chaucer* (1970), Jill Mann's *Chaucer and Medieval Estates Satire: The Literature of Social Classes and the General Prologue of* The Canterbury Tales (1973), Derek Brewer's *Chaucer* (1973), and Donald Howard's *The Idea of* The Canterbury Tales (1976).

The first edition of *Approaches to Teaching Chaucer's* Canterbury Tales, as we noted in our preface, was the inaugural volume of the MLA's Approaches to Teaching Masterpieces of World Literature series. The word "masterpieces" dropped out of the series name after ten volumes (between Milton and Wordsworth!), but it is hard not to wish it back as *The Canterbury Tales* volume returns in a new second edition. Everything that has taken place critically, as noted above, and pedagogically, as is evident in what follows, only reminds us that it is a text that richly deserves the designation, handsomely repays our attentions, and will continue to offer an abundantly rewarding experience in the classroom.

NOTES

[1] Included are the GP; the KnT, MilT, RvT, WBT, ClT, FrT, SumT, MerT, FranT, PardT, and PrT; a brief selection from Mel, NPT, ManT, and the ParsT; and the Ret.

[2] Included here are the GP, KnT, MilT, RvT, CkT, WBT, FrT, SumT, ClT, MerT, FranT, PardT, PrT, NPT, Parson's prologue, and the Ret.

[3] The nine tales are the KnT, MilT, WBT, ClT, MerT, FranT, PardT, PrT, and NPT.

[4] The MilT, WBT, PardT, and NPT are included.

[5] Also included are the GP, MilT, FranT, PardT, Ret; "Gentilesse" and "Truth"; "Roundel," from *The Parliament of Fowls*; "Cantus Troili," from *Troilus and Criseyde*; "Balade" and "The Legend of Thisbe" from *The Legend of Good Women*; "To Rosemounde"; "The Complaint of Chaucer to His Purse"; and "Chaucer's Words unto Adam, His Own Scribe."

APPENDIX
SURVEY RESPONSES: A SELECTED CENSUS

1. Please describe the course(s) in which you teach *The Canterbury Tales*, indicating the course title, type, and level.

A majority of those responding to the survey teach *The Canterbury Tales* in one of two ways—either as part of a survey of medieval or premodern British literature (usually offered to lower-level students) or in a class focusing on Chaucer's works generally or more selectively on *The Canterbury Tales* (typically for upper-level students). Respondents regularly include some tales as central texts in thematic courses with a medieval focus in a variety of other courses, sometimes paired with works by other writers.

2. Which tales do you find most successful and which least successful in the classroom?

As illustrated in the list below, which orders the tales from most to least successful, the Wife of Bath's Tale is always a smash success; the Miller's Tale, the Pardoner's Tale, the Knight's Tale, and the Nun's Priest's Tale are consistently popular; and the Tale of Melibee and the Parson's Tale are consistently deemed the least successful:

1. Wife of Bath's Tale
2. Miller's Tale
3. Pardoner's Tale
4. Knight's Tale, Nun's Priest's Tale (tied)
5. Franklin's Tale
6. General Prologue, Clerk's Tale, Prioress's Tale, Reeve's Tale (tied)
7. Merchant's Tale
8. Man of Law's Tale
9. Manciple's Tale, Shipman's Tale (tied)
10. Cook's Tale, Friar's Tale, Physician's Tale, Second Nun's Tale, Tale of Sir Thopas (tied)
11. Squire's Tale, Summoner's Tale (tied)
12. Monk's Tale, Tale of Melibee (tied)
13. Parson's Tale

3. What do you find are the primary challenges of teaching *The Canterbury Tales*? What strategies do you use to overcome these challenges?

With only one or two exceptions, respondents single out the language barrier as their primary challenge in teaching Chaucer; yet they are almost universally committed to helping students become as proficient as possible in reading and understanding Chaucer's language. (For classroom stratagems employed to this end, see responses to question 5, below.)

The other major challenge is the "alterity" of the Middle Ages—many students tend to think of Chaucer as "old" and "musty." To address the medieval-modern gap, many instructors provide an overview with general lectures on medieval culture, often relying on visual aids (medieval manuscripts, medieval maps, medieval art forms, images of pilgrims, etc.); others offer minilectures on historical, cultural, economic, and political matters whenever classroom occasions demand. Some address the alterity challenge with imaginative creative assignments, such as a class compilation of a medieval cookbook or a book on medieval housekeeping. Also popular are writing assignments comparing and contrasting elements in Chaucer's milieu and elements in contemporary culture; however, as respondents warn, it is often difficult to keep students from overmodernizing—the Wife of Bath might morph too easily into a hippie feminist. One respondent invites her students to give each of the pilgrims moral rankings, medieval and modern, leading to a discussion of their similarities and differences. Another asks each student to invent a character and a tale (medieval or modern), and the class eventually fits the portraits and narratives together as "our tales." Finally, another respondent invites students to research a pilgrim's medieval profession and then assume that character's identity in a class-centered on-line discussion.

4. Which texts or editions do you find best for teaching these works and why? The hardbound *Riverside Chaucer* remains the most highly valued edition of Chaucer's complete works; as one respondent puts it, it simply "has everything." A few prefer to order the *Riverside Chaucer* paperback for classroom use because it is lighter and somewhat less expensive. The other text of choice is V. A. Kolve and Glending Olson's Norton casebook, The Canterbury Tales: *Fifteen Tales and the General Prologue.* An inexpensive paperback of the most often taught tales, it includes a clutch of time-tested critical essays. Jill Mann's Penguin *The Canterbury Tales* is also well regarded as reliable, inexpensive, and reader-friendly. A frequently used anthology in survey courses is *The Norton Anthology of English Literature: The Middle Ages through the Restoration and the Eighteenth Century.* And although translations are regarded with ambivalence, a few respondents recommend A. Kent Hieatt and Constance Hieatt's Bantam Classic edition of *The Canterbury Tales* for student use because it has the original text and translation on facing pages.

5. If you teach *The Canterbury Tales* in Middle English, how do your students learn to comprehend and pronounce Middle English? If you teach *The Canterbury Tales* in translation, how do you address issues of language?

With few exceptions, survey respondents are ardently committed to teaching *The Canterbury Tales* in Middle English. As a way of familiarizing students with the sounds and rhythms of Chaucer's language, many read key passages aloud throughout the term. Just as many rely on recorded and dramatized readings of Chaucer, such as those made available by the *Chaucer Studio* and Harvard's *Geoffrey Chaucer Page.* To assist in students' pronunciation, respondents use a variety of pedagogical devices: reciting the first lines of the General Prologue together, reading a line and having all students repeat it, assigning each student to read one or more lines aloud, requiring students to memorize and then recite a passage (oftentimes the first eighteen lines of the General Prologue) or asking students to read aloud outside class. For additional assistance, roughly half of the respondents provide their students with pronunciation handouts and lists of useful vocabulary.

A few respondents go further. One reports using an online voice recorder available through *Blackboard* called *Wimba,* which allows students to speak and review their recordings without being put on the spot in class. Another has her students engage in a performance of the parliament scene from *The Parliament of Fowls.* A third starts her course off by having students read "The Three Little Pigs" in Middle English, while another has his students compete to see who can write the best fake "Middle English."

While almost all instructors teach *The Canterbury Tales* in the original, some encourage their students to engage with translations as well, at least early in the course. Those who countenance the use of translations usually require students in class discussions as well as in tests and papers to cite

Chaucer's texts in the original. All instructors encourage their students to work especially hard on their comprehension of Chaucer's Middle English, asking students to appreciate what these words actually mean. To this end, some ask students to work in breakout groups, but the most common method is giving a sequence of linguistic exercises and quizzes. Other aids for learning Middle English are the *Oxford English Dictionary*, the *Middle English Dictionary*, and the glossary, glosses, and notes provided in the classroom text; Larry Benson's notes on grammar in *The Riverside Chaucer* are especially recommended.

A small number of respondents report that they do not make an effort to have their students learn to pronounce Chaucer's language, but instead are content with having them learn to comprehend it on the page. One instructor in particular objects to making his students learn a pronunciation scheme that he does not believe is necessarily an accurate representation of how English was spoken six hundred years ago. Yet those who do not focus on pronunciation nevertheless work intensively with their class on Chaucer's lexicon, grammar, and syntax. In teaching students how to comprehend and appreciate Chaucer's language, respondents emphasize, above all, the values of "close reading," "patience," and "lots of encouragement."

6. What kinds of assignments do you find most helpful? How are these assignments aligned with the larger goals of the course, and how are they assessed?

Respondents describe a number of common assignments: assignments that help students focus on the language of the tales by having them memorize a portion of Chaucer's poetry or translate a portion of Chaucer's verse into modern English; work that requires the use of the *Middle English Dictionary* or *Oxford English Dictionary*, ranging from looking up every word in a ten-line segment of *The Canterbury Tales* to glossing a passage or investigating one or several words in the context of a passage; the close reading essay, which varies in length, from 1–2 to 5–8 pages; and research papers (typically 8–10 pages). Several respondents have students work throughout the term on an annotated bibliography that is not necessarily connected to a final paper in order to encourage students to engage with critical sources, and many instructors require a paper that summarizes and analyzes a scholarly article.

7. What kinds of critical approaches or methodologies have you found most helpful in teaching *The Canterbury Tales*? What approaches or methodologies do your students find most helpful?

Many instructors say that they usually do not emphasize theory when teaching Chaucer to undergraduates and that the only approach they really use is close reading. One instructor said that he seeks only "to convince his students to read slowly and with attention." While most do not require their students to do extensive secondary reading, some assign essays that students find more accessible. As one instructor puts it, anything that helps students see *The Canterbury Tales* as relevant to their lives is helpful in engaging them, and several point out that both they and their students enjoy the fact that there are a variety of critical approaches that they can examine and compare with one another in order to come to conclusions of their own about the tales. Thus a number incorporate psychoanalysis, Marxism, postcolonial theory, queer theory, structuralism, postmodern theories of textuality, and Robertsonian, Jungian, or Bakhtinian methodologies into class discussions, often with a particular approach tied to a particular tale.

Instructors draw most commonly on feminist and historicist approaches. Some instructors explore the latter by having their students read other primary documents from Chaucer's time and examine sources and analogues, manuscripts, or contemporary and historical reception of *The Canterbury Tales*. A generic approach to *The Canterbury Tales* is also fairly common. One instructor notes that he likes to approach the *Tales* from the point of view of translation theory, since most of his students are acquainted with another language. Those who show film adaptations of the tales to their students open the door to the discussion of film theory, the gaze, and so on.

8. If you have been teaching *The Canterbury Tales* for some time, how has your pedagogical approach changed?

Those who feel that their methods have evolved over time now generally lecture less and invite student discussion and participation more. Several instructors say that they are now more open to seeing what discussion of the tales yields in the classroom, allowing students' interests to guide the class. Instructors often focus less on making students learn facts about medieval history and culture and memorize word lists and instead spend more time helping students engage with the text. This means more time with the language. Similarly, some choose to cover fewer tales and spend more time on the ones that they do assign.

Some specific changes instructors mentioned include a greater focus on gender issues or on codicology and problems of textual authority. One instructor spends more time looking at the interlinks between the tales to help students study issues of audience and performance, while another has added more focus on the analogues to allow students to make comparisons with matters outside the tales, whether contemporary or modern. There is also a greater focus on interactive materials; for example, one instructor encourages her students to look at pilgrimage sites from around the world on her Web site and offers pictures of the various pilgrimage sites visited by the Wife of Bath. In addition, a few instructors note that they now assign much shorter writing assignments, or, in one case, a short paper for presentation instead of a longer traditional research paper. Finally, several instructors note that they make better use of technology now. They use more audiovisual aids, *Blackboard* or a Web site created for the course, and more images from the text or other sources. And, of course, so do their students; another respondent observes that with so many more sources available now, he focuses on helping students develop criteria for evaluating and choosing which sources to use.

Part Two

APPROACHES

Introduction: A Survey of Pedagogical Approaches to *The Canterbury Tales*

The results of the MLA survey that preceded this volume affirmed many of our intuitions about the state of Chaucer materials, the use of technology, and the place of theory in the contemporary classroom. We were at the same time somewhat surprised and definitely impressed by the degree to which the responses reflected the wide variety of situations in which *The Canterbury Tales* are being taught in the twenty-first century, a testament both to the robust status of the *Tales* and to the value of the proposed volume: this variety at the level of the institution (not just traditional university and college settings but also two-year colleges, technical institutes, and high schools) and the curriculum (single-author courses but also surveys and general education, world literature, English education, and composition courses) was perhaps not adequately captured by the first Approaches edition. Accordingly, we have tried to put together a collection of essays—all of them proposed by survey respondents—that reflects this infinite pedagogical variety and that captures the wisdom of Chaucerians, ranging from emeritus professors drawing on a career's worth of experience to first-year instructors reporting, as it were, from the trenches.

The essays in this volume are subdivided into five sections, the first of which, "Chaucer's Language," addresses the difficulties of Middle English, which can be daunting to instructors and students alike. In this section of the volume, essays by experienced teachers of *The Canterbury Tales* take up the language issue in its multiple aspects. In "Teaching Chaucer's Middle English," Peter Beidler describes how he uses the International Phonetic Alphabet to lead students across the great vowel shift toward a grasp of Chaucer's iambic pentameter, which lets them read with confidence and fluency. The next two essays, William Quinn's "The Forms and Functions of Verse in *The Canterbury Tales*" and Howell Chickering's "Teaching the Prosody of *The Canterbury Tales*," take up the artistry of Chaucer's verse and describe the basics of scansion and recital exercises, which, once mastered, can let students highlight "the brilliant local effects of Chaucer's prosody—moments when his acoustic strategies significantly support or subvert the diction, syntax, and rhetoric of his narration" (Quinn). Jane Chance's "Teaching Chaucer in Middle English: The Joy of Philology" brings new life to a familiar assignment—using the *Middle English Dictionary* and the *Oxford English Dictionary* to study etymology and the range of meaning of Chaucer's richly nuanced diction. Such an assignment helps students see that they can do actual, original linguistic research and experience "the joy of philology." Tara Williams, in "Worrying about Words in *The Canterbury Tales*," discusses how to move students from comprehension to interpretation to "a full-fledged argument" about a text in an unfamiliar language through close reading and prewriting exercises. And Andrew Cole offers genre- and language-based strategies for fostering the kind of textual immediacy and intimacy necessary for "getting Chaucer's jokes."

The volume's second section, "Individual Tales and Fragments," could be a collection in and of itself; in practice, this section serves as an implicit index of some of the more popular and more consistently taught tales, including the routinely anthologized General Prologue. It begins at the beginning, with Robert J. Meyer-Lee's "The Problem of Tale Order" and his discussion of one of the most basic questions about teaching *The Canterbury Tales*: should we represent the tales as structurally whole, an incomplete but essentially ordered sequence, or as a fundamentally provisional collection whose incompleteness is its chief feature? Roger Ladd's "Chaucer and the Middle Class; or, Why Look at Men of Law, Merchants, and Wives?" seeks to turn the "happy coincidence" that "Chaucer focuses on the middle stratum and that students often hope to rise in our own society's middle stratum" into an opportunity to bring issues of social class to the fore in discussions of the General Prologue. Similarly, in "Professions in the General Prologue," Alexander Kaufman connects the fact that most of his students work full- or part-time outside the classroom with the representation of labor in the General Prologue by having them research one of the poem's professions in depth. In "Teaching Chaucer's Obscene Comedy in Fragment 1," Nicole Nolan Sidhu argues for the importance of getting students to move beyond their initial reactions to Chaucer's fabliaux—amusement, disgust, confirmation in their ideas about the bawdy Middle Ages—in order to think about obscenity as a cultural discourse and explore vexing questions about gender, violence, and social hierarchies. Michael Calabrese takes up a tale that, according to the survey, does not always succeed in the classroom in order to argue for its unusually great potential. In "The Man of Law's Tale as a Keystone to *The Canterbury Tales*," he argues that while the tale has recently been at the center of feminist and postcolonial Chaucerian criticism, it invites a wider variety of critical approaches involving issues of religion and causality, reading and interpretation, and style and narrative strategy. Just as Sidhu takes us "beyond the Miller's Tale," Emma Lipton seeks to take us past the "marriage group" in "Beyond Kittredge: Teaching Marriage in *The Canterbury Tales*." She demonstrates how literary representations of medieval marriage do not simply locate it in the private sphere but link it to competing social and political values, particularly the conflict between conventional clerical strictures and the late medieval consensual, sacramental model derived from Augustine. Turning to another of the marriage tales, Peter Travis, in "The Clerk's Tale and the Retractions: Generic Monstrosity in the Classroom," demonstrates how he connects the Clerk's Tale's resistance to "any single and unifying generic template" to his students' own dramatically varied reactions to the tale, a process that reveals them to be exactly the kind of readers that Chaucer is trying to create: readers who "will interrogate everything creatively and independently, pushing back against even the most straightforward-seeming work." Robert Epstein's "Students' 'Fredom' and the Franklin's Tale" describes how to get the Franklin's "demande"—"Which was the mooste fre, as thynketh yow?"—to do real work in the classroom. Epstein suggests casting the students as the "lordynges" being prompted and making them own their reactions to, and readings of, the tale. The last two essays in the section address the tales typically considered the most and least volatile in Chaucer's text. Larry Scanlon, in "The Prioress's Tale: Violence, Scholarly Debate, and the Classroom Encounter," discusses how to build one's pedagogy precisely around the tale's challenge to its modern readers, seeking in place of an impossible consensus a coherence that acknowledges that "in many respects the history to which [the tale] belongs has yet to come to a close." Jamie Taylor's "Chaucer's Boring Prose: Teaching the Melibee and the Parson's Tale" advocates teaching two less frequently taught tales, arguing that the pair are crucial to understanding Chaucer's playful and complicated vision of authorship and to broadening students' understanding of fourteenth-century literary production.

Our "Strategies for Teaching" section provides a glimpse of not only the "sondry" folk who teach and study Chaucer but also the "sondry" institutions and the various curricular organizations that influence (but evidently do not constrain) their pedagogical experiences. Those experiences begin even before the semester starts, claims Michelle Warren. Her essay, "How to Judge a Book by Its Cover," offers a comparative reading of the several French and English manuscripts that provide cover images for various editions of *The Canterbury Tales* and illustrates how primary sources can enliven and deepen students' understanding of the *Tales*, medieval culture, and modern scholarship—even before they open their books for the first time. Bryan Davis's contribution, "Chaucer's *The Canterbury Tales* in the Undergraduate English Language Arts Curriculum," grows out of his experience preparing teacher certification candidates for positions in K–12 education and demonstrates how *The Canterbury Tales* and course goals constructed around it can be used to meet the NCTE standards that those future teachers must later observe. Jacob Lewis, in "A First Year's Experience of Teaching *The Canterbury Tales*," describes bringing *The Canterbury Tales* into a variety of classes: a literature and composition course, a world literature survey, and a British literature survey. Each class served different needs and constituencies, and each presented distinct opportunities for challenging students and challenging his own ideas about *The Canterbury Tales*. Yet another body of students features in Deborah Sinnreich-Levi's "Teaching *The Canterbury Tales* to Non-Liberal-Arts Students." She describes the strategies she has developed—a mix of the electronic and the traditional—to teach Chaucer to her students at a technological institute where the most popular majors are mechanical and civil engineering and business technology. Teaching *The Canterbury Tales* at a historically black university, Donna Crawford has had to address a double alienation that the study of medieval literature can give rise to: according to her essay, "Chaucer and Race: Teaching *The Canterbury Tales* to the Diverse Folk of the Twenty-First-Century Classroom," understanding medieval texts' construction of difference requires students to negotiate a past outside the historical definitions of race that inscribe the colleges they attend. In "Making the Tales More Tangible: Chaucer and Medieval Culture in Secondary Schools," Kara Crawford draws on her experience teaching the tales to tenth and twelfth graders. The secondary school classroom, she argues, can be a place to preempt the narrow, stereotypical view of medieval culture that might otherwise take root in the minds of young readers. Through a focus on what is tangible, concrete, and sensory—images and manuscripts, the sounds of the language—this approach takes advantage of the fact that younger students are often more concrete thinkers than their college-age counterparts. Picking up on this material, experiential approach, Bethany Blankenship, in "Producing *The Canterbury Tales*," describes how her students create an actual manuscript page while studying *The Canterbury Tales* by integrating explication and illumination.

Surveys of new and not-so-new theoretical approaches to Chaucer abound; one could argue that, particularly in the last decade (and for various reasons), the profession has been rather scrupulous about charting its evolution and its integration of newer critical methodologies. But it is rare that these surveys approach matters from a specifically pedagogical perspective, an omission that the section called "Theory in the Classroom" seeks to address. The first essay in the section is Katherine L. Lynch's "Reading Food in *The Canterbury Tales*," which draws on the work on play, game, and theatricality by such critics as John Ganim and Carl Lindahl. The essay alerts teachers of Chaucer to the role of food as a structuring motif and a material and imaginary presence throughout *The Canterbury Tales*. Tison Pugh brings queer theory to bear in "Teaching Chaucer's *Canterbury Tales* with Queer Theory and Erotic Triangles." Pugh suggests that students, once equipped with the concept of the erotic triangle drawn from the work of Eve Sedgwick, can learn to read both rivalry and love as expressions of desire that exist along the same continuum and discover the manifold "triangulated permutation[s] of desire" in the *Tales*. Through these permutations, widely different characters express their erotic drives in ways that can be disruptive to prevailing mores. "Chaucerian Translations: Postcolonial Approaches to *The Canterbury Tales*," by Patricia Clare Ingham, outlines strategies for considering Chaucer's linguistic, temporal, and representational strategies in the light of the insights offered by postcolonial cultural studies, particularly such topics as the politics of language and translation, questions of history and temporality, and the political tensions of community structures and their vicissitudes. For Becky McLaughlin, "*The Canterbury Tales* provides a perfect example of how the unconscious functions" as it undercuts attempts to achieve mastery, both within and without the text. In her essay "Chaucer's Cut," she describes how approaching the pilgrimage as a Lacanian "journey into the symptom" can reveal how the text tells the tale of psychoanalysis. In "Performance and the Student Body," David Wallace describes how he encourages students to move beyond their typical assumption that Chaucer is a great storyteller by calling on a variety of pedagogical tactics that can reveal the discursive strategies that govern *The Canterbury Tales* and lead to the recognition that he is "a great discursive performer." Contemporary gender theory governs "Hidden in Plain Sight: Teaching Masculinities in *The Canterbury Tales*." In this essay, Holly Crocker describes the pedagogical swerve she uses in her course on Chaucerian masculinities. To preserve for students a sense of the diversity of masculinities depicted in the General Prologue, she suggests that one should turn not to the usual suspects in fragment 1 but to the tales of the more formally varied fragment 7, which put the construction of masculinities explicitly at issue in a variety of medieval genres. The final essay of the section is "The Pardoner's 'Old Man': Postmodern Theory and the Premodern Text." In this piece, Leonard Michael Koff uses the mysterious encounter at the center of the Pardoner's Tale to explore how Chaucer, like Emmanuel Levinas, examines ethical and ontological issues through imagined cases, as in the revelers' challenging encounter with the Old Man as radical other.

Nothing has changed as much since the 1980 *Approaches* volume as the variety of classroom technologies available to teachers of Chaucer. The last section of essays, "*The Canterbury Tales* in the Digital Age," functions as a sort of practical companion to the "Aids to Teaching" portion of the "Materials" section, offering examples of the use of both online materials and Web-based technologies (blogs, discussion groups, social networking software, podcasts, streaming video) in course design, individual assignments, student writing, and discussions. The first and longest essay is Lorraine Kochanske Stock's "Designing the Undergraduate 'Hybrid' Chaucer Course." Confronting head-on the current trend toward "blended learning" courses, Stock recounts her careful development of a hybrid Chaucer course that meets half the time in a traditional classroom and half the time in cyberspace, describing in detail the hurdles involved in designing a course that preserves as much as possible "the human social interaction expected by humanities students." Martha W. Driver is another experienced professor looking to connect the promise of cutting-edge technologies with strengths of traditional pedagogical practices. In "Public Chaucer: Multimedia Approaches to Teaching Chaucer's Middle English Texts," Driver describes how an enhanced awareness of audience that derives from the classroom use of multimedia approaches (filming, videoconferencing, interaction in the online virtual environment *Second Life*) can lead students to focus more intently on Chaucer's texts. In "Chaucer's Pilgrims in Cyberspace," Florence Newman recounts how she takes advantage of students' adeptness with social media by having them create *Facebook*-like pages for the Canterbury pilgrims, which grow in depth and complexity throughout the semester as the tale-telling contest unfolds and enlarges the students' understanding of the relation between tellers, tales, and audience. Timothy L. Stinson, in "Translating *The Canterbury Tales* into Contemporary Media," explains an assignment that asks students to recast some of the tales into more contemporary literary and entertainment genres, a process that not only enhances their understanding of the dramatic character of the tales but also provides them with a direct opportunity "to experience the processes of recomposition and reinterpretation integral to medieval authorship." Also interested in active student learning is Alex Mueller, who, in "Digitizing Chaucerian Debate," describes his use of a classroom role-playing blog that, because it is designed to mimic the "quitting" structure of *The Canterbury Tales* itself, encourages student engagement and interaction with the material and with one another.

The final essay in the collection is an overview offered by Susan Yager. In "Signature Pedagogies in Chaucer Studies," Yager draws from educational theory the idea of "signature pedagogies"—"types of teaching that organize the fundamental ways future practitioners are educated for their professions" (Shulman 52)—and asks whether it is possible to identify a "signature pedagogy" for Chaucer studies based on the evidence collected in this volume and what benefits might follow from identifying our common underlying assumptions as readers, scholars, and teachers of *The Canterbury Tales*. Her conclusion might serve as an epigraph for this new edition of *Approaches to Teaching Chaucer's* Canterbury Tales:

> The classroom is becoming more virtual, the atmosphere more egalitarian, and theoretical approaches more numerous, but the "joy," in Chance's words, of teaching is a constant. What then might be our signature pedagogy, the practice at the heart of Chaucer studies? Perhaps it is our constant drive to make Chaucer new, to create again the "sudden electric shock of recognition" of a poet and thinker who provides such a heady combination of enjoyment and learning.[1]

NOTES

Translations of Middle English that appear in this volume are those of the contributors or editors unless noted otherwise.

[1] Yager here quotes Ridley xv.

Teaching Chaucer's Middle English

Peter G. Beidler

Three large obstacles confront those of us who want our students to learn to read and pronounce Chaucer's Middle English: our students come to us with virtually no knowledge of a phonetic alphabet, they have never heard of the great vowel shift, and they lack familiarity even with iambic pentameter. While it may be true that "[t]he best way to learn [Middle English] is to hear it spoken, by a teacher or on records or tapes" (Chaucer [ed. Kolve and Olson] xv), hearing Chaucer read aloud does not remove these obstacles. Of course teachers should read Middle English aloud to their students, and the Chaucer Studio recordings (see creativeworks.byu.edu/chaucer/) are delightful accessories to the learning process. Listening to others read aloud helps our students understand Chaucer and gain fluency, but in my experience if students are to learn to read Chaucer's verse as it sounded in fourteenth-century London, they need to be active doers, not just receivers.

Because most Middle English consonants are identical to those of modern English, our students catch on quickly enough to Chaucerian consonants. We need to tell them that Chaucer spelled phonetically, which for consonants means that letters that have now become silent were for Chaucer meant to be pronounced. Thus, the *l* in Middle English words like *folk*, *calf*, and *wolde* was pronounced, whereas we now pronounce such words "foke," "caff," and "wood." We need to tell them that the *k* in initial *kn-* combinations was pronounced and that whereas in modern English we have made *gh* either silent, as in *thought* and *night*, or into an *f*-sound, as in *enough* and *cough*, in Middle English it was palatal, similar to the end sound in the German *ich*. Thus, while the word *knyght* has become for moderns simply "nite," for Chaucer it was more like "kaneecht."

I've found that students learn best when they see something in writing, but how do we convey in writing the sounds of Middle English? How do we write that palatal *gh* sound? How do we write the vowel sound of *y* (a letter usually equivalent to *i*) in *knyght*? Does it sound like the *i* in our *line*, the *i* in our *this*, or the *i* in our *elite*? Vowels are a special problem for those learning Middle English. The letter *a*, for example, has different sounds in the modern English *father, fathom*, and *fame* but had essentially one sound in Middle English—the sound it has in the modern English *father* (though sometimes it perhaps had a longer duration). And what about the paired letters *ou*? In modern English that combination of letters has several different pronunciations—consider *rough, mouse, fought, uncouth*, and *boulder*—but Middle English had only one or two. Since our modern letters for vowels have so many possible pronunciations, we cannot reliably use them to indicate sounds. We need a different way to convey in writing to our students what the sounds for *y*, *a*, and *ou* were. We need, that is, the International Phonetic Alphabet, or IPA.

The IPA is a set of symbols, each of which represents one sound and one sound only. In theory, a student who knows no English but who knows the IPA could read aloud to his roommate the IPA sounds for "I'm hungry" [ɑɪm hʌŋɡɾi], and his roommate would take him to the dining hall. IPA symbols are set off in square brackets to make it clear that they represent sounds, not letters. Using the IPA symbols, then, the modern English *knight* is pronounced [nɑɪt], while the Middle English *knyght* was pronounced [kniᵪt]. Note that in the modern word the vowel [ɑɪ] is a diphthong, whereas in the Chaucerian word it [i] was not. Diphthongs—that is, vowel glides—are represented by two symbols, one showing the first vowel sound and the other showing the sound into which it glides.

To help our novice students understand why the vowel in the Middle English *knyght* [i] became a diphthong [ɑɪ] in the modern English *knight*, we need to introduce a second key concept, the great vowel shift, or GVS. Until the nineteenth century, when language historians succeeded in recognizing and reconstructing the great vowel shift, literary scholars thought that Chaucer had failed at consistent rhyming. For example, in lines 3 and 4 of the General Prologue, Chaucer rhymes *licour* and *flour*. The Modern English *liquor* and *flower* don't rhyme, but once scholars figured out that certain vowels had different sounds for Chaucer, they saw that in the fourteenth century, *licour* did rhyme perfectly with *flour*. Because the changes that modern scholars have come to call the great vowel shift were for the most part consistent and regular, modern readers, knowing how a word is spelled or pronounced in modern English, can leap back across the GVS—can in effect "unshift" it—and make reasonably accurate assessments of the way Chaucer's poetic lines were pronounced.

This short essay is not the place for a detailed discussion of the vowels and diphthongs affected by the GVS or of the special complexities of transcribing and pronouncing the letters *o* and *e* in Middle English. Suffice it to say here that not all vowels were affected. The vowels sometimes termed "short" today, like the *i* in *his, fish,* and *till* and the *e* in *the, dress,* and *fell,* did not change. Rather, the GVS affected mostly those vowels termed "long" today, like the *i* in *white, cried,* and *bright* and the *e* in *free, deep,* and *she.* Teachers may want to consult Helge Kökeritz's thirty-two-page *Guide to Chaucer's Pronunciation,* but I have found that it is too complex to assign to beginning students. I have over the years developed my own fifty-five-page *Student Guide to Chaucer's Middle English,* now available commercially. The third major obstacle that teachers of Chaucer must immediately face if they want their students to be able to read Middle English with some degree of accuracy, fluency, and confidence is Chaucerian iambic pentameter. With a few exceptions, English majors come into our classes knowing little about scansion. We need, then, to explain terms like "iamb," "meter," "foot," "penta-," and "unaccented." I have found it most efficient to start with modern English iambic pentameter—"five iambs in a line, count 'em":

> Sweet Alison played quite a clever trick.
> She dumped old John and then enjoyed young Nick.

Substituting "Beautiful" for "Sweet" in the first line lets us show that the resulting "Beautiful Alison played quite a clever trick" is neither beautiful pentameter nor sweet iambic. Not only are there now two too many syllables for a pentameter line, but the initial foot is no longer iambic.

Before we can begin transcribing into phonetic symbols Middle English iambic pentameter couplets, we need to tell our students about the Chaucerian unaccented *e,* which was always pronounced as an eleventh syllable at the end of a line and sometimes, if the iambic pentameter required it, in an interior word.

All this is a lot to learn, especially since students need to learn everything almost simultaneously, but with encouragement and a series of homework exercises, they quickly begin to catch on. In my classes, the first of these assignments is a list of modern English words for students to transcribe into IPA symbols. Then we move on to transcribing a list of individual Middle English words. Finally, I have them transcribe a series of individual lines and couplets, keeping in mind the possible dropping of unaccented *e*'s. By the end of the second week of our fourteen-week semester, my students are ready to transcribe into IPA symbols lines 35–36 from the General Prologue:

> But nathelees, whil I have tyme and space,
> Er that I ferther in this tale pace

By now my students have read and reread my *Student Guide* and have come a long way toward removing the three obstacles to reading and pronouncing Chaucer. These lines cannot be properly transcribed without knowledge of the IPA, the GVS, and Chaucerian iambic pentameter. With this knowledge, students know that they should pronounce the final *e* in both *space* and *pace* as eleventh, unaccented, end-of-line syllables, and they know too that they should pronounce as a separate syllable the final *e* in *tale* but not the ones in *have* and *tyme*. They would then come up with a transcription something like this for the two lines:

> ɓʊt naθəlɛs, hwil i hɑv tim ɑnd spɑsə
> ɛr əɑt i fɛrthɛr ɪn əɪs tɑlə pɑsə

During a typical class I have students write their transcribed words and lines on the board, and we then spend some class time correcting one another's lines and defending our choices. My own contributions sound something like this: "For the word *tyme*, look on the vowel chart for *i* in your *Student Guide*. Since that *i* is a diphthong today—'ah-ee'—as we pronounce *time*, it would have sounded like 'teem' for Chaucer. Note that he would not have pronounced the final *e* because the next word begins with a vowel." "Now read those lines aloud. Good!" "Stomp it out: *ta-DUM, ta-DUM, ta-DUM, ta-DUM, ta-DUM*—and don't forget that final *e* there at the end of that line, that final *ta-DUM*." "I know it's confusing, but stick with it, and next week when you come in for your individual appointment, you'll sound terrific!"

As we work on removing the three obstacles in the first three weeks of the term, we also read our way through the General Prologue and the Knight's Tale. Our fourth week is given over to testing. By then my students have completed the homework transcription exercises, listened to and taken part in several oral readings of lines from the General Prologue and the Knight's Tale, and completed a couple of practice tests in class. They are now ready for the written exam, which typically starts something like this:

> Quoted below are several passages, given in order, from the Knight's Tale. In the bracketed space to the RIGHT, give the phonetic transcription of the underlined word in the line. In the space to the LEFT, write either the meaning of the word highlighted in **boldface** in the line or, if the word is a pronoun, the person to whom the pronoun refers.

> _____   "**He**, for despit and for his tirannye,   [   ]
> _____   To do the **dede** bodyes vileynye   [   ]
> _____   Of alle oure lordes whiche that been **yslawe** [   ]
> _____   Hath alle the **bodyes** on an heep ydrawe ." [   ]

This closed-book exam, which typically goes on in that fashion for fifteen more lines that I quote from different parts of the Knight's Tale, takes students about a half hour to complete.

At the end of the exam, before the students leave the room, they sign up for individual twenty-minute appointments with me later in the week. These conferences are crucial to the process, since they reinforce what I had been telling my students almost every day: that the purpose of all this IPA-GVS-pentameter stuff is not for them to put squiggly marks on a sheet but to help them pronounce Chaucer's lines pretty much as he did. Students have three tasks to perform in our twenty-minute conferences, all of them directly related to pronunciation. First, they recite in Middle English eight lines they have memorized from the description of one of the pilgrims in the General Prologue. I make a game of it: "Don't tell me who you are describing. This is in part a test of me, to see if I am good enough to identify your pilgrim." Second, students have to read aloud a passage from the Knight's Tale that they know about in advance and that I had read aloud to them. Third, they have to read a longer passage from the Knight's Tale that I select on the spot: "OK, now turn to page twenty-seven and start reading at line 1451. Let me remind you of the context: Arcite was released from prison seven years ago, but poor Palamon remains there in the darkness."

How do they do in week four? I am happy to report that almost all my students do very nicely. They speak their memorized lines well enough that I can identify the pilgrim being described. They read with confidence the lines they have had a chance to prepare from the Knight's Tale. I am always particularly interested in how they will do on the longer passage they read "cold." While some of them stumble, most surprise both themselves and me with their ability to pronounce most of the words correctly and place them gracefully in lines of passable iambic pentameter. Occasionally I will interrupt: "Try that line again without pronouncing the final *e* in 'passe'" or "What do you think Chaucer means by 'aventure' in that line?" or "Well done! So what's going on in the passage you just read?" For reasons I cannot fully explain, each year some of my students read the lines they have not had a chance to practice better than the lines they have memorized or the lines they can practice before they come in. Almost always there is at least one student who reads, in that fourth week, more fluently than I do.

For most of the rest of the semester we discuss Chaucer's tales as literature, but I find that I need to keep the language before us. The transcription into IPA symbols ends with week four, but I try to keep the students' language skills alive by having them perform in class, in Middle English, a series of skits from various tales and by giving them additional assignments on iambic pentameter, culminating in their writing a "Chaucerian" scene in modern English couplets. (For more on the skits and the iambic pentameter assignments, see Beidler, "Low-Tech Chaucer.")

Some students complain a little about having to learn Middle English: "Man, this is hard!" or "I thought this was going to be a literature course." But almost all, by the end of the fourth week, are pleased with themselves and with the praise I can honestly give them. In my anonymous course evaluation at the end of the term, I ask my students whether, in retrospect, they are sorry I made them learn to read and pronounce Chaucerian poetry in the original Middle English. Virtually none claim to be sorry. I am far more likely to get comments like these: "Are you kidding? It wouldn't be Chaucer if I couldn't pronounce it!" "It was hard, but I'm glad to know the IPA—it's helping me learn Italian for my spring study abroad." "That was my favorite part of the course." "I was thrilled to suddenly understand why so many of Chaucer's lines start with one-syllable little conjunctions and prepositions like 'And,' 'But,' 'For,' and 'As'—because the first syllable always has to be unaccented!" "Chaucer's Middle English is music; I love knowing how to sing it."

The Forms and Functions of Verse in *The Canterbury Tales*

William Quinn

The precise scansion of a number of lines in *The Canterbury Tales* remains a heated controversy for a very few prosodists. For new students, it may be sufficient to affirm that all of Chaucer's verse lines can be read as regular rather than rough. The grace of Chaucer's verse needs not so much to be proved as recited and performed. Once this recital skill is achieved, class discussion can then focus on particular passages that demonstrate the brilliant local effects of Chaucer's prosody—moments when his acoustic strategies significantly support or subvert the diction, syntax, and rhetoric of his narration.

Sixteen of the twenty-four extant tales, including fragments, and all the framing links, including the General Prologue, are pentameter couplets (purportedly first used by Chaucer in the prologue to *The Legend of Good Women*). It is often assumed that the "riding rhyme" of *The Canterbury Tales* guaranteed the future triumph of the heroic couplet, though John Gower remained perfectly content with the tetrameter form. By John Dryden's time, not only did Chaucer's lines seem irregular—largely because of mispronunciation—but his end rhymes came to sound too loud (end-stopped), too pat (predictable), or too contrived (rime riche). Nevertheless, most readers think that most of Chaucer's couplets sustain a remarkably fluid, colloquial style. Again, this easy flow is more the product of recital skill than prosodic dictates. Unfortunately, reading too rapidly can muffle the often subtle complexities of Chaucer's allegedly rough lines and conventional rhymes.

The most frequently memorized lines of *The Canterbury Tales* are the first eighteen. Chaucer's first couplet seems a little wrenched, however—a curiously unusual linking of "soote" and "ro[o]te." Presumably, this rhyme demands an exact repetition of the long vowel [o:], rather than a mixing of [o:] and [u:] sounds. The postpositive placement of the adjective "soote" makes this rhyme's emphasis only more conspicuous. Furthermore, "soote" seems a fairly rare word form in Chaucer's rhyming lexicon. It occurs only three other times in *The Canterbury Tales* and only once more as an end rhyme (SqT 389). Variations of "sweet" (e.g., GP 5) are much more common and are included twelve times as end rhymes in the *Tales*. Perhaps Chaucer meant to suggest an extremely subtle distinction between *suavis* and *dulcis*. Perhaps Chaucer simply delighted in the rarer rhyme. Perhaps, for starters, Chaucer was merely reaching for a rhyme. This segment also ends with a peculiarly conspicuous pairing of "seke" and "seeke" (GP 17–18)—possibly an approximate rather than an exact rhyme. In the middle of this overture, Chaucer's rhymes "melodye" with "ye" (GP 9–10), employing both senses needed to appreciate (and reproduce) Chaucer's song, the eye and ear. The most provocative question remains, How should the iteration of such couplets be performed? As artsy? wrenched? playful? purple? Much depends on each reader's *pronuntiatio*, or oral interpretation, which in turn is often informed by each reader's critical preferences.

The Man of Law has his own prejudices, complaining he can tell no "thrifty [suitable] tale" that Chaucer has not anticipated (46), "thogh he kan but lewedly / On metres and on rymyng craftily" ("although he [Chaucer] only ignorantly knows how to meter and rhyme skillfully"; MLT 47–48). The basic irony of Chaucer's having the fictional lawyer mock his own real abilities as a poet is rather obvious: Chaucer's contemporary readers as well as his most proximate imitators thought him a laureate poet primarily because of his craftsmanship, his ability to rival the formal excellence of French verse in English. For many modern fans of free verse, however, it seems remarkable that Chaucer could have achieved such a "natural" or "conversational" style despite the fixed artifice of end rhyme. The Man of Law's distinction between lewd metrics and crafty rhyming is curiously vague; the adverb "lewedly" can insult everything Chaucer "kan" do as a regular poet. Yet the rhyming of antonyms, "lewedly" and "craftily," itself exemplifies just how crafty Chaucer's rhyming can be.

In a still, though often indirectly, influential essay, James Wimsatt found Chaucer's rhyming relatively weak compared with that of Alexander Pope, who far more frequently deployed a witty "kind of fixative counterpattern of alogical implication" (Wimsatt 153). Whereas Dryden considered Chaucer's metrics lewd, Wimsatt thought Chaucer's rhymes insufficiently subtle. Wimsatt voices a modern sensibility produced by a (normatively "silent") reading that finds the musical effect of end rhyme weak at best. Merely competent rhymes are only "strong enough" or "neutral" or "tame." Post-Pope readers require a more sophisticated deployment of a poem's rhyming diction, which will reward the scrutiny of readers who can discover syntactically disconnected words that play against each other's coincidence of sounds.

The overall quality of Chaucer's rhyming need not be assessed simply in terms of the raw quantity or the proportionate frequency of "good" (because they are surprising) rhymes. Chaucer may not have thought this wordplay the most necessary or desirable effect of end rhyme per se; nevertheless, the tonal potential of Chaucer's rhyming is often overlooked if not amplified by recital (that is, by audible emphasis in the classroom). For example, many of the pilgrims' portraits in the General Prologue contain one or more rhyme pairs that provide an opportunity to discuss some implied dilemma or limitation in the given character's point of view. For the Knight, it is the implied conflict between his former "viage" and his present "pilgrymage" (GP 77–78); for the untroubled Squire, it is the exuberant iteration of "nyghtertale" by the "nyghtyngale" (97, 98); for the Prioress, it is the confusion of courtly "reverence" and true "conscience" (141, 142); for the Friar, a similar confounding of "penaunce" with "pitaunce" (223, 234); for the Monk, the absurdity of "cloystre" and "oystre" (181, 182); for the Clerk, the complementary (or competing) demands of "scoleye" and "preye" (301, 302); for the Franklin, the synonymity of "pleyn delit" and "felicitee parfit"

(337, 338); and so on. These are not necessarily Chaucer's most original rhymes, but they can be amplified in recital as telling moments.

End rhymes often punctuate Chaucer's punch lines. At the end of fragment 2, for example, the Parson objects when the Host exclaims "for Goddes bones." Chaucer uses "for the nones" (MLT 1165, 1166), itself a nonce phrase, for the required rhyme, making a seemingly throwaway couplet — one that thus defuses the full force of the Host's curse. Chaucer enhances the Parson's objection, however, by giving rhyme emphasis to "swere" (1171). The Host then swears again with a habitual, semantically void oath, "by Goddes dignitee," which the Parson seems to match with a similarly pat exclamation: "Benedicite!" (1169, 1170)— another nonce rhyme, unless rhyme itself reinvests the Latin imperative with its full semantic import: "Speak well!"

Intonation can give even Chaucer's apparently weakest rhyme choices suggestive strength in context. The Squire, for example, with studied modesty, apologizes in advance if he will speak "amys," which Chaucer rhymes with "this" (SqT 7–8), promising immature hackwork. Some rhymes seem ironic as if by position. The Squire ends his "secunda pars" with "bigynne" (670), and the Franklin begins his polite termination of the Squire's third installment with "yquit" (673).

When Chaucer is taught as part of a survey class, there is a high probability that only a very few of his works, all of these in pentameter couplets, will be experienced. If so, a main point of discussion can be how Chaucer avoids tonal monotony (unlike Pope on occasion) despite the formal homogeneity of such disparate tales as the Miller's, the Wife of Bath's, the Pardoner's, and the Nun's Priest's. But, to appreciate Chaucer's use of the couplet itself as part of his greater prosodic experiment, some attention must be paid to his alternative formal choices in *The Canterbury Tales*, including his occasional preference of prose.

Four of the tales use the rhyme royal stanza (MLT, ClT, PrT, and SNT), thought to be Chaucer's invention, though its pattern (*ababbcc*) merely omits the third a rhyme of the ottava rima pattern (*abababcc*) favored by Boccaccio. The rhyme royal stanza also has close affinities to the highly musical ballade form. Many of Chaucer's rhyme royal lyrics are designated "ballades." The eight-line ballade stanza (*ababbcbc* or *ababbccb*) was also one of Chaucer's favorite lyric patterns (found in "An ABC," "Former Age," "Fortune," "To Rosemounde," "Womanly Noblesse," "The Complaint of Venus," and "Bukton"). Rhyme royal is probably so called because it was perceived to be a modification of the ballade or chant royal (not because these "sevins" were subsequently used by King James I of Scotland). Unlike either ottava rima or the French ballade patterns, however, rhyme royal concludes with two strong couplets, and punctuation often gives the second some particularly strong rhetorical emphasis, much like the closure of an English sonnet.

It has become conventional to assume that Chaucer employs the rhyme royal stanza for tales that have a feminine focus or female narrator. (For Chaucer's immediate audience and for Chaucerians, this impression within *The Canterbury Tales* is greatly reinforced by the stanza's precedent use in *Troilus and Criseyde*.) Conversely, the Wife of Bath, who rides forked like a man, uses riding rhymes. But marrying one verse form to one tonal function is hardly so simple or stable in the *Tales*. Indeed, those occasions when Chaucer apparently changed his mind are particularly fascinating. Although the Man of Law had promised a prose tale (MLT 96), which the Host afterward approves of as a "thrifty tale" (1165)—perhaps initially praising the Melibee—Chaucer imposes rhyme royal on his account of an abused queen received from some "marchant" (132). The Man of Law's Tale sometimes achieves sincere pathos, often in direct quotation (e.g., 827–68). More often, however, Chaucer's favorite stanza sounds overblown in the lawyer's mouth, but that (parodic) effect is attributable to the pilgrim narrator's professionally excessive use of apostrophes and rhetorical questions, not the poem's pattern.

The Clerk's use of the rhyme royal stanza sounds far less stilted than that of the Man of Law's, and his tale of an abused wife has proved far more disturbing. As a translation of a translation, the Clerk's Tale invites class discussion of poetic equivalence—that is, the deliberate substitution of one form for another—and thereby the re-creation (or distortion) of perceived tone. In the couplets of the prologue, the Host invites the coy Clerk to speak, with one proviso: that he relate some simple merriment, the appropriate union of style and tone (ClT 15–16). The Clerk consents and pays homage to Petrarch, even though his source's proem seems impertinently digressive (54). The following tale is neither merry nor simple. Chaucer's choice of rhyme royal seems a formal heightening of Petrarch's prose, yet Chaucer's English represents a fall from Latin; analogously, Griselda's patience seems both saintly and stupid. Chaucer's formal translation of prose into verse displays the art of hiding art. The inherent musicality of the rhyme royal stanza often seems silenced, an inconspicuous scaffolding for the pervasive sadness of the tale, with occasional eruptions of a repressed outrage (e.g., 995–1001).

In sharp contrast, the appended "Lenvoy de Chaucer" (ClT 1177–1212) is very loud. If read as part of the Clerk's Tale proper, this odd envoy would represent the only instance in the *Canterbury Tales* when Chaucer seems to change his form in midtale (as occurs in "Anelida and Arcite"). Chaucer here uses a six-line stanza (*a*10 *b*10 *a*10 *b*10 *c*10 *b*10) that seems a truncated parody of the double ballade (three stanzas repeating the same rhymes with a refrain). Chaucer's six stanzas are all linked by the same three rhyme sounds (-ence, -aille, -ence, -aille, -ynde, -aille); a number of unaccented *a* and *b* rhymes produce technically and perhaps aggressively "feminine" endings. The masculine *c* rhyme repeats only across stanzas, like an anemic tail rhyme. Chaucer's envoy (as a palinode to a tale prefaced by a critique of Petrarch's proem) acts like Echo, who always answers in "countretaille" (1190). Following such a tirade, returning to rhyme royal, the merry Host accepts the futility of his "wille" (that wives be patient) and surrenders to silence with a rhyme: "lat it be stille" (1212 f–g).

In *The Canterbury Tales*, Chaucer does employ the rhyme royal stanza with both tonal sincerity and formal success. All of his other stanzaic experiments fail spectacularly—and deliberately. Chaucer's comic rhyming proves most crafty when his pilgrim persona seems most lewd as a minstrel. In the Tale of Sir Thopas, Chaucer obviously abuses a six-line pattern typical of tail rhyme romance (*a*8 *a*8 *b*6 *c*8 *c*8 *b*6) that itself did not seem inherently amusing to late medieval readers.[1] But Chaucer attempts to duplicate the same rhyme in all four tetrameters (*aabaab*). His rhyming word choices seem at best tedious and sometimes ludicrous, requiring learned explication: "Olifaunt" "Termagaunt" (Th 808, 810), "Fayerye" "symphonye" (814, 815), "aketoun" "haubergeoun" (860, 861), "hawberk" "Jewes werk" (863, 864). The stanza pattern itself falters (by being further complicated) four times in a row and then again at the end of the second fit (790–826, 881–90). In each case, an extra foot is added to the second *b* line, adding a *c* rhyme formatted as a disyllabic line. In the first case (790–96), this hypermetric foot usurps the tail rhyme role, and the b rhyme is used instead of a repetition of the a rhyme for the second couplet (*a*8 *a*8 *b*6 *c*2 *b*8 *b*8 *c*6). All these syllable counts are questionable—that is, dubiously competent.

In the remaining anomalous stanzas, there are three *a* couplets (*a*8 *a*8 *b*6 *a*8 *a*8 *b*6 *c*2 *a*8 *a*8 *c*6), resulting in a singsong ten-line tail rhyme pattern, the final four lines of which sound like a deformed bob and wheel. In the last of these too-exuberant patterns, the *b* and *c* rhymes (-ounde/-onde) are very proximate and so the worst. The final formal joke of Sir Thopas is its midline interruption of the mock minstrelsy: "Til on a day–" (918). Were this stanza concluded, we can assume the rhyme pattern would continue "something, something," rhyming with "Percyvell" and "well," and all too predictably "it befell." Less obvious is the fact that the interrupted half line at 917 and line 918 together form a pentameter, which, with near assonance ([aɪ:]/ [e:]), conjoins to the first line of the Host's interruption (Th 919). On the one hand, by exaggerating certain formal features of English verse, Chaucer apparently invented "rym dogerel" (925), both the term and the deliberately comic effect. On the other hand, with the pentameter couplet and the rhyme royal stanza, Chaucer repressed the inherent singsong quality of regular verse and established a new standard of serious narrative verse that prevailed (at least until Surrey or Pope or Whitman).

The infrequently assigned Monk's Tale aspires to be most serious but fails—as tragedy in order to succeed as comedy. Chaucer deploys his very familiar ballade stanza, which, nevertheless, looks very odd (indeed, sui generis) among the extant tales. Chaucer's lyric use of this pattern usually entails the repetition of rhymes between stanzas and a refrain. The Monk's Tale lacks this musical feature. If the verse homily had not already died as a genre, the Monk's Tale would surely have killed it. After seventeen minihistories, Chaucer apparently aborted this narrative experiment and never tried it again. The Knight, somewhat rudely, stops the Monk as if his 135 stanzas were a runaway horse, "Hoo!" (NPT 2767). The Knight dislikes the Monk's tragic redundancy. But the Host despises the mere loudness of the Monk's poetic efforts (2781).

In the Monk's prologue, Chaucer had all but predicted this narrator's inability to have form fit function. The Monk repeats rightly that the most common foot for tragedy is the hexameter (MkT 1978), though he is probably referring to the hackwork of John of Garland, not the artistry of Vergil. Chaucer's mangled macaronic rhyme "*exametron*/oon" only highlights the comic potential of the Monk's formal incompetence (1979–80). Excepting only the twelve syllables—give or take—of the first line of his prefatory stanza to his tale (1991), the Monk's measure is pentameter. But the Monk has conceded that tragedy can also be composed in prose: "And eek in meetre in many a sondry wyse" (MkT 1981)—that is, any which way.

It is frequently noted that Chaucer has the Parson voice a certain contempt for "rum, ram, ruf," but the Parson simultaneously renounces "rym" (ParsT 43–44). And Chaucer does employ alliteration, much more than is normally noted by silent readers. Chaucer's use of alliteration, unlike its sustained use by poets of the alliterative revival, is ornamental or rhetorical (e.g., NPT 3398–99), not structural. The most discussed example of sustained alliteration in *The Canterbury Tales* occurs in the melee scene of the Knight's Tale (2605–16). This instance seems a dramatic heightening of a sincere *descriptio*, but it raises again the same series of formal and tonal, and so interpretive, questions that pertain to doggerel (an equally barking metaphor for rhyme): at what point does conspicuous artificiality become excessive, and therefore comic, and, if so, deliberately so, for ironic effect (as, for example, in *LGW* 635–49)? This recurrent though intermittent consideration of such tonal particulars in Chaucer's versecraft should provoke a far more fundamental class discussion: to what extent did the father of English verse initiate its protocols of sound and sense—even for Dryden?

Two of the tales (Melibee and the Parson's Tale) are prose. Both are, in fact, translations. Therefore, neither needs to be read in terms of a fictional narrator's peculiar voice, though each is appropriate to its assigned pilgrim. Chaucer's Retraction is also prose; it, however, supposedly preserves the author's extrafictional confession. Ironically, close attention to Chaucer's formal ploys demands that the significance of these prose texts be addressed as such—that is, as not verse. Each requires Chaucer to renounce poetic artifice in favor of thematic substance; each seems a self-conscious act of formal abstinence. At the very conclusion of the prologue to the Parson's Tale, Chaucer quotes the Host and provides the final rhyme of his entire *Tales*: "'Sey what yow list, and we wol gladly heere.' / And with that word he seyde in this manere" (73–74). Chaucer's last couplet explicitly demands attention to the manner of hearing words, so we should indeed look and listen still.

NOTE

[1] See Thomas Chestre's "Sir Launfal" for an example of such a tail rhyme romance.

Teaching the Prosody of *The Canterbury Tales*
Howell Chickering

Offered in an open curriculum, my *Canterbury Tales* course is not required, has no prerequisites, and is taken by freshmen through seniors. I can't assume students will know anything about prosody or have had a prior poetry course, yet the catalog promises them "a rapid mastery of Chaucer's English and an active appreciation of his poetry." Many will not take another course in Chaucer or in poetry. I get one chance to teach both subjects.

I welcome this constraint. It gives me the opportunity to focus on how Chaucer's poetic rhythms enhance, and at times create, his literary effects, especially his humor, irony, and narrative and dramatic designs. I stick to this exclusively literary approach at the expense of historical and thematic concerns because I want students to see Chaucer first and last as a poet. It is important to me that they enjoy reading him and understand his nuances. That means reading him aloud in every class, which in turn requires knowing how to articulate his lines. Understanding his prosody enables students to bring his poetry to life in their own voices.

Basic Terms

Most of the tales are written in iambic pentameter—that is, five iambs (an unstressed syllable followed by a stressed syllable) and thus ten syllables per line. It is a very flexible meter. Its lines may contain from nine to twelve syllables. Sometimes a reader will hear only three or four heavy stresses, and occasionally six. Chaucer found this meter as a nonaccentual ten-syllable line in French and Italian poetry and adapted it to the native accentual patterns of English speech. Because his prosody can be described in the terms we use for later English poetry, in my class I call it iambic pentameter, a term English majors may recognize, though Chaucer probably would not.

All poets writing in English must take the language as they find it, using the natural stress patterns of spoken English when they fashion their lines. This makes reading Chaucer's poetry aloud fairly easy, once students have learned to pronounce Middle English. "Do not count feet," I tell them, "but instead let the stresses fall where they would in modern English according to the sense, and you usually will end up with a good iambic rhythm to the line." (Only a few Middle English words have shifted accents in modern English.)

Most of Chaucer's lines have a break, or caesura, somewhere within the line, usually at the boundary of a phrase or clause. This break is represented in the scansion below by an x, and its variable placement helps create the cadences of living speech. Chaucer's lines are either end-stopped—indicated in modern editions by a comma, semicolon, or period—or else the sense and rhythm run on to the next line, in which case the line is called "enjambed" (from the French for "to stride"). Enjambment is usually cued by a lack of punctuation at the line end, in which case readers should run right on to the next line without pausing, or they may choose to pause very briefly, in half-enjambment, to honor the weight of the first line if it is a phrase complete in itself. Since the modern punctuation of medieval texts is only editorial, readers can choose to fully enjamb a line that has a final comma if the sense demands it.

Lines 15–16 of the General Prologue show these features:

   ᴗ   / ᴗ / ᴗ / ᴗ / ᴗ /
And specially from ev(e)ry shires end(e)
   ᴗ / ᴗ / x ᴗ / ᴗ \ ᴗ(x) ᴗ / ᴗ
Of Engelond   to Caunterbury   they wende

Line 15 has no caesura and is also fully enjambed. Line 16 is end-stopped and has a heavy caesura. A second light or optional caesura is indicated by (x) in line 16.

Half-enjambed lines often occur when a clause ends a line but not the sentence and a dependent clause starts the next line, often with "that," as in these two selections from the portrait of the Prioress:

   / ᴗ   ᴗ / ᴗ / ᴗ(x) ᴗ / / ᴗ
Wel koud(e) she carie a morsel   and wel kepe
  \ / / ᴗx ᴗ/ ᴗ / ᴗ   /
That no drope   ne fille upon hir(e) brest.
. . . .
   ᴗ / ᴗ / ᴗ(x) / ᴗ / \ / ᴗ
Hir over-lippe   wyped she so clene
   \ / ᴗ /   ᴗ ᴗ / / ᴗ   /
That in hir copp(e) ther was no ferthyng sen(e)
   ᴗ / ᴗx / ᴗ / ᴗ /   ᴗ   / ᴗ
Of grece,   whan she dronken hadd(e) hir draughte.   (130–31; 133–35)

The second selection is half-enjambed at "clene," and then fully enjambed so that in "sene / Of grece" the final e of "sene" is elided before the following vowel.

Multiple heavy caesuras are possible:

   ᴗ   / x ᴗ   / x \ᴗ / ᴗ   / ᴗ
Som this, som that, as hym liketh shifte. (WBT 104)

And caesuras are moveable, too, as in line 1918 of the Knight's Tale:

   /   xᴗ ᴗ /   ᴗ / ᴗ / ᴗ /
First, in the temple of Venus maystow se

Or you can read it thus:

$$ / \;\; \smile \;\; \smile \;\; / \;\; \smile \;\; / \smile \text{x} \;\; / \;\; \smile \;\; / $$
First in the temple of Venus maystow se

You place the caesura where you hear the pause in the grammar. "First" can introduce the whole sentence, or it can go with "in the temple of Venus." Because the line contains both potential meanings, you must choose where to pause. Either is a correct reading.

Chaucer's Prosody Is Flexible

English speakers naturally use and can readily hear three levels of stress: full (/), medial (\), and light or unstressed (⌣). The abstract pattern of English meter, however, uses only stressed (/) and unstressed (⌣) syllables to identify its various feet.

Poets typically try to live up to this abstract template as much as they can, without sacrificing natural stress and sense. It is an artificial pattern to keep in mind while reading aloud, in order to appreciate the interplay between the formal pattern and the natural rhythms that articulate it. However, you should not force the stresses so much that they sound unnatural.

Elision and partial elision of pronouns or vowels may occur to keep the meter. But how to enunciate it is often unclear. The final vowel of a word may be omitted or joined with the following vowel. This is especially true for the articles "a" and "the." For instance:

$$ \smile \;\; / \;\; \text{x} \smile \;\; / \;\; \text{x} \;\; \smile \;\; / \;\; \smile \text{x} \smile \;\; / \;\; \smile \;\; / \;\; \smile $$
Th'estaat, th'array, the nombre, and eek the cause (GP 716)

In addition, lines can often be heard more than one way, especially when more than one meaning is possible. In fact, how we interpret the sense directly affects how we articulate the line. For example, upon introducing Chauntecleer in the Nun's Priest's Tale, Chaucer writes that "In al the land of crowyng nas his peer" (2850). If the caesura is heard after "of crowyng," it creates the phrase "the land of crowyng"; if it comes right after "the land," the line means "In all the land [there] was not his peer for crowing." This is a straightforward hyperbolic assertion, while "the land of crowing" is a delightful metaphor for the chicken yard. Both readings make good sense, so we should not try to choose between them but rather entertain both in our mind's ear.

Once students also learn the three most common variations from Chaucer's usual prosody, they will know how to read aloud ninety-five percent of his poetic rhythms in iambic pentameter. They encounter the first variation, a "headless" initial iambic foot, in the first line of the *Tales*:

[˘] / ˘ / ˘ x \   ˘   / ˘ / ˘
Whan that Aprill with his shoures soote (1)

The initial unstressed syllable is omitted, and thus here, as often, it gives the
line a trochaic rhythm (a trochee is the reverse of an iamb: / ˘). The caesura
splits the light iamb of "-rill with," increasing the trochaic feel. Line 2 redresses
these irregularities with a regular iambic five-stress rhythm that establishes the
norm for the General Prologue:

˘   / ˘   / x ˘   / ˘ \ ˘   / ˘
The droghte of March hath perced to the roote

The second metrical variation is an inverted first foot—that is, a trochee substi-
tuted for an iamb—easily seen in the word "Redy" below:

˘   / ˘   \ ˘   / ˘ \ ˘ /
In Southwerk at the Tabard as I lay,
/ ˘ ˘ / ˘ / ˘ / ˘ / ˘
Redy to wenden on my pilgrimage (20–21)

The third common variation is a similar substitution: trochaic inversion within
the line. This is sometimes confusingly called "the Lydgate line," since Chaucer's
successor John Lydgate was fond of it, and it is sometimes derided as a "broken-
backed line." But that implies it is a defect in Chaucer's prosodic practice, when
in fact, by following the stresses of sense, it merely replaces internal iambs with
trochees, often following a caesura. For example (trochees italicized):

˘   / ˘ / x / ˘ /   ˘   / ˘
Eek Plato seith, *whoso kan hym rede* (741)

Chaucer's Couplet Rhymes

The first two rhyme pairs in the General Prologue, "soote" / "roote" and "licour" / "flour," are typical of most of Chaucer's rhymes. The two rhyme words
have the same stressed vowel sound, and both end in the same consonant. If
there is an unstressed final e, it must occur in both words.

  In modern parlance, "licour" and "flour" are called masculine rhymes; the
words end on a single stressed syllable. In feminine rhymes, the rhyming
stressed syllables are followed by identical unstressed syllables, as in "evene" /
"swevene" (KnT 1523–24). Some scholars treat Chaucer's unstressed final e as

creating feminine rhymes, but I would limit this modern term to identical consonantal syllables, which receive slightly more stress than the schwa of final *e*, as one can hear by comparing "evene" / "swevene" to "soote" / "roote." Since so many of Chaucer's words could be written with or without a final *e* depending on their rhythmic contexts, an unstressed final *e* seems more a property of the meter than the rhyme.

Prosody as Poetry

Chaucer often uses his rhymes and rhyme schemes to make comic or thematic points. In the four tales in rhyme royal (MLT, ClT, PrT, SNT), he is especially adept at using the rhyme scheme *ababbcc* of the seven-line stanza to emphasize themes. The final *cc* couplet frequently expresses the narrator's judgment on the action or reinforces a concept central to the tale, such as "entente" or "wille." In the Prioress's Tale, the triple *b* rhymes create a repetitive singsong texture that well suits the Prioress's sentimental brand of piety. Chaucer learned to thematize his rhymes well before composing *The Canterbury Tales*: in *Troilus and Criseyde*, also in rhyme royal, the rhyme pair "Troye" and "joye" echo throughout the seven thousand lines of the poem, first brightly and then sadly.

Comic couplet rhymes—some obvious, some subtle—are everywhere in the Miller's Tale. No reader will miss the broad strokes of rhyming "kisse" with "pisse" or shifting from Absolon's plaintive "I not nat where thou art" to Nicholas letting fly "a fart" that then enjambs into a mock-epic simile (lines 3797–98, 3805–06). But couplets in the Miller's Tale also serve a structural function: the first line of a couplet often finishes one narrative section and the second line switches to a new section. To my mind the funniest and most artful instance of this is Chaucer's rhyming on the innocuous little words "do" and "to" right after Absolon's "nether kiss":

> He felte a thing al rough and long yherd,
> And seyde, "Fy! allas! what have I do?"
> "Tehee!" quod she, and clapte the wyndow to,
> And Absolon gooth forth a sory pas. (3738–41)

This is superb management of dramatic pace, closing off the rhyme as Alisoun closes the window.

Meter itself can also create comic effects, as when a moment later Absolon tries to rid himself of the nether kiss:

> Who rubbeth now, who froteth now his lippes
> With dust, with sond, with straw, with clooth, with chippes,
> But Absolon . . . (3747–49)

Five simple iambs in a row (with four caesuras) enact the desperate comic rhythm of his actions. Chaucer has used the most basic property of his meter to create a memorable image. Of course, the meter itself carries no intrinsic meaning and only gains its effect when combined with the sense of the lines, and the sense itself gains meaning from the rich narrative context. Chaucer is thus able to use the same meter to gain many different effects. Consider, for instance, "He was a verray, parfit gentil knyght" (GP 72). The steady trochaic beat of the three adjectives confirms our sense of the Knight's ideal qualities. It would be wrong for students to hurry through reading the line aloud.

But read it aloud they must, if they want to hear it as poetry. In lines 456 through 462 of the Clerk's Tale, the Clerk comments on his story with apparent distaste for Walter but also with a humorous glance at the Wife of Bath. How ironic he means to be depends entirely on where you hear his stresses. My students find three to four prosodic ambiguities in the lines. We sound out the possibilities and debate their merits, focusing on the relationship of the teller to his tale. They understand that deciding where to put the stresses is fundamentally an act of literary interpretation.

Teaching Chaucer in Middle English: The Joy of Philology

Jane Chance

We enjoy the rigor of discipline, but for some of us this
enjoyment would be spoiled if we acknowledged it.
—Aranye Fradenburg

Chaucer's choice of Middle English words informs and shapes his poetry visu-
ally and aurally—and should inform our pleasure in teaching it. One means of
encouraging an appreciation for his exquisitely nuanced poetry is to ask students
in a short research paper (two to four pages) to zero in on the etymology and
varied Middle English denotations of a single word in the General Prologue. A
carefully selected word illuminates the motives and inclinations of a Canterbury
pilgrim as well as the interpretation of the portrait as a whole. In addition to
familiarizing students with Chaucer's poetics and acquainting them with Middle
English, this deceptively simple exercise more importantly introduces students
at any level, undergraduate or graduate, or in any major, whether English or
engineering, to the joy of original research through the use of primary sources
and the exploration of philology, a pleasure few anticipate beforehand.

This opportunity arrives in my fourteen-week, junior-level Chaucer course
at Rice University (open as well to graduate students) after an initial several
weeks devoted to the short poems and the *Book of the Duchess*. By the time
students actually begin a close reading of the General Prologue, they have
already familiarized themselves with the pronunciation of Middle English
through daily practice of reading aloud. The class spends a fairly long period of
three weeks reading the General Prologue while also researching and writing
the Middle English word paper. Because the selection of a richly meaningful
word is key to the success of the exercise and is much trickier in practice than
it might appear, I employ several teaching strategies to clarify how to select an
appropriate one.

First, in up to two seventy-five-minute classes, we focus initially on the portraits of the Knight and then, briefly, on those of his Squire and the Yeoman and
their triune familial and chivalric relationship. Here, students begin to see how
carefully Chaucer has drawn his not so "parfit" aristocrat, particularly in the major epithet used five times to describe him—"worthy" (lines 43, 47, 50, 64, 68).
Although at first glance the abstraction *worthy* seems exactly the type of word
a student should choose to research, it is not, for several reasons. The Middle
English denotations of *worthy* do not vary much from the modern English
(or Latin, for that matter), and class discussion of its implications, while valuable for understanding Chaucer's methodology in the General Prologue, tends
to involve the interpretive rather than the philological—whether, for example,

Chaucer the narrator is exaggerating the knight's worth through such repetition and thereby undercutting it. Subsequently, to sharpen the students' sophistication in word selection, I occasionally ask them in class to pick a word that might carry the requisite polyvalence necessary for multiple interpretations and then defend that choice. What works best appears to be a word that is not image, symbol, or abstraction—often an adjective, but one whose denotation differs from its modern cognates and bears multiple meanings. In this regard, I urge students in their reading for class to check the glossary and notes at the end of the *Riverside Chaucer*.

Second, for actually researching their individual words, I refer them to the *Oxford English Dictionary* (now conveniently virtual at my university library and, presumably, at others) and the *Middle English Dictionary*, both of which frequently include thirteenth- or fourteenth-century examples from appropriate texts. Because students' success will depend on the medieval social and cultural differences in denotation (and on the perceptivity and intelligence of the student in understanding a portrait and in marshaling evidence), I offer my opinion, in advance of the exercise due date, of any word they are considering, ideally accompanied by this word's specific Middle English denotations and literary citations from the above-named dictionaries. By this means I help steer them away from very common or technical words for which there is little interpretive possibility (*fair* or *boil*, for example) or from words whose literal meaning would require more extensive historical research beyond the philological scope and length of the assignment (words such as *manciple, mortreux, sautrie, fee*, and so forth).

Third, I also hand out copies of two or three previous student essays that successfully unpack the complexity of a single word through careful attention to its philology and etymology. Generally, students are drawn to the most complex and best-known pilgrims, especially those ecclesiastics at the front end of the General Prologue, namely the Prioress, the Monk, and the Clerk—most likely because we spend so much time on them at the beginning of the General Prologue, when students are in the process of selecting their word—and, always, the enigmatic Wife of Bath. The best essays, even those about Chaucer's most ruthlessly satirized pilgrims, transcend more obvious analysis because of students' ability to perceive often subtle connections elsewhere in the portrait and to offer multiple interpretations based on different denotations of their word.

In one prizewinning essay, "Human Transaction in the Marchant's Prologue," the undergraduate Robert L. Forrest, Jr., chose what seemed an ordinary word, *bisette*, used to describe the Merchant's relationship with his own mind in line 279: "This worthy man ful wel his wit bisette." The student observes that *bisette*, in the *MED*, denotes "employed" ("Bisetten," def. 6), which suggests that the Merchant uses his cleverness to establish greater material worth (as in the illegal sale of French coins at line 278) or to cover up his indebtedness (line 280). This denotation kicks off the economic imagery in the portrait: according to the student, the Merchant's wit is also "bisette" in the sense of being "fixed" in purpose ("Bisetten," def. 4)—that is, obsessed, unmoved, particularly in relation to his material goods and business. The wit that earns him greater wealth and, paradoxically, so cleverly conceals his debt fails to help the Merchant acknowledge and comprehend his spiritual "dette": the student notes that the Merchant remains the "Old Man" whom Peter describes as "corrupted according to the desire of error" and whom he urges us to put off for the "New Man," who "according to God is created in justice and holiness of truth" (*Bible*, Eph. 4.22–24). Yet another meaning of *bisette*, the student continues, is "arranged" or "managed" ("Bisetten," def. 7). The Merchant uses his head in so cool and rational a way that in his pride he has cut himself off from support by others (including God). For this reason his wit can be considered *bisette* in yet one more sense: it is besieged and hemmed in ("bisetten," def. 2; "beset," def. 4), just as he is himself.

In a second example, "'Fat' and Chaucer's Monk," a history graduate student, Patricia R. Orr, begins with the physical associations of the word *fat* (GP, line 200). In addition to referring to the corpulent, as it does in modern English, *fat* (when used for land) refers to its fertility and, more abstractly, means "prosperous" ("Fat," defs. 2b, 6, 7a). Both of the latter meanings are appropriate for Chaucer's well-off outrider, who patrols the monastic estates. Less obviously, *fat* can also denote a "vat," the large open vessel used for cheese making or brewing (defs. 1b and 2). Therefore, Orr suggests, it can more figuratively and ironically apply to the Monk's body as a vessel for the soul (def. 3). This vessel the Monk stuffs full of literal food, particularly the fat, roasted swan (GP, line 206), which he resembles, given his shiny, steaming head (lines 198 and 202). Or perhaps more figuratively, the steaming head reveals the Monk as the prey of the devil, its steaming triggering the infernal image of a "forneys" under a boiling cauldron (line 202).

In a third example, "The Wife of Bath: 'Deef' as More Than a Hearing Problem," the undergraduate Brandi E. Braud starts with the fact that Alisoun was "somdel deef, and that was scathe," or unfortunate (line 446). Noting that Chaucer never returns to the Wife's deafness in the portrait, Braud turns to its denotation of "not giving ear, unwilling to hear or heed, inattentive" ("Deaf," def. 2, figurative) to link her deafness to her "wandering by the way," particularly her adulterous relations and her sacrilegious behavior at church offerings. In addition, Braud picks up the medieval attribution of *deef* to the adder ("Deaf," def. 2) from its source in Psalm 57.5–6, where the wicked are said to resemble the deaf adder that will not hear the charmer's voice or that of the wise wizard. Through this association of Chaucer's Wife and the deaf adder, Braud finds precedent for the Wife's spiritual deafness in the first woman created, Lilith, who, according to an earlier and apocryphal version of the book of Genesis, ignored the voice of God and returned to Eden transformed into a snake to tempt Eve to sin (Hoffeld 434). The serpent Lilith was punished by the Virgin Mary after the Fall of Adam and Eve, when Mary stamped on Lilith's head, which symbolized the birth of Christ and the promise of eternal life. So are all women punished, by mortality and the pain of childbirth—such an association becoming doubly ironic in relation to the aging Wife, who may be "deef," finally, in the sense of "hollow, empty, barren" ("deaf," def. 6a). We never hear in Chaucer about Alisoun's children, the student reminds us.

Such efforts in research and literary interpretation do boost students' confidence in their handling of Middle English and their understanding of medieval polysemy (and Chaucerian irony) in preparation for reading the more complex pilgrim tales. Some of the more resonant words that students have selected over the years crop up in the descriptions of those associated with the first two estates (the aristocracy and, especially, the clergy), possibly because of the disjunction between the pilgrims' obligations and the reality of their desires. Listed in order of their appearance in the General Prologue, they include "dresse" (Yeoman; line 106); "symple," "coy," "ooth," "semely," "fetisly," "desport," "tretys," "pitous" (Prioress; lines 119, 120, 122, 123, 124, 137, 143, 151, 152); "venerie," "prikyng," "enoynt" (Monk; lines 166, 191, 199); "wantowne," "daliaunce" (Friar; lines 208, 211); and "holwe," "hente," "cure" (Clerk; lines 289, 299, 303). The words the students take from commoners' portraits mostly refer to the bourgeoisie: "medlee" (Sergeant of Law; line 328); "praktisour," "kepte," "boote" (Physician; lines 422, 424, 442); and "wrooth," "boold," "wandrynge," "bokeler" (Wife of Bath; lines 451, 458, 467, 471). The more rustic commoners and the final reprobates are, surprisingly, less represented by complex words, perhaps because these pilgrims are either more obviously very good, as in the case of "substaunce" (Parson; line 489), or deceptive and evil, as in the case of "knarre," "brood" (Miller; lines 549, 553); "wise," "lewed," "wood" (Manciple; lines 569, 574, 582); "felawe" (Summoner; line 648); and "smal," "wynne" (Pardoner; lines 688, 713).

One ancillary benefit of this exercise, I have learned over time, is that it has convinced me that undergraduate students are capable of conducting original research. And in regard to graduate students, an exercise such as this one, involving a methodology of checking the etymologies and denotations of words in one primary text against those in another, can shape a student's life or career in unexpected ways. Laura F. Hodges, a former Rice English graduate student, volunteered a comment on the transformative nature of her own experience researching her Chaucer paper on *floytynge* in the Squire's portrait (GP, line 91). Having rechecked the original medieval literary sources for all the citations listed in the *MED* for her word, Hodges developed what she calls a "feel for the usage" (Message). The word *floytynge* is glossed at the bottom of the page as "fluting (or whistling)" in John Fisher's Chaucer anthology, but in the *MED*, she found, it is linked in Chaucer's day to *floute*, meaning "[a] flute; a shepherd's pipe," and only later, around 1430, to the verb "floutyn." Through this pastoral denotation, she identifies the Squire, in his colorful tunic embroidered with red and white flowers like a meadow, as a natural man in his whistling or as Pan-like in his fluting but also as a piping shepherd or courtly lover. She observes, "The fact is that this *MED* exercise was an 'open sesame' for my research from the time of the assignment, 1983, onward," meaning that it introduced her to a valuable philological and cultural method of inquiry she used subsequently in *Chaucer and Costume* and *Chaucer and Clothing* (Hodges, Message); it also contributed to a section on the Squire in one of those books (*Chaucer and Costume* 67–70, n58). In addition to the etymologies in the *MED*, Hodges found particularly helpful Anglo-Saxon and Old French dictionaries and glossaries and those on more specialized topics, such as fabric, law, and business (see W. Beck; H. Black; and Edler for historical context).

Chaucer's choice of Middle English words and their nuances informs and shapes his poetry—and our pleasure in reading it. Whoever insists that our teaching and research activities must be mutually exclusive practices, without an intersecting reflex or a significant consequence within our lives, surely has not experienced the virtuous circle that is fed into and illuminated by both. To open the door for students to experience the possibility of the joy of this philological reading—in its most exacting form—despite the drudgery and false starts is a pleasure in itself. There, I've admitted it.

Worrying about Words in *The Canterbury Tales*

Tara Williams

Anxieties over words pervade *The Canterbury Tales*. The narrator cautions us that he merely records the other pilgrims' speech because "The wordes moote be cosyn to the dede" ("The words must be cousin to the deed"; GP, line 742). His Tale of Melibee goes on to examine the various effects of "sweete wordes," "viciouse wordes," "plesante wordes," "egre wordes," "wordes of flaterye," and "goodliche wordes" (1114, 1128, 1152, 1177, 1180, and 1733). The Manciple's Tale revisits the concern from the General Prologue, insisting that "[t]he word moot nede accorde with the dede" and "cosyn be to the werkyng" ("the word must accord with the deed"; "cousin be to the working"; 208, 210), even as it shows how that relationship can go awry in fatal as well as trivial ways. In the final tale, the Parson warns that "ydel wordes" are not only "withouten profit" but "been somtyme venial synne" (647–48).

We, as scholars and teachers of Chaucer, also worry about his words. *The Canterbury Tales* is both the text in which students are most likely to encounter Middle English and the one for which translations are most readily available. But persuasive interpretations rely on a comprehensive understanding of the original language—what does it mean, for example, for the Miller to call Nicholas "hende" or the Wife of Bath to claim that she will not be "daungerous" (MilT, line 3199; WBP 151)? The recent resurgence of interest in close reading only reminds us how it has always been the foundation of the most influential scholarship. So which editions of *The Canterbury Tales* are best? Would assigning a modern English version be a venial or a mortal sin? How can we ensure that students understand Middle English, and how much time should be spent on that effort? These questions are foundational in Chaucerian pedagogy, and excellent work has been done on how to introduce students to Middle English and on the larger significance of that enterprise.[1] Introductory exercises necessarily focus on comprehension and, while crucial, comprehension is only the first phase in teaching students to work with Chaucer's language. Instructors can most profitably approach teaching Chaucer's language as a means to an end—an end that provides students not only a nuanced understanding of the text but also an enhanced ability to build strong readings of it.

When first reading Middle English, students often focus on the plot rather than on the shades of meaning involved in individual words and may have particular trouble with words that seem deceptively familiar, like *sad* or *sentence*, as well as those that appear to be entirely foreign, including *wight* or *wode*. To equip students to attend to such words as complex signifiers, we must teach them to mine resources like the *Middle English Dictionary*. Asking students to work with the *MED* presents some challenges—such as discussing how to use a dictionary without standardized spelling and how to recognize the limitations of the evidence base—but those are far outweighed by the benefits. The *MED* allows students to see the first noted appearance of a word in the written record, its full range of meanings, and when specific meanings were current. They can look up any term they find intriguing or puzzling, locating definitions absent from their text's notes or glossary and supplementing or querying the information that is there.

After introducing students to the *MED*, I ask them to apply through close-reading exercises the knowledge they gained.[2] Each student writes a one-paragraph analysis of a brief passage (five to ten lines) of his or her choice from an assigned tale, attending to specific words, phrases, and images and explaining how those elements affect meaning. When working on the Clerk's Tale, for instance, one student might examine the beginning of the third part to work through the thorny question of why Walter tests Griselda, while another might consider the first lines of the envoy in an attempt to tease out whose voice is being represented. Students must also identify at least one word that seems particularly critical or problematic in their passage and investigate its medieval meanings through the *MED*. I only require one word because of the short length of the assignment and the learning curve involved in using the *MED*, but once students get a taste of how useful it can be, many will look up each of the key words in their interpretation. For example, a student focusing on the friar's assertion in the Summoner's Tale that "[t]her nys, ywys, no serpent so cruel, / Whan man tret on his tayl, ne half so fel, / As womman is, whan she hath caught an ire" ("There is, indeed, no serpent so cruel / When man treads on his tail, nor half so dangerous / As woman is, when she has become angry"; lines 2001–03) discovered that *fel* could mean not only dangerous—the gloss the textbook supplied—but also evil and wicked or subtle and clever. This discovery allowed her to make a stronger claim about how the tale represents the effects of anger and reveals the Friar's hypocrisy.

I repeat these exercises across the term—with one due every week in which no other major deadline falls—to keep students attuned to Chaucer's language and to help them feel more confident and comfortable analyzing it. The close readings also have an immediate payoff: they improve the quality of discussion. A class that wrote about the Summoner's Tale, I found, was much more engaged with it than previous classes had been. As a result, I assign close readings on texts with which I anticipate students will struggle (whether because of the subject or the tale's complexity).

For a longer essay, the same skills and resources come into play, but the shift from interpreting a passage to mounting a full-fledged argument presents new challenges. The stage between generating ideas and writing a draft seems particularly tricky for students, though even composition studies, where the focus on writing as process rather than product is commonplace, overlooks this phase.[3] While a prewriting exercise would be useful for any paper, it is especially so when students are working closely with Middle English and may be likely to get stuck in the language or stretch it to fit their argument. Designed to precede a full research paper, the prewriting exercise requires students to articulate their argument and explore how they might support it with textual evidence before they produce a complete draft. The assignment walks the students through the critical elements of the paper: they articulate their argument, identify several quotations relevant to it, and analyze each, considering what the important language in the quotation suggests and how this evidence develops the argument. Students respond to the steps in list or bullet form, using complete sentences but not attempting to construct paragraphs yet, as in this excerpt adapted from a student response:

> Argument: The Man of Law's Tale represents loyalty differently in different religious contexts.
>
> Quotation:
> They trowe that no "Cristen prince wolde fayn
> Wedden his child under oure lawe sweete
> That us was taught by Mahoun, oure prophete."
>
> And he answerde, "Rather than I lese
> Custance, I wol be cristned, doutelees." (MLT 222–26)[4]
>
> Analysis: The Sultan's conversion to Christianity at the outset of the tale seems to be a positive move inspired by Custance. However, his advisers describe Islam as "oure lawe sweete" and, according to the *MED*, *sweete* could mean "spiritually pleasing or satisfying" or even "of God." This portrayal of Islam as holy and beloved by its believers suggests that the Sultan's speedy conversion is more problematic than it first appeared.

The student went on to analyze two other relevant quotes, one describing the Sultaness's adherence to Islam and one describing Custance's enduring Christian faith.

I encourage students to take risks and even to include questions for me when they are not sure of their interpretation. The exercise may also include more advanced elements like connections to secondary research or literary theories, recognition of what is at stake in the argument, or awareness of alternative interpretations. This hybrid activity works as a more structured kind of free writing or a fuller type of outlining, and it helps students begin to explore their ideas while leaving them in an open-ended format that is amenable to meaningful revision. While a student who has produced a full draft may be reluctant to do more than tinker with it, a student who has put together an argument and some possible interpretations may be willing to rethink those as part of the process of working them into a draft.

The prewriting exercise encourages students to focus on the fundamental elements of their paper before worrying about stylistic or sentence-level concerns, allowing them to engage with the weighted meanings of Chaucer's words, both in Middle English and within their own developing interpretations. Classic examples would include *mastery* or *gentilesse* in the Wife of Bath's Tale, *intent* in the Friar's Tale, and the Host's characterization of Chaucer as *elvish*. But there are many cases that have received less attention: when Chaucer names the land of the Amazons "Femenye," for instance, how does that affect the representation of those female warriors in the Knight's Tale (line 866)?

Because the prewriting exercise asks students to work closely with Chaucer's words before committing to a fully defined argument, it acts as the beginning of a conversation: they can make audacious or tentative claims, and the instructor can respond by showing how students might add nuance to their interpretations or bolster their points (in the sample above, for instance, I might ask the student to say something more specific about *how* the tale represents loyalty "differently" or to consider the source of the description of Islam as "sweete"). Prewriting also helps students develop confidence in their own ideas rather than borrow from secondary or online sources. In short, this assignment makes students' work stronger—students begin thinking about the issues earlier, have the benefit of targeted feedback from the instructor, and practice balancing the elements they will need in the final paper, such as close reading and critical contextualization. The improvement in those final papers is well worth the instructor's investment of a few minutes spent responding to each prewriting exercise.

Within *The Canterbury Tales*, Chaucer employs the formulation "[a]nd with that word" nearly three dozen times. Instead of seeing this phrase as a line filler, we might see it as a signal to attend to his words and their multivalent effects. This approach means not simply learning vocabulary but examining how texts create and deploy meaning. It has a philological dimension, but, instead of reverting back to the traditional form of that practice, it participates in the ongoing reclamation of philology. "By unsettling seemingly secure foundations," Michelle Warren argues, "philology can support the elaboration of more nimble humanisms" ("Introduction" 286). For students of Chaucer, a thoughtful focus on words imparts the linguistic foundation to support more nimble interpretive work.

NOTES

[1] See Goodmann; Ross; B. Stevenson; Sylvester.

[2] For a similar assignment in a different sequence, see Kruger, "Series" 34–36.

[3] The assumption seems to be that the hurdle is coming up with something to say; as a result, composition scholars focus on "invention" instead of on constructing analysis.

See, for instance, Kytle; Rohman. James Beck suggests using a "predraft," but this is still a form of a first draft.

[4]"They judge that no 'Christian prince would be willing / To marry his child under our sweet law / That was taught to us by Mohammed, our prophet.' // And he answered, 'Rather than I lose / Custance, I will be christened, doubtless.'"

Getting Chaucer's Jokes

Andrew Cole

Chaucer is funny. But it's no joke: the bibliography on Chaucer's humor is not as extensive as one would expect. Most scholarship is oriented toward the poet's handling of precedent authors and satiric and comedic traditions, and while this work improves on earlier research on Chaucerian irony, it does not, frankly, laugh with Chaucer in the way teachers and students do in the classroom—no doubt because academic writing runs afoul of the rule about jokes: "it's not funny if you have to explain it." In other words, while analyzing Chaucer's humor is not easy or always desirable, getting his jokes is an almost instantaneous process, involving an intimacy with the text of *The Canterbury Tales* and a sense of their immediacy that few hermeneutical protocols can claim. It is on account of such immediacy that Chaucer's humor is best experienced in collective fashion in the classroom. To help foster such an experience, I offer some general reflections about humor in relation to genre and language and propose some keywords students might find useful for both discussion and analysis in their essays.

To begin with, students can approach the comic aspects of Chaucer's poetry by assessing various interpretive frames for humor, starting with genre, which includes estates satire, fabliau, comic exemplum, and comedy in its classical sense—a genre Chaucer never purely adopts and seems to fuse with the tragic, as in the peripeteiac, jocoserious Knight's Tale. Students can then move to the more minute frames at the level of the line, differentiating sarcasm from irony, jokes from physical comedy, and double entendre from outright profanity. From there, they can think about laughter, which is almost an entirely separate matter from questions of genre and rhetoric because it is not always clear that when Chaucer's characters laugh, we are meant to laugh as well, even though so much of the fictive frame of *The Canterbury Tales* involves "mirth" and "quityng," an aesthetic competition in which it's fair game for one teller to rib another.

Consider, for example, the Miller's Tale, a narrative whose genre, the fabliau, carries with it the expectation of readers' laughter. After John the Carpenter falls from the rafters while sitting in his doomsday tub, only to break his arm (line 3829), the villagers gather round and "gan laughen at his fantasye; / . . . / And turned al his harm unto a jape [joke]" (lines 3840, 3842). Is laughing at an old man breaking his arm really *that* funny? Must Chaucer's physical comedy always involve injury? When characters laugh, with whom do we identify, the laugher or the laughee? As students answer these questions, it helps to bear in mind that most of the laughter in Chaucer's *Canterbury Tales* is directed at someone's "woodness" ("insanity")—"he was holde wood in al the toun" ("he was considered crazy in all the town"; 3846)—or motivated by "stryf," conflict, and pain: "And every wight gan laughen at this stryf" ("and every person began to laugh at his strife"; 3849). While one may chalk up these instances to comic relief, not all examples conform to that mold, as made clear by the evil laughter of none other than "Woodnesse" himself, "laughynge in his rage," depicted in the temple of Mars in the Knight's Tale (2011). Chaucer understood, avant la lettre, the B-movie "mwahahaha" of the mad scientist and other contriving deviants.

In the same way that medieval fabliaux, the essence of short and raunchy comedy, can violate generic expectations in offering up no laughing matter, religious genres can supply plenty of humorous stuff. Indeed, the Second Nun's Tale—an example of hagiography—briefly entertains the fabliau setup of the cuckolded husband when Cecilia explains to Valerian, "I have an aungel which that loveth me, / That with greet love, wher so I wake or sleepe, / Is redy ay my body for to kepe" ("I have an angel who loves me, / Who with great love, whether I am awake or asleep, / Is always ready to protect [hold] my body"; 152–54). (Some medieval plays use this awkward setup to good effect in the scenes following the Annunciation, when Mary must tell Joseph she is pregnant, to his great surprise and worry.) It takes no stretch of the imagination to hear a term of endearment in Cecilia's words, a declaration that she has a paramour called "angel." Yet before Chaucer reveals this "angel" to be a genuine divine intermediary, he has fun with the scenario and writes what I believe is the queerest line in the entire Tales: Cecelia tells Valerian that in certain circumstances, her angel "wol yow loven as me" ("will love you as he loves me"; 160). Perfect.

The penitential Parson's Tale, rarely assigned in the undergraduate classroom and never considered funny, allows teachers to create assignments that encourage students to adopt a jocund hermeneutic in reading its disquisition on sins. Students will easily see the comedy in descriptions of sins like Pride, in which the Parson excoriates people who wear tight and scanty clothes that "ne covere nat the shameful membres of man" and "shewen the boce of hir shap, and the horrible swollen membres . . . . ; / and eek the buttokes of hem faren as it were the hyndre part of a she-ape in the fulle of the moone" ("do not cover the shameful sex organs of man"; "show the bulge of their shape, and the horrible swollen genitals . . . . ; / and also the buttocks of them appear as if they were the hind part of a she-ape in heat"; 422–24). Does the Parson's vivid language exceed his moral point? Because this tale is chock-full of such stunning statements, students discover an accessible entry into straightforward and straitening religious materials, and teachers can ask questions about the epistemology of humor in the Tales—how the "Canterbury frame" forces us to see even the dourest of penitential expressions as hypothetically Chaucerian, playful, and genuinely funny.

To get Chaucer's jokes requires a background in one intellectual tradition or another, but the poet always helps his readers by using words riddled with innuendo, as if saying the word with raised eyebrows brings forth the meaning just below the surface. Take, for example, Dame Alice's description of her fifth husband: "in our bed he was so fressh and gay, / And therewithal so wel koude he me glose, / Whan that he wolde han my *bele chose*" ("in our bed he was so fresh and happy, / And therewith he could so well flatter me, / When he would have my *pretty thing*"; WBP, lines 508–10). Dame Alice has already made it resoundingly clear that "*bele chose*" means her sexual organ (447). But what of "gloss"? *Gloss* typically means to "comment" on a text. But here, when referring to *gloss* in a description of how Jankyn performs "in . . . bed," a new reading emerges, which invites us to recognize what *gloss*, from the Greek γλῶσσα (*glóssa*) means: its primary definition is "tongue," the organ of taste. Knowing that information, we can say something more specific about this passage than the prevalent and persuasive idea offered by Carolyn Dinshaw that male readers do things to female texts, figured as bodies (3–14, 22–26): Alice, quite bluntly, is speaking of the pleasures of cunnilingus, how well Jankyn glosses her.

As is invariably the case in Chaucer, however, what's funny is not so much the punch line as the setup, the ways in which the poet brilliantly juxtaposes and conflates the high and the low to great comedic effect. Students can find other puns in Chaucer, other conflations of the high with the low, when they study the meaning of words. Using the online *Chaucer Concordance*, they can search for jocund vocabulary in his canon and study the variations of meaning between passages. In my experience, terms that work especially well in such comparative assignments are *corage, pricke, thinge, queynte, orgon, melodie, grope, privee/privetee*, and *hende*. Students can be asked to choose one of these words and also to find a second, seemingly innocent term that may have been press-ganged in the service of humor. They can also collect the poet's ludic expressions, such as *laugh, jolif, joie, mirth, revel, jubilee, jape, mery, jocund, gay, glad, chere*, and Alisoun's *tehee* in the Miller's Tale (line 3740; the only onomatopoeia of laughter in the entire *Canterbury Tales*), and discern the nuances of meaning such words exhibit: does *laugh* correspond with *joie*, or *mirth* with *chere*? Finally, they can observe the absence of certain terminology both in Chaucer's works and in the lexicon of humor over the centuries. Never, that is, does the poet utter the word *comedye* in *The Canterbury Tales* (though he speaks of *comedye* in relation to *tragedye* in the famous ending of *Troilus and Criseyde*), and the pair *fun* and *funny* didn't appear until some 350 years after the poet's death. Likewise, *humour*—a medieval medical term denoting the four fluids that comprise a person's disposition—slowly merges with the sense of ridiculousness some two hundred years later ("Humour, humor," def. I.2.a and 7.b). Clearly, our words for humor differ from those used by medieval people, but does this difference mean that, correspondingly, medieval people thought and felt differently about humor? Or does humor know no historical distinctions between them and us? Is laughter, rather, our way to identify with the past and fundamentally get what people then were experiencing, even if momentarily? Students, by availing themselves of the *Middle English Dictionary* and the *Oxford English Dictionary*, can muse on how the traditions and cultures of humor change over time.

To laugh with Chaucer, then, is not simply to have a dirty mind or to be comfortable speaking in academic tones about Chaucerian vulgarity. Rather—and this point is very significant for students—to be in on the joke requires readers to be in the know in a very specific way. Not only must they focus on the intellectual and linguistic histories that inform *The Canterbury Tales* but also, and most important, they must pay primary attention to the line, to the words on the page that make up each tale. Chaucer's humor tells us about his craft, the techniques of poetic "makyng," and the assembly of sources in an original fashion. Making fun and "makyng" are one and the same process.

The Problem of Tale Order

Robert J. Meyer-Lee

I have had the unusually good fortune of studying *The Canterbury Tales* with Lee Patterson and Derek Pearsall, two of the most inspiring and influential teachers of Chaucer over the last several decades. Yet as much as I learned from each of them, their combined influence has been rather unsettling, like that of two parents who give their child precisely opposite advice. For, famously, Patterson's and Pearsall's conceptions of what *The Canterbury Tales* actually is—what, as a literary work, it consists of—are virtually antithetical.[1] While both acknowledge that the work is unfinished, for Patterson it is nonetheless structurally whole, and to understand it as anything less is profoundly to misrepresent the work and impoverish criticism. In contrast, for Pearsall, the incompletion of *The Canterbury Tales* is one of its most fundamental features, and Chaucer's design for its structure, inasmuch as he had one, was so manifestly provisional and opportunistic that attributions of meaning to this structure risk critical irresponsibility, if not simple foolishness. Corresponding to these views are, as one would expect, rather dramatically different notions about the proper way (and I use this phrase with all its moralistic implications) to teach *The Canterbury Tales*. For Patterson, the work is best taught from beginning to end, as an intensive study of an evolving, thematically linked, ordered sequence of twenty-four tales, which divide into different levels of groupings. For Pearsall, the work is best taught with a focus on individual tales with little or no regard to sequence and with cross-tale considerations emphasizing generic and other formal similarities. (Hence in the introductory course on *The Canterbury Tales* that I took with him, after the General Prologue we leapt all the way past fragments 1 and 2 to the Wife of Bath, the shock of which transition I still feel;

next up was the Pardoner.) Consequently, while students left the classrooms of both scholars with a robust and sophisticated sense of Chaucer's accomplishment, their respective understandings of what this accomplishment consists of differed in some radical ways.

The important question this difference prompts is not the facile one of which of the two is right. There are, after all, countless pedagogical approaches falling somewhere between these poles, including the common one of emphasizing continuities within the work's fragments but avoiding considerations that cross fragment boundaries. Instead, the Patterson-Pearsall polarity highlights the fact that, when one teaches *The Canterbury Tales*, one must make some sort of decision about the significance, if any, that one will attach to the structure of the work and specifically to tale order, a decision that will greatly influence students' understanding of the work. The crucial question, then, is: on what basis can we make this decision?

Any rigorous answer to this question requires a consideration of the surviving manuscript witnesses to *The Canterbury Tales*, which number over eighty, including fifty or so of the work in its most complete form. Since few teachers of Chaucer are in a position to survey this evidence, they rely on the conclusions of those who have done so, such as, most extensively, John Manly and Edith Rickert in their eight-volume study, *The Text of* The Canterbury Tales. In their second volume's chapter, "The Order of Tales," Manly and Rickert confidently declare, "That Chaucer cannot be held responsible for any one of the [tale] arrangements in the [manuscripts] seems perfectly clear" (2: 475), and this pronouncement has been taken by many as disabling all critical considerations of the significance of tale order, at least across fragment boundaries. If, as Manly and Rickert assert, all extant tale orders are posthumous, scribal attempts to make sense of the materials Chaucer left behind, then in ascribing meaning to any one of these orders we are mistaking scribal necessity for authorial intention.[2] This understanding of the situation lies behind Pearsall's oft-quoted call for an edition of *The Canterbury Tales* that presents the work "partly as a bound book (with the first and last fragments fixed) and partly as a set of fragments in folders" (*Canterbury Tales* 23). It also informs the critiques of modern Chaucer editions leveled by scholars who have contributed to that movement in medieval literary criticism, sometimes given the label "manuscript studies," that combines historicism and detailed appreciation for manuscript evidence with a poststructural skepticism of such conventional critical categories as authorship and organic unity (e.g., Machan).

Less well known than Manly and Rickert's conclusion about tale order, however, is their reasoning behind it, which in fact rests on the very critical categories that some manuscript studies scholars would now suspend in the name of historical authenticity. To support their claim, Manly and Rickert first target the tale order represented in the very early, lavishly produced Ellesmere manuscript (San Marino, California, Huntington Lib. El.26.C.9), which, with its famous pilgrim portraits, emblematizes literary completeness perhaps more than any other witness and was the basis for the two most important editions in Manly and Rickert's day, those of W. W. Skeat (*Complete Works of Geoffrey Chaucer*) and F. N. Robinson. In respect to the Ellesmere tale order, all the other orders appear inferior, and hence if the authority of Ellesmere falls, so does that of the others. Yet in discrediting this authority, Manly and Rickert merely repeat the observations of several generations of scholars before them: namely, that in the Ellesmere order the positions of some of the few geographic and temporal details mentioned in the tales and links result in a nonsensical sequencing of events in the trip from Southwark to Canterbury. Chaucer, they are certain, never intended such nonsense.

Almost all Chaucer critics today find this assumption about Chaucer's intention deeply problematic. For the poststructurally inclined reader, this view rests on the discredited critical category of organic unity, undergirded by the equally dubious assumption of an all-controlling authorial consciousness. For the historicist, it anachronistically projects the requirements of novelistic realism onto the rather different aesthetic conventions of premodern narrative. For the close reader, such a simplistic interpretation of the geographic and temporal details in question ignores the dramatic and rhetorical contexts that shape their meaning. And the practically inclined reader will find it difficult to defend the implication that, in a manifestly unfinished work, these details are somehow more finished than the tale order—that is, that Chaucer had necessarily settled on these details but not on tale order, rather than vice versa (or neither).

These and other objections have been raised, however, not so much about Manly and Rickert's use of this critical position but rather about its initial use by the Victorians Frederick Furnivall and Henry Bradshaw. Notoriously, as Furnivall describes in *A Temporary Preface*, he and Bradshaw took the details in question as the basis for rearranging the tales, against all manuscript evidence, so that the geographic and temporal references make sense. And for many years, despite objections raised from the start, this rearrangement (which came to be known as the Bradshaw shift) gained wide acceptance, especially after Skeat adopted it in his edition. Today, even while the shift's editorial residue survives in the de facto standard edition, the *Riverside Chaucer*, virtually all agree that it was fundamentally misconceived, finding absurd, for example, Furnivall's table of precisely when and where each tale was supposedly told on the journey to Canterbury (42–43). Manly and Rickert, like Skeat in such later writings as *The Evolution of* The Canterbury Tales, expressed misgivings about the shift on the principle that speculations about what Chaucer might have done if he had finished the work are not editorially valid inferences, and hence an editor's decisions regarding the structure of *The Canterbury Tales* must instead derive from a rigorous consideration of the manuscripts themselves. Yet as we have seen, Manly and Rickert's conclusion about the manuscripts was in fact guided by the Bradshaw shift's assumption about the significance of historical and temporal details; if today we are unwilling to make this assumption, what then do the manuscripts tell us?

The answer to this question rests on the tantalizing but murky evidence offered by the Hengwrt manuscript (Aberystwyth, Natl. Lib. of Wales Peniarth
392D). Virtually all scholars believe Hengwrt to be the very earliest surviving
manuscript, and most also believe it to share the same principal scribe as Ellesmere, although the textual relations between the manuscripts remain obscure.
Ever since the efforts of Manly and Rickert, editors and textual scholars of *The
Canterbury Tales* have tended to favor the text of Hengwrt as the most faithful to what Chaucer wrote. However, not only is the order of tales in Hengwrt
unique in the corpus of manuscripts, but by most accounts it is also simply
wrong. For example, it includes a sequence of Squire-Merchant-Franklin in
which the two links between the three tales appear sloppily altered to fit this
order of tellers, in contrast to the forms of the same two links in the Merchant-
Squire-Franklin sequence in Ellesmere and other manuscripts.[3] While a few
scholars have argued for the priority of the Hengwrt links and the overall better
(but still non-Chaucerian) authority of that manuscript's order,[4] the vast majority accept Hengwrt's apparently paradoxical combination of good text and bad
order. Given this situation, our question then becomes, if the earliest manuscript is a reliable witness to what Chaucer wrote yet contains a faulty order,
should we conclude that Chaucer did not himself order the tales and that hence
the orders of later manuscripts, and in particular Ellesmere, are scribal?

The answer to this question lies, first, in one's interpretation of the significance of some of the odd paleographic and codicological details of Hengwrt.[5]
From such physical features as changes of ink and evidence of inserted leaves,
scholars have concluded that the Hengwrt production team did not receive an
exemplar of the entire work but rather, over time, a series of exemplars of pieces
(of tales, links, and even portions of tales) and that, moreover, the team was fully
aware neither of the contents of the entire work nor in what order they were
to receive the pieces. Hence, while the principal scribe copied the individual
pieces faithfully, the faulty order of the whole reflects the uncertainties of the
production process. Scholars have generally surmised that these uncertainties
reflect some difficulty in obtaining an exemplar of the work or in understanding
the organization of one, in the aftermath of Chaucer's death. However, their
various (and sometimes heatedly voiced) explanations of this difficulty support
a wide range of opinions about what Hengwrt in fact represents.

For example, depending on the explanation, one may understand Hengwrt
as either a corruption of a more or less ordered whole (Patterson's view) or a
reflection of the disorder of the materials Chaucer left behind (Pearsall's view).
Lengthy arguments have been made for the relative probability of one option or
another, and the current majority probably favors Pearsall's position. Nonetheless, any such argument is necessarily speculative, since it depends on an imagined reconstruction of events for which we do not and are never likely to have
any record. Moreover, recent suggestions that Ellesmere may have been copied
very shortly after Chaucer's death and hence Hengwrt copied within Chaucer's lifetime (K. Scott), and the identification of the scribe of both Hengwrt

and Ellesmere as Adam Pinkhurst—who appears to have had a long working relationship with Chaucer (Mooney)—have not so much helped to resolve this mystery as intensified it. For if Chaucer was alive during Hengwrt's production and if Pinkhurst did have knowledge about his literary activities, then the fact of Hengwrt's disorder seemingly becomes more difficult, rather than easier, to account for.

The second part of the answer to the question of Chaucer's responsibility (or lack thereof) for tale order rests on the equally inherently speculative foundation of what one imagines to be the basis for Ellesmere's much more coherent order (and its overall more "finished" presentation), given Pinkhurst's repeat performance as primary scribe. While the simplest scenario is that Ellesmere represents the product of what Pinkhurst learned from his mistakes in Hengwrt (along with whatever knowledge he had about the production of intervening manuscripts), this scenario begs the question of what exactly he did learn, answers to which may range from merely his own insights about how *The Canterbury Tales* should be ordered to some belatedly arriving information about what Chaucer intended. Once again, while many arguments have been marshaled in support of various explanations, they all depend on an imaginative reconstruction of events that are permanently lost to history. To be sure, some of these reconstructions are easier to imagine than others, and yet ease of imagination is by itself scarcely definitive and indeed—if the cliché of "truth is stranger than fiction" reflects any experiential wisdom—may actually be misleading.

In the end, then, we do not possess a firm basis for deciding whether to teach *The Canterbury Tales* as Patterson conceives of the work, as Pearsall conceives of it, or as any moderating conception between—and yet we cannot avoid making some sort of decision. Whatever approach we choose, therefore, will likely reflect our more general beliefs about the aims, methods, limits, and theoretical undergirding of literary criticism. Consequently, our decisions about how we present the significance of tale order may serve as a spark to the powder keg of our critical assumptions. If we foreground, rather than cover over, the profound indeterminacy that we face at the very outset of our reading of *The Canterbury Tales*, Gerald Graff's famous exhortation to "teach the conflicts" may take very concrete, practical form in the Chaucer classroom. The intractable uncertainty about the structure of *The Canterbury Tales* may become a pedagogical asset rather than a liability, and the Chaucer classroom can be a site par excellence of the reflexive criticism that, whatever its specific theoretical orientation, has become one of the primary objectives of twenty-first-century literary pedagogy.

In practice, this approach may take the form of an enchantment-disenchantment dialectic, like the lie about Santa Claus that we know our children may someday repeat to their own. For example, every fall when I teach *The Canterbury Tales* as part of the British literature survey, I have students first read the General Prologue, and in discussion I limn for them the marvelous structure of the work as a whole that this prologue prospects. As a supposed example of this structure, when we later reach the Wife of Bath I have them read the Man of Law's end-link, and we spend much of a class period uncovering the intricate thematic relations between that link and the Wife's prologue that Patterson taught me to see. Only once most students are convinced of the brilliance of this tale sequence and link do I disclose the Pearsallian truth—that in none of its versions does the link give the Wife of Bath as speaker and that the link appears in neither Hengwrt nor Ellesmere. Unfailingly, this sudden demystification provokes some of the most critically far-reaching discussion of the semester. The students are thenceforth in on the decision regarding our basic conception of *The Canterbury Tales*, and they become conscious that their interpretive claims in discussion and papers are contingent on that original and fundamentally uncertain decision. Thus, whether they ultimately hold with Patterson's view or Pearsall's is not as pedagogically important as their confrontation with the necessary assumptions and exclusions constituting any critical position.

I won't say, however, that I haven't been keeping a count.

NOTES

[1] See, e.g., Patterson, *Temporal Circumstances* 19–35; Pearsall, "Pre-empting Closure."

[2] There are many different tale orders in the manuscripts, although they fall into four general patterns; see Manly and Rickert 2: 474–94 and the three unnumbered pages following.

[3] The *Riverside Chaucer* and other editions put a fragment break within the link between Merchant and Squire, but this is an error. See Meyer-Lee.

[4] Blake, most notably, supports the priority of the links. He also argues that they are non-Chaucerian in toto (*Textual Tradition* 79–95).

[5] For these details, see Doyle and Parkes.

Chaucer and the Middle Class; or, Why Look at Men of Law, Merchants, and Wives?

Roger A. Ladd

Why teach social class in Chaucer? It is no secret that for many students, higher education is all about social mobility, often understood directly in class terms. Regardless of our own critical or theoretical orientations, class issues cannot be entirely abstract in our classrooms. Because students have passed through a class-stratified educational system, many students' critical thinking skills can be quite underdeveloped. The "banking" (Freire 72) or "domesticating" (Finn 94) education still offered in many working-class schools inhibits both social mobility and critical thinking by approaching students as information receptacles and socializing them into the intellectual passivity of test preparation. For such students, and even for those benefitting from more empowering educations, class is everything. The need then to approach Chaucerian social class in these terms arises from a paradox: we care about class no less than Chaucer does, but we talk about it with a completely different language and conceptualize it through very different ideologies. If, however, we resort to explaining those sociocultural differences through lecture, we risk reinforcing students' passivity.

Bridging that alterity gap is worth our time, both because it helps students read *The Canterbury Tales* and because it can push their critical thinking beyond the limited ways encouraged by their previous education. Carolyn Whitson articulates this latter need passionately when she describes focusing on "the tools of medieval studies" with working-class junior-college students in hopes that they will learn, among other things, to interrogate the discourses of the past and to recover "from history the strategies that oppressed groups have used to effect social change" (44–45). With such goals in mind, I find that the General Prologue can provide students an unusual opportunity to discuss conflict between social classes without the emotional weight of addressing their own aspirations. With an analysis of the Merchant's portrait as an example of the approach I recommend, I hope to establish how the General Prologue destabilizes the familiar gestures of social satire, especially for the middle-class pilgrims who do not fit neatly into the three-estate model. One advantage of this approach to the Merchant's portrait and the General Prologue is that the availability of the Ellesmere tale-teller portraits allows us to avoid reinforcing students' passivity through extensive lecture.

That the General Prologue participates in estates satire is well established,[1] if not universally endorsed. I use the Merchant's portrait as an example of Chaucer's challenge to estates satire in the General Prologue because it briefly focuses on a problematic "middle-class" group and because it is so hard to be sure just how positive or negative the portrait is, an uncertainty that undermines the corrective function of traditional estates satire. The utter lack of critical consensus on the Merchant's portrait effectively demonstrates Chaucer's refusal to commit to clear satire. The Merchant's "forked berd" (GP, line 270), for example, might be a satiric sign of duplicity (J. Crane 84), but it also represents a popular style probably worn by Chaucer, as evidenced in the Harvard portrait included in the *Riverside Chaucer*'s frontispiece (v).[2] Perhaps the Merchant's speech about his earnings and open sea lanes is "typical of his class" (M. Bowden 147), or it emanates from a "professional façade" (Mann, *Chaucer* 102), or it represents a sign of depraved greed (J. Crane 83–84). Business terms like "eschaunge" (GP, line 278), "bargaynes" (282), and "chevyssaunce" (282) name commercial activities that antimercantile satire traditionally condemns. William Langland and John Gower both list and condemn the terms *exchange* and *chevisance* along with *usury* (Mann, *Chaucer* 100), which always denotes sin. Chaucer, however, pairs these terms with the more neutral *bargains*, thus undermining the collocation's satiric power.

As an interpretive crux, this passage's resistance to the much more direct critique of traditional estates satire goes beyond an aesthetic appreciation of ambiguity or merely a deliberate "transferring of responsibility from the text to its readers" (Fish 467). This observation matters in terms of thinking critically about class because of the social function of estates satire—the genre's defining approach of outlining the flaws of different social types creates an expectation of critique that Chaucer declines to meet. H. Marshall Leicester, Jr., made a similar point twenty years ago, arguing that Chaucer's substitution of ambiguity for direct critique reveals the contingency of traditional satire's social categories ("Structure," 246–47, 255), but I am interested in this sense of contingency as a spur to students' critical thinking. With the Merchant, Chaucer strikes such a fine balance between positive and negative elements that any initial bias for or against merchants will nudge it either way. In the absence of any bias, a reader might well remain ambivalent about merchants on the basis of this passage, and this latter case is most likely for modern students accustomed to seeing class issues through their own experience. Resolving or embracing the text's ambiguity thus requires students to think directly about how class discourse works.

Elsewhere in the General Prologue, Chaucer's discourse on class abounds with similar interpretive cruxes, including the Knight's "gypon / Al bismotered with his habergeon" ("tunic / All stained with his mail-coat"; lines 75–76), the Prioress's "Stratford atte Bowe" French (125), the Wife's "coverchiefs" ("linen head-coverings"; 453–55), and the Man of Law's "purchasying" ("legal conveyance of property"; 320). Even with pilgrims typically seen negatively, like the Pardoner, details evade certain extrapolation—surely being perceived as "a geldyng or a mare" matters (GP, line 691), but we cannot agree on why (Patterson, "Chaucer's Pardoner" 659–63). Chaucer's choice of which social groups to represent in the General Prologue also foregrounds the contingency of class discourse; although the careful placement of the Knight, Parson, and Plowman directly invokes the three estates, Chaucer does not represent the estates proportionally or in a strict hierarchy.[3] Simply following Chaucer's ostensible reliance on the three estates by categorizing the pilgrims by estate (for a class handout, perhaps) reveals the limitations of social categories, as the General Prologue presents a society of the middle, focusing primarily on the least stable social categories—kings and villeins would be easily placed, but Chaucer's presentation of a figure like the Merchant requires us to follow the poet's critique of his own society's class discourse. Since that critique consists in large part of interpretive cruxes, any reading of the General Prologue's approach to the middle class must address how class distinctions are supported by ideologies like the three estates and how descriptive details both enable and challenge class-based critique. Given the level of metacognition required to apply such concepts, it seems reasonable to expect students to leave a close study of the General Prologue with the intellectual tools to consider ideology and fine social distinctions in other contexts. That Chaucer focuses on the middle stratum-and that students often hope to rise in our own society's middle stratum is a happy coincidence.

At the same time, students are initially granted considerable critical distance by Chaucer's alterity, so they can argue whether individual details are positive, negative, both, or neither without being caught up in their own ideological battles. The fine balance that characterizes Chaucer's challenge to estates satire relies on his cultural milieu, but we know that a lecture outlining each pilgrim's social world provides an excellent cure for insomnia and reifies the passivity of the banking method. We can both address this challenge and develop students' critical thinking on class more broadly through an exercise using the Ellesmere tale-teller portraits.[4] Since the Ellesmere portraits represent two unknown artists' very early readings of *The Canterbury Tales*, close comparison of them to the General Prologue places students in dialogue with early readers of the text. Those areas where the portraits do follow the General Prologue are helpful; it is easier to look at the Wife of Bath's "foot mantle" than to explain it (Beidler, "Chaucer's Wife of Bath's 'Foot-Mantel'" 389–91). Details that do not match, such as showing the Knight in a *houppelande* ("a loose belted overgown") rather than the armor-stained "gypon" ("a tight tunic of varying length") described in the text, pose problems for students (or student groups) to resolve: are the artists updating the fashion (Mullaney 37), deflecting satire by omitting critical details (Rosenblum and Finley 140), misreading the text, or something else?[5] Already accustomed to thinking of class in terms of their own style and appearance, students can apply considerable nonacademic interpretive skills to a developing analysis of class structures and their expression through language. Students may not know what a *houppelande* is, but they expect clothes to mean something. This "problem-posing" approach (Freire), in which a student group disputes why an artist might reduce the Prioress to a sedate nun (Rosenblum and Finley 145), must rely on the instructor and edition as resources, but if sufficiently student centered it can provide an experience of finding or creating meaning through analysis of both text and context. If students can do that, they will be better readers of both Chaucer and the discourse of social class.

NOTES

[1] See Mann, *Chaucer*; M. Bowden; Leicester, "Structure"; Lambdin and Lambdin.
[2] See also Hodges, *Chaucer and Costume* 80–86; Pearsall, *Life of Geoffrey Chaucer* 285–305.
[3] See Leicester, "Structure."
[4] See Schulz for good color reproductions of the portraits.
[5] See the entries for "Hopeland" and "Jupon" in the *Middle English Dictionary*.

Professions in the General Prologue

Alexander L. Kaufman

Quite early in my teaching career, I began to understand the significant role that work played in the lives of my students. At my university, a large portion of the student body works full-time or part-time. Many are returning to college after several years (or decades) away from higher education, while others are first-time college students who have worked in various sectors for some time. With the recent reintroduction of the GI Bill, there has been an increase in service men and women at my institution. Even most of those who fall into the typical college-age demographic (18–24) work at least part-time, and many hold down full-time jobs, all while taking classes and attending to family concerns. With the background of my students in mind and the desire to have them connect in a very real way with Chaucer, I decided to create an assignment that would introduce them to the professions represented in the General Prologue.

At the beginning of my sophomore-level Survey of English Literature I course, I generate a list of all the professions that are found in the General Prologue. I then assign each student (sometimes two students) a profession to research. The document that I instruct them to generate is two pages (four pages if two students work together), double spaced, and written in MLA format. The assignment counts for ten percent of the grade for the course. I also inform my students that they will be asked to provide a brief overview of their chosen medieval profession in the form of a one-page handout to distribute (in bullet-point form and with significant quotations from primary and secondary sources) and a short, two-to-three-minute oral presentation in which they report what they have learned.

Fundamentally, the assignment is a "definition paper." Students must describe the basic responsibilities of their assigned profession in England during the Middle Ages. But I also ask that my students consider other lines of inquiry: Did the scope and duties of the profession change over the course of the Middle Ages? Were the responsibilities of the profession the same in other countries? How valuable was the profession to society, and why? Very importantly, what is the attitude of the narrator of *The Canterbury Tales* (and the attitudes of other pilgrims) toward the profession and the pilgrim who represents it? In regard to these questions, I advise my students to reflect on Jill Mann's general assertion: "The Prologue proves to be a poem about work. The society it evokes is not a collection of individuals or types with an eternal or universal significance, but particularly a society in which work as a social experience conditions personality and the standpoint from which an individual views the world" (*Chaucer* 202). Finally, I ask, How is the medieval profession related to a modern profession (if at all)?

One of the aims of this assignment is to acquaint students with our library and with library research. To help guide their research strategies, I instruct them to first look at the footnotes in our text (I use *The Norton Anthology of English Literature*) and to then broaden their research by looking at the explanatory notes from *The Riverside Chaucer*. To gain a deeper understanding of key terms, I introduce them to the online versions of *The Oxford English Dictionary*, *The Middle English Dictionary*, and *The Catholic Encyclopedia*. I require that they use at least two print sources for the assignment, suggesting texts (and placing a few on reserve) that describe the activities of labor in the Middle Ages and how labor is represented in medieval texts, such as James Bothwell, P. J. P. Goldberg, and W. M. Ormrod's *The Problem of Labour in Foureenth-Century England*, Christopher Dyer's *Making a Living in the Middle Ages: The People of Britain, 850–1520* and *Standards of Living in the Later Middle Ages: Social Change in England, c. 1200–1520*, and Maurice Keen's *English Society in the Later Middle Ages, 1348–1500*. However, for defensible pedagogical reasons, I purposefully do not place certain volumes on reserve that could be one-stop research items (Lambdin and Lambdin's *Chaucer's Pilgrims*).

In my survey, I typically spend at least a full week of class time on the General Prologue. Other Chaucerian texts include the Miller's Prologue and Tale, the Wife of Bath's Prologue and Tale, and the Nun's Priest's Tale. After an introduction to Chaucer's life and work and a discussion of the genre of *The Canterbury Tales* and the General Prologue, I tend to move deliberately through the text. The labor assignment, I find, serves as a perfect controlling guide. We discuss each pilgrim and his or her "condicioun" and "degree" as well as "what array they were inne" (GP, lines 38, 40, 41). With each new portrait, I ask the student whose mission it was to research that pilgrim's profession to inform the class what he or she discovered.

The reports on the Knight's Yeoman have always generated good class discussions on labor. Most students admit that they have heard of the term "yeoman" but do not know exactly what a yeoman did. Turning to the *Middle English Dictionary* and the word *yēman*, the students were surprised to discover that a yeoman could be many things: a low-ranking military officer, a seaman, an attendant in a royal or noble household, or a hired laborer, to name just a few. A yeoman, they discovered, could also own land and might even have a small estate. They are quick to determine that yeomen served a valuable and large role in the English economy. When discussing Chaucer's Yeoman, the students are most interested in his gear (the expensive peacock arrows; the sword, shield, and bright dagger; the silver image of Saint Christopher on his chest), his very dark complexion (much like the Shipman, who could be a yeoman but is never identified as such), and that he is, or so the narrator guesses, a forester. It is here that the reports provide detail on the responsibilities of a medieval forester, and we learn that some are gamekeepers who are responsible for protecting their lord's game. We also learn that sometime before 22 June 1391, Chaucer was himself appointed deputy forester of the royal forest at North Petherton, Somerset, a position with a significant amount of responsibility (Crow and Leland xxv). At this point, the class often debates how much of Chaucer's life and skill is perhaps present in the Yeoman. A key descriptor of the Yeoman, and one that often is misinterpreted, is that he knew "wodecraft" (GP, line 110). This is a word that our Norton anthology does not gloss, and so many students mistakenly describe the Yeoman as one who also knows how to carve wood or make furniture. A few keen students read Larry Benson's explanatory note in the *Riverside Chaucer* and discover that one who was skilled in "wodecraft" knew of the ceremonies of the hunt ("Yeoman" 802). In my geographic area, hunting is quite common, and many students describe not only the skill that it takes to hunt but also the labor-intensive work of breaking (or "processing" as it is now called) the game. We are also reminded of the skill of the hunters in Bertilak's three hunts in *Sir Gawain and the Green Knight*. In short, the class arrives at a "thick reading" of the Yeoman's profession: he has considerable expertise and knowledge, provides a valuable service for the Knight, and may in fact command a hefty wage for his duties. Most important, an in-depth reading of the yeoman's work leads the class toward a richer appreciation of the complexities of medieval culture.

Labor is a topic that prevails throughout my survey course, interrelating a number of other texts that we read, such as selected Arthurian romances, *Piers Plowman*, *Doctor Faustus*, *Gulliver's Travels*, and *Oroonoko*. In general, my students enjoy the General Prologue assignment. Its research component gives them more insight into various forms of medieval labor, including the work of the medieval poet, and since they are always aware of their own work lives, students realize that the act and value of labor can transcend temporal and geographic boundaries.

Teaching Chaucer's Obscene Comedy in Fragment 1

Nicole Nolan Sidhu

As many teachers of Chaucer can testify, reading the fabliaux of fragment 1 can be an exhilarating experience for students. Absolon's kissing of Alisoun's "nether ye" ("lower eye"; line 3852), Nicholas's fart, and the subsequent scalding of his "towte" in the Miller's Tale ("buttocks"; line 3853)—as well as the ludicrous bed hopping of the Reeve's Tale—all wreak havoc with the seriousness and sexual reserve that students expect from canonical British authors. In this respect, Chaucer's obscenity can spark student interest in a time period that many initially approach with groans and the rolling of eyes. At the same time, the fabliaux of fragment 1 also present challenges to the instructor. Students who come from cultural or religious backgrounds wherein sexuality and bodily functions are deemed private matters may be disturbed at Chaucer's explicitness. Feminist students often dislike the treatment of women in Chaucer's obscene comedy, particularly the intimations of rape in the Reeve's Tale. Even for those students who delight in Chaucer's obscenity, the initial thrill can end in a blind alley, leading them to regard Chaucer and the medieval period as naturally "earthy" or simple in ways that belie the sophistication of the author and his culture.

If, however, we ask students to step back from their initial reactions and invite them to think about obscenity as a cultural discourse, we can foster a deeper understanding both of Chaucer's fabliaux and of obscenity's powerful role in Western culture. Those who enjoy Chaucer's obscenity will be prompted to consider the reasons for their interest and to think about how Chaucer uses obscene comedy to explore questions of gender, violence, and social power relationships. Those who are disturbed by Chaucer's obscenity can see how the medieval author might share some of their own concerns. Encouraging students to think more fully about obscenity is much more valuable than simply ignoring their discomfort or patronizingly excusing them from engaging with works they find difficult.

I introduce the broader cultural context of obscenity during discussions of the Miller's Tale by identifying the tale as a fabliau and asking students to read one or two Anglo-Norman fabliaux like *Le chevalier qui fesoit les cons parler* ("The Knight Who Could Make Cunts Talk") or *Les.iv. sohaiz saint Martin* ("Saint Martin's Four Wishes"). These two fabliaux provide excellent background for studying the Miller's Tale because their English origin and flamboyant obscenity help students to interrogate the extent to which the tale might have shocked or offended its original audience. In discussing the fabliaux, I point out that the genre was consumed by the same aristocratic audiences who enjoyed the romance, a theory that is strongly supported in the English context by the fact that all of the extant fabliaux in English manuscripts before Chaucer are written in Anglo-Norman, the language of the aristocracy.

Also useful for placing the Miller's Tale in a broader context is the visual evidence for obscenity in the Middle Ages, much of which can be obtained from published photographs. Obscene marginalia in medieval romances and books of hours are widely available in published monographs (Camille; M. Jones; MacDonald). Such marginalia includes images of nuns picking penises from a penis tree, a lover defecating in a bowl as a "gift" for his lady, and secular badges featuring such images as a vulva riding on horseback and winged phalluses. Photographs of the obscene stonework in many medieval churches—including carvings of ithyphallic men and women exhibiting their vulvas—have also been published, as have the obscene scenarios that often bedeck English misericords (Weir and Jerman; Grossinger).

Knowing that obscene scenarios and images appeared in mainstream venues like churches and prayer books invites students to question the extent to which medieval people perceived obscenity as anti-authoritarian and leads to discussions about the ways that medieval obscenity supported the gender status quo. At the same time, the fact that medieval obscenity is cordoned off into certain genres (it appears in the fabliau but not in the romance) and spaces (on the margins of manuscripts and in the marginal spaces of medieval architecture like corbels and misericords) shows students that these representations are not simply the unselfconscious productions of a culture that lacked a notion of obscenity.

This context allows students to read Chaucer's Miller's Tale from a new perspective. The remarks Chaucer the narrator makes in the Miller's Prologue apologizing for the Miller and Reeve's "harlotrie" and advising every "gentil wight" who might find it offensive to "turne over the leef and chese another tale" ("turn over the leaf and choose another tale") might now be read as playfully ironic, assuming a distaste for the obscene that was highly unlikely among Chaucer's original audience (lines 3184, 3171, 3177). More important still, the popularity of obscenity in aristocratic circles leads students to regard the Miller's claim to "quite" the Knight more critically, opening up the possibility that, in spite of its rudeness, the Miller's Tale might share certain assumptions with the Knight's romance. This is particularly relevant to commonalities in the two tales' attitude toward gender, a point that has been made by many feminist readers of the Miller's Tale, such as Karma Lochrie and Elaine Tuttle Hansen, but can be difficult for students to grasp in the absence of the broader cultural context.

Opening students' eyes to the possibility that the Miller's Tale may not be the sine qua non of opposition to the Knight's Tale gives new importance to the Reeve's Tale. The tale told by the Reeve includes descriptions of sexual violence whose frank brutality diverges from fabliau convention. For that reason, scholars have often dismissed the Reeve's Tale as the artistically inadequate product of an embittered narrator (Muscatine, *Chaucer* 204; Patterson, *Chaucer* 276).

Viewing the tale in the broader context of medieval obscenity, however, allows students to see how the Reeve's violation of fabliau conventions allows him to engage with a number of issues—like rape, male competition, and social power relations—that are obfuscated in the more conventional Miller's Tale (Sidhu).

A canvassing of student opinion after a first reading of the Reeve's Tale will often reveal a recognition of the tale's brutality and spark debates over whether the coitus between Aleyn and Malyne is rape. These discussions can be improved by a comparison of how Chaucer represents sexual violence in the Reeve's Tale and how the authors of the fabliaux represent it. While it is productive to read the Reeve's Tale in the context of its two fabliau analogues, *Gombert et les deus clers* ("Gombert and the Two Clerks") and *Le meunier et les deus clers* ("The Miller and the Two Clerks"), I also recommend reading it in the context of fabliaux that represent nonconsensual sex, like *La damoisele de la grue* ("The Crane") or *La damoiselle qui songoit* ("The Dreaming Damsel") in order to demonstrate how the tales soft-pedal rape in ways the Reeve's Tale does not. Diane Wolfthal's work is helpful in this context because it demonstrates that there were a variety of different discourses of rape in the Middle Ages, some treating it as a comic event and others condemning it as a sorrowful act of violence. These insights attune students to the possibility that Chaucer's brutal representation of coitus in the Reeve's Tale may be a deliberate choice that aims to comment on the gender politics of both fabliau and romance, inviting us to think about how neither genre is willing to admit how women are endangered by a patriarchal culture that accords high status to men who dominate through violence.

This insight can be deepened by pointing to a progression of violence against women throughout fragment 1 and its relation to masculine contests, moving from the frightening but still protected position of Emily as the object of love for two violent suitors in the Knight's Tale, through the near-scalding of Alisoun with the hot colter in the Miller's Tale, intensifying in the rapes of the Reeve's Tale, and concluding with the Cook's Tale. The Cook's Tale is fragmentary and unfinished. Thus, it is difficult to tell where the Cook's Tale might have taken these themes. Chaucer's continuing interest in the relations of power, sex, and gender is evidenced in the tale's reference to the wife who "swyved for hir sustenance" ("screwed for her living"; 4422).

Reading fragment 1 in the context of medieval obscenity also helps students see how Chaucer uses the fragment's sequence of romance-fabliau-fabliau to expose the tendency of traditional obscene comedy to obfuscate the political sources of masculine violence. Again, pointing to a progression through the tales of fragment 1 is helpful. Students can see Chaucer moving from the romance interpretation of masculine battles as a matter of honor and love in the Knight's Tale to Nicholas's simple drive for sex in the Miller's Tale to a recognition of politics in the socially ambitious male characters of the Reeve's Tale.

Studying fragment 1 in the light of medieval obscene comedy thus helps students understand that Chaucer did not deploy obscenity uncritically but was aware of both the strengths and limitations of this important late medieval cultural discourse. Making medieval obscenity into an object of critical study is also of great use to the modern instructor of Chaucer's fabliaux, helping to move us beyond an indulgence in shared guffaws, which may alienate many students by assuming a uniformity of opinion about obscenity and its functions that does not actually exist. In both Chaucer's world and our own, obscenity is a potent discourse whose capacity to help us reconsider our most treasured assumptions about sex, gender, and the body is matched by only its restrictive power to degrade, shame, and alienate.

The Man of Law's Tale as a Keystone to *The Canterbury Tales*

Michael Calabrese

Nation and Race

The Man of Law's emotionally epic, high-seas adventure of a sixth-century Roman princess can try students' patience and shake their confidence. The teller's
lofty rhetorical style—and the shifting tone and subject matter of his confusing introduction and prologue—is alienating, the topics are uncomfortable, the
themes ambiguous, the tale and teller relationship possibly random and unpro-
ductive. The story itself is bizarre: a Christian royal woman is forced (gender
studies nightmare) to marry a Syrian Muslim (race and religious controversy)
whose mother-in-law (the first of two treacherous ones) kills her own son. Add
another brutal murder, a matricide, two attempted sexual assaults, some Christian nation building, and a vengeful slaughter of Muslims, and we see what a
minefield of politically incorrect events threaten to overwhelm our presentation
of the tale. As with the Prioress's Tale, then, the Man of Law's Tale must be
understood in both modern and medieval interpretive contexts; this means confronting in class the obvious themes of religious hatred—and their relevance to
a post-9/11 world—but then listening closely to Chaucer's language and tran-
scending a purely emotional or ideological reaction to the tale's brutalities. The
issues of nation, race, and religion in the tale are important and fecund, as are
history, economics, and geography (Lynch, "Storytelling"; Heffernan; Lavezzo),
but these issues must be balanced with an awareness of medieval spiritual narrative and the exegesis required to explicate the images and events in the tale.
Despite these pitfalls and despite its traditional low rank as a classroom favorite,
the Man of Law's Tale can also be one of the most rewarding assignments in
Chaucer class, serving, in fact, as a keystone tale that anchors the presentation
of fragment 1 to the tales that follow.

Style and Narration

But before even getting to the tale and to its sensitive issues, the very introduction and prologue can bog down class discussion. The introduction is a comic
episode in which the Man of Law, lost for a tale, contrasts himself to no less a
figure than the prolific love poet Chaucer, jabbing at once at Chaucer's friend,
the poet John Gower, who went too far and told a tale of incest. This infight-
ing among Ricardian poets may be lost on modern readers, but students can
appreciate how Chaucer, as *The Canterbury Tales* apparently begins anew in
fragment 2, looks back over his achievement as a poet. The tone of the Host's

opening calculation of time and his exhortation not to waste it are meditative and contemplative. Were the godless pagan philosophizing in the Knight's Tale and the fabliaux in the Miller's, Reeve's, and Cook's tales all a waste of time? Has Chaucer himself, as he surveys his own corpus, done right to be a love poet? English majors will appreciate questions about the artist's personal and public responsibility and learn here the fundamental ethical poetics of the Middle Ages. The Man of Law's Prologue, a curious text that praises wealth and disparages poverty, has no apparent link to the introduction or to the tale. But the prejudicial praise of money and harsh mockery of the poor misrepresent the text's source, Pope Innocent III's *De miseria*, by omitting a parallel attack on wealth; in fact, the Man of Law is grateful to rich merchants who taught him the tale.[1] The prologue thus makes us question the accuracy, reliability, and moral understanding of the Man of Law, rendering him pompous and potentially ridiculous. As a lawyer, he is all about words and pleading (see "submitted," "assent," and "biheeste" in the introduction, lines 33 and following), and he intervenes in the tale frequently not only with legalisms but with astrological ramblings, emotional outbursts, classical and biblical analogies, personal concern for his heroine, and venom for her enemies. Since the meaning of the story risks being lost in a sea of histrionic rhetoric, I ask students to find and analyze the Man of Law's grand intrusions throughout the story and to try to determine how this teller relates to the tale (Barlow; Caie; M. Nolan; Reed). (In the unfinished state of *The Canterbury Tales*, the tale may have been independently produced and not initially assigned to him. A. C. Spearing has powerfully challenged the fixation on this teller in his essay "Narrative Voice," arguing that the tale itself contains relatively little of his clear narrative voice.)

Religion, Gender, and Causality

But no Chaucerian teller goes away willingly, and Chaucer makes us fend off a narrator to get to the narrative. Our goal is to get to, as the Man of Law himself says, the "fruyt of this matiere" (MLT, line 411). Perhaps Barbara Nolan best isolates the spiritual core of the tale: "Custance overcomes the bizarre wonders of her mortal life by her movingly human, heartfelt, prayerful appeal to, and identification with, Christ, Mary, and the promise of eternal bliss" ("Chaucer's Tales" 27). Chaucer often makes us fight through the bizarre to perceive the eternal. But will students embrace Nolan's mystical reading or Carolyn Dinshaw's equally compelling historical awareness of Custance's subjugation to patriarchy? Or will they engage with both? The tension between these readings and their simultaneous applicability point to the complexity and richness of trying to read women's experience in medieval Christian texts.

　　With these issues of female power and human agency in mind, I base my class on the Man of Law (and *The Canterbury Tales* as a whole) on a series of questions about will and causality: How do things happen? What can people control? Where, if anywhere, is God? The Knight's Tale summons planets, gods, political rulers, careful stadium architecture—all to order the animalistic human passions of two men fighting over a woman. All systems of control fail, as does Nicholas's inventive but severely punished hijacking of scripture to bed the carpenter's wife. Finally, in the Man of Law's Tale we get purely divine causality; Custance lives biblical narrative, and readers can enjoy her adventures without fearing that God's enemies will ever get to her. Has Chaucer, however, solved the problems of free will and providence, or is the divine protection that secures Custance, kills her enemies, and reunites her family just part of another fictive fantasy, as remote from real human life as the sparring planetary influences of the Knight's Tale? The question itself makes us wonder what sort of literary world we are in with the Man of Law's Tale: is it a secular saint's life, an "Oriental" romance, or, finally, a puzzling patchwork of too many conflicting texts and contexts?

To answer these questions, I have students trace and read the visual images, as famously seen by V. A. Kolve, that allegorically align Custance's sea voyage to the soul's journey to God: here the church and the cross protect the faithful Christian through time, and the tale confidently links Custance to the Israelites, Daniel, David, and Judith while echoing hymns and prayers from the Good Friday liturgy (Kolve, *Chaucer*; B. Nolan, "Chaucer's Tales"). Do students agree that these exegetical moments and analogies express the tale's primary, that is to say "medieval," meaning?

Reading and Interpretation

Related to scriptural exegesis is the broader theme of reading throughout the tale. "Thus wole [says] oure text" says the Man of Law to the Host (MLT 45), acknowledging his debt to tell a story, and he frequently refers to some nebulous source story told by merchants, a story that he evidently trims and glosses in recounting Custance's tale. One can ask students to isolate every instance of reading, of interpreting, texts, laws, and doctrines in the tale, while they trace as well Chaucer's own additions to his sources.[2] The Man of Law cites legal books and quotes Innocent III; the stars are a book that reveals everyone's death; hijacked, lying letters lead to the unjust exile of wife and child and, later, to vengeful matricide; a gospel book, abused, ensures violent justice for a perjurer; and Christian Scripture battles the Koran, which nonetheless inspires submission among its own faithful. I teach the tale not only as a violent conflict of faiths but also as an adventure about books, reading, interpretation, and the comprehensive struggle to perceive and create meaning with words, spoken or written. When Custance reaches England, she speaks incomprehensible Latin to the locals and fails to identify herself; she can't communicate well but "all hir loven that loken in her face" ("everyone that looked into her face loved her"; 532). At this deeply Dantean moment, Custance radiates a love beyond language and identity, beyond rhetoric, law, doctrine, or nation. Students can here ponder the limits of analysis and exegesis in response to spiritual poetry. When did Chaucer imagine his readers would stop chasing down allusions and begin a process of religious contemplation? When should we?

In addition to such potentially glorious moments of transcendence, the Man of Law's Tale also explores *The Canterbury Tales'* more earthy themes of passion, love, and marriage. When Custance says woman is born to man's "governance" or the Man of Law that "housbondes been alle goode" ("all husbands are good"; 238, 272), Chaucer develops the marriage question that will continue to dominate the *Tales*. The "yong knight who loves her so hoote" with his "foul [perverted] affeccioun" recalls Nicholas, Palamon, and Arcite (586), while the inciting Satan anticipates the Prioress's Tale. The tale thus takes its place in the old marriage debate and claims a central location in Chaucer's study of men and women, provoking students to make many associations to other characters and tales. In tracing the tale's allusions, anticipations, and cross-references, they will discover how tightly Chaucer weaves his art.

So, finally, I advise my fellow Chaucerians that if you are deep "ystert in loore" ("steeped in learning"; MLT 4); if you succeed in tracing out many of Chaucer's allusions, anticipations, and revisions; and if you also commit yourself to teaching the tale as a medieval story in and about translation, you and your class will enjoy a slow, careful engagement with the Man of Law's Tale. Take it from the margins, fight through the political and ideological firestorms, play or read it aloud (see *Chaucer Studio*), and give yourself and your students over to the "wilde see" of the Man of Law's Tale (506). With any luck (or is it divine guidance or fortune or astral fate?) you'll find your way home, or at least to the Wife of Bath's Prologue.

NOTES

[1] On the role of Innocent in the Man of Law's texts, see Caie; Lawton; and, most recently, Zieman.
[2] The *Riverside* tracks Chaucer's additions to Nicholas Trivet's *Chronicle* and Gower's *Confessio Amantis*. See Correale and Hamel.

Beyond Kittredge:
Teaching Marriage in *The Canterbury Tales*
Emma Lipton

Recent work by scholars such as David Wallace (*Chaucerian Polity*), Glenn Burger, Lynn Staley, and others has suggested a variety of ways in which marriage should be understood as both a political and a domestic arrangement in *The Canterbury Tales* and in medieval culture more broadly. Yet it is George Lyman Kittredge's famous 1912 essay on the "marriage group" that is reproduced in the critical section of the most recent Norton edition of *The Canterbury Tales* (ed. Kolve and Olson [2005]) and that continues to draw students' attention. Here Kittredge argues that from the Wife's Prologue to the Franklin's Tale, *The Canterbury Tales* should be understood to offer a "dramatic dialogue" about the proper relationship between husband and wife in marriage, a dialogue in which the Wife maintains that "wives should rule their husbands" (Kittredge, "Chaucer's Discussion" 439), the Clerk counters that the husband should "rule his wife absolutely" (446), and the Franklin promotes a "relation of mutual love and forbearance" (467). In my experience, students are drawn to this essay not only because of its accessibility but also because of its focus on marriage and love as located in private life, which allows them to draw connections between Chaucer's poem and their own lives. I suggest that the discourse of marriage in the tales can also be linked to social and political values. Teaching marriage in this way helps students grasp a central insight of the tales: even our most personal values are constructed by our social and class positions. I have found that teaching love and marriage as social constructs and political institutions can help overcome students' resistance to the idea that social class is relevant to their daily lives. Indeed, current debates about gay marriage highlight the important place of marriage in the complex nexus of civic, legal, and religious discourses in modern life and remind us that marriage remains a deeply political institution.

My students often assume that medieval marriage was patriarchal and oppressive. Indeed, medieval marriage sermons frequently instructed spouses that wives were subject to the authority and correction of their husbands (D'Avray and Tausche 105). This precept can be found in a wide range of texts, including the colorful passage in the conduct book *Le ménagier de Paris* in which a young wife is instructed to obey her husband as a dog obeys his master (*Good Wife's Guide* 102). In medieval law, wives were known as *couverte de baron*, meaning that they had no independent legal status and were completely under the legal authority of their husbands (Bennett 110–14; Pollock and Maitland 2: 405–08).

Medieval theologians contributed to the bad reputation of marriage. Saint Jerome and later writers invoked Saint Paul's injunction that "it is better to marry than to burn" to establish marriage as a last resort for those who could not maintain continence (1 Cor. 7.9). Marriage was tolerated only as a remedy against carnal lust, a prophylactic measure against fornication and greater evils. Since the doctrine of the marital debt required spouses to have intercourse if one spouse requested it, many theologians saw marriage as defined by sex and thus as incompatible with the pious life. This idea was behind the "three grades of chastity," which valued virginity above widowhood, assigning marriage to the bottom. The association of marriage with sex and thus with sin was confirmed and maintained by the twelfth-century laws against clerical marriage, which established celibacy as the truly pious life and bolstered clerical prerogative.

But in a competing model, marriage was also defined as a sacrament based in love and grounded in mutuality and friendship. Known as the sacramental model, it was based in the writings of Augustine, who drew on the biblical example of the marriage of Mary and Joseph to argue that marital affection instead of sexual relations defined marriage. For Augustine, marriage was not just a relative virtue in that it was better than fornication but had three specific "goods": *proles*, *fides*, and *sacramentum* ("offspring," "faith," and "sacrament"). In the more elaborated formulations of twelfth-century theologians, the substance of the marriage sacrament was the mutual love between the members of the couple; this love in turn was both the sign and substance of God's grace (Hugh of Saint Victor 326). The sign of the couple's love was expressed in the exchange of consent featured in the marriage ceremony (*Sarum Missal*). Medieval ecclesiastical courts upheld this definition of marriage as consent between two parties; the approval of families and the presence of clergy was not strictly necessary (McSheffrey 4–14; Helmholz 25–73). This ideal of mutuality allowed sacramental marriage to become a paradigm for horizontal social relations.

The tension between the marital debt and the sacramental model of marriage was a means of negotiating clerical prerogative and lay authority in Chaucer's England. While medieval theologians thought sex was sinful, the doctrine of the marital debt required marital sex among the laity, reinforcing clerical authority and superiority. On the other hand, by dignifying marriage—and lay life generally—as a spiritual practice, disassociating it from sex and defining it as love, sacramental marriage blurred the boundary between laity and clergy that the laws against clerical marriage sought to impose. The definition of the sign of the sacrament of marriage as an exchange of consent between lay people was thus potentially challenging to the idea of priest-mediated sacraments. In fact, late medieval Lollards made marriage part of their challenge to clerical authority and the validity of the sacraments. Understanding that the hierarchy of virginity over marriage bolstered clerical monopoly, the Lollards criticized clerical celibacy and promoted marriage as a vocabulary for moral and religious life. A broad-ranging growth in lay piety made marriage and the family increasingly central to late medieval religious practices. The idea, so familiar to modern students, that marriage should be at the center of Christian practice was not a traditional family value (to invoke modern parlance) but a late medieval innovation that challenged the clerical monopoly on piety and was tied to the emergence of a growing and powerful lay middle stratum of society.

As this brief summary suggests, I teach the contradictions and tensions within marriage ideology and encourage students to explore how *The Canterbury Tales* uses marriage to analyze shifting social and religious authority in the period. Although I would argue that Chaucer's concern with marriage is everywhere in *The Canterbury Tales*, I have chosen three prologues and tales—the Wife's, the Clerk's, and the Franklin's—that preoccupied Kittredge and are frequently taught.

The Wife of Bath is often seen—as Kittredge paints her—as a dominatrix who challenges the familiar medieval paradigm in which the husband rules over his wife. Indeed, this reading is easy to sustain, since the wife gleefully describes in the prologue her sovereignty over her first three husbands, and in the tale the "correct" answer to the question of what women most desire is sovereignty. By contrast, with her latest husband, Jankyn, she is willing to abandon the "mastery" she has gained when she learns that he cares enough about her to grant it, suggesting that what she desires most is mutuality in marriage (Patterson, "'Experience'" 141). Similarly, at the end of the tale the knight is rewarded for placing himself in his wife's wise governance (line 1231). As a result, the couple apparently achieves happiness in marriage: "and thus they lyve unto hir lyves ende / In parfit joye" ("And thus they lived in perfect joy until the end of their lives"; lines 1257–58). I ask students how to reconcile the ideal of mutuality embraced by the endings of both prologue and tale with the texts' earlier preoccupation with sovereignty. By asking what role the Wife's lesson on "gentilesse" (as based on behavior rather than birth) plays in the tale and in the Knight's decision to abandon mastery, I suggest that the tale draws a correlation between mutuality in marriage and the emergent social values of merchants like the Wife (Burger; Lipton).

The Wife of Bath not only engages with the tensions between mutuality and hierarchy in medieval marriage but also makes marriage a weapon in her own personal challenge to clerical authority. In the very first lines of her prologue, she cites experience as her authority to discuss marriage, which, of course, the celibate clergy did not have, despite their role in prescribing marital conduct. The Wife challenges clerical authority by adapting the voice of a preacher and theologian to dispute the idea that virginity is superior to marriage (Galloway, "Marriage Sermons"). Using a strategy familiar from both theological treatises and marriage sermons, she quotes from the Bible to support her case. I assign students the biblical passage 1 Corinthians 7, which is repeatedly cited by the Wife in her prologue and was (not coincidently) the basis for Saint Jerome's influential antimatrimonialism and for medieval lay instruction about the marriage debt.[1] We begin with an analysis of the proper reasons for having sex according to Saint Paul (to avoid fornication, satisfy marital debt, and procreate). A close reading of the first third of the prologue shows how the Wife enlists the specific language of the Apostle but misreads her source and upends the hierarchy of celibacy over marriage. She does not dispute the association of marriage with sex (as did Augustine) so much as argue for the virtues of marital sex. The Wife also challenges clerical authority through her parody of clerical antimatrimonialism and misogyny. She begins her prologue, like many antimatrimonial poems, by saying she will "speke of wo that is in mariage" (3), and through the middle section of the prologue she invokes commonplaces of the genre through a refrain of "thou sayst," which marks her discourse as a rehearsal of conventional wisdom. I assign students examples of antimatrimonialism, such as "Against Marrying" (Blamires, *Woman Defamed* 125–29) and the oft-cited Theophrastus passage (357–58), so they can see that the Wife exemplifies virtually every fault of which wives are accused. I ask students to consider what making a misogynist stereotype into an appealing character implies about the prologue's perspective on clerical authority and antimatrimonialism and to identify the rhetorical strategies the tale uses to manipulate the reader's sympathies for the Wife.

Like the Wife of Bath's Tale, the Clerk's Tale also uses marriage as a political vocabulary for sovereignty, as a close analysis of diction in the opening passages shows. Resisting his people's desire for the stability of an heir, Walter contrasts the "liberty" of his single state with the "servage" of marriage. In an effort to convince Walter to marry, his people describe marriage to him as "that blisful yok / Of soverayntee, noght of servyse" ("that blissful yoke of sovereignty, not of service"; lines 113–14), drawing a parallel between marriage and rulership. Walter's resistance to marriage is characterized as a focus on his own individual interests in contrast to the concerns of his subjects. It also invokes the conventional depiction of tyranny in mirrors for princes as the valuation of singular over common profit, establishing marriage as a vocabulary for exploring tyranny in the tale (Wallace, *Chaucerian Polity* 295). I assign a short excerpt from *Le ménagier de Paris*, one of many conduct books to use the Griselda tale, to provide a context for the tale's Aristotelian idea that household and polity are interwoven (Staley 265–338; Collette, *Performing* 59–78). I also assign an excerpt from Petrarch's letter to Boccaccio, in which Petrarch identifies the patience of Griselda as a model for those who would "submit themselves to God with the same courage as did this woman to her husband" ("Francis" 138). On day two of discussion, I divide the class into three groups to analyze the political, religious, and domestic aspects of the tale, and then we discuss the ways that the tale is complicated by their interactions. Although the hagiographic elements lend support for the Clerk's and Kittredge's vision of the tale as an argument for the virtues of female passivity and suffering in marriage, the exaggerated torture of Griselda by Walter can also be seen as a critique of domestic and political tyranny. Thus, the Clerk's Tale shows that political and religious discourses both shape and are shaped by the discourse of marriage.

I invite students to consider how the Franklin's Tale's depiction of marriage reworks the paradigms and genres of the Clerk's Tale and other earlier tales, using marriage to construct an ideology that suits the Franklin's social class. I ask students to compare the opening five lines of the Franklin's Tale with the Knight's Tale so that they recognize the latter as a highly condensed form of a conventional romance plot: the tale recounts the knight's labors and famous deeds inspired by the love of his lady and ends with marriage. The Franklin invokes the romance convention of depicting marriage as an apotheosis of battle and thus a confirmation of the aristocratic public world of honor. After this initial passage, the tale deviates from the conventions of romance (and from the depiction of vows in the Clerk's Tale) by granting Dorigen the choice of husband offered by marriage law without mentioning the role of family, property, or money in her decision. Dorigen's pledge of "trouthe" and her vow "til that myn herte breste" ("till my heart break") echo the "tyll deth us departe" of the marriage vows in the *Sarum Missal* and come after Arveragus's vow to "hym take no maistrie" ("[upon] himself take no mastery") (FranT, lines 759, 747). By emphasizing the exchange of vows, the tale draws on the sacramental model that represents mutual love as the basis of marriage. Immediately after discussing the exchange of vows, we move to an analysis of the "sermon on marriage," in which the Franklin expounds, "[F]reendes everych oother moot obeye, / If they wol longe holden compaignye. / . . . Love is a thyng as any spirit free" ("Friends must obey each other / If they wish to keep company long / . . . Love is a thing like any spirit free"; lines 762–63, 767). Here the Franklin echoes the diction of contemporary marriage sermons, which often used a classical vocabulary of friendship, describing spouses as equals and partners, to comment on mutuality in marriage (Lipton 34–40). Later, we note that the vocabulary of friendship used to describe Dorigen and Arveragus's marriage is applied in the end of the tale to the relationship between the Clerk, the Squire, and the Knight, suggesting that marriage has become a model for social relations (Jacobs). Kittredge's notion that the tale provides a model for a marital mutuality that resolves the "problem" of marriage posed by the Wife's and Clerk's tales can be difficult to sustain with students who question Dorigen's absence at the end of the Franklin's Tale and want to explain Arveragus's death threat against his wife. Indeed, the focus on male bonding in the tale and the failure to address Arveragus's violent threat suggest that the tale may be more invested in using marriage to articulate a horizontal ideology of social equality than in constructing truly egalitarian gender relations. The tale can be seen not so much as Chaucer's ideal of marriage or as an answer to the problem of marriage in the tales, as Kittredge argues, but as the Franklin's own use of marriage to reflect and formulate his emergent social values.

As my comments suggest, Chaucer does not develop a single vision of marriage but shows how medieval marriage was both hierarchical and mutual, based in sex and centered on love. Chaucer uses marriage both to depict relations between husbands and wives and also to comment on rulership, to articulate the values of the middle stratum of medieval society, and to explore tensions between lay and clerical authority. By including many tales about marriage and attributing them to speakers from so many different walks of life, Chaucer's

Canterbury Tales demonstrates that there was no single homogeneous idea of medieval marriage. Instead, marriage was a means of negotiating a variety of social and religious interests in Chaucer's time, as it is today. Studying marriage in *The Canterbury Tales* can show students that ideas such as love and marriage that often seem to them simultaneously private and universal have their own public histories.

NOTE

[1] Jerome's essay "Against Jovinian" appears in R. Miller 415–36 and in Chaucer [ed. Kolve and Olson] 359–73.

The Clerk's Tale and the Retraction: Generic Monstrosity in the Classroom

Peter W. Travis

In an article published more than forty years ago, Francis Lee Utley argued that the Clerk's Tale needs to be appreciated as a complex conflation of at least five genres: drama, exemplum, fairy tale, novella, and religious allegory. In dozens of articles published since then, the Clerk's Tale has proved receptive to a multitude of similarly provocative generic interpretations. Focusing on the tale's allegorical substrate, its biblical symbolism, its political analogies, its affective strategies, its gender dynamics, its novelistic inflections, its folk tale registers, or myriad other salient aspects, each of these interpretative ventures must eventually contend with the tale's complex and even violent yoking together of different generic categories. "[A]n offensive monstrosity to some, an alluring and subtle fable to others," the tale has proven to be a site of such narrative hybridity and heuristic irresolution that it might properly be termed, writes J. Allan Mitchell, a "perverse *exemplum terrible*" (117, 135). Offensive to some, yet alluring, subtle, perverse, beautiful, exemplary, and terrifying to others: how is it possible to teach such a tale?

In my *Canterbury Tales* course, my first maneuver is to fully honor students' dramatically different reactions to the tale because these responses actually cover much of the conflicted critical reception previewed above. To empower their insights, I write a numbered sequence across the blackboard (1 standing for "worst" and 10 for "best") and ask students to locate the Clerk's Tale somewhere on the grid, writing out a short paragraph by way of justification. Last autumn, in a class of about thirty, the overall average was (perhaps surprisingly) 5.8, but the range of responses (quite unsurprisingly) was extreme. "I give the Clerk's Tale a 2," writes one student; "Griselda's lack of agency and sickening devotion repulse me, as does Walter's ego and need for control." Another writes: "I give this story an 8 because I think that the hermeneutic obstacles posed both within the tale itself and in a reading of the tale within the context of its frame give the tale an exemplary depth." And a conflicted centrist explains:

> I give the Clerk's Tale a 4 because I am horrified by the repugnant way
> Walter treated his wife, but I am also intrigued by the notion that, despite
> its apparent lack of moralizing, maybe this tale could be a condemnation
> and exposé of marital psychological abuse to the modern reader. Further-
> more, although the tale is horrible in its temporal context, if we took it as
> an allegory for the devotion we should have to God, it could be a much
> more intriguing and complicated moral statement.

Moving progressively along the grid, emphasizing the persuasive aspects of every student-held position, within a half hour we have accorded credence to a multitude of readings while acknowledging their collective resistance to any single and unifying generic template.

After this preliminary brainstorming, we enter the text itself. Writing *ababbcc* on the board, I encourage off-the-wall speculations about how the Clerk's rhyme royal stanza provides a number of opportunities: in its sonic contact points and directional turns, its aural recollections and thematic counterpoints, each stanza is a minipoem demonstrating artistic control realized within predefined formal constraints. What I try to encourage—with some nudging—is that students begin thinking about how the sophisticated design of this new prosodic form might actually contain some of the generic tensions, interpretative counterpressures, and logical disputations at play in the tale itself.

My next move is to focus on the first four stanzas of "Secunda Pars" (lines 197–224), where Griselda, moderately fair to physical sight, embodies the inner virtues of a secular saint; her poor village (counterpoised to the marquis's palace) likewise resonates with spiritual immanence, for, as the narrator reminds us, Christ's Incarnation occurred in a humble ox's stall. Composed in the plain style of Christian low-mimetic pastoral, these stanzas are not entirely realistic; rather, they embrace a host of nonverisimilar narrative forms—including folk tale, exemplum, parable, apologue, and allegory. In this exercise in close reading, my intent is to slightly decenter students' novelistic predispositions by focusing on how this passage (and then the tale at large) engages an array of distinctly different medieval genres—literary kinds with which students are less immediately familiar but with which, they discover, they are still quite conversant.

In the first day's final exercise, I bear down on the Clerk's exacting description of Walter and Griselda's egregiously one-sided marriage contract. If as interpreters we are here being asked to suspend our modern and reality-based disbelief (and this may ultimately be an impossibility), according to what medieval literary-critical rules might we do so? Should we point in the direction of Stith Thompson's folklore index entries on extreme "tests connected with marriage"(389–411)? Should we discourse anagogically, gesturing toward God's inscrutable power, his *potentia absoluta*, as articulated within certain late medieval theologies? Should we talk historically about the vertical power dynamics typical of medieval marriages? Should we contrast the actualities of medieval chauvinism with the quite equitable vows of affection between man and woman celebrated in the Sarum Use (see "From the *Sarum Missal*")? Riffing rapidly through these questions, I bring my first class to a close not like a responsible teacher, by detailing a summary of stable vantage points from which the tale may now be confidently interpreted, but by further disequilibrating any sense of generic balance or hermeneutical certainty. For students, the overall effect of this first class tends to be empowering, liberating, and confusing. The viability of their individual responses has been honored, but the disharmony among those responses has evidently deepened. Key passages have revealed the tale's refinements as a well-wrought narrative; yet precisely because of its author's sure-handedness, the Clerk's Tale seems increasingly a problematic and self-subverting literary puzzle. At any rate, the jam-packed hour is up, and perhaps there's no need to worry; the next class should be interesting, and—who knows?—all the right answers might be waiting in the wings.

My reading assignments for the second class are all included in V. A. Kolve and Glending Olson's Norton Critical Edition of *The Canterbury Tales*: namely, Boccaccio's *Decameron*, day 10, novella 10; Petrarch's revision of Boccaccio's Griselda story (and relevant epistles); and a passage from *Le ménagier de Paris*. Focusing on Chaucer's crucial changes to his narrative sources, students are now able to appreciate how these interventions further enhance the Clerk's Tale's generic complexities. Chaucer, in his revision, intensifies Griselda's silent suffering, thus adding an even deeper degree of "pathetic realism." In contradistinction to Boccaccio's and Petrarch's accounts, Chaucer interweaves a series of explicit editorial commentaries, leaving no doubt that Walter's tests of his wife are "yvele" ("evil"; line 460), "crueel" ("cruel"; 740), and "wikke" ("wicked"; 785). And in a powerfully cathartic scene of his own design, Chaucer dramatizes Griselda's long-suppressed maternal love: reunited with her "dead" children after years of stoic self-restraint, Griselda embraces them with such force that, even in her swoon, it is only with great difficulty that men manage to prize her arms away (1079–1106). How, we wonder—especially in the light of all these striking additions—could any reader embrace Griselda's torments as a model of wifely devotion?

Yet, responding to quite similar versions of the tale, many medieval readers did just that, choosing to interpret the Griselda story *ad litteram* as a positive domestic exemplum, a "mirror for wives." Petrarch reports two reactions to his own account: his first reader, apparently in admiration of Griselda's perfection, wept so inconsolably that he could not finish the tale; the second remained skeptical only because he was certain no women exist in the world who are "the equal of this conjugal devotion" ("Two Letters" 419, 420). But such responses were by no means universal: in *Le ménagier de Paris*, a fifteenth-century husband explains to his wife that although he had asked her to read the story of Griselda, it was "not because I wish such obedience from you. . . . [I] know that I may not properly assault or assay you thus, nor in any such fashion" (421). So even when narrowly interpreted as a unidirectional marriage manual, the Griselda story provoked some disapprobation as well as approbation among medieval (male) readers.

Chaucer, apparently anxious that even his fully evolved revision could still be misconstrued as a model for virtuous wives, counsels at tale's end that it would be "inportable" ("intolerable") were women to try to live in imitation of Griselda's life: "This storie is seyd nat for that wyves sholde / Folwen Grisilde as in humylitee, / For it were inportable, though they wolde . . ." ("This story is told not so that wives should emulate Griselda in humility, for that would be intolerable, even if they wished to"; lines 1142–44). This is a powerful and important caveat, but does Chaucer (and do we) actually expect one authorial intervention to settle all matters of a tale's meaning? D. H. Lawrence's famous words, "Never trust the artist. Trust the tale," are worth invoking here (14); however, in the case of the Clerk's Tale, is it actually possible to trust the tale when it seems impossible to determine which parts of the tale it is best to trust? Chaucer nevertheless extends his interpretative counsel into the tale's coda, where he parodies two brands of wrongheaded critical response. In an essay included in this volume, William Quinn anatomizes the prosody of the Clerk's envoy:

> Chaucer here uses a six-line stanza (*a*10 *b*10 *a*10 *b*10 *c*10 *b*10) that seems a truncated parody of the double ballade (three stanzas repeating the same rhymes with a refrain). Chaucer's six stanzas are all linked by the same three rhyme sounds (-ence, -aille,-ence,-aille, -ynde, -aille); a number of unaccented *a* and *b* rhymes produce technically and perhaps aggressively "feminine" endings. The masculine *c* rhyme repeats only across stanzas, like an anemic tail rhyme.

By emphasizing the envoy's unique stanzaic form, its sonic clangor, and its "aggressive" feminine and "anemic" masculine rhyme schemes, Quinn spotlights many of those prosodic elements that, in my class, I insist must be heard as entirely parodic in tone and intent. That is, by counseling wives to answer at the "countretaille" ("reply" / "countertally") like a "greet camaille" ("great camel") in order to make their husbands "waille" ("wail"; 1212), the Clerk mimics an imaginary, arch-feminist, hypermilitant voice that is responding not to the tale itself but to an equally hypermilitant and arch-masculinist misapplication of the tale's apparent point. Lest there be any doubt about the popular currency of this misaligned masculinist reading, Chaucer (in a sometimes canceled stanza) deftly closes the tale's end-link with Harry Bailly's meathead announcement to his fellow pilgrims: "Me were levere than a barel ale / My wyf at hoom had hered this legende ones" ("Even more than a barrel of ale, / I had rather my wife at home had but once heard this saint's life"; lines 1212c–12d). Precisely because these crude examples of marriage-debate literalism both fall flat, they succeed in directing readers centripetally, like so many of Chaucer's unsatisfactory endings, back to the work's spiritual center. But then, does the Clerk's Tale have a spiritual center? As a final maneuver, I close out my second and last class pondering the metaphor of the soul's stressful marriage to God.

With Petrarch's concluding gloss serving as his model ("Two Letters" 417), Chaucer at tale's end applies Saint James the Evangelist's radical distinction between diabolical temptation and divine testing: that is, whereas Griselda was wrongfully tempted by her mortal husband, God rightfully tests our spiritual mettle so that we may learn to "live in virtuous suffraunce" ("patience"; line 1162). Of all the tale's conundrums, this piece of analogical and anti-analogical reasoning proves to be the thorniest hermeneutical problem debated in my class. Alluding earlier in the tale to Job's miseries, to Isaac's narrowly averted sacrifice, and to Christ's crucifixion, Chaucer has clearly been bending his Griselda story in an allegorical direction. But where does this bending, culminating as it does

in his Saint James's application, ultimately lead us? Is the tale finally a justification of God's ways to man or a theodicy (perhaps a fourteenth-century cosmic
kvetch) or an attenuated variant of the Passion? Committed to desentimental-
izing and defamiliarizing the Passion, I point toward the unspeakable horrors
of Calvary as staged in the medieval plays of Corpus Christi; and, appropriating
a crucial term Slavoj Žižek and others have recently been employing in their
studies of Christianity (Žižek and Milbank), I underscore the "monstrosity" of
theological explications of God's impositions of pain, suffering, and death on an
innocent subject. My concluding point, then, is that even a purely theological
reading of the tale, while absolutely crucial, is far from fully adequate because it
brings with it a plethora of even more interpretative problems.

Thus, at the end of our extensive classroom interrogations, we are left pondering the postulate that there is absolutely no adequate way of understanding
the Clerk's Tale. As J. Allan Mitchell has put it, this is a work "where no explanation is totally persuasive, no decision sufficiently justified, no response good
enough" (135). What these critical insufficiencies help confirm is that my students' original conflicted and conflicting assessments of the tale remain, in their
entirety, entirely right. Logically, the tale is an *insolubilium*; aesthetically, it is a
"problem poem" that defies generic classification. Yet this does not mean that
the tale is in any way an artistic failure. While it may still appear "monstrous"—
that is, offensive, alluring, subtle, perverse, exemplary, and terrifying—there
should now be no question that it is also a thing of beauty and a work of absolute
genius. My centrifugal teaching strategies thus leave a hefty number of critical
questions suspended in midair. However, the short supply of adequate answers
does not appear too great a disincentive for further thought. My more adventur-
ous students, at any rate, oftentimes choose to write their papers on the challenges of the Clerk's Tale. And, provoked at least in part by all the uncertainties
raised in class, many of these students succeed year after year in writing critical
papers that are scholarly, well-researched, and remarkably self-assured.

If the Clerk's Tale is a "problem poem" that raises so many questions that it
leaves the reader in a quandary, should the Chaucer professor set things right
by providing at the eleventh hour the "right interpretation"? I think not, at least
if that interpretation muscles to the side most of the complexities the tale contains. A signature element of Chaucer's genius, I emphasize in my class, is his
trust in his readers, his expectation that they will interrogate everything creatively and independently, pushing back against even the most straightforward-
seeming work. In other words, he wants his readers to create their own generic categories, thinking self-reflexively in a hypercritical fashion. He does this
everywhere: in spades in the Clerk's Tale, in myriad ways in the Nun's Priest's
Tale, and even in the Retraction.

The Retraction is in fact a generic "monster" designed with such audacious
subtlety that I find I need all of my final two classes to open up Chaucer's last
words. I maintain, rather aggressively, that the Retraction is not a monologic
speech act; rather, it is a double utterance that counterpoints two aesthetic posi-

tions, the first articulating an *apologia pro arte sua*—an all-embracing benediction of all writing—the second condemning almost all that Chaucer has written as his "giltes" ("guilts"; Ret 1082). In the chasm between these two pronouncements there stands a single word, "Wherfore." So: wherefore "Wherfore"? I eventually want to address this pointed question, but I scarcely begin with it. As in my first class on the Clerk's Tale, I invite as many responses to the Retraction as possible, writing out a shorthand version of each on the board and providing my own supportive glosses. By the end of the first class, with a cornucopia of seemingly unharmonizable positions, we find ourselves in a state of ruminative uncertainty, a massive *kankedort* ("state of insoluble complexity"; *TC* 1752). And as a supposed *auctoritas* I have said precious little in my own voice that might help stabilize matters. So in my final class I take things slowly: I reread the Retraction closely and very carefully, fleshing out the arguments and suppositions of the two countervailing aesthetic positions and emphasizing the enormous gulf between them. Then I turn to a sustained meditation on the monstrous mysteries of "Wherfore." Elsewhere, I have tried my hand at demystifying this "Wherfore" ("Deconstructing"); even so, every year when I teach *The Canterbury Tales*, I find that my final lecture hasn't much in common with its predecessors.

And this may be as it should be. If the Clerk's Tale is a work "where no explanation is totally persuasive, no decision sufficiently justified, no response good enough" (Mitchell 135), so too is the Retraction. It may be that no response is good enough, but each of us must nevertheless define for ourselves the potential meanings of that one most critical word, for ultimately, I find, it is our essence as readers that constitutes the essential dialectics of Chaucer's "Wherfore." In other words, there possibly may be ways of bringing Chaucer's two countervailing evaluations of his literature into alignment, just as there possibly may be many ways of bringing the Clerk's generic conflicts into harmony. And there may not. In my end-of-term lecture on the Retraction, I give it my best shot, all the while insisting that what I am saying is *my* response in the present moment and need not be yours, for Chaucer grants each of us license to interpret his works as each of us chooses individually to do. Perhaps that explains why, at the end of the term, as I read thoughtful student papers dealing with the significance of the Retraction—papers that show little if any influence of my heartfelt closing lecture—I feel I may have succeeded in teaching Chaucer just the right way.

Students' "Fredom" and the Franklin's Tale

Robert Epstein

My first teaching experience came as the graduate teaching assistant for a lecture course on *The Canterbury Tales*. The position had a host of duties, but for the lecture on the Franklin's Tale, I had one additional role: election official. During the lecture, the professor asked the students to answer the tale's famous *demande* ending, "Lordynges, this question, thanne, wol I aske now, / Which was the mooste fre, as thynketh yow?" (lines 1621–22). I distributed ballots, collected them, tallied the scores, and reported the results to the professor, who announced those results at the end of the lecture.

That was more than twenty years ago. Since then, in every survey and seminar in which I have taught *The Canterbury Tales*, I have repeated this exercise. The class on the Franklin's Tale has invariably been the most successful of the semester. It is also the one that comes closest to achieving my goals, not just for the discussion of this particular tale but for teaching Chaucer and, in fact, for manifesting my ideals for the study of literature, which perhaps are best described by the Freirean term "problem-posing education."

Since I teach smaller surveys and seminars rather than lecture classes, I do not use secret ballots. Before class, students compose a response paper on the Franklin's Tale, identifying their choice for the "mooste fre" of the characters and justifying their decisions. In class, we invariably begin by collectively reviewing the major events of the tale and taking note of the crucial ambiguities. Why does Arveragus add to his proposal of equal marriage his caveat that he must preserve "the name of soveraynetee" (751)? Why does Dorigen make her oath to Aurelius? Is Aurelius a true lover? Does Arveragus's reaction to Dorigen's confession make sense? Then, one by one, students announce their choices and defend them as a running score is tallied on the blackboard.

This exercise is fruitful in a number of ways. First, it forces students to see how the Franklin's Tale, like the best romances, challenges its own assumptions and principles. In making their selections—most often, they explain, by a process of elimination—and defending their choices, students see how morally compromised each candidate is. Aurelius and Arveragus almost always vie for the lead. But advocates of Aurelius are obliged to consider his final act of generosity in the light of the insipidity of his original petition of Dorigen as well as the fundamental selfishness of his demand of payment. Supporters of Arveragus, meanwhile, can point to the equanimity of his reaction to the news of the oath, unbelievable even to Dorigen, and the magnanimity of his insistence that she keep her "trouthe." But they must also consider the outburst that immediately ensues and Arveragus's threat to kill Dorigen if she ever reveals her tryst with Aurelius—all of which suggests that Arveragus may be less concerned with "trouthe" or with egalitarian marriage than he is with his own masculinity and reputation.

Many students discount the clerk from consideration since his involvement in the cascade of generosity at the conclusion entails a sacrifice only of monetary compensation. Some, on the other hand, vote for the clerk for precisely the same reason, maintaining that a contract requiring payment for services rendered is so sacrosanct that the clerk's voiding of it trumps all other value measurements. There have been times in my career when this view has actually predominated—in the early 1990s, conspicuously, though seldom since. My sample set is not large enough to allow me to extrapolate greater sociological significance from the trends. I do see significance, however, in a more consistent response. In any given semester, very few students, sometimes none, vote for Dorigen. Indeed, it is rare that students even consider Dorigen as a candidate, as if the Franklin, in asking "Which was the mooste fre," did not intend her to be on the ballot. It is a tendency both telling and puzzling: Do the sequential acts of generosity by the male characters erase the moral agency of the one female character, even though it is her volition and her body being contested? Whose values are at the core of this romance? One might say that part of Arveragus's generosity is his extension of "trouthe," a quintessentially chivalric value, to his wife. But he seems completely insensitive to the specifically feminine value system that Dorigen had been using to measure her own options, an ancient code based not on "trouthe" or "fredom" but rather on chastity, by which suicide is the ultimate assertion of female agency and autonomy.

Even if they do consider voting for Dorigen, my students—not exclusively the male students—commonly eliminate her from contention on account of her putatively irrational obsession with the "grisly rokkes blake" (859) or her rash oath. This is the point in the discussion when I am least able to restrain myself from asserting my own opinions, as opposed to simply interrogating the reactions of the students. Although the tale asks its readers to adjudge the characters' generosity, there seems to be a reluctance to recognize that both Dorigen's complaint against the rocks and her rash oath are motivated by her concern for Arveragus's safety and possibly for Aurelius's feelings.

But I am seldom able to persuade anyone to transfer allegiance to Dorigen, and this too is revealing. When discussing other tales, students are often inclined, in the face of the quasi-Socratic badgering that is the essence of my pedagogy, to concede or change sides, apparently under the impression that I want them to take a different position. But in answering the Franklin's question, students in fact become firmer in their positions and defend them more forcefully than they do any other issue. To me, this is the ultimate value of the exercise: it encourages students to respect their own interpretive instincts and to take ownership of their readings. Even many strong students, I have found, suspect their English professors of possessing secret keys to interpretation that they are withholding from the class. But any reader can see that the *demande* has no definitive answer. Its point is to place the tale's conclusion in the hands of the reader; the tale's conclusion is therefore in the reader's present tense, and its ultimate meaning is unmistakably his or her construction. In my experience, most students are empowered in their responses. Just as important, the class discussion, which necessarily places each student in opposition to some class-mates and in alliance with others and which places the meaning of the tale up for grabs, dramatizes the social nature of interpretation. Meaning becomes the ongoing project of a community of readers.

I should note that this was not the intended lesson of the lecture class when I was a teaching assistant. This was at Princeton, and the vote on the Franklin's Tale was a multigenerational tradition initiated decades earlier by D. W. Robertson. The lecturer would, after announcing the results, inform the students that they were all wrong. No one in the tale was truly generous, so there could be no winner. This represented Robertson's reading of the Franklin and his tale. The Franklin himself is an avatar of bourgeois materialism, an Epicurean whose ostentatious generosity is meant to obscure the class anxiety of a grasp-ing social climber. He imagines the characters in his tale to embody generosity, but they are motivated not by liberality but by cupidity. And if modern readers are inclined to sympathize with the tale's characters, it is because they share the Franklin's fallen mentality and therefore warp the author's ironic intentions. "Chaucer," Robertson complained, "had no way of knowing that the spiritual descendents of the Franklin would one day rule the world" (*Preface* 472). The purpose of the vote was to disabuse the students of their presumption of inter-pretive agency.

Robertson may well be right that none of the Franklin's characters are truly generous. Many students confess to difficulty in declaring any one of them truly "fre." One can easily validate such responses by pointing out that many modern critics share such reservations. Despite Robertson's disparagement, contempo-rary Chaucerians seem to agree with his suspicion that the "fredom" the tale extols is a self-serving false-consciousness of the socially and materially privi-leged. But if this is the students' determination, the important thing is that they arrive at it on their own and not because any figure of critical or magisterial authority imposes an overriding hermeneutic paradigm.

So, though my only emendation to the exercise has been to lop off the moral-izing conclusion, I think I have inverted its meaning. I always vote, too; I think it is important to show the students that I am a reader with them and that my own reactions are, like theirs, fluid and ambivalent. In fact, I usually assert that as professor I get multiple votes, and I then try to stuff the ballot box for Dori-gen. But I am pleased to say that they never stand for this. They have seen that it is their story as much as anyone's and that neither authors nor authorities but readers, individually and collectively, make meaning. It is to the reader that Chaucer says, "Now telleth me, er that ye ferther wende [go]. / I kan namoore [no more]; my tale is at an ende" (FranT 1623–24). This is the essence of his generosity as author.

The Prioress's Tale: Violence, Scholarly Debate, and the Classroom Encounter

Larry Scanlon

The Prioress's Tale, Chaucer's version of the blood libel legend, brings its readers into direct contact with one of the grimmest, most persistently disturbing strains in the long history of Western culture. The challenges the tale poses to the classroom instructor do not differ in kind from those they offer the modern, post-Holocaust reader; the addition of pedagogical obligations simply intensifies them. On the one hand, there is the tale's visceral expression of anti-Semitic or anti-Judaic stereotypes; on the other, there are Chaucer's characteristic poetic mastery and intellectual nuance. The teacher's responsibility as professional medievalist to convey as accurately as possible the specificities of Chaucer's historical moment sits uneasily with the even more basic responsibility to unearth, convey, and explain the complexities of literary form. These challenges are best met head-on. Chaucer scholarship itself remains deeply divided by the tale. Any attempt to bring some consensus to one's undergraduates is doomed to fail; it is much better to recognize that fact from the beginning and build one's pedagogy around it.

The urgency of this tale and its relation to the legacies of anti-Semitism are abundantly evident in the fractious scholarly debates that surround it. Teachers who make students aware that their own reactions do not differ markedly from those who study Chaucer for a living will give their students an intellectual stake in a field that in other ways seems out of reach. Such students should also be more receptive to the wealth of recent historical scholarship on late medieval Jewish-Christian relations. Many of the findings will strike them as surprising, including the basic facts that Christian charges of Jewish ritual murder were a late medieval innovation and that the very first occurred in England. Both the critical history and the social context should return students with fresh urgency to Chaucer's text itself—the goal of any literature teacher of any text.

Critical History

The most basic division in the Prioress's Tale's modern reception lies between readers for whom its anti-Semitism defines its poetic and intellectual horizons and readers for whom its anti-Semitism is ultimately a by-product of its Christian piety. Sherman Hawkins's 1964 "Chaucer's Prioress and the Sacrifice of Praise" offers a classic statement of the latter position. Hawkins flatly declares that "[a]nti-Semitism in the usual sense is quite beside the point" (604); the Jews are little more than incidental stand-ins for the dangers of reading literally. The clergeon recalls the martyrs, and in his martyrdom he dramatizes the imperative to read spiritually. The "greyn" ("seed") on his tongue that keeps him singing even after he has his throat cut represents "the word of God" (Hawkins 617). A decisive shift occurred in 1989 when L. O. Aranye Fradenburg argued that any responsible view of the tale must take "into account the historical experience of the Jews in Western Europe" ("Criticism" 77). Without denying the tale's piety, she nevertheless maintained that it is "a text of torture": its intensity and the "emotional vividness" of its piety "depend on its characterization of Jews," from which it "cannot be split off" (83–84). There is no doubt that Fradenburg's essay has largely set the agenda for subsequent discussion of the tale. No one would now dismiss the tale's anti-Semitism as beside the point. Instead, the more traditional approach now concentrates on recovering Chaucer's own conscious intentions and his assessment of the blood libel tradition.[1] Similarly, those following Fradenburg's approach have concentrated slightly less on the sheer brutality of the tale and a bit more on its position within the broader discourses and traditions that structured late medieval Jewish-Christian relations.[2] More recently, some feminist scholars have added another dimension to this latter, discursive approach by concentrating on the highly gendered specificity of the tale's protagonists and teller (e.g., E. Robertson; Lampert). Finally, Bruce Holsinger modulates this gender reading into an analysis of the violent practices of medieval musical pedagogy (259–92).

Social Context

The anti-Semitism specific to late medieval Europe, especially in the north, was a curious mix of material relations and ideology. During this period, the dependence on Judaic tradition, which has always haunted Christianity, became a particular focus of cultural anxiety. As ecclesiastical authorities struggled to intensify Christian devotion and the range of their own authority, they often made Jews scapegoats. Novel forms of cultural hostility like the blood libel reworked such venerable themes as the Jew as carnal infidel and betrayer of Christ. They also reflected social and historical developments. There were virtually no Jews in northern Europe until the late tenth century, when settlements of what would come to be termed Ashkenazic Jewry began, drawn by the new political stability and economic opportunities in the north (Chazan, *Medieval Stereotypes* 1–6). Protected by the sovereign, these new immigrants found themselves in commercial competition with the nascent Christian bourgeoisie and in an uneasy alliance with their aristocratic and royal protectors. During the eleventh century, as economic activity in northern urban centers quickened, Jews moved away from other commercial enterprises and into money lending, filling the void left by ecclesiastical prohibitions of usury. While making the Jews an even more prominent target of Christian anxiety and ambivalence, this change made them even more valuable to their royal protectors, at least initially. Chaucer's text clearly engages these social realities.

First, he positions the Prioress's Tale after the Shipman's Tale, whose plot turns on the merchant's astute manipulation of the credit market; and second, he sets it in a great city in Asia, where there was "[a]monges Cristene folk a Jewerye, / Sustened by a lord of that contree, / For foule usure and lucre of vileynye" ("Among Christian folk a ghetto, / Maintained by a lord of that country / for foul usury and shameful profits"; lines 489–91). That this literary refraction occurs nearly a century after the English Crown expelled the Jews makes it that much more remarkable. Jewish migration to England started shortly after the Norman Conquest. Jews experienced the same pattern of relative tolerance punctuated by violent attacks as they encountered elsewhere in northern Europe. Nevertheless, English anti-Semitism was particularly severe. It owns the dubious distinction of the first recorded instance of the blood libel, in the case of William of Norwich in 1144. A rash of murderous incidents, including the massacre of some 150 Jews at York, occurred between 1188 and 1190 after the coronation of Richard I and during the lead-up to his crusade. The case of Hugh of Lincoln, which Chaucer cites at the end of the tale, was a fabrication, said to have occurred in 1255. Anti-Semitism continued to intensify until Edward I expelled the Jews in 1290.[3]

The blood libel recapitulates a central strain of anti-Jewish polemic that extends back to Christianity's origin: the Jews as Christ's betrayers. The new legend makes the charge more general, the Jews' murderous intentions toward Christ now becoming a thirst for all innocent Christian blood almost always expressed in the murder of a Christian child. The concomitant charge of cannibalism can be seen as a predictable extension of the traditional polemic. It may also reflect contemporary doctrinal struggles over the meaning of the Eucharist. The blood libel circulated with host desecration stories, which were also used to justify anti-Jewish violence. The latter portray Jews pursuing a profane interest in the actual physical evidence of transubstantiation similar to that of unlearned Christians in sermon exempla. As Miri Rubin notes, "The host desecration tale was told by Christians to Christians to make them act and redefine that which made them Christian" (5).

Teaching the Tale

In my experience the student response to the tale should guide the way we introduce the Prioress's Tale scholarship into the classroom. Since I want that response to be as unmediated as possible, I do not assign extra reading. Instead, I begin simply by asking for general reactions. Typically, it does not take very long for positions to emerge that correspond to those in recent critical debate. Some students will suggest that Chaucer needs to be seen in his own time, while others will express discomfort with the tale's obvious anti-Semitism. Once these positions are out on the table, I take my own role to be twofold: first, to introduce the relevant scholarly findings and positions into the conversation and, second, to point out specific places in the tale where the issues at hand are particularly vexing or concentrated. The point of the former is not to resolve the argument but to refine, elaborate, and complicate the positions. The point of the latter is to bring the positions back to the text. Some quick examples: the tale's use of the "greyn" on the clergeon's tongue to figure the word of God provides a compelling illustration of medieval exegetical tradition.[4] Indeed, considered purely in relation to the internal dynamics of that tradition, this aspect of the tale is largely independent of the issue of anti-Semitism. At the same time, Pauline origins of Christian exegesis link it to anti-Judaic polemic. Similarly, the tale's brutal imputations of violence to the Jews are so closely tied to the quasi-hagiographical logic of the narrative that they can easily encourage a more general discussion of the aesthetics of violence and its possible relation to the Christian notions of suffering. Or one can point to the many places where suffering and violence become gendered: the Prioress's eroticized portrait and her hymn to Mary in the General Prologue and the clergeon's widowed mother and the relatively extended portrayal of her experience of loss. Finally, what should we make of Satan's speech inflaming the Jews and the paradoxical sense it makes (PrT, lines 558–64)—does it not grant to Jews the same right of religious intolerance this tale more generally arrogates for itself?

All these maneuvers constitute very traditional pedagogical practice. The only difference is that I take my own role not to be the provision of some magisterial synthesis but, on the contrary, to convey the unresolved state of scholarly debate. It is crucial that I deploy my scholarly expertise in response to student response. This enables me to avoid arbitrating the difficult and still unresolved political issues the tale raises. It also enables me to drive home the point that no amount of erudition can resolve such questions on its own. Although I do not necessarily refrain from expressing my own views, particularly toward the end of class, that is much less important than ensuring that the students have gotten some clear sense of the depth of the tale's complexities. And to the extent that there is a single point of my own I want to drive home, it is simply this: the Prioress's Tale continues to produce such sharply divided responses because in many respects the history to which it belongs has yet to come to a close.

NOTES

[1] The most thorough and rigorous instance of this approach would be Patterson, "'Living Witnesses.'" See also Delany, "Chaucer's Prioress."
[2] For a particularly impressive recent instance, see Krummel, "Globalizing."
[3] For additional historical background, see Chazan, *Jews* and *Medieval Stereotypes*; Huscroft; Mundil. For the blood libel, see Dundes.
[4] On this point, Hawkins remains an extremely useful resource.

Chaucer's Boring Prose: Teaching the Melibee and the Parson's Tale

Jamie Taylor

After the dazzling courtly display of the Knight's Tale, the bawdy physical comedy of the Miller's Tale, and the startling violence of the Prioress's Tale, students run smack up against the somber prose of the Tale of Melibee. Though the Melibee starts excitingly enough with a sudden act of violence, it quickly devolves into a seemingly interminable series of citations. The Parson's Tale is even worse. After making it through the Melibee, students are rewarded with the dramatic martyrdom of Saint Cecilia and the alchemical experiments of the Canon's Yeoman's Tale only to be confronted with the Parson's dreary lecture. Perhaps the Melibee and the Parson's Tale are often left out of undergraduate classrooms, even in courses specifically dedicated to *The Canterbury Tales*, because students (and scholars) sense their tedium.[1] Yet I want to advocate for teaching these tales to undergraduates and offer a few pedagogical strategies for incorporating them into medieval studies courses, even at an introductory level. Both the Melibee and the Parson's Tale introduce students to two important medieval genres: the mirror for princes and the penitential treatise. Moreover, the Melibee and the Parson's Tale allow students to think about what prose, as opposed to poetry, might offer both Chaucer the pilgrim and the Parson.

Indeed, there are multiple, even surprising, payoffs to examining these texts in the classroom. Students can expand their sense of what medieval literature looked like (not all of it was in verse or addressed to a saint or an absent lover), and they can consider the relation of literature to bureaucratic or didactic writing, a distinction that would have seemed odd to Chaucer but is often strictly fixed for our students. Additionally, discussions of these tales often lead students to important thinking about their own writing practices as they seek in their essays to balance their voices and arguments with citations in support of those arguments. More than a tangential turn away from Chaucer and onto their impending essay deadlines, these self-referential discussions demonstrate how the Melibee and the Parson's Tale can serve as the basis for deep considerations about the relation between authorial invention and citational authority—a relation persistently confronted by both Chaucer and our students.

The Tale of Melibee follows the truncated Tale of Sir Thopas, the meandering story told by Chaucer the pilgrim. Outraged with Chaucer's "drasty rymyng" ("worthless poetry"), the Host interrupts Chaucer to insist on a prose tale that provides "som murthe or som doctryne" (Th, lines 930, 935). The ensuing back-and-forth between Chaucer and the Host provides a succinct debate on the nature of authorship, and this debate sets up some terms by which students can test and refine the common assumption that an author is someone who invents new stories out of his or her own imagination. A careful reading and guided discussion of the Thopas-Melibee link has helped my students map out various models of authorship useful for thinking about *The Canterbury Tales* in particular and medieval writing more generally. Indeed, once students articulate Chaucer's argument in support of translation and compilation in the Thopas-Melibee link, I briefly lecture on medieval vocabulary that describes literary authorship (e.g., *compilator, narrator, auctor*). These terms quickly become interpretive opportunities for students, leading to examinations of Chaucer's key words for his own literary practices (such as *makyng, sentence, endite*). A discussion of these terms further presents an opportunity to teach students to use the *Middle English Dictionary*.

By the time students read the Tale of Melibee itself, they are primed to think about the tale as fundamentally interested in both authorship and form. I often begin by lecturing on the *Furstenspiegel* as a powerful genre in the fourteenth century, offering a short explanation on both the legacy of the *Secreta secretorum* and related works as well as the political events at the end of the fourteenth century, such as the revolt of the Lords Appellant against Richard II. Then, to explore Chaucer's deep engagement with his generic avatars and his interest in political events occurring in the 1380s and 1390s, I ask students to work carefully with Chaucer's immediate sources, Albertano of Brescia's *Liber consolationes et consilii* and Renaud de Louens's *Livre de Mellibee et Prudence*. Tracking Chaucer's additions, omissions, and changes from his source texts, however subtle, gives students invaluable practice reading closely. This exercise presents multiple opportunities to discuss Chaucerian translation and authorship as well as to think about the status of Middle English with respect to Romance languages.

In our discussions about the Tale of Melibee, I have found that students are often surprised by Prudence's ability to cite from patristic and scriptural authorities. With access to a facsimile of the Ellesmere manuscript, students can examine the marginal glosses, which emphasize the names of *auctores* like Seneca and Cicero and, significantly, include Prudence's name alongside them, treating her as though she were an *auctor* as well.[2] How, I ask them, does this important manuscript announce Prudence's authority, both as a political counselor and compiler? What does conceptualizing Prudence as a compiler or an *auctor* tell us about the way the Melibee imagines the role of wives in a political household? Students will sometimes return to the Wife of Bath's Prologue as a comparison; the Melibee thus turns out to be particularly helpful in encouraging students to read across fragments.

When we turn to the Parson's Tale having dedicated some thought to the discussion of textual production in the Thopas-Melibee link, students often immediately point to the Parson's interest in authorial choices, apparent in his prologue when he claims he cannot "rum, ram, ruf" like an alliterative poet (line 43). The Parson's Prologue and Tale thus offer a neat shift into discussing the structure and purpose of medieval penitential manuals.

The Ellesmere manuscript can offer a way to assess the Parson's Tale's organization. As it does with the Melibee, the Ellesmere provides signposts in the margins, giving the names of *auctores* and locating the sins and remedies the Parson discusses. Unlike the Melibee, however, the Parson's Tale lends itself to sectioning and separation, and the *Riverside Chaucer* retains each sin's taxonomic headings. I often begin our discussion of the tale's organization by asking students to choose their favorite sin, which leads to a lively debate that almost always must be cut off. I then group students according to their choice and ask them to read carefully through the Parson's explanations, examples, and remedies. Do they make sense? What seems odd or incongruous?

These introductory questions usually lead to short discussions about medieval taxonomies of sin and the structure of penitential manuals. "The Boke of Penance" is a good example of the kind of penitential tract the Parson draws on. Included in the Early English Text Society's edition of the *Cursor mundi*, the "Boke" offers its own descriptive list of the sins. I often hand out copied selections from the "Boke" and group students into pairs, asking them to compare its version of their chosen sin and the Parson's. This assignment works well in smaller seminars, when students can quickly read through the text together and work in pairs or small groups. (For larger courses, one could project specific quotations onto a screen and discuss them as a class, or one could create an assignment in which small groups of students read portions of the "Boke" outside class and compare it to the Parson's Tale.) We then discuss how both the "Boke" and the Parson's Tale understand the relation between sin, penance, and salvation. Again, such source study hones their critical reading skills. Moreover, because the "Boke" is written in rhyming couplets, it allows us to think about the limitations and benefits of writing didactic literature in verse and prose.

After discussing how the "Boke" and the Parson's Tale categorize sins and conceptualize penance, I ask students to find other contemporaneous descriptions of their chosen sin, whether literary, didactic, or visual. This can be done outside class; I ask each group to spend time at the library finding two or three particularly interesting examples of their sin to present at our next meeting. The exercise is valuable in providing students a sense of the various media through which the taxonomy of the sins were promulgated, and it can prompt questions about how and where laypeople encountered the kind of penitential schema outlined by the Parson. Through Internet searches, my students have found, for example, a fifteenth-century painting of the tree of the seven deadly sins, located in a parish church in Suffolk, as well as stained glass portrayals of sins in the York Minster.

What I have sought to provide here is neither a manifesto nor an apology on behalf of these two "boring" tales but a proposal to include them in undergraduate syllabi. Despite their length and their putative tedium, these tales have much to offer about Chaucer's playful and complicated vision of authorship and provide examples of medieval bureaucratic and formulaic writing. Close reading and source study can introduce students to critical tools like the *Middle English Dictionary*, while the tales' prose offers unique opportunities to teach students about the scribal technologies designed to help readers navigate their way through dense text. Though they are perhaps not the most scintillating reads, the Melibee and the Parson's Tale can be enormously exciting to teach.

NOTES

[1] Notably, in the syllabus appended to Thomas Garbáty's contribution to the 1980 *Approaches to Teaching* The Canterbury Tales, neither the Melibee nor the Parson's Tale appear. They do appear in the syllabus appended to the essay by Emerson Brown, Jr., in the same volume.

[2] Woodward and Stevens have edited an accessible black-and-white version.

How to Judge a Book by Its Cover

Michelle R. Warren

Students' understanding of *The Canterbury Tales* is shaped at least partly by the book their instructors ask them to carry around. Here, then, I propose methods for bringing some of these modern books into classroom discussion. By treating books as objects of analysis, instructors can empower students to approach with confidence the experience of reading "old texts" in contemporary times. Students can also grasp the many ways in which modern ideas shape what we call medieval. By focusing on students' reactions to books, instructors can engage students in reflection on the complexities of medieval literary culture through questions including how the book makes them feel and what details of its design create those feelings. Instructors can thereby create effective bridges between students' preexisting ideas and historical nuance. In the process of interpreting their books, students come to see themselves as active players in the ongoing construction of Chaucer's *Canterbury Tales*; they enter a transactional relationship with their reading materials. By repositioning the status of the "authoritative" edition (Warren, "Post-philology"), instructors can enhance accessibility while deepening students' understanding of material history. This kind of analysis, moreover, focuses students' attention on the impact of even the smallest details, training their eyes to question whether things that look the same in fact mean the same thing (an important skill for sorting through the false friends of Middle English).

The archive of cover designs for *The Canterbury Tales* offers numerous possibilities for broadening students' awareness of the effects of editorial packaging. Alongside the obvious choices of Chaucer portraits and pilgrim groups, one also finds images related to Canterbury (trans. Raffel [2008]), the Knight's Tale (trans. Wright [1998]; trans. Tuttle; trans. Hill [2007]), the Prioress's Tale (ed. Fisher and Allen), and, obliquely, the Wife of Bath's Tale (ed. Cawley [1995]). Each selection offers a distinct thesis about the book's meaning. For example, Francis Philip Barraud's 1887 watercolor of Canterbury Cathedral (depicted on the cover of Raffel's 2008 translation), places the viewer in the position of a pilgrim approaching the end of a journey—a moment never in fact represented in *The Canterbury Tales* (the 2009 reprint of Raffel's translation, by contrast, makes the medieval synonymous with the Arthurian and the documentary by sporting a photograph of a sword in a stone). Images from the Knight's Tale (Emily or knights in combat) prepare readers for scenes of "high romance" that actually play little role in the tales as a whole; these images also foreground the first tale, one told by a traditionally privileged social actor.

Comparisons with covers' source images can extend the analysis. The cover of David Wright's 1998 translation features Emily in Boccaccio's *Teseida*, from MS 2617, Osterreichische Nationalbibliothek, Vienna, folio 53r, available on the "Geoffrey Chaucer" page on *Luminarium* (www.luminarium.org/medlit/garden.htm). Referencing the Knight's Tale, the image underscores Chaucer's techniques of "translation" and broader relations to continental literature. Emily and the imprisoned knights also appear on the cover of Hill's 2007 translation, in a nineteenth-century etching by Edward Burne-Jones and William Morris. Another Knight's Tale image, "Palamon Desireth to Slay His Foe Arcite," by Walter Appleton Clark (trans. Tuttle), points to American medievalism as another dimension of translation. Meanwhile, the image of a naked couple in bed (ed. Cawley [1995]) feeds expectations of overt sexuality. Excerpted from a manuscript of the Old French *Roman de la Rose*, the scene illustrates a misogynistic passage (line 16393) in which Genius warns of the danger of husbands' confiding in their wives (http://romandelarose.org/#read; Douce195.118r.tif). This cover, then, aligns *The Canterbury Tales* with the spirit of the Wife of Bath's fifth husband—and the teachings of the book she grew to hate. It also focuses attention on gender politics throughout *The Canterbury Tales*.

Cover images that portray Chaucer emphasize the univocality and stability of his authorship. These books tame the tales' cacophony and yoke Chaucer's own reputation to modern editing and translating (trans. Coghill, from MS Additional 5141, British Lib., London; trans. Nicholson; ed. Mann, from MS Ellesmere, Huntington Lib., San Marino). The pilgrims, however, are by far the most popular covering: they communicate polyvocality and the unpredictable vibrancy of social interactions (the 2003 reprint of Coghill's translation has replaced Chaucer with the pilgrims). Thomas Stothard's *The Pilgrimage to Canterbury* (www.tate.org.uk/art/artworks/stothard-the-pilgrimage-to-canterbury-n01163; see "Pilgrimage") is the most popular modern painting of pilgrims depicted on covers (trans. Hieatt and Hieatt; ed. Cawley [1992]; ed. Howard; ed. Fisher and Allen). Comparison with the original image can lead to discussion of the thematic implications of the selected or excised portions (e.g., the image included on Hieatt and Hieatt's translation centers on the Wife of Bath). Other modern representations include William Blake's *The Canterbury Pilgrims* (found on the 2000 edition of the *Riverside Chaucer*) and *The Pilgrims Set Out* and *Therewith He Brought Us out of Town*, by Clark (trans. Wright [2008]; trans. Tuttle). All these images foreground *The Canterbury Tales*'s performance context and the idea of pilgrimage.

Two of the most widely used editions feature pilgrims—the Norton Critical Edition and the *Riverside Chaucer*.[1] Each can introduce students to manuscript contexts in appealing ways. The Norton editions (ed. Kolve and Olson 1989, 2005) both feature a cover image from John Lydgate's *Siege of Thebes* (see folio 148r at www.bl.uk/manuscripts/Viewer.aspx?ref=royal_ms_18_d_ii_f148r; "Royal MS"). (The image also appears on Glaser's and Coghill's translations.) This illustration, which was added to the manuscript in the sixteenth century, depicts Lydgate in black among Chaucer's pilgrims, returning from Canterbury. By alluding to a post-Chaucerian moment, the image opens conversation concerning the role of other writers in shaping both "Chaucer" and his tales. The *Riverside Chaucer*, meanwhile, has appeared with two different pilgrim images: Lydgate's in the 1998 British paperback edition and Blake's in the 2000 abridged edition. The repackaging of the Lydgate image with different colors, words, and physical dimensions prompts discussion of the unique impressions created by each object. How do "Chaucer" and the tales change in each context? How does the image's significance change when it introduces all of "Chaucer" as in the *Riverside Chaucer*, versus "Fifteen Tales and the General Prologue" as in the Norton edition? Or when Lydgate is identified as "a disciple of Chaucer" on the back cover of the 1988 *Riverside* edition while not explained at all in the Norton? What does it mean for the cover of the "complete works" to refer exclusively to *The Canterbury Tales* (through the cover image)?

The Riverside *Canterbury Tales* has actually appeared in four different forms, each with a distinct framing strategy. In the United States, the book is most commonly known through the red cloth cover of the "original" third edition (1987). The image reproduced here, extracted from a manuscript of the thirteenth-century Old French *Image du monde* depicts the three estates—a clerk, a knight, and a laborer (British Lib., MS Sloane 2435, folio 85). Their mere description succinctly frames social dynamics, referencing stable divisions often undermined in the tales. Students can look for textual examples of the three types on the cover while attending to the ways in which characters play against their ostensibly fixed roles. The *Image du monde* upholds the power of the clerical class while offering an encyclopedia of world knowledge. The figures appear in a *C* representing *Clergie*: in this context, the clerk, rather than the knight, commands the center of attention. We might ask students in what sense *The Canterbury Tales* functions as a kind of encyclopedia—and what kinds of authority it embraces or rejects. Finally, the cover image's French origin can open into discussion of multilingualism in Chaucer's literary practice as well as more broadly in fourteenth- and fifteenth-century England.

The most recent *Riverside Chaucer* (printed in 2008) features the painting *Chaucer at the Court of Edward III*, by Ford Madox Brown (1845–78).

Historical figures gather around Chaucer, who reads from his book. The entire scene offers students a marvelously varied allegory of reading—from attentive to distracted, admiring to dismissive, high status to low, women to men. At different moments, students may adopt the posture of the focused note takers (seen in lower right corner) or turn away to intimate conversations with other readers (seen in the lower left). Brown himself identified the tale that Chaucer reads as the Man of Law's ("the Legend of Custance," lines 834–40); the listeners include John of Gaunt, John Gower, a troubadour, a never-sleeping squire (GP 10), and a priest "on good terms with the ladies" (Bendiner 131–33).

The *Riverside Chaucer*'s visual variety offers productive tensions between medieval and modern, multiplicity and singularity, narration and authorship (Trigg 1–39). The very fact of variability belies the singularity that the editions themselves put forward. This variability illustrates the multiple voicing of the tales and the importance of detailed contextual observation as the basis of literary interpretation. Meanwhile, the text that frames these images remains relatively stable and laconic. What are the effects of naming or not naming an editor? Why does one copy have to declare itself complete? These discussions can lead to broader editorial considerations: What makes an edition "critical"? Why do we need more than one edition in the first place? What would happen if everyone in class had a different book? From close attention to titles and subtitles, discussion can move easily into the multiple ways in which the text between the covers also results from many different interpretations, decisions, and ideological presuppositions. From this perspective, the notion of the fragment, which organizes the tales in the *Riverside Chaucer*, becomes clearly both material and theoretical. In what ways do parts cohere or not into a whole?

When the path to a "real" medieval manuscript begins with a modern reaction to a modern book, students experience how they as innocent readers can serve as entry points into historical understanding. One of the ongoing challenges of text-based teaching in the twenty-first century is connecting textual analysis to visual analysis, establishing meaningful relations that vivify texts and make images readable. The covers of our books—not to mention the portals of our Web sites and the screen designs of any number of electronic devices—have shaped students' expectations before we even meet them. Directly analyzing these materials provides students with powerful methods for assessing texts and images of all kinds.

NOTE

[1]The *Riverside Chaucer* is currently produced by Cengage Learning as the *Wadsworth Chaucer*. In an editorial sleight of hand, bibliographic entries list the publication date as 1986 (first publication of the third edition of the *Riverside Chaucer*), with a new ISBN and slightly different dimensions. So far, the cover image remains the same.

Chaucer's *The Canterbury Tales* in the Undergraduate English Language Arts Curriculum

Bryan P. Davis

> The pedagogical aspect of moving [toward a student-centered pedagogy] is quite simply to make a generous outreach to students and try to reformulate—even at the expense of re-thinking them for ourselves—understandable answers to their questions about the value of humanistic scholarship.
>
> —Charles Muscatine, "'What Amounteth Al This Wit?'"

My first remembered encounter with Chaucer occured during my junior year of high school, when Sister Julia read the Miller's Tale aloud to our class in Middle English. I do not want to suggest that I decided then and there to become a Chaucerian, but I do want to suggest that this aural moment clearly contributed to my development and that such early encounters with Chaucer are crucial to the maintenance of medieval studies. Since then, not long before the first edition of *Approaches to Teaching Chaucer's* Canterbury Tales was published, much has changed in education, particularly in university education, where the importance of teaching as part of a scholar's portfolio increases annually. An emphasis on student learning has led to increased scrutiny by federal and state departments of education, university boards, and accrediting organizations, which are designed to ensure adherence to standards generated by regional and national discipline-based accreditation organizations.

Regional and national standards have created, among other things, the need for English programs to assess their effectiveness in graduating critical readers, writers, and thinkers who possess the skills to continue learning and adapting beyond the classroom. Part of the effectiveness puzzle is the variety of postbaccalaureate lives envisioned by our students and by our English programs, including the life of a literary scholar, a K–12 teacher, and a professional or creative writer. In this essay, I focus on the challenges presented by K–12 teacher candidates and the National Council of Teachers of English's gold-standard content benchmarks for English language arts candidates. I will argue that this challenge is also an opportunity for university teachers of *The Canterbury Tales* to develop critical readers, writers, and thinkers with a love of Chaucer and the skills to articulate how his study meets recognized educational standards (see app. 1 for a complete list of the NCTE Standards for English Language Arts).

When I first arrived at my current institution, we had a traditional literature program that required a number of broad survey courses at the sophomore and junior levels, even for the professional-writing and teacher-certification tracks within the program. Between the four surveys and track-specific requirements, little room was left for senior-level surveys in any period or author, much less Chaucer. Over the years, the junior-level surveys have been replaced by sophomore-level surveys that double as general education requirements and by senior-level seminars on individual authors, such as Chaucer, and specific periods, such as medieval English literature. These literature seminars, as well as classes in advanced composition, introductory linguistics, and theories of rhetoric, now form the core of the curriculum for all English majors. Therefore, when I teach a senior-level Chaucer or English medieval literature seminar, the class roster includes traditional literature students, professional-writing students who may not attend graduate school (and who will not study literature, if they do), and teacher-certification candidates who may spend the bulk of their professional lives in K–12 education. While Chaucer has practical virtue for each group, I believe the third or more of my students who are teacher candidates have the most influence on the future of Chaucer studies.

Teacher candidates encounter *The Canterbury Tales* in one of two undergraduate classes—a senior seminar in Chaucer or in medieval English literature. As a prerequisite for both classes, students must take a course that introduces such basic linguistic concepts as phonology, morphology, and syntax. I teach both senior seminars, in which I require at least some acquaintance with Middle English, and I assign readings from *The Canterbury Tales* in their original language. In order to show how *The Canterbury Tales* meets the NCTE standards, I produce for teacher candidates a separate syllabus that not only includes the course learning outcomes that are shared with all students but also maps how particular outcomes relate to the NCTE standards. Since teacher candidates usually come to their content classes familiar with the NCTE standards and with mapping course learning outcomes to program outcomes, they begin to see the practical virtue of Chaucer's *Canterbury Tales* as soon as they read the course syllabus (app. 2 charts how the learning outcomes of my Chaucer course relate to the NCTE standards). For instance, the course learning outcome specifying that "a student will apply an understanding of the culture and history of medieval England to the interpretation of Chaucer's texts" maps directly onto NCTE standard 2: "students read a wide range of literature from many periods in many genres to build an understanding of the many dimensions (e.g., philosophical, ethical, aesthetic) of human experience ("NCTE/IRA Standards").

Since each description explains how the assignment relates to course learning outcomes, teacher candidates can use their course maps to find the associated NCTE standards. For instance, the descriptions show that translation assignments address the course outcome that states, "A student will understand the vocabulary, morphology, and syntax of Middle English," and the syllabus has already indicated that this course learning outcome relates to NCTE standards 6 and 9. While the metacognitive practice of stating expected outcomes improves learning for all students, its specific application to teacher candidates has the additional benefit of showing them how their learning can relate to their future careers. Since honest, self-reflective practice underpins successful learning and teaching, the reflection and writing I require of students has also benefited my thinking about how and why I teach Chaucer's *Canterbury Tales* in the first place.

Each assignment I use in senior seminars, including translations, class presentations, and writing assignments, can be adapted to address NCTE standards. Furthermore, gearing assignments toward teacher candidates develops self-monitoring abilities in which students learn "how to consider their own understandings of a text and learn how to proceed when their understanding fails" (*NCTE Principles* 6). Development of self-monitoring requires students not only to complete assignments but also to reflect on the process of completing them. Thus, I structure many assignments in a way that encourages students to ask questions about what worked best in completing an assignment, what did not work well, and how to proceed in the future to overcome difficulties. While I build reflection into most assignments for all students, I encourage teacher candidates in particular to think about how they might help their own prospective students identify and overcome difficulties in reading and writing.

My approach to teaching students to read and translate Middle English exemplifies how the theory of metacognitive reflection addresses NCTE standards and how it can influence future teacher practice. Since I can assume that students have some familiarity with basic linguistic concepts, I begin by describing and giving examples of how Middle English differs from modern English on these points. After participating in a discussion of the most important differences, students write a "one-minute paper" on which differences are the most clear and which the least (Light 66–69). Reading these papers provides me with direction for the next class, and writing them demonstrates to teacher candidates a simple method of gauging what students learn from a given lecture or discussion.

After addressing their concerns, I work with students to translate one of Chaucer's lyrics, often "Truth." Before the next class, students post a short paper on the class discussion board about what they found most difficulty in the translation exercise or what they anticipate will pose the greatest difficulty in translating individually; teacher candidates may opt, and are strongly encouraged, to post about what difficulties they believe present greater pedagogical challenges. (These assignments are based on Salvatori and Donahue, esp. 9–11.) I use the posts to locate difficulties for discussion and to generate small groups for collaborative translation of individual stanzas from "The Complaint of Chaucer to His Purse" or a similar lyric. This method helps ensure that I do not create groups in which every member has similar difficulties. Before I evaluate the collaborative translations, students submit short individual reports on whether their anticipated difficulties arose and why or why not. If teacher candidates exercise their option, they report on the pedagogical challenges they anticipated. It should be noted that not all student difficulties arise from the language itself, so we discuss issues of genre, form, imagery, and historical context as we translate, and I model ways of overcoming these difficulties as well.

In the next stage of learning the language, we again work together as a class to translate the first forty-two lines of the General Prologue, and students again write a one-minute paper on the clearest and most unclear thing about this passage. We continue by collaboratively translating the next couple hundred lines, and then the balance is divided equally for individual translation. Before I grade the individual translations, students post reports on the class discussion board on what difficulties they have overcome and how, as well as on remaining difficulties. For this assignment, teacher candidates have the option of reporting on what methods they anticipate using in the future to help their prospective students overcome obstacles.

Since students can access online resources such as glossaries, dictionaries, and translations while they work, especially outside class, I show and critique various translations during class discussion of the General Prologue. Groups or individual students who use online resources to produce their translations must document their sources and give a rationale for choosing one source over another if multiple sources are available. Teacher candidates have the option of giving a rationale for using such online resources in their future classrooms. Throughout the time spent learning to read Middle English, I make a point of discussing how classes and assignments are designed to promote learning that will allow student success in the class. At the same time, I make the point that less immediate goals, such as the abilities to collaborate and devise strategies to overcome difficulty, can lead to success after graduation.

Presentation and writing assignments can also be adapted for teacher candidates by the methods used for translation assignments. Depending on the size of the class, I typically assign either an individual or a collaborative presentation during the middle weeks of the semester; in larger classes I tend to go the collaborative route. After observing my introductions to the tales that complete fragment 1, each group or student chooses a tale from the reading list to introduce before we discuss it. Whether the presentations are collaborative or individual, students produce two types of reflective assignments about the presentations. Immediately after students or groups present, each individual writes a report about what parts went well, what parts did not go well, and why he or she made these assessments. Teacher candidates are encouraged to apply to this assignment knowledge and skills they may have acquired from their education curriculum, through field observation, or from observing other classes they have taken. We have a general discussion of criteria for an effective presentation. After all groups or students have presented, each individual writes a report about which presentation she or he felt was the best and why. Teacher candidates are again encouraged to apply their educational knowledge, skills, and experience to the task.

Adapting the research essay that is typically the capstone of my Chaucer seminar to the needs of teacher candidates does not follow exactly the same model as other assignments. Since the opportunities for reflection after submission are limited, most reflection must be done with a research proposal. The typical timetable for such a seminar essay requires a proposal at or about midterm, a working bibliography a couple of weeks after the proposal, and a preliminary draft two to three weeks before submission of the draft for evaluation near the end of the term. Teacher candidates are given the option of producing detailed lesson plans for a unit on *The Canterbury Tales* in place of the traditional research essay, while being held to the same standards for writing and documentation as the other students in the seminar. In addition, teacher candidates are required to indicate what NCTE standards their lesson will meet at the beginning of the assignment and to provide a statement at final submission that asserts and supports how their finished lesson meets the specified standards.

Giving teacher candidates options that relate to their professional goals helps them see and reflect on "the value of humanistic scholarship" to life after graduation (Muscatine, "'What Amounteth'" 54), while giving newly minted teachers at least one preplanned unit on Chaucer and the strategies to produce more. In addition, student reflections give me invaluable feedback that helps me keep my practice fresh by forcing me to adapt to changing student audiences. Collaborating with teacher candidates in composing their lesson plans also keeps me in touch with the education curriculum. This approach benefits not only the glad student but also the glad teacher.

APPENDIX 1
THE IRA/NCTE STANDARDS FOR ENGLISH LANGUAGE ARTS[†]

1. Students read a wide range of print and nonprint texts to build an understanding of texts, of themselves, and of the cultures of the United States and the world, to acquire new information, to respond to the needs and demands of society and the workplace, and for personal fulfillment. Among these texts are fiction and nonfiction, classic and contemporary works.
2. Students read a wide range of literature from many periods in many genres to build an understanding of the many dimensions (e.g., philosophical, ethical, aesthetic) of human experience.
3. Students apply a wide range of strategies to comprehend, interpret, evaluate, and appreciate texts. They draw on their prior experience, their interactions with other readers and writers, their knowledge of word meaning and of other texts, their word identification strategies, and their understanding of textual features (e.g., sound-letter correspondence, sentence structure, context, graphics).
4. Students adjust their use of spoken, written, and visual language (e.g., conventions, style, vocabulary) to communicate effectively with a variety of audiences and for different purposes.

[†] *Standards for the English Language Arts*, by the International Reading Association and the National Council of Teachers of English, copyright 1996 by the International Reading Association and the National Council of Teachers of English. Reprinted with permission.

5. Students employ a wide range of strategies as they write and use different writing process elements appropriately to communicate with different audiences for a variety of purposes.
6. Students apply knowledge of language structure, language conventions (e.g., spelling and punctuation), media techniques, figurative language, and genre to create, critique, and discuss print and nonprint texts.
7. Students conduct research on issues and interests by generating ideas and questions and by posing problems. They gather, evaluate, and synthesize data from a variety of sources (e.g., print and nonprint texts, artifacts, people) to communicate their discoveries in ways that suit their purpose and audience.
8. Students use a variety of technological and information resources (e.g., libraries, databases, computer networks, video) to gather and synthesize information and to create and communicate knowledge.
9. Students develop an understanding of and respect for diversity in language use, patterns, and dialects across cultures, ethnic groups, geographic regions, and social roles.
10. Students whose first language is not English make use of their first language to develop competency in the English language arts and to develop understanding of content across the curriculum.
11. Students participate as knowledgeable, reflective, creative, and critical members of a variety of literacy communities.
12. Students use spoken, written, and visual language to accomplish their own purposes (e.g., for learning, enjoyment, persuasion, and the exchange of information).

APPENDIX 2
CHAUCER-NCTE OUTCOMES MAP

Chaucer Course Learning Outcomes	Related NCTE Standards
A student will	
understand the vocabulary, morphology, and syntax of Middle English;	Standards 6, 9
understand the culture and history of medieval England;	Standards 1, 2
apply an understanding of the culture and history of medieval England to the interpretation of Chaucer's texts;	Standards 1, 2
understand the interaction between medieval visual and literary texts, especially in Chaucer;	Standards 4, 12
compose effective analytic and interpretive responses to Chaucerian texts.	Standards 3, 4, 5, 7, 8, and 12

A First Year's Experience of Teaching *The Canterbury Tales*

Jacob Lewis

One of the many generous aspects of *The Canterbury Tales* is its versatility in the classroom. Chaucer can be taught well in a variety of circumstances and contexts, each of which changes our students' and our own understanding of his poetry. Such was my experience in my first year of teaching *The Canterbury Tales* to undergraduates. In that year, I taught Chaucer in three different classes: first, a literature and composition course; second, a survey of world literature; and finally, a survey of British literature. Each course required me to present *The Canterbury Tales* differently, and each in turn caused me to rethink some aspect of the *Tales*.

The Composition Course

Admittedly, *The Canterbury Tales* is not entirely at home in a composition course, even one that is literature based. The advantages of teaching the tales (they're fun, they make an interesting contrast with modern fiction and poetry) do not sufficiently outweigh the disadvantages (the teaching-in-translation debate, issues of culture shock). In that first year, I tried teaching *The Canterbury Tales* as part of a "writing about literature" course. I divided the course into four sections: fiction, poetry, drama, and film. Each section focused on developing close-reading skills and taught students basic formal features (plot, theme, point of view, tone, and so on). *The Canterbury Tales*, naturally, showed up in the poetry section, although I didn't introduce them until later in the unit, when my students had more practice reading poetry. I started with a brief handout on Middle English, largely drawn from the *Riverside Chaucer*'s introduction. After a lecture on the language, I walked them through the Miller's Tale and the Wife of Bath's Prologue (readily available, for example, on Harvard's *Geoffrey Chaucer Page*). I encouraged them to read the Middle English first and to use resources like *SparkNotes* only for clarification, although most of them ended up going straight to the study guides.

Despite my preparation, my students—a diverse group of lower- and upperclassmen from a variety of majors—were not comfortable with Middle English. While most were able to at least get some sense of the narrative, much of the three days of class discussion was spent clearing up their misconceptions about both the Middle Ages in general and the plot of the tales in particular. In discussion, they tended to react to only the most dramatic and isolated moments—for example, the window scene in the Miller's Tale. Their lack of analysis was all the more frustrating since my students had shown themselves capable of solid textual criticism when we read works like Ha Jin's "The Bridegroom" and

e. e. cummings's "in Just-." In those cases, my students were keener to discuss the text and even commented on issues of race, sex, and gender. Clearly something was amiss.

Few students were willing to write on the Chaucer selections; those who did avoided clear argument in favor of plot summary. While the recourse to summary seems like an attempt to make sense of the text, it taught me what is now painfully obvious: Middle English, even Chaucer's, does not work well in a composition course. It might be possible to teach composition with Middle English, but doing so would take a lot more preparation and would take away from the overall goals of the course. In other words, do I want my students to read Middle English or to improve their analytic and writing skills? At best, a few students have learned to appreciate Chaucer; at worst, they have left feeling that English is confusing and irrelevant to their needs.

The World Literature Course

Thankfully, the stakes are not so dire in a world literature course. The Canterbury Tales almost certainly belongs there; it is one of the most influential texts in the Western canon and can also fit into a variety of thematic units. In my class, the Wife of Bath's Tale was part of a unit on tricksters. While that word is more at home describing culture heroes—Anansi, Coyote, Prometheus—I focused on people who were clever with their words: the Wife of Bath, Shahrazad from The Arabian Nights, and Hunahpu and Xbalanque from the Popol Vuh.

The general thread connecting these works was the use of storytelling as a device to extricate oneself from difficulties. For example, while the sons of the Hunahpu twins in the Popol Vuh tell stories about their powers in order to trick the Lords of the Underworld into killing themselves, Shahrazad heals Shahryar of his compulsive violence toward women through her storytelling, a talent she shares with the Wife of Bath. I used the storytelling gambit to foreground the Wife of Bath's Tale and encouraged my students to read the prologue as a supplement to the tale. The Wife of Bath–Shahrazad pairing works very well, especially since the Norton Anthology of World Literature (our department-mandated text) prints only the frame narrative and the opening two stories of the Nights, which focus especially on Shahryar's compulsive violence.

Because we studied the Wife of Bath's Prologue and Tale in modern English, my students were better able to analyze the narrative and make connections across the texts during class discussion. They were primarily interested in the ways that both Alisoun and Shahrazad explored the power of speech to change circumstances and even heal their antagonists' deep psychological issues. They pointed out that the problems of both the rapist-knight and Shahryar stem from their objectification of women, although the gender and power issues are reversed. While the queen may control the knight's fate, Shahryar still controls Shahrazad's. I encouraged my students to pursue these connections in their papers. The cultivation of thematic connections among a variety of premodern texts and cultures, I found, provided students with a gateway to a literary world with which many had been unfamiliar and revitalized those stories they already knew.

The Survey of British Literature Course

My third opportunity to teach *The Canterbury Tales* came when I was asked to teach our medieval and Renaissance literature survey. Even this opportunity came with a bit of a challenge, since it was a sped-up six-week summer course. I covered all the tales in the anthology: the Miller's Tale, the Wife of Bath's Tale, and the Nun's Priest's Tale. I pared down the reading of the General Prologue to the first forty-one lines and just the portraits of the Miller, the Wife, and the Prioress, the latter so we might discuss the connections between her and Pertelote. Despite my reservations, teaching Middle English through the General Prologue worked better than my handout on Middle English because the students were able to use narrative and textual clues to make better sense of the language. Meeting every day likely helped as well because it let my students get better feedback on their understanding of the language and the text. Compared with my previous classes, the students in my survey course were able to make stronger connections between the individual tales and the prologue. Moreover, the addition of the Nun's Priest's Tale enriched conversations about gender and power, conversations that had tended to be tentative in my other classes.

These conversations (and the rapid pace of a summer session) were also beneficial when my students read both book 1 of the *Faerie Queene* and a selection of Elizabeth I's letters and speeches. As we once more discussed issues of gender—Elizabeth's "heart and stomach of a king" (326), for example, or Redcrosse's encounters with Error and his seduction by Duessa—my students pointed back to both Alisoun and Pertelote, and we talked deeply about the relation between misogyny and power over the intervening two centuries.

My first year of teaching *The Canterbury Tales* was largely a process of experimentation. I would encourage first-time teachers of the *Tales* to be a little daring in their syllabi, whether by pairing the *Tales* with a non-Western analogue or by springing our favorite poet on freshman writers. And don't be afraid of the big conversations about class, gender, and religion; in fact, such conversations can be a way for students to jump the "ye olde" language hurdle. Finally, even the worst gamble can still give us opportunities for interesting class discussions, creative paper topics, and the sharing of our abiding love of *The Canterbury Tales*.

Teaching *The Canterbury Tales* to Non-Liberal-Arts Students

Deborah M. Sinnreich-Levi

I teach medieval literature to future engineers, scientists, and managers—and a tiny handful of literature majors and minors—at a school where faculty club lunch conversations range around the hilarities of teaching thermodynamics and nanotechnology and where the students are an interesting mix: seventy-five percent men, about fifty-five percent from New Jersey, forty percent from across the United States, and more than five percent international (predominantly from Malaysia, China, South Korea, and India). The three most popular majors are mechanical engineering, civil engineering, and business technology. My students tend to have little context for the study of the Middle Ages, so I help them find it both in class and through electronic tools. The course I inherited from a now-retired colleague was titled Chaucer: A Literary Study and included selections from Dante and Boccaccio and the practice of reading aloud in Middle English. But now my course, which covers *The Canterbury Tales* and the dream visions, is called Chaucer: The Journey and the Dreams. Not only the course title but also the tools of my pedagogy and the skills, attitudes, and needs of my students have changed. This essay describes one way of teaching Chaucer to non-liberal-arts students, which includes providing them a Web site with links to my slide shows, texts, art, history, and other related topics and having them build a virtual study guide.

I teach *The Canterbury Tales* in translation. I read aloud in Middle English, especially early in the semester: I want my students to hear what I hear in my head: Robert O. Payne reading Chaucer out loud, the cadences of the poetry in its original language, the sharp tongue of Chaucer the social critic, and the jibes, complaints, and lyricism of the many voices of *The Canterbury Tales*. But my students are not asked to read in Middle English. They would be too daunted to remain in the course, although they would probably cite constraints on their time or a perceived lack of relevance. So I prefer complete verse translations at reasonable cost and settled some years ago on Ronald Ecker and Eugene Joseph Crook's serviceable volume coupled with Rob Pope's useful study guide. Class discussion is predominantly an informed version of reader response. Topics we keep returning to include genre studies, religion and culture, and the voice of the poet: What can we learn from the poet's sometimes transgressive use of genres and motifs? What is a saint? What is the role of organized religion in medieval society? How do people function in a tightly organized community? What medieval social mores does the poet challenge? How does the poet use the personae of the pilgrims to speak to his contemporaries and to us?

Engaging with primary texts is the principal activity of the course, and to help my students wrestle with the reading, I rebuild my course's Web site annually—syllabus, slide shows, discussion questions, outside links.[1] Great online resources are readily available, aiding both instructors and students.[2] My syllabus used to be interactive, but the instability of the Web, the time sink of compiling links, and a required syllabus template have separated assignments from ancillary readings. Keying Web sites to each assignment gets students to visit the links, so I still list specific ancillary readings with information and images about pilgrimages (for example, to Canterbury and Santiago de Compostela), art and architecture (Lady Fortune and Canterbury Cathedral), and historical, cultural, and sociological topics (the Three Estates, hagiography, dreams, medicine, and manuscript production).

Before students come to class each day, they are expected to have done four things: read the assigned tales, explored relevant Web sites, reviewed PowerPoint slides they will see in class, and posted to the class discussion board. These last two activities are related: the discussion-board questions for each tale are taken from the questions posed in my slide shows. Questions begin with reading comprehension: "Who are Averagus, Aurelius, and Dorigen?" More analytic questions include, "What unusual relationship do the knight and his wife enjoy?" Then questions widen in scope: "Contrast Dorigen and Averagus's ideas on marriage with the Wife of Bath's" and "What is a Breton lai?" Students are expected to reply to at least some study-guide questions at least twice a week. What sells students on the extra writing is that if they all participate, they build a set of shared notes for the course, which are only as successful as the amount of work each student contributes. Students are, therefore, prompted to prepare better for class. If they can't respond to the study-guide questions, they know they should be reading more deeply. Reading other students' posts presents alternative interpretations before class even starts. The walls of the classroom are stretched with four good results: students can ask questions in the middle of the night that I can respond to in class; the conversation can go in unpredicted directions; the conversation can last longer than the three hours per week we will be in the same room; and students reread the discussion threads and *PowerPoint* slides as exam preparation. One additional benefit can accrue: the semester I wrote this essay, I had a great group of students, who were all, unfortunately, consistently silent in class. If I hadn't included asynchronous discussion, there might have been no conversation at all, but instead debate raged in the middle of the night, during lunch, and on weekends.

The following is an example of such a discussion from this same semester. For the Cook's Tale, I posted three study guide questions: "What theme in the frame is continued?" "What is the theme of this tale?" and "Why bother reading an incomplete tale?" There were twenty-six responses from seven students. The conversation ranged over a variety of predictable as well as unexpected topics, including the rare depiction of a working-class character, the possible rivalry between the Cook and the Host, the impact of education (and what it means that the Cook, unlike many of the pilgrims, is uneducated), theft as a theme (and whether Chaucer is trying to indicate something stolen from him or his society), who was really insulting whom (that is, whether the Cook is mocking himself and who is the object of Chaucer's mockery), and an 820-word post on the economics of the Cook's position and what it implied about him and his tale. This last post summed up the other students' arguments, noted that the Cook and the characters were not mere fast-food workers with only a couple of days of experience using the deep-fryer, discoursed on the apprenticeship system, and drew a distinction between Perkyn's resigning pending the master's approval and the master's declaring Perkyn's training ended but with the master's imprimatur. I wove these comments and queries into the actual class on the Cook's Tale.

I use slide shows in every class. Available to students from the first day of the semester, these files are expanded versions of the bulletin discussion plus the Web links and include questions comparable in range to those in the *Power-Point* files (comprehension questions and more open-ended discussion) as well as other materials. The slides sometimes have a seminal quotation ("Experience, though noon auctoritee / Were in this world, is right ynogh for me / To speke of wo that is in mariage" ["Even if there were no formal precedent to cite, my own experience is all I need in this world to speak about the affliction found in marriage"; WBT 1–3]), an image (Chaucer's grave in Poets' Corner), or a chart (the symmetrical structure of the Knight's Tale or the three parts of penitence). Students know that if they master the materials covered in the slide shows and discussion boards, they are well prepared for both class and exams. Unforeseen circumstances such as snow days can disrupt a tightly organized syllabus, but live conferencing using services such as *Wimba* can rescue the day. This easy-to-use tool lets me upload my slide show and open a "classroom" in which students can speak both through microphone and text. Instead of losing a day, having to cram two days' material into one, or scheduling a makeup day, I am able to hold class during my regularly scheduled slot and record the session for students who don't get my emergency notification before class time.

For my students, and perhaps for many nonliterature majors, rereading the online material is more efficient than completely rereading the primary texts. Electronic aids prepare students for class, reinforce materials in advance of exams, and function as study guides in the most active sense—if and only if students participate actively, which can be urged by carrot-and-stick methods. The stick: nonparticipation costs ten percent of the final grade. The carrot: participation in the threaded discussion builds a guide for all to profit from in a form familiar to information-age students (that is, threaded topics and hierarchical information). Hypermeticulous students save the slides and record answers to all the questions (a habit I find rather limited and see only rarely). Engineering students in particular like collaborating and having orderly review materials, which are learning styles to be cultivated in most students. Most college students are also further down the information highway than most of their faculty members. We do not have to immediately adopt every novel technology—I do not yet see any pedagogical benefit to social networking—but electronic ancillary materials and discussion possibilities are as transparent and useful to our students as water is to fish.

NOTES

[1] I had used *WebCT* since it was in beta testing, but all the popular platforms provide suitable functionalities, including my sine qua non, the discussion board. My school has switched to *Moodle* both for its pricing and open sourcing.

[2] See "Aids to Teaching" in the "Materials" section in this volume.

Chaucer and Race: Teaching
The Canterbury Tales to the Diverse Folk
of the Twenty-First-Century Classroom

Donna Crawford

Perhaps it should not have surprised me when a student in a class reading the
General Prologue to *The Canterbury Tales* asked whether the Yeoman was African. After all, the Yeoman is described as having a "not heed . . . with a broun
visage" ("a closely cropped head . . . with a brown face"; line 109), and the
Knight, of whose small entourage the Yeoman is part, as having traveled as far
away as Belmarye (57) and Tramyssene (62). The conjunction of the Yeoman's
dark skin with the Knight's crusading in North Africa makes the question plausible enough. Still, it isn't one that students at predominantly white schools are
likely to ask. This question stands as an example of how teaching at the historically black college or university (HBCU) requires some rethinking of expectations about how to teach Chaucer—and this rethinking has value for professors
working in any of the twenty-first century's diverse classrooms.

HBCUs, as these schools are known, have their origins in the United States'
racially divided past. Whether the schools taught the traditional liberal arts or
trained students for careers, they have long been centers of black intellectual life
in the American South and have participated in resistance to inequality from the
era of Jim Crow through the civil rights movement and into the present. This
heritage continues to define the over one hundred institutions that are classified
as HBCUs and to condition the assumptions and sense of identity of the students who attend them (for an overview of these schools, see Gasman et al.).

Chaucer obviously does not appear to pertain directly to this history and
heritage. The student who asked about the Yeoman in the General Prologue
was doing what so many student readers do: looking for herself in the text. But
Chaucer, while distant and potentially alienating for any modern student, can
be especially disquieting to those in the HBCU classroom. Like most present-
day students of literature, HBCU students have learned to be attuned when
they read to who is being marginalized and to which voices are being left out.
However, the silences and omissions in Chaucer are not the same as the ones
produced in the literary works of later centuries. Only after helping students
reach some awareness of the cultural assumptions within Chaucer's text (a process that necessarily requires them to consider some of their own cultural assumptions) can a teacher bring students to see a distinctive array of silences,
omissions, and stereotypes, which were based on the hierarchies of difference
that mattered in fourteenth-century England. In turn, recognizing those hierarchies of difference can help students better understand some of the systemic
inequalities that persist in our own society.

Race in the Middle Ages

Medieval ideas of race were notably different from those in the present day. The difference matters both in terms of the long history of diverse peoples invading and being incorporated into the regional cultures of England before Chaucer's career and in terms of the development of the Atlantic slave trade, which arose in the centuries after his death. Current scholarly discussions of race as it was understood and lived in the Middle Ages make general points that are important for twenty-first-century students of Chaucer to understand. Even now, the term *race* does not have a precise or unchanging meaning; as a medieval term, it could refer to characteristics that included genealogical background, language, law, customs, physical appearance, and, most important, religion (Hahn; Loomba and Burton). By leading students to consider how such characteristics create the ambiguities of modern racial categories, the professor of a diverse classroom can prepare students to notice the significant details of difference in Chaucer.

What may be most important for the professor teaching at an HBCU, however, is to emphasize that skin color, which carries so much emphasis in modern understandings of race, is just one feature, and not necessarily a central one, in medieval ideas of race. Still, matters of skin color had begun to gather significance by Chaucer's time. Geraldine Heng notes that medieval European literature and art offer examples of "a colour dualism in which white is valued positively, as the colour of the noble-born and Christians, and black is valued negatively, as loathly and foul, and the colour of infernal heathens and killers" (261). Yet even as they recognize this, students must be brought to understand that though somatic features held meaning within a system of hierarchical value in the Middle Ages, slavery and skin color were not linked in the period before the trans-Atlantic slave trade as they would later be. Although students know that slavery as an institution has endured since ancient times, they are often startled to learn that the etymology of the word *slave* derives from a period of Mediterranean trade when persons of Slavic ethnicity were bought and sold. Here, ethnic distinctions take precedence over skin color, and when students think through such ethnic differences, they are encouraged to take yet another look at the geographic locales through which Chaucer's Knight is described as having crusaded.

Reading Difference in The Canterbury Tales

Students in literature survey courses might read only the General Prologue to *The Canterbury Tales*, while those in advanced courses will read more. In the General Prologue, the representation of the estates bears consideration: student readers are often puzzled about many of the occupations and social positions cataloged in the prologue, and making clear what the pilgrims are and how the dynamics of hierarchy are presented is important.

In addition, the prologue's references to skin color are worth having students notice and discuss. For example, the contrast in skin color between the Monk, who "was nat pale as a forpyned goost" ("was not pale as a tormented ghost"; line 205) and the Friar, whose "nekke whit was as the flour-de-lys" ("neck was white as a lily"; 238), suggests the satirical working of the text: these pilgrims' modes of being in the world are obviously at odds with the expectations of their estates. Likewise, considering the face of the Wife of Bath ("Bold . . . and fair, and reed of hewe" ["red of hue"; 458]) or the "fyr-reed cherubynnes face" of the Summoner ("fire-red cherub's face"; 624), with its apparently untreatable "whelkes white" ("white pustules"; 632), impels students to learn different ways of understanding in order to draw meaningful conclusions about these figures.

In addition to the Yeoman, another provocative example of darker skin color is the Shipman: "The hoote somer hadde maad his hewe al broun" ("The hot summer had made his hue completely brown"; 394). Students can be encouraged to wonder about the import of this detail during an April pilgrimage. They might also consider how his description as "a good felawe" ("fellow"; 395) accords with his drinking the chapmen's wine and kicking opponents into the water, where they would presumably drown. What connections should a reader draw between dishonesty, brutality, skin color, and occupation as a shipman?

Discussing these details of skin color and the associations they carry is just one of the ways that even those students who read only the General Prologue can learn the importance of otherness and the values implicit in the dynamics of social hierarchy. Students in more advanced courses will have the chance to consider Chaucer's representations of racial others: the Syrians of the Man of Law's Tale, the Tartars of the Squire's Tale, the Jews of the Prioress's Tale. In each of these tales, elements of a specifically medieval orientalism filter through the narrative. Clearly, the exotic spectacle of the warriors Lygurge and Emetreus in the Knight's Tale and the narrator's admiration of the noble Cambyuskan and the marvels of his court in the Squire's Tale contrast sharply with the virulence of Christian feeling against the Muslims in the Man of Law's Tale and the Jews in the Prioress's Tale. The differences allow for discussion of how racial attitudes can be enacted under varying circumstances and how the consequences of these attitudes can range from stereotypes to violence.

Still, none of these tales engages the color emphasis that African American students most centrally associate with race. Such color descriptions, when they do appear, bear careful attention. It is especially critical for a professor in a diverse classroom to be aware of how objectionable some students of color find the associations of blackness with the devil. In the Friar's Tale, for instance, the widow curses the summoner "unto the devel blak and rough of hewe" ("unto the devil black and rough in appearance"; 1622). And in the Nun's Priest's Tale,

Pertelote compares the red choleric humor she blames for Chauntecleer's dream with

> ... the humour of malencolie [that]
> Causeth ful many a man in sleep to crie
> For feere of blake beres, or boles blake,
> Or elles blake develes wole hem take.

> ... the melancholy humor [that]
> Causes many men to cry in their sleep
> For fear of black bears, or black bulls,
> Or else for fear that black devils will seize them. (2933–36)

Even if the use of blackness in these descriptions can be explained, it is important that it not be simply explained away: no explanation can erase the explicit presence of blackness in a demonic context. Here, a professor should engage students to consider what they have learned about race in the Middle Ages and how it might be juxtaposed with what they know of race from their own experience and understanding.

So, how should I have responded to my student's question: Is the Yeoman in the General Prologue an African? It is hard to be convinced that he is, for aside from the color of his skin, Chaucer's text provides no evidence to set him apart from the other pilgrims "from every shires end / Of Engelond" (15–16). Still, a professor teaching students of color who wonder about the Yeoman's identity would do well to encourage a reading of *The Canterbury Tales* that notices his relatively brief description and his place, along with the Plowman and the Five Guildsmen, as a pilgrim whom Chaucer does not provide with a tale. Recognizing the various ways, in various historical circumstances, that human differences have been arranged into hierarchies of worth is one of the many valuable lessons Chaucer has—beyond his clear literary merit—for students to whom race matters.

Making the Tales More Tangible: Chaucer and Medieval Culture in Secondary Schools

Kara Crawford

I was inspired to consider the impact of "things tangible" during a visit with Lee Patterson's National Endowment for the Humanities (NEH) seminar class to the Beinecke Library for a viewing of several medieval manuscripts. My personal response was visceral: the vellum, the pigment, each hairline detail allowed me to imagine the movement of the scribe's hand. Back in my classroom, I soon realized that sharing detailed images with my tenth- and twelfth-grade students had a similar effect. While visual artistry always has its appeal, it seems that in the era of the virtual, things concrete have become increasingly rare and intriguing. In "Keeping It Real: Why, in an Age of Free Information, Would Anyone Pay Millions for a Document?" James Gleick discusses the eight-figure price tag, determined at public auction, of an extant copy of the Magna Carta and explains the value placed on such items: "It's a kind of illusion. We can call it magical value as opposed to meaningful value. . . . A physical object becomes desirable, precious, almost holy, by common consensus, on account of a history—a story—that is attached to it." Because our students know a world in which seemingly endless information exists in the abstract realm of the virtual, they are intrigued by the opportunity to experience a singular and sensory artifact. As Gleick sums up, "Why? Because the same free flow that makes information cheap and reproducible helps us treasure the sight of information that is not. A story gains power from its attachment, however tenuous, to a physical object. The object gains power from the story."

I suggest that better engaging students requires us to move away from pedagogical approaches in secondary education that distance students from the original work: not Chaucer for children, not Chaucer as a rap, not even modern analogy. Rather than offer contemporary parallels that may be misleading and that give little opportunity for students to explore the subtleties of differing perspectives, we can design lessons and curricula that focus less on "making it real" and more on the "real" that is tangible, concrete, and sensory. In this endeavor, we need not lament that younger students are often more concrete thinkers but rather make use of the opportunity to provide the more concrete elements of language and context on which we can build for further scholarship. The beauty, intricacy, and oddity of illuminated manuscripts, a topic of study often delayed until graduate school, is one that secondary students most readily appreciate. In both my tenth-grade survey course and a senior elective, my medieval unit begins with a packet of handouts complete with a full-page coloring-book version of an illuminated letter on the cover, a pronunciation key and flashcards to assist with Middle English, a map of the trip to Canterbury, a diagram of medieval cosmology, a chart indicating the socioeconomic position of each pilgrim, and a list of links to Web sites for browsing illuminated manuscripts. We spend much of the first day coloring and exploring the images that create each letter. (And, yes, when my twelfth graders saw the colored pencils set out for the other classes, they wanted to know when they would get to color as well.) While coloring beautiful designs, students become curious about the unusual creatures (griffins, dragons, and a variety of fantastic hybrids) as well as odd representations of both human and animal forms. The activity also quickly brings them to note the prevalence of religious iconography (saints, halos, images of martyrdom). While students explore and I describe the contents of the packet, I project onto the screen sample illuminations from online resources, many of which anticipate the playful quality of the stories to come. One of my favorite images for capturing students' interest is the Arthurian Romances manuscript at the Beinecke Library. Its margins are alive with a host of figures, including monkeys and rabbits that appear to be telling their own version of the story (see pp. 94v, 106v, 287r, 295r, and 325r). We also search for a broader variety of illuminated capital letters through the Hill Museum and Manuscript Library and conclude the day with an online video from the Getty Center entitled "The Making of a Medieval Book." The evening's homework is to view the introduction tour of the *Catalogue of Illuminated Manuscripts* on the British Library Web site and browse the catalog glossary ("Introduction"). The experience of exploring manuscript images also exposes students to the increasing number of online reference resources and teaches them how to search for and read resources that they can continue to use.

On the second day of the unit, we explore sound. I read from Chaucer in Middle English, and we discuss how to move our mouths and breathe to make new sounds (inevitably amid much laughter). With regard to the study of basic vocabulary and to hearing and pronouncing language, I advocate as much practice and exposure as is manageable. While online audio files of Middle English offer support, placing students in coaching pairs and supplying them with flashcards that cover vowel sounds and diphthongs quickly leads to successful recitations of simple passages.

Our first attempt at reading aloud and paraphrasing is taken from the early Robin Hood ballad "Robin Hood and the Monk." Each student pair prepares a stanza to share with the others. I project the *Middle English Dictionary (MED)* Web site onto the screen and perform a few searches for the more challenging words to familiarize students with this resource. Inevitably, the simple form of the ballad and the familiar characters of Robin Hood and Little John provide confidence. We review a summary of the ballad, a tale in which a pious Robin Hood and optimistic Little John overcome a minor challenge to their friendship and establish that the fellowship of merry men far exceeds the power of the false brotherhood of a "gret-hedid munke" ("large-headed monk"; line 75).

For homework, students examine excerpts of key passages that detail the piety that first draws Robin into the church, Little John's sense of social equality, the monk's willingness to cast aside his vow to uphold religious sanctuary and instead seek personal vengeance, and the king's final admiration of the yeomen's loyalty to one another. This brief introduction helps students appreciate the richness of Chaucer's anticlerical satire and his admiration of true Christian piety, as evidenced in the Pardoner's Prologue and Parson's Tale.

A second ballad, "Robin Hood and the Potter," depicts Robin Hood earning the friendship of a potter and enjoying an evening with the sheriff's wife and introduces themes and conventions students will see again in the fabliaux and the marriage tales. The next day, I prompt the class with questions concerning medieval culture. Why is there an emphasis on fellowship and generosity? How is violence depicted? Instead of asking students to relate these scenarios to contemporary times, our discussions begin to supply the vocabulary for understanding Chaucer's medieval world.

Finally, we are ready for Chaucer. I use a dual-language text (Hopper) to construct an interpretive dialogue between the Middle English and the modern word. In the General Prologue, we focus on characters whose tales we later read (Knight, Squire, Miller, Pardoner, Franklin, Wife of Bath, and Friar). Before we take a close look at images of the Ellesmere pilgrims, students examine the more concrete details offered in each portrait: my tenth-grade students create their own images on posters, and my twelfth-grade students compare their impressions with those rendered by the artist Arthur Szyk for Frank Hill's 1946 translation of *The Canterbury Tales*. The students' posters—either hand drawn or made with photographs of students posed in improvised costumes and perhaps edited in *Photoshop*—provide visual reinforcement of character details throughout our reading.

Reference resources like the *Oxford English Dictionary* (*OED*) and *MED* are essential to meaningful comprehension of *The Canterbury Tales*, even in secondary schools. Not only does a detective-style *MED/OED* word hunt lead to the discovery that each word has a story and a history that can bring new meaning or clarity to a passage, it also provides students with a sense of independence about how to arrive at an interpretation without consulting study notes or secondary criticism. For example, an exploration of the range of meaning of the word *gentil* helps establish qualities of character in a passage such as, "He was a verray, parfit gentil knight" ("He was a truly perfect noble knight"; GP 72). And it is always a surprise to students that *fre* might refer to generosity rather than independence.

Within the discussion of the Knight's Tale and the Miller's Prologue and Tale, we examine the following key words: *chivalrie, curtesie, gentilesse, honour,* and *pitee.* In excerpts from the Wife of Bath's Prologue and Tale we discuss *worthinesse, maistrye,* and *fre,* and I often provide some background about medieval "feminine estates." We conclude with the Franklin's Tale, which offers opportunities to explore the significance of *trowthe* and *fredom*.

At the conclusion of a standard six-week unit, the final project emphasizes the tangible: students become makers of text themselves—scribes, illuminators, annotators, and performers. Though reading aloud in Middle English in secondary school is often avoided beyond memorization of the first eighteen lines of the General Prologue, sufficient familiarity with the pronunciation of Middle English allows students to hear and appreciate the use of sound in Chaucer's poetry and to recognize the importance of prosody.

The specific assignment requires each student to create a unique illuminated manuscript leaf on a single sheet of art-quality paper. The students choose their favorite passages to read aloud and comment on how their exploration of the original sound and vocabulary enhanced their understanding of the passage. To reinforce and develop comprehension based on accurate definitions, I ask each student to closely examine a selected passage of about twenty lines and to research three to five words in the *MED*. Students are also encouraged to research any other curious elements, such as references to animals in the Aberdeen Bestiary. The assignment inspires some students to explore the art of calligraphy further. For the presentation, each student displays a manuscript leaf in which handwriting and illumination skills enhance the text and delivers a reading of the passage in Middle English with a couple of comments about interpretation. In addition, a short written explication allows students to articulate all their research discoveries and insights. Not surprisingly, an experience that is tactile and visual makes once strange words on a page come alive; performance infuses the text with voice, and research provides students confidence in presenting a meaningful interpretation. Student work unveiled on presentation days always shows a variety of richly conceived forays into the medieval world. Each student's physical creation, having gained its own story, seems to take on magical value.

Producing *The Canterbury Tales*

Bethany Blankenship

I teach *The Canterbury Tales* in the context of a class called The Manuscript Tradition. The course allows instructors to teach any text not originally produced with the aid of a printing press. Teachers can use anything from the journals of Lewis and Clark to the letters of Anaïs Nin, but I take a more traditional route and teach Middle English literature, including *Sir Gawain and the Green Knight*, *The Book of Margery Kempe*, and *The Canterbury Tales*. Despite my traditional canon, I employ a nontraditional approach for content delivery. I believe that experiential learning practices are among the most effective in teaching *The Canterbury Tales*, whether the *Tales* stand alone or are included in a survey class. Colin Beard and John Wilson describe experiential learning as the engagement of a student's intellectual and physical worlds. For example, in composition classes, students learn to write by writing. In a broader sense, Beard and Wilson contend that experiential learning is effective because it incorporates the whole person on emotional, intellectual, and physical levels (2). Numerous studies show us that service learning and other experiential learning activities positively impact our students' ability to learn, use, and retain information.

How, then, can students physically connect with a six-hundred-year-old manuscript such as *The Canterbury Tales*? In my class, students experience the material conditions of Chaucer's poem by producing a manuscript of their own. In their final project, students choose five lines from *The Canterbury Tales* to explicate and illuminate. The assignment ensures that the students understand not only what their lines mean but also how they look on a page.

Students buy George Thomson's *Illuminated Lettering Kit*. At less than thirty dollars, the kit includes a wooden stylus, nib, ink reservoir, watercolors, black ink, paper, and an explanatory booklet. I provide gum arabic, toothpaste, drawing and tracing paper (I advise the students to buy extra to practice at home), paper towels, hand-sized pieces of cloth (cut up from old towels), kitchen-sized trash bags, and masking tape.

I begin the class by showing the film version of Umberto Eco's book *The Name of the Rose* (1986). Students benefit from seeing the conditions of manuscript production in the Italian scriptorium as well as from learning the film's central message about the power of the written word in a largely illiterate society. After seeing the film, students read excerpts from Thomas Cahill's *How the Irish Saved Civilization*. In particular, I assign the chapter of the same name, which describes how Irish hermits began a monastic tradition that valued books and, eventually, manuscript production as ways to teach people about Christianity.

As students read Cahill's text, I describe several existing manuscripts of *The Canterbury Tales*. *The Ellesmere Chaucer: Essays in Interpretation*, an anthology edited by Martin Stevens and Daniel Woodward, is an excellent resource that has color illustrations and detailed descriptions of manuscript production. Specifically, M. B. Parkes's "The Planning and Construction of the Ellesmere Manuscript" describes in great detail the physical makeup of the manuscript. During my lecture, I also show images from Columbia University's *Digital Scriptorium*, which houses several dozen images of the Ellesmere manuscript as well as many other medieval and Renaissance manuscripts. This is also a good time to talk with students about how the production of manuscripts such as the Ellesmere Chaucer affects the ways scholars interpret *The Canterbury Tales*, especially with regard to tale order. Robert Root's article about the 1940 Manly and Rickert edition of *The Canterbury Tales* describes John Manly's and Edith Rickert's exhaustive process of looking at numerous manuscript fragments, faded ink, and torn pages in order to determine which fragments were meant to go together.

During these discussions and while reading *The Canterbury Tales*, I keep the students on an experiential track by interspersing "manuscript-making days" with discussion days, weekly if the class meets three days a week or bimonthly if the class meets only twice a week. We begin our manuscript production by learning from the *Illuminated Lettering Kit* how to manipulate the pen, which is dipped by hand into an inkwell. This step can be the longest and most arduous. To prepare for this, students draw lines on paper (cheap drawing paper will do) and tape trash bags to their desks (the housekeeping staff thanks me for this). After rubbing toothpaste onto the pen's nib and ink reservoir to texturize the brass surfaces, I give each student a drop of gum arabic (or CMC powder mixed with water) to rub onto the nib and ink reservoir, which eases the flow of ink. After slipping the reservoir on the nib, students dip their pens into ink bottles (Elmer's Poster Tack stabilizes the bottoms of the bottles). It may take the entire class period for students to feel comfortable dipping their pens and making consistent marks on their papers without the ink splattering or running out before a letter is completed.

I should admit that I am not an art teacher, nor have I had any formal training in art. After I taught this class the first time, I did take a community college class on uncial calligraphy, which taught me the few basics that I have related here. Mostly, I rely on art professors at my university as well as the students themselves. Invariably there are two or three students who have taken art classes, and they always have good tips on painting and drawing for their fellow students.

I encourage students to find calligraphic letters online that appeal to them, but I also give them several examples from *Calligraphy Alphabets Made Easy*, by Margaret Shepherd, and Marc Drogin's *Medieval Calligraphy: Its History and Technique*. I favor Margaret Shepherd's *Learn Calligraphy: The Complete Book of Lettering and Design*. This affordable text includes outlined shapes of pens against which students can lay their own pens and check the angle of their nibs. This is extremely helpful for students when they practice their calligraphy at home.

Sporting hands semipermanently stained with india ink, the students at this point have a firm grasp of how difficult manuscript production was for medieval copyists, who did not have brass nibs and premade ink. Eventually, though, class production time must be devoted to creating and illuminating versal letters. Using an exercise in the *Illuminated Lettering Kit*, students trace designs and paint them with watercolors from the kit. Though I allow some time during class for students to work on their graded manuscripts, they mostly complete their final projects on their own. I require that their manuscript be accompanied by a versal letter and a drollery or artwork of their choice; however, I also assure students that I do not grade the quality of their artwork, merely their attempt (the explication, however, follows stricter grading guidelines).

While producing their manuscripts and writing their explications, I ask them, "How does making a manuscript change the way you think about *The Canterbury Tales*?" Some of the answers include the following:

> Nothing I have ever done before caused me to understand the outright diligence someone had to enforce on their own willpower in order to complete an entire page, let alone a manuscript. (Phillip)
> Talk about a realization! We take for granted the options we have today. When I sat down with the calligraphy kit, it took me as long to write seven lines with pen and ink as it would've taken me to type a seven-page paper! Not to mention that I knocked the ink bottle over and made a huge mess on my dining room table. (Dana)
> I got a better understanding of why these pieces of literature were altered and why many pieces were lost or never copied. While trying to pick out what I wanted to illuminate, there were times where I felt like putting my own thoughts or words into the text, as the scribes had done throughout history. (Brian)

By the end of the semester, students develop a deep appreciation for manuscript production. How much that production affects the explication is not evident until the final day of class, when students give short presentations on the main arguments of their explications. Students tend to describe their lines not only in intellectual terms (figurative language, theme, etc.) but also in physical terms (copying, tracing, drawing, and so on). These descriptions enact Beard and Wilson's definition of experiential learning, "the sense-making process of active engagement between the inner world of the person and the outer world of the environment" (19).

When I evaluate the explications at the end of the semester, I find them more detailed and thoughtful than explications I receive in other classes because of the amount of time Manuscript Tradition students spend studying *and* illuminating the poetry. Copying lines with painstaking care while analyzing their use of alliteration, imagery, and rhyme scheme helps students learn the art of poetic creation as well as the art of writing and illuminating. After learning about the process of medieval manuscript production and reading *The Canterbury Tales*, students who produce the *Tales* for themselves actively experience Chaucer's poetry.

Reading Food in *The Canterbury Tales*

Kathryn L. Lynch

Most courses on *The Canterbury Tales* present students with a governing paradigm for the work—a unified structural account of what the text means and how its different parts fit together. Students crave an overarching narrative, which the very concept of a course seems to demand. From about 1950 through the early 1980s, the solution to this problem was easy: the reigning paradigm for understanding *The Canterbury Tales* was pilgrimage, and readers generally shared an understanding that the tales were ultimately headed both metaphorically and literally to the same place, the shrine of a Christian saint, with all that was involved in worshipping there. This paradigm, dominant for thirty years, was first fully articulated by Ralph Baldwin in his influential monograph *The Unity of* The Canterbury Tales. The 1980 first edition of the MLA *Approaches to Teaching Chaucer's* Canterbury Tales, edited by Joseph Gibaldi, shows the dominion of pilgrimage over teaching practice in several essays (e.g., Julia Bolton Holloway's "Medieval Pilgrimage"). But times have changed, and recent readers have grown resistant to a single structural paradigm, preferring instead modes of understanding that, to borrow a term from the Russian theorist M. M. Bakhtin, stress the "dialogic" nature of the work (Ganim, *Chaucerian Theatricality*; Kendrick; Knapp, *Chaucer*). New styles of reading *The Canterbury Tales* have brought the playful and folkloric aspects of the storytelling contest to the forefront, enabling us to see how these ludic elements subtly offer a counterpoint to the earnestness of religious pilgrimage, which as a historical practice could even include festive interludes (Lindahl). But the centrifugal force of this kind of criticism creates problems in the classroom. As a practical matter it is difficult in a thirteen- to fifteen-week semester to dramatize the festive, disruptive reading with the cogency that a single theme like pilgrimage might once have allowed. Pilgrimage is a unifying, ordering device, while play is a disordering, scattering one. This is where food comes in, for Chaucer uses food, though diversely in diverse parts of *The Canterbury Tales*, as a unifying shorthand for the festive elements in his poem; in other words, elements that collide with and supersede each other nonetheless can be traced throughout the text through their common relation to the culinary arts and gustatory appetites. In *The Canterbury Tales*, the social production and consumption of food provides an alternative, circular, and festive ethos that is in dialogic relation with the linear, inner-directed, ascetic dynamics of pilgrimage. Food, however, is a huge topic. It relates to many other themes and image patterns that form part of Chaucer's broad scheme, including institutional regulations controlling food consumption, food preparation, food taboos, the Eucharist, agriculture and hunting, manners, and more. The General Prologue, Chaucer's primer on how to read the overall poem, provides an excellent crash course in the syntax and vocabulary of this variegated motif.

The range of food references in the General Prologue offers a foretaste of the remarkably divergent ways in which food can signify throughout *The Canterbury Tales*. Food references, for example, include allusions to the pilgrims' table manners and the ways that food practices can enforce (or disrupt) filial, feudal, and ecclesiastical hierarchies. In his description of the Squire, Chaucer closes the wide geographic circle of foreign adventuring in which both the Knight and his son engage by bringing the pair back to the domestic table in the last line of the Squire's description, when the son shows due respect by carving before his father at table (line 100). The Prioress's fastidious "conscience" is matched by her impeccable manners as she patrols the cleanliness of her lips, her cup, and her garments to ensure that no droplet of grease pollutes them. Her tenderheartedness is revealed in the culinary treats she sets aside for her "smale houndes" (146). Similarly, the Franklin expresses a hospitable nature by keeping his table at the ready and stocking his house with whatever "deyntees" ("delicacies") are in season (346), in addition to wine, ale, bread, pies, fat partridges, and freshwater fish from his own pond (340–54). These references provide a window into medieval culture and also raise subtle questions of interpretation. Is the Squire's final demonstration of courteous humility at the dining table sufficient to counterbalance his preoccupation with fashion and fluting, or are we meant to see him as shallow and feckless? Is the Prioress a woman of truly refined sensibility, or is she too dainty or persnickety? Should the "rosted flesh" ("roasted meat"), milk, and "wastel breed" ("fine white bread") she saves for her pets be donated instead to the poor (147)? Is the Franklin likewise too hospitable? Are his generosity and taste on show to advance his reputation and political career in the local shire, or is he motivated by a genuine spirit of altruism? These questions will again emerge in the individual pilgrims' tales.

Elsewhere, turning from manners to diet, we find abundant examples of food used in the General Prologue to instruct the reader on the intemperance or, less often, the sobriety of an individual character, as when we learn of the Summoner's preference for "garleek, oynons, and eek lekes" ("garlic, onions, and also leeks") and strong wine "red as blood" (634–35). As various scholars have demonstrated, these details reflect the disorder of the Summoner's humors and suggest a venereal disease (Kaske, "Summoner's Garleek"; Wood). They help us begin to construct a lexicon of food, looking forward, for instance, to other references to the leek, either as anthropomorphized by the Reeve for its hoary head and green tail (RvT, line 3879) or as a thing of little value (WBT 572, MerT 1350, CYT 795). They also, as references to food often do in *The Canterbury Tales*, possess religious significance, alluding to the longing for these three pungent vegetables experienced by Jews who had fallen away from God (Num. 11.5). The Summoner's description even contains Eucharistic overtones, for not only does he favor blood-like wine, he also carries a buckler made of an oversized wafer (GP 667). Conversely, if rich, peppery foods are morally problematic, plain fare suggests homely virtue. Passing references to food are wrapped into metaphors that are easy to overlook unless one is alert to them. The Parson, for instance, makes no "spiced conscience" (526), meaning that he attends to moral substance and not display as he circulates among his parishioners.

The General Prologue not only introduces the literal food of the Middle Ages and Chaucer's use of it as a device for exploring character, it also presents food as the second large structuring device of the entirety of *The Canterbury Tales*. For the Host proposes that each member of the company of pilgrims regale the others with two tales on the trip to and two on the trip from Canterbury, with the promise of a supper (expenses paid by the whole group) as the prize for the most entertaining and enlightening story (GP 790–801). Whether Chaucer abandoned this plan or simply failed to complete it remains unknown. The General Prologue nonetheless provides a circular and reiterative design for the journey that remains in tension with the teleological structure of pilgrimage and that permits storytelling a playful, re-creative purpose as well as an improving, instructive one, just as the repetitive and pleasure-providing nature of the appetite for food mirrors the perennial human desire for a good story told well. To reflect this tension in the links between tales, food and drink function as placeholders for tale-telling of a sort that has ambiguous moral value. It becomes immediately clear, for example, that entertaining stories flow forth like (and with the assistance of) liquor. The Miller is soused, anything uncouth that he speaks, "[w]yte it the ale of Southwerk" ("blame it on the ale of Southwerk"; MilT 3140), a disavowal that reminds us of the narrator's own fictional alibis (e.g., GP 725–46, MilT 3170–86). The Pardoner, too, pausing in a tavern like the one that generated the whole tale-telling project, responds to the Host's request for a comforting draught of "moyste and corny ale" ("fresh and malty ale"; PardT 315) with his own demand for drink, needed to stimulate the poetic imagination (328).

But the Pardoner's performance also reveals that the severing of the playful from the true is morally dangerous, laying bare the ambiguities of human appetite and the perils of theatrical suasion. The Pardoner's Tale fittingly explores the sins of the tavern and builds on images of literal and moral digestion, culminating in the conclusion of the tale, where the Host suggests that animal waste—a hog's turd—might serve as an appropriate resting place for a certain part of the Pardoner's anatomy (955). Here, as at many points along the way, Chaucer uses excrement to demonstrate pollution and the threat of a failure of signification (Morrison). What goes in comes out unchanged, as references to the digestive process dramatize: "O stynkyng cod, / Fulfilled of dong and of corrupcioun! / At either ende of thee foul is the soun" ("Oh stinking belly, / Filled with dung and putrefaction! / At both of your openings the sound is foul"; PardT 534–36). In fact, the whole of the Pardoner's Tale can be seen as an exploration of sin as the breakdown of signification and moral digestion, for in the monastic and penitential traditions within which the Pardoner is working, a failure to understand was understood as a failure to digest what was read and studied (Lynch, "Pardoner's Digestion"). Indeed, in the link leading into the Manciple's Tale, the intoxicating power of drink becomes so mighty that it tips the balance of earnest and game entirely toward the latter and paradoxically leads to the silencing of the inebriated Cook, who cannot resist taking one swill too many. The ironic blessing bestowed by the god Bacchus, "That so kanst turnen ernest into game!" ("that so can turn seriousness into game"; ManT 99), foreshadows the silencing of the crow in the Manciple's Tale. There, even as Phebus Apollo's "mynstralcie" (267) is broken apart, so also the "ernest" truth telling of the crow is abruptly silenced. Food, drink, and poetry increasingly have become interchangeable terms in a developing argument about the incompatibility of fable making with moral truth.

In a larger sense, food and drink widen to stand for not just fiction but for the ephemeral nature of life itself, a meditation that emerges both explicitly and implicitly. In the Reeve's Prologue, the tun of wine, traditionally a merry icon, becomes a frightening "tappe of lif" that is almost run out "[t]il that almoost al empty is the tonne [barrel]" (lines 3890, 3894; discussed by Kolve, *Chaucer* 225–27). With guidance from the relevant historical dictionaries, the attentive reader may hear an echo of this image later, at the opening of the much jollier Nun's Priest's Tale, which is "attamed" ([NPT 2818] rather than simply "begun," the *Riverside* gloss for this word). This example suggests the value of dictionary work for students exploring a strange culinary lexicon; attention to historical dictionaries will show them that "attamed" has a tun metaphor at its heart. It signifies the piercing that broaches a cask, which allows the liquid to pour out. That word thus both foretells the amusing tale the Nun's Priest will tell (itself full of food references) and, taken in its larger context, provides a melancholy foreshadowing of the end of *The Canterbury Tales* as it comes down to us, which is nearing the bottom of the barrel. I also make sure that the students look up the word *host* in both the *Oxford English Dictionary* and

Middle English Dictionary. *Host* is, of course, not only an innkeeper but a synonym for the bread of Christ's body as consecrated in the ritual that creates a Christian community. When my class reads the Parson's Prologue, we keep in mind the full range of meanings this word can have and note how it has circulated throughout the tales.[1]

Perhaps the most important medieval food metaphor is one that has been rehashed in criticism so frequently we've almost ceased to recognize its comestible and noncomestible root: the metaphor of fruit and chaff. The Parson returns us to this oft-used comparison when he promises to sow not "draf" ("chaff," "husks") but the wheat of truthfulness in his "tale" (lines 35–36). And yet even this seemingly stable trope has had many careers in the tales, shaded by complicated ironies, all carried forward into this final reference. The Wife of Bath interprets "flour" (distinguished from "bren" ["bran"]) as youthful beauty (WBT 477–78). In the epilogue to the Man of Law's Tale, when the Parson is called on to speak, a competing narrator complains that the preacher wants to spread weeds in the pilgrims' "clene corn" (1183). The Host, a figure not known himself for attention to the kernel of truth, worries that the Parson is a "Lollere," that is, a perpetrator of a heresy whose very name recalls a Latin word for *weed* ("lolium"; see *Riverside* 863 [note to line 1173]). The Nun's Priest disingenuously attempts to disentwine the two at the end of his complex performance of the beast fable (which turns on the frustrated attempt of one character to eat another), when he advises, "Taketh the fruyt, and lat the chaf be stille" (NPT, line 3443), all the while knowing that his lively tale has made this winnowing especially difficult.

Students find sifting through the topic of food inherently attractive. Especially in a class devoting a couple of weeks to the General Prologue, one can ask students to research an aspect of a specific pilgrim's description that has an emphasis on food habits. Numerous useful sources are available, from Alan Davidson's *The Penguin Companion to Food* to guides specifically focused on the General Prologue that synthesize dietary and sumptuary imagery (e.g., M. Bowden; Lambdin and Lambdin). This kind of research, whether presented orally to the rest of the class or in a brief paper, makes students feel like instant experts on an individual character. Among the many handy supplementary sources that focus on medieval dining and food preparation are recent books by Peter Hammond, Bridget Henisch, and Terence Scully (Paul Freedman provides remarkable insight into the importance of spices). Starting the students out with research on medieval food also explodes their preconceptions about the Middle Ages as an unsophisticated era. Far from the joints of fowl and herb-basted potatoes (all handled by greasy fingers) that students may remember from visiting the theme park Medieval Times, courtly cuisine in the age of Chaucer swam in rich, spicy sauces; eschewed the plain vegetable whenever it could; was heavy on meat, custards, and pies; and craved spectacle at great feasts. The potato was unknown in Europe until the very end of the fifteenth century. While forks were not used in England until around the same time, spoons and knives did the job admirably with no fingers needed. This kind of background encourages skepticism about stereotypes of the medieval period that students may have received from the general culture or in earlier classes and prepares them for Chaucer's literary "subtlety" (a word that at Chaucer's time could signify an edible confection).

On the final day of the term, I ask the students to come prepared to identify not only which tale they think would have won the supper contest but also what fare they think their winner would have picked for the victory supper. This is a task that reminds them, even as *The Canterbury Tales* draws to its communal and penitential close, that it is also a long poem about individual points of view and shifting perspectives. Mindful of those perspectives, most students select the Nun's Priest's Tale because they remember that Harry Bailly has set himself up as judge, and there is evidence that Harry admires this well-fed narrator (3447–62). But my students are usually more interested in talking about what some of the runners-up for the prize might choose for supper—or what they might reject. The Wife of Bath, with her penchant for traveling and her craving for sensual pleasure, might, they speculate, have a taste for fruitcake or gingerbread; she definitely would not be asking for bacon (WBT 418)! The point of such exercises is to keep a festive spirit alive just as *The Canterbury Tales* themselves have done. In that spirit, don't be surprised if, after all this talk of medieval food, students want to experience it themselves. There is no point in resisting this urge, for some wonderful Web sites and cookbooks can facilitate a very satisfactory class feast (M. Black; Hieatt, Hosington, and Butler).

NOTE

[1] The importance of the Host's identification as "oure hoost" is underscored by the fact that his given name is used only once in the entire work, in the prologue to the Cook's Tale (4358).

Teaching Chaucer's *Canterbury Tales* with Queer Theory and Erotic Triangles

Tison Pugh

Geoffrey Chaucer does not directly address homosexuality in his *Canterbury Tales*: even his most sexually ambiguous character, the Pardoner, cannot be definitively identified as a medieval homosexual.[1] *The Canterbury Tales* nonetheless abounds in sexual tensions and transgressions, and an observation of this provides a foundation for teaching students to read Chaucer's masterpiece queerly. From a theoretical perspective, homosexuality and queerness often overlap, though they are not and should not be construed as synonymous. While *homosexuality* refers to sexual acts and identities predicated on same-sex eroticism, *queerness* encompasses sexual acts and identities deemed nonnormative through an ideological lens. If a given culture accepts homosexuality as an unexceptional expression of erotic desire (as was the case in ancient Greece and is increasingly the case in the Western world), homosexuality need not be queer at all.[2]

Given this potential division between homosexuality and queerness, employing queer theory in the classroom necessitates attuning students to the ways in which cultures regulate sexualities and the sociohistorical contexts of such policing. Queer theory asks readers to examine how and why certain sexual desires become marked as transgressive. David Halperin points to the oppositional nature of queerness: "As the very word implies, *queer* does not name some natural kind or refer to some determinate object; it acquires its meaning from its oppositional relation to the norm" (63). Jeffrey Jerome Cohen suggests that "queer theory's tremendous strength is its insistence upon the historical instability of epistemological categories, especially those involving sexuality" (*Medieval Identity* 38). As ideologically constructed systems of desire and transgression, sexualities need to be investigated for their historical contingencies and contradictions rather than accepted as transhistorical truths. Thus an initial set of questions that pertains to virtually any text and can elicit dialogue in the classroom revolves around how erotic desires are expressed and how they are responded to. Chaucer's *Canterbury Tales* provides strikingly vibrant portraits of men and women expressing erotic drives in ways disruptive to prevailing mores.

To help students locate queer moments in *The Canterbury Tales*, instructors can introduce the theoretical and structural model of the erotic triangle. In establishing queer theory as a remarkably adaptable theoretical perspective, Eve Sedgwick famously observed, "in any erotic rivalry, the bond that links the two rivals is as intense and potent as the bond that links either of the rivals to the beloved. . . . [T]he bonds of 'rivalry' and 'love,' differently as they are experienced, are equally powerful and in many senses equivalent" (21). With these words, Sedgwick founded a critical school that over the last twenty-five years has spawned numerous groundbreaking interpretations of texts throughout and beyond the literary canon. She introduced scholars to the ways in which some readers' predisposition to seeing heterosexuality occluded the same-sex desires latent in countless plots. While employing Sedgwick's interpretive paradigm, students need a critical lexicon for interpreting same-sex relationships that emphasizes a continuum of desire ranging from homosocial to homoerotic to homosexual.

In the *The Canterbury Tales*, many of the pilgrims' narratives feature some triangulated permutation of desire along the homosocial to homoerotic continuum: Palamon and Arcite for Emily in the Knight's Tale, Nicholas and Absolon for Alisoun in the Miller's Tale, John and Symkyn for Symkyn's wife in the Reeve's Tale, Januarie and Damyan for Maius in the Merchant's Tale, Arveragus and Aurelius for Dorigen in the Franklin's Tale, the merchant and the monk for the merchant's wife in the Shipman's Tale, and Phebus and the "man of litel reputacioun" for the deity's wife in the Manciple's Tale (line 199). Even texts not explicitly concerned with sexual desire often evince the skeletal structure of the erotic triangle. In the Man of Law's Tale, when Custance's mothers-in-law plot against her, though their motivations are founded primarily on allegiance to their native religions, these motivations simultaneously involve their sons' marital decisions. The intersection of religious belief, filial devotion, and unresolved family conflicts hints at least obliquely at illicit maternal desires. In the Physician's Tale, Apius and Virginius struggle for sexual control of Virginia while the corrupt judge seeks to defile her and her father to preserve her virginity. Likewise, in the Second Nun's Tale when Cecile spurns Valerian on their wedding night because of her chaste devotion to God, Valerian rejects the divine rivalry at the heart of his human romance and accepts his secondary position to his wife's heavenly love. In these texts, Chaucer's attention to the ways in which narrative tensions arise from triangulated desires asks for a queer analysis, particularly one aware of the intertwined wranglings of sex, love, desire, and amatory competition.

The Knight's Tale well illustrates the queer tensions and subliminal erotics sparked by men seeking heterosexual consummation. When readers first meet the knights Palamon and Arcite, their defining feature is their sameness. Discovered nearly dead in a pile of bodies, the two men share the same arms, and the narrator reports that they "weren of the blood roial / Of Thebes, and of sustren two yborn [born]" (lines 1018–19). More than cousins, Palamon and Arcite have sworn an oath of brotherhood to each other, as Palamon reminds Arcite when their argument over Emily begins:

"It nere," quod he, "to thee no greet honour
For to be fals, ne for to be traitour
To me, that am thy cosyn and thy brother
Ysworn ful depe, and ech of us til oother,
That nevere, for to dyen in the peyne,

Til that the deeth departe shal us tweyne,
Neither of us in love to hyndre oother,
Ne in noon oother cas, my leeve brother,
But that thou sholdest trewely forthren me
In every cas, as I shal forthren thee—
This was thyn ooth, and myn also, certeyn." (1129–39)

"It would be," said he, "to you no great honor
To be so false or to be a traitor
To me, who am your cousin and your brother
Sworn full deep, each of us to the other,
That never, though we die in torture's pain,
Until death shall depart us two,
Neither of us in love hinders the other,
Nor in any other case, my beloved brother,
But that you should truly further me
In every case, as I shall further you—
This was your oath, and mine also, truly."

These lines underscore that the homosocial bond between the two knights should take precedence over courtly, heteroerotic amatory pursuits, as well as that each man should privilege his brother's good over his own. The phrase "[t]il that the deeth departe shal us tweyne" echoes those in marriage rites (K. Stevenson 79), which further cements the image of the brothers' homosocial union as a sacrosanct and lifelong pact. Although these observations do not construe Palamon and Arcite as homosexuals, such moments reveal that male bonds carry latent hints of eroticism, even when such eroticism is not fully realized.

Sedgwick's contention that the bonds of rivalry and love are congruent aptly suits readings of the Knight's Tale, for Palamon and Arcite's brotherhood dissolves into animosity when they argue heatedly over Emily. Palamon threatens Arcite with his imminent demise: "I drede noght that outher thow shalt dye, / Or thow ne shalt nat loven Emelye. / Chees which thou wolt, or thou shalt nat asterte!" ("I doubt that either you shall die, / Or that you shall not love Emily. / Choose which you will, or you shall not escape!"; lines 1593–95). Indeed, the many death threats that the two men cast at each other foreground necrotic desires over erotic ones (e.g., 1649–60). Surprisingly, when Arcite dies unexpectedly after triumphing in the combat for the right to marry Emily, he awards her to his enemy Palamon with his final words: "As in this world right now ne knowe I non / So worthy to ben loved as Palamon" ("In this world right now I know of no one / As worthy to be loved as Palamon"; 2793–94). Given that the bulk of the narrative has emphasized Palamon's hatred of Arcite, his reaction to his sworn brother's death is somewhat surprising: "Shrighte [Shrieked] Emelye, and howleth Palamon" (2817). The subsequent description of Palamon stresses the suffering he endures after his sworn brother's death:

Tho cam this woful Theban Palamoun,
With flotery berd and ruggy, asshy heeres
In clothes blake [black], ydropped al with teeres;
And, passynge othere of wepynge, Emelye,
The rewefulleste of al the compaignye. (2882–86).

Then came this woeful Theban Palamon,
With fluttering beard and shaggy, ashy hair,
In clothes black, saturated with tears;
And, surpassing all others in weeping, Emily,
The most pitiable of all the company.

Rather than the joy of victory, Palamon experiences the pain of loss. Significantly, his homosocial bond is paradoxically strengthened through Arcite's death. His suffering bears the symptoms of the melancholy of unrequited love, such as that which afflicts Troilus in his despair over Criseyde. Queer theory does not ask readers to locate homosexuality where it does not exist, but it does ask readers to trace the surprising routes of desire in a text. The fluctuating homosocial bonds of the Knight's Tale highlight how male friendship is most fully realized in Palamon's marriage to Emily.

By focusing analysis on erotic triangles, teachers can encourage their students to generate unique readings that are cognizant of how conflicting desires create narrative tension and complicate simplistic views of homo- and heteroeroticism. Chaucer's Knight's Tale showcases the ways in which otherwise "straight" texts welcome queer readings, and the interpretive strategies behind this foundational example can be fruitfully employed with texts throughout Chaucer's canon. Looking for a medieval forebear of modern homosexuality in *The Canterbury Tales* may be an exercise in anachronism, but reading the latent and triangulated eroticisms of the Canterbury narratives reveals the surprisingly queer trajectories of Chaucerian desire.

NOTES

[1] For conflicting views on the Pardoner's sexual indeterminacy, see Kruger, "Claiming," and R. Green.

[2] For more on the history of homosexuality, see Spencer. On the challenges of describing medieval sexuality under the rubrics of homosexuality and heterosexuality, see Lochrie xviii–xxviii and Schultz 51–62. For an overview of queer theory, see Hall. For homosexuality in ancient Greece, see Dover.

Chaucerian Translations:
Postcolonial Approaches to *The Canterbury Tales*
Patricia Clare Ingham

The notion of a postcolonial Middle Ages no longer seems oxymoronic in the way that it did in 1995, when I first began taking an implicitly "postcolonial" approach to teaching Chaucer's *Canterbury Tales*. Over the past fifteen years, medievalists have shown the mutual relevance of medieval and postcolonial studies in any number of ways: by engaging premodern scenes of conquest and annexation with postcolonial theories of culture, by considering medieval traditions of *translatio studii* and *translatio imperii*, by analyzing the periodizing divide of medieval to modern as covert justification for the colonial civilizing mission, by querying the status of the medieval in the rhetoric of global empire, and most recently by investigating whether medieval cosmopolitanism might contribute to a desire for more inclusive accounts of global citizenship.[1] The pertinence of some such work to the undergraduate Chaucer course may seem obvious enough, and for more than a decade now postcolonial readings of some Canterbury tales have been very much on the table (e.g., Schibanoff, "Orientalism").

Prompts to a postcolonial consideration of Chaucer have also been provided by nonmedievalists. Accounts of contemporary postcolonial poetics have turned to questions of vernacularism with the Middle Ages in mind: in a 1995 essay, the Irish-language poet Nuala Ní Dhomhnaill objects to biased assumptions of the irrelevance of "old," "archaic," "pre-modern," and precolonial vernaculars (in her case, Irish), situating her own work amid the complexities of diasporic history, Ireland's colonial status, and the Irish-language politics of the Gaeltacht. Even more directly on point for Chaucerians, David Chioni Moore has compared the contemporary Nigerian writer Ngũgĩ wa Thiong'o's decision to write in his vernacular (rather than in the global literary language of English) to Chaucer's vernacularism. If these two critics share a provocative, surprising (and exceedingly useful) mixing of temporalities, they do so to different effect: where Ní Dhomhnaill emphasizes the problems with an account of history that dismisses older languages as "other" and hence irrelevant to the contemporary age, Moore stresses the relevance of literary history to current scenes of writing by borrowing Chaucer's canonical status to advance both the language politics and the literary power of a Nigerian novelist.

In my experience, such temporal crossings have enormous power in the classroom. They can serve, for one thing, as provocations to reading Chaucer in his original Middle English. But they have also helped me guide students toward a deeper knowledge of the complexities of Chaucer's poetry, language, and context and its continued relevance today. Quotations from Ní Dhomhnaill's, Moore's, and Ngũgĩ's works that I sometimes use on the first day of class awaken students' curiosity about what a Middle English poet might have in common with contemporary writers and about the difference that difference (whether communitarian, linguistic, or temporal) makes.

Here I outline an approach to teaching Chaucer's *Canterbury Tales* in contrapuntal relation to three topics about which postcolonial cultural studies has taught us: community and its vicissitudes, the politics of language and translation, and the problems of history and temporality. These three issues are not built into my syllabus as explicit units or topics; instead, they serve as a kind of deep structure for the course as a whole, emerging regularly in questions posed throughout the term and offering three different ways with which students might trace a "through-line" over the various weeks of the semester. For clarity's sake, I take each in turn here; in the classroom, however, these issues frequently converge with one another.

Community

It is hardly news that Chaucer's *Canterbury Tales* can shed light on the vicissitudes of community. Yet a postcolonial consideration of these issues would be committed not only to the nature and meaning of community but to the "discourses of opposition" and problems of exclusion that nationalist or colonialist definitions of community engender. Any wholly celebratory account of an inclusive and wide-ranging pilgrim community duplicates the claim that nations regularly promise but on which they can rarely deliver. Chaucer's frame story (the tale-telling competition, the diversity of pilgrims, the poem's persistent concern with aggression, rivalry, disagreement among the pilgrims) explicitly raises the tensions between diversity and unity, tensions drawn out in a careful reading of the General Prologue.

Students benefit from considering how the General Prologue has been construed by critics: as an idealized celebration of a happily, hierarchically ordered band of diverse folk with the Knight at its head; as estates satire offering a send-up of the foibles of diverse figures and types; as a contentious crew, jockeying for prestige and position and led by Harry Bailly as their own lord of misrule. Many students at first easily follow the idealized reading suggested by the Knight's apparent preeminence in both narrative and tale-telling order, since it fulfills their expectations of the Middle Ages as an orderly, hierarchically obsessed society. I ask students to take account of the General Prologue's counterevidence: the tattered nature of the Knight's description (and his list of disastrous crusading battles) and the final description of the drawing of straws. As critics like Paul Strohm (*Social Chaucer*) and Peggy Knapp (*Chaucer*) have pointed out, Chaucer's narrator uses terms associated with governance and rule, like "governor" (line 813), "rebel" (833), or "judgment" (778, 805, 833), simultaneously raises questions of communitarian order and of misrule and dissent.[2] What does it mean that the text both gestures toward communitarian assent of the whole and shows the Knight to be the noble, rightful head of that whole? And just as the cut falls to the Knight ("were it by aventure, or sort, or cas" ["whether by fortune, or chance, or luck"]; 844) the text raises the possibility that this game of chance is played with a stacked deck. Here, a postcolonial approach shares interests with other political approaches to the tales, such as materialist or feminist ones. The Knight's crusading history sets the stage for a larger consideration of the history of the Crusades (further developed later in the semester).

An emphasis on the prologues, epilogues, head-links, and end-links similarly helps students consider the communitarian stakes in *The Canterbury Tales*, by drawing out the complications and contentiousness of Chaucer's group of pilgrims. My students and I attend to the judgments, reactions, or rebelliousness of particular pilgrims and to the according shifts in status vis-à-vis the larger group. Rather than emphasize the personalities or pathologies of particular pilgrims (as in the dramatic approaches to *The Canterbury Tales*), a postcolonial approach draws attention to the recurrent structures of aggression, the inclusions and exclusions, embedded in Chaucer's larger work. Ultimately—although the question must be allowed to accrue over time—I ask students to reflect on the persistence of such textual moments and on how those moments stage problems of communitarian order, judgment and reaction, or threats of violence and exclusion. In some cases the head-links and end-links guide my selection of the tales we read: fragment 1, of course, but also the Man of Law's Tale (including its introduction and epilogue) and the communitarian matters raised by the tales of the Squire, Franklin, Physician, Pardoner, and Prioress.

Particular tales offer opportunities to address the vicissitudes of community in terms especially pertinent to ethnicity and racialization, internationalism, or cosmopolitan culture. Treatment of the Wife of Bath's Tale draws on my own work on the regional and ethnic variety of the Arthurian tradition and the diverse valences of the "Britons" in Chaucer's text and its larger context (see, e.g., Ingham, "Pastoral Histories"). Such issues obviously emerge in the Man of Law's Tale. One recent change in my syllabus has been the inclusion of the Squire's Tale to emblematize the regularity of representations of sophisticated eastern courts in texts of romance and as a counterpoint to the account offered by the Man of Law. At two specific points throughout the term, students are asked to summarize a scholarly disagreement about a particular tale: I regularly use the Man of Law's Tale as an occasion to teach how critical disagreements on postcolonial matters (like the place of Syria, the legacies of Roman imperial rule, the question of orientalism) can change our understanding of Chaucer's work.[3] By the time we turn to the Prioress's Tale, students have been thinking about such issues and are well prepared to take on critical accounts of the tale's anti-Semitism (e.g., Fradenburg, "Criticism"; Delany, "Chaucer's Prioress"; Cohen, "Flow"; Lampert; Despres; and Krummel, "Semitisms").

Language

The politics of vernacularism ground the accounts of poetry offered by Ní Dhomhnaill and Moore with which I began. Their work usefully inaugurates a consideration of the relevance of Chaucer's poetry to the politics of global English, the (historically variable) meanings of the vernacular, and the protocols by which writers ascend to canonical status and stay there. In a lecture and discussion on Chaucer's language early in the term, Moore's comments set up our consideration of fourteenth-century vernacular politics in England, but not only there. There are two aspects to this consideration, one insular and the other international.

In the first place, I emphasize the point that fourteenth-century England was a polyglot society in which translation was regular and ubiquitous. Here, I usually can rely on students knowledgeable about polyglot cultures. A representative Chaucer class at Indiana University is likely to contain students ready to critique any assumed correlation between linguistic identity and citizenship or the ascriptions of superiority to a monolingual society. (This has not, however, been my experience teaching at other universities.) We query the politics of prestige languages and the risks and benefits of eschewing them, which helps students consider linguistic history and genealogy: in a lecture, I trace the process by which Chaucer's marginal English vernacular became the prestige language that nevertheless would eventually be rejected in the twentieth century by certain writers choosing to return to their own native languages.

Ngũgĩ's rejection of English suggests the unsettled nature of contemporary language issues for postcolonial writers. Similarly, Chaucer's situation can show the unsettled nature of language in England's late medieval polyglot culture. Students are surprised to learn that regularized spelling of English was a postmedieval development. They were also surprised by differences of dialect across the range of British regions. In this context, facts in the history of the English language (that Parliament was opened in English for the first time in 1362 or that by 1400 Henry IV would claim his rights as king in English) take on new force and relevance. The politics of language can thus provide an excellent avenue into aspects of Chaucer's historical background as a context for his writing.

Yet the postcolonial impulse of Moore's essay also provides an opportunity to warn students not to ascribe a primarily nationalistic impulse to Chaucer's decision to write in English. I stress both Ardis Butterfield's recent point that Chaucer had "more than one vernacular" ("Chaucerian Vernaculars" 25) and the degree to which Chaucer's turn to English was part of a vernacular literary movement that can only be called international. While such a case can be made in an early lecture on Chaucer's language, it is developed further with reference to Chaucer's indebtedness to Boccaccio and Dante.[4] The Clerk's Tale is most useful here—and I teach the tale in the context of controversies over Italian vernacular writing, directing students to the letters of Petrarch and Boccaccio printed in Robert Miller's still useful *Chaucer: Sources and Backgrounds*.

One assignment asks students to consider the nature of translation and vernacularism while also increasing their familiarity with Chaucer's Middle English. Early in the term, students select a brief passage of their choice (of no more than one hundred or so lines) and prepare two translations of that passage: a literal translation into modern English, performed with the help of the *Middle English Dictionary*, and a literary or interpretive translation, which is a freer rendering prepared with a particular audience in mind. For the second translations, students refer to recent adaptations and translations of Chaucerian material, some of which might be termed postcolonial, such as a transposition of *The Canterbury Tales* to contemporary Nigeria (Brinkman; Nelson; King-Aribisala). In conjunction with class lectures on Chaucer's work on the Griselda tradition, this assignment helps students understand some of the metacritical concerns that attend the politics of translation then and now.

Temporality

Crossings of temporality have been implicit throughout this essay, and they are made explicit regularly throughout the term. Ní Dhomhnaill's essay helps the class think about rhetorics of irrelevance or primitivism that all too frequently attend assumptions about medieval literature. Her ironic analogy, describing the Irish language as a kind of linguistic zombie (the corpse who sits up and talks back) queries what it means to call a language (or literature) dead. This is an issue that is, of course, not unique to postcolonial approaches. Here some care is required, for not all older languages necessarily engage postcolonial considerations; to be sure, Ní Dhomhnaill might look askance at the uses of her work in a class on the "father" of literature in the language of the English colonizer.

And I use her essay to raise precisely these issues, continuing our semester-long conversation about the colonizing history of English even in the Middle Ages (England's conquest of Ireland began with Henry II, after all). Yet students also feel the force of her critique of dead languages and her passionate manifesto about the power of reanimation. This topic provides, moreover, an opportunity to think through the uncanny relevance of many of the issues Chaucer's poetry raises, and a reconsideration of what it means to read older texts (or study older languages) in the present moment. I address the category of the medieval in contemporary political culture—as, for instance, in the unfortunate reference to the Iraq war as a "crusade" or the assessment of the "medieval" culture of the 9/11 hijackers. Such issues were first raised (actually by a student) in discussions of the Knight's Tale in 2002. The events of 9/11—and the subsequent war—have raised the stakes on student interest in the kind of sacrificial warrior culture represented by Palamon, Arcite, and Chaucer's crusading Knight. Some students have found Theseus's famous charge to "make a virtue of necessity" uncannily familiar in that it is a sentiment that raises philosophical and ideological problems of our current moment (KnT 3042). Such classroom conversations are, of course, charged. But that very fact has contributed to the seriousness and focus of our work.

As I am keen to help students think about the ways in which Chaucer's work comes to us, I draw attention to the history of editions and anthologies. Near the last day of class, students are asked to assess the selection of Chaucer's work included in various literature survey anthologies since the early 1970s. Working in groups, students examine the tables of contents in anthologies used in survey courses in British literature.[5]

Having now read nearly all the tales, students consider how these anthologies have packaged Chaucer differently. What observations can they make about how the principles of selection have or have not changed over time? What do they think about the virtually unanimous editorial popularity of the Miller's Tale, Wife of Bath's Prologue and Tale, the Pardoner's Tale, and the Nun's Priest's Tale? What do they make of the fact that only the *Broadview Anthology of British Literature* (ed. Black) pairs the Knight's Tale with the Miller's? Since the advent of the *Broadview Anthology* (which seems to students, accurately in my view, the collection of tales most engaged with the issues we've been pursuing all term), these questions have resulted in a sparky debate. In my opinion, this exercise offers an alternative to the usual end-of-term conversation about which pilgrim the students judge to be the winner of the tale-telling competition.

I wish, by way of conclusion, to point out that my "postcolonial" approach to *The Canterbury Tales* seeks neither to praise nor to bury Chaucer. I do not engage a postcolonial approach so as, finally, to judge Chaucer as either cosmopolitan or provincial. I am instead interested in drawing out how we might evaluate the various Chaucers available to us and the degree to which Chaucer's poetry will reward a broad array of cultural questions that are still important, still very relevant today.

NOTES

[1] Notably, Biddick, "Coming"; J. Bowers, "Chaucer after Smithfield"; Kruger, "Fetishism"; Ganim, "Native Studies"; and Cohen, "Introduction: Mid-colonial"—all in Cohen's *Postcolonial Middle Ages*; Stein, esp. 65–66; the introduction and essays in Ingham and Warren; and Biddick, *Shock* and *Typological Imaginary*.

[2] Also useful are Ganim, "Cosmopolitan Chaucer" and Schildgen.

[3] Students consider Schibanoff's essay alongside Lynch's "Storytelling." See also Lynch's "East Meets West."

[4] My reading of the Clerk's Tale draws on Wallace, *Chaucerian Polity*.

[5] I include those with material available on the Web: seven editions of *The Norton Anthology of English Literature* (www.wwnorton.com/college/english/nael/middleages/welcome/html and www.wwnorton.com/college/english/nael/publication_chronology/index.html), two editions of *The Broadview Anthology of British Literature* (www.broadviewpress.com/product.php?productid=968&cat=49&page=1), and two editions of *The Longman Anthology of British Literature*.

Chaucer's Cut

Becky McLaughlin

Now draweth cut, er that we ferrer twynne;
He which that hath the shorteste shal bigynne.

Now draw for cut, and then we can depart;
The man who draws the shortest cut shall start.
— Chaucer, *The Canterbury Tales*

One might call what I do when I teach *The Canterbury Tales* a pedagogical form of catoptric anamorphosis, whereby a mirror is placed on a drawing or painting to transform a distorted image into a three-dimensional picture. In this scenario, Chaucer's text is the anamorphic blot and Jacques Lacan the mirror through which that blot is transformed into a readable image. Instead of taking a frontal approach, my students and I sidle up to *The Canterbury Tales*, viewing it aslant through a number of key psychoanalytic concepts. This does not mean that we use Lacan as the instrument of Chaucer. In fact, it might be more accurate to say we do the opposite. But then Freud set the precedent when he used Sophocles's play to formulate the Oedipus complex, and Lacan followed suit when he used *Hamlet* to elaborate on the nature of desire. From its inception, psychoanalysis has been in fruitful dialectical exchange with literature.

Like Roland Barthes's fetishistic reading of a tutor text, my students and I cut up (with) *The Canterbury Tales*, rearranging its order for the purpose of telling the tale of psychoanalysis—a tale that begins with its most important concept, the unconscious, and ends with one of its most complex, the relation between desire and the drive. When justification is needed for this assault on the rule of right order, I point out to my students, generally upper-level English majors, that even Chaucer himself seems to have made no final decision about the ordering of his tales.

The Canterbury Tales provides a perfect example of how the unconscious functions, for despite the fact that its narrative is premised on contest or one-upmanship, what gets undercut at every turn is precisely mastery. Things begin to go awry both diegetically and extradiegetically almost from the start: if a contract exists between writer and reader, it gets broken when the narrative fails to deliver the promised goods. The pilgrims leave the Tabard with the plan of return, but they remain suspended somewhere between inn and cathedral. Thus, they and we fail to hear who is announced the winner of the storytelling contest.

Like the drunken Miller, who rides halfway out of his saddle and refuses to obey that censoring agent, Harry Bailly, the unconscious makes itself known through tricks such as parapraxis and misprision, through the puckers and gaps in language. In other words, Chaucer always says more or less than he intends to say, and what his work unavoidably points to and urges us to look at are precisely those moments of surplus and lack that shatter the mirror game the subject is supposed to know into a million whispering shards. Certainly, Chaucer is the maker of a text called *The Canterbury Tales*, but he is not its master. Had he been, the one character who is never acknowledged—the unconscious—could not have cut the strings that would otherwise allow Chaucer to control his pilgrim marionettes.

What this psychoanalytic axiom means is that Chaucer's text cannot be mastered, for if its writer is subject to unconscious forces, so too are its readers. And thus *The Canterbury Tales* forces us to return to it time and again without ever having "cracked its code." It keeps desire in play (as Lacan says, "desire . . . is interpretation" [176]), and because desire arises out of lack, it is appropriate that the storytelling contest be initiated with the draw of the "cut." If Chaucer as writer wields the concept of the cut for narrative purposes, it is with the cut (as rupture or lack) that Chaucer as narrator seems to identify, for when we examine the position his pilgrim takes up, we find it is consistently that of one who has been rendered invisible, wounded, or eliminated. In the General Prologue, for example, the pilgrim with whom we associate Chaucer is not the one who sets dialogue or action in motion until Harry Bailly enters the scene and creates a contract with his assembled guests. And although Chaucer as pilgrim paints a brilliant portrait of each of his fellow pilgrims, he elects not to paint one of himself. Because of this omission, he comes to occupy the position of lack itself. As he says of himself in relation to his fellow pilgrims, he "shortly . . . was of hir felaweship anon" ("quickly . . . became one of their fellowship"; lines 30, 32). What this wording suggests is the dyadic bond of mother and child, which is experienced as a nonrelation. In other words, not only does Chaucer as pilgrim lack an image, he also cannot successfully establish himself as a subject until Harry enters the scene, for Harry functions as father, rupturing the dyadic bond and introducing language as a substitute for the mother.

To further flesh out the concept of Chaucer's cut or Lacan's lack, my students and I talk about the repetition compulsion—as Lacan does in his commentary on Poe's "The Purloined Letter"—noting that in *The Canterbury Tales*, the fantasy of difference (twenty-nine pilgrims of various estates) collapses into a repetition of the same. Every story told is the same traumatic story, the drawing of straws initiating a string of cuts or tales about the subject's cut or wound. For example, the Miller's Tale illustrates how the primal scene cuts or wounds, the carpenter awakening in the night to strange noises and then falling into the scene of coitus, where he breaks his arm and—no doubt—his heart; meanwhile, the Wife of Bath's prologue reveals a gap or cut residing between her desire for mastery and her desire for a husband. It is her need for mastery that leads to the annihilation of her husbands: she can have mastery or a husband but not both at the same time.

As my students and I discuss the stories and their tellers, we acknowledge the temporal gap that exists between Chaucer and us. This allows us to begin thinking about the nature of the split subject and the role castration plays in its dehiscence. Like the split subject, Chaucer's text is castrated, its fourteenth- and twenty-first-century iterations not coincident with each other. Psychoanalysis understands this noncoincidence as the inevitable condition of the subject or, in this case, the text. Perhaps if oedipal law functioned perfectly, there would be no "aberrant" subjects, no symptoms. Yet it seldom does, and so my students and I approach Chaucer's pilgrimage as a journey into the symptom and thus into the unconscious itself. Beginning with the spectacle of hysteria, moving through the perversions of fetishism, masochism, and sadism, and ending with paranoia and psychosis, we explore the ways in which conflicts with oedipal law play themselves out on the pilgrims' flesh and language.

We start with the Prioress, examining the contradictions of her name, Madame Eglentyne, the relation between the spectacle she stages and the neurotic symptoms she exhibits, and her desire for the Virgin's feminine jouissance. Using hysteria as a divining rod, we discuss the difference between the Wife of Bath's response to authority and the Prioress's, noting that while the Wife of Bath directly addresses the question Freud placed at the center of psychoanalysis—"What does woman want?" (E. Jones 421)—the Prioress has the much more torturous role of acting it out, dramatizing the question on the stage of her body.

Following the Prioress, we discuss the Pardoner's perverse performance in terms of masochism. We explore his fetishistic sale of false relics through the mechanism of disavowal, whereby his repeated performance of the abject lie he tells his innocent and gullible parishioners becomes a repetition of the moment of trauma in which he recognized and refused sexual difference. Next, we explore the violence of founding law and its relation to the exalted role of the obscene "anal" father in sadism, focusing on the Man of Law, the Clerk, and the Physician. Each tells a sadistic tale, and each represents one of what Immanuel Kant will later call the higher faculties: law, the logic connected with theology, and medicine. The question I pose to my students is why these storytellers recount narratives based on beautiful but tortured young women. Do these storytellers, whose authority is based not on reason but on rule books, identify with the submissive roles played by the women in their tales? Does the nature of their authority make them feel powerful or powerless?

Finally, we turn to paranoia and psychosis, focusing on the Reeve's and Miller's tales of doubling. I argue that the tale told by the Miller is a recounting of the Reeve's primal scene, drawing a parallel between the Reeve's lengthy prologue and Lacan's mirror stage. What this parallel makes apparent is the split between an image that appears whole or together and one's experience of the awkward, uncoordinated limbs that fragment one's body.

To get my students up to speed on the necessary concepts for this approach, I assign selections from two glosses of Lacan's work by Bruce Fink: *The Lacanian Subject* and *A Clinical Introduction to Lacanian Psychoanalysis*. The first fleshes out Lacanian concepts such as the real, the symbolic, and the imaginary, while the second explains the structures of neurosis, perversion, and psychosis—all in sophisticated but still lucid and readable fashion. Because my students are in the process of discovering their own sexual identities, they respond positively to both the reading assignments and the psychoanalytic approach, a response reflected in the sophistication of their final papers, which they share with one another during an end-of-semester miniature conference. What is this grand finale but a kind of pedagogical "talking cure"?

Performance and the Student Body

David Wallace

Students typically enter our classrooms primed to believe that Chaucer is a great storyteller. While not wishing to dislodge that notion, we might work to refine it: Chaucer tells some good tales, but he is preeminently a great discursive performer. By way of unpacking this proposition, which surely sounds like professor-speak to the undergraduate ear, I like to begin a *Canterbury Tales* course not with the General Prologue but rather with the Physician's Tale. The General Prologue is a bad place to begin the teaching of Chaucer. Its opening and closing passages are quite wonderful, but the substantial tranche of pilgrim portraits forming its substantial middle is relatively static, with some baffling trade-related vocabulary that never returns and is hence soon forgotten. But the Physician's Tale, full of incident, stirs mightily the emotions of all concerned: the characters within the tale (the wicked judge Apius, the unyielding aristocrat Virginius), those listening within Chaucer's tale world (especially the Host), and those attending to it now—which is to say, the students themselves. How horrible that a young girl (just a little below undergraduate age) should perish in a power play between men, that her head, deployed by her father like a jack-o'-lantern, should swing from her hair, her sightless eyes mocking the judge who lusted for her body. Students can get really riled up by this tale and may turn on Chaucer or even his teacher; it is disgusting medieval stuff. But this is all pedagogically good: the rebellious readerly body itself forms part of the performance that Chaucer (text and author) has in mind. Appalled and emotionally exercised but not bored or baffled, the students are likely to return for the second class: an important consideration in the new collegiate economy of "add and drop," when every class early in the semester is conducted, so to speak, in a shop window.

The Physician's Tale, then, gets everyone emoting and performing right away, characters and readers and listeners alike. A great deal happens in this very short tale, yet fewer than half of its 286 lines advance the plot: indeed, the story really does not get going at all until our heroine, still nameless, leaves home in line 118. Much of this tale's content is actually dedicated to the verbal performativity of the Physician and to the rhetorical personifications that he invents. These begin with an extraordinary eighteen-line speech by Nature, who asserts her absolute superiority to "countrefete" art (of the kind, of course, that the Physician is laboring to produce [line 13]). We are then treated to more than thirty lines of apostrophizing, directed to governesses and then fathers and mothers, who oversee children. The relevance of all this to the story is moot but can hardly be overleaped: it forms part of the strange but distinctive discursive performance of a Canterbury pilgrim, a physician, who nearly succeeds in inducing (through narrative art) cardiac arrest. Harry Bailly, worrying that he has "caught a cardynacle" (line 313), believes that only medicinal liquor, alcohol, or "a myrie tale" might save him: and so we are delivered into the hands of the greatest discursive performer of all, the Pardoner (316).

Medieval Catholicism demanded expressions of emotion as outward and visible signs of changing, and hopefully reforming, mental states. The content of medieval tale-telling could induce strong physiological reactions in an audience, but so too could the form, style, or *modus agendi*. The Franklin, for one, cannot further endure listening to the Squire's botched narrative performing. *Decameron*, day 6, novella 1, tells of a lady who, trapped in the company of a knight who is butchering and mangling his tale telling, feels physically sick; John Florio, translating in 1620, understands her plight most empathetically:

> Madame Oretta, being a Lady of unequalled ingenuitie, admirable in judgement, and most delicate in her speech, was afflicted in soule, beyond all measure; overcome with many colde sweates, and passionate heart-aking qualms.

The only cure that Oretta can shape for herself is to interrupt this "discourser": a delicate task, since her interruption must not be taken to cut at his manhood. Chaucer's most celebrated discourser, the Wife of Bath, rides out several attempted interruptions by men. But there are times in his *Canterbury Tales* when Chaucer recognizes that the collective mood (again, within and beyond the tale world) calls for a differing style of narrative performance. When the Prioress's Tale, for example, leaves "every man" feeling "sober" (lines 791–92), the Host turns to the pilgrim Chaucer to lift the mood, which he does not by introducing substantial narrative matter but rather through discursive performing that may be enjoyed but then judged and rejected as comically inept. Again, our surrogate listener in chief, the Host, is emotionally stirred: Sir Thopas moves him to speak of shittiness, turds, and castration. But the very energy of the Host's interrupting sustains the forward momentum of the collective discursive project; there is no time to pause and wonder quite what made hearing the Prioress's Tale quite so "sober" an experience.

A comparable response to emotional impasse and moral complexity was adopted by the Royal Shakespeare Company's two-part *Canterbury Tales* in 2006. The audience at Stratford-upon-Avon was contradictorily interpellated by the Prioress's Tale. On the one hand, they were lulled and reassured by the beautiful choral singing with which the dying "litel clergeon" was processed to church (line 503): for this was the sonic landscape of *Choral Evensong*, the radio program first broadcast from Westminster Abbey in 1926 by the BBC and the touchstone of all things English. On the other hand, they had just witnessed the simulated murder of actors wearing big-nosed masks: a reminder of an older English tradition, the anti-Semitic pogrom. Relief from spectatorly paralysis, however, came with the next tale, that of the Nun's Priest's, a glorious barnyard romp that swept away everything with a flurry of dancing chickens. The curtain then fell for intermission, and the audience was free (it being England) to find ice creams. It is out of Ellesmere order to bring on Chauntecleer and company after the Prioress's Tale, but the strategy is Chaucerian: to move on from a moral *kankedort* or away from disturbing images simply by initiating new and different discursive performance.

Various strategies might encourage students to begin thinking about discursive performance. Early exposure to the Physician's Tale helps them feel their own bodies being played upon, nudged by narrative into pathos or outrage. But we want students to themselves become performers, proficient enough to express emotions that—like the Pardoner—they may not personally feel. It is easy to identify two or three students in a class who enjoy performing: theater studies majors or those of antic disposition. But for things to work properly we need the whole class to buy in, to become invested in performing Chaucer, and so we start with baby steps. I generally begin by reading a single line of Chaucer and then have the whole class repeat it. The next step is for each student along a row to read one line of a passage under consideration. This sacrifices syntactic flow a bit but preserves a happy anonymity for shyer students (who can keep their heads down while reading, and the moment will soon pass). The next step, several weeks in, is for each student along the row to read a sentence aloud. This is more nerve-racking, but also more fun: students are playing a sort of Russian roulette, since they may get a short sentence or a very long one—and of course, you can get into debates about what constitutes a medieval sentence or period. From there you can progress to groups prepping passages to be delivered before the class or to full-blown dramatic productions. I once saw my career coming to a premature end when a group performing the Miller's Tale really did feature Nicholas taking a piss. But thankfully, it turned out, he was just discharging a squirt gun into a bucket. Video, of course, raises whole new worlds of possibility for out-of-class assignments; *YouTube* has many examples, good and bad.

Our Chaucer rapper, Baba Brinkman, can help inspire students, since he has transposed a number of Chaucer's tales into a contemporary musical idiom very much aware of, and interactive with, its audience. Brinkman writes suggestively on how Chaucer's tale-telling context might be likened to the freestyle battle of hip-hop culture: again, matters of style (associated primarily with the body of the performer rather than with the written page) are front and center. Brinkman supplies links to a number of his performances, but classroom hacks might try a performance for themselves, for it so happens that Chaucer's Tale of Sir Thopas is written in a meter that aligns perfectly with rapping rhythm. The teacher can thus begin by reading from the text, quite soberly, but then ease gradually into a rapping rhythm that might be combined with a few dance steps. You will, of course, sound and look ridiculous, but any interruption from the floor will only parallel that initiated by the Host to end the ridiculous rhyming of Sir Thopas.

Chaucer's most prolifically discursive performer, the Wife of Bath, awaits no invitation to speak: she speaks unbidden, at the beginning of fragment 3. To bring out quite how brilliant the voicing of her performance is, we might attempt, as a classroom exercise, a little reediting. Take her opening thirteen lines, for example. On first acquaintance, students will have little idea how to voice and stress the Wife. Emphasizing that every revoicing is an act of reinterpretation, we might try breaking up the lines and accentuating particular words as a guide to spoken performance:

Ex-*per*-i-ence
Though noon *auctoritee* Were in this world
is right ynogh for *me* To speke of wo
that is in mari-age;
For lordynges
sith I twelve yeer was of age
(Thonked be God that is eterne on lyve)
Housbondes
at chirche dore
I have had *fyv*e
(*If* I so *ofte* myghte have
ywedded bee)
And alle were *worthy* men in hir degree.
But me was toold
certeyn
nat longe agoon is
That *sith* that Crist ne wente nevere but *onis* To weddyng,
in the Cane of Galilee,
That by that *same* ensaumple taughte he me
That I ne sholde wedded be
but ones.

The aim here is to bend pronunciation and all else to the needs of meter, rhythm, and (above all) sense while yet sustaining a genuinely Chaucerian language. Such a performative model guides the greatest Shakespearean actors; the "sense" they seek to serve is, of course, the understanding of their audience. Fidelity to a Chaucerian sound world, adapted to address matters of acute contemporary interest, has been marvelously essayed by multilingual poet Caroline Bergvall. See (and hear), for example, her "Banned in Poland: The Summer Tale (deus hic 1)," which contemplates the addiction of a Polish pope to marrons glacés ice cream, and her "Franker Tale (deus hic 2)," which speaks of a dying pope and women's rights ("Caroline Bergvall").

Chaucer's Pardoner produces flowing verbal *copia* to rival that of the Wife of Bath (he interrupts her *as* a rival at line 163), coupled with intensified emphasis on the *techne* of bodily performance:

Thanne peyne I me to strecche forth the nekke,
And est and west upon the peple I bekke,
As doth a dowve sittynge on a berne.
Myne handes and my tonge gon so yerne
That it is joye to se my bisynesse. (PardT 395–99)

Then I take pains to stretch forth my neck,
And east and west upon the people I nod,
As does a dove sitting on a barn.
My hands ands my tongue move so eagerly
That it is a joy to see my busyness.

In Web-linked classrooms, the highly mannered protocols of this performing might usefully be compared with and considered voguing, a highly stylized dance form that evolved in Harlem before being mainstreamed by Madonna's "Vogue" and by movies such as *Zoolander*. Certain gestures employed in hip-hop and voguing, such as momentary but emphatic pointing, loop back to equivalent gestures in Chaucer: to the Pardoner, certainly, but perhaps even to the famous Hoccleve portrait (where a painted Chaucer points to a written text attesting to his own "lyknesse"). Class can wrap up with the walk-off from *Zoolander*, which sees two white actors deploy a whole battery of gestural and voguing techniques. Two questions to end with: How does the film allay homophobic anxieties arising from this camp, male-male encounter (frequent cuts to a blond girlfriend figure and David Bowie showing up to declare it "a straight walk-off")? And how does the film both acknowledge and repress the origins of the cultural form it is appropriating (frequent cuts to Ben Stiller's "second," or corner, man, an African American in cornrows, for example)? Such questions lead back to those larger discussions of race and gender, or the gendering of race, that form part of any contemporary *Canterbury Tales* class. They usefully suggest that we need not confine ourselves to the usual-suspect tales—that of the Man of Law for Islam and of the Prioress for Judaism—in matters of race and its performance.

Hidden in Plain Sight:
Teaching Masculinities in *The Canterbury Tales*
Holly Crocker

Teaching masculinities in Chaucer's *Canterbury Tales* is frequently all too easy. To begin with the General Prologue is to present students with a rich and varied catalog of masculinity, a collection of men differentiated by characteristics including social rank, spiritual status, and sexual potency. Through close readings of Chaucer's well-known portraiture, students can easily see that medieval masculinities are a complex, contingent, and constructed mash of social, moral, and sexual traits. The sheer plurality of the General Prologue has the potential to demystify masculinity's cultural authority or the idea that lived maleness is a totalized, seamless experience of gendered sameness. I typically introduce students to medieval masculinities by having them read an introductory essay by Jeffrey Jerome Cohen and Bonnie Wheeler.[1] As students quickly learn, gender has no single, fixed meaning in the General Prologue, so they must piece together their own readings of masculinity in *The Canterbury Tales*. While the General Prologue can be the best place to start a course on masculinities, moving directly from the General Prologue to fragment 1 is frequently far more troublesome in terms of gender analysis.

Rather than see the porous interchangeability between the Knight, Miller, Host, and Monk, students naturalize each man's masculinity in order to privilege the social contest. (The "knight versus laborer" motif will be familiar to many students, even those whose knowledge of medieval social history derives only from the "anarcho-syndicalist commune" episode from *Monty Python and the Holy Grail*.) To avoid this potential reduction, I deliberately skip fragment 1. In order to confront students with medieval masculinities that are less typified in the modern imagination, I ask students to extend their thinking about Chaucer's masculinities by moving first to fragment 7. This grouping of tales provides a helpful generic variety from fabliau to beast fable, but it also includes some of the more difficult forms of medieval representation — allegory and tragedy — in narratives that put the construction of masculinities explicitly at issue. In other words, homosocial competition offers a way for students to see the allegory of the Tale of Melibee or the tragedy of the Monk's Tale as significant to the formation of different masculinities. The Shipman's Tale's engagement with gendered notions of social respectability underscores the high stakes of masculine reputation, especially a woman's power to affect a man's identity in the public domain. This theme is also evident in the Prioress's Tale, where childish Marian devotion transforms developing masculine piety into jarring anti-Semitic martyrdom. But the homosocial production of masculinity most pointedly inflects the Thopas-Melibee sequence.

166 TEACHING MASCULINITIES

Focusing on masculinities in Chaucer, therefore, offers a way to teach those tales that might otherwise remain hidden in plain sight. In seeking a tale to lighten his mood, Harry Bailly turns to pilgrim Chaucer, who, as Lee Patterson points out ("'What Man'"), puzzles the Host to such a degree that he asks with a kind of bewildered frustration, "What man artow?" (Th, line 695). That question, at the heart of any course exploring masculinities in *The Canterbury Tales*, underscores masculinity's contingent dependence on femininity in the following narratives. By describing pilgrim Chaucer as a "popet in an arm t'enbrace" ("doll in an arm to embrace"; Th 701), the Host emphasizes the diminutive aspects of Chaucer's fictive persona. Is pilgrim Chaucer "feminized," as Jill Mann argues (*Geoffrey Chaucer* 129–45)? If so, does that mean he is inscribed within a binary that associates masculinity with agency and femininity with passivity? Many agree that he is, particularly in the light of the tales he goes on to tell. The masculinity Harry Bailly seeks to institute, therefore, depends on a differential recognition of femininity. But it also leads to considerations of genre, including the methods and limits of description in romance as well as allegory. The joke that is Sir Thopas, students agree, establishes pilgrim Chaucer's ability to resist the Host's dominance. The extended blazon of Sir Thopas's beauty, which Jeffrey Jerome Cohen helpfully calls students to notice, frequently prompts them to argue that Chaucer critiques Harry's hypermasculinity (Cohen, "Diminishing" 145).

The ironic fluidity of gender, which Chaucer establishes through the plasticity of genre, is equally central to his Tale of Melibee. If critics find the Melibee unreadable on account of its formulaic dullness (Foster, "Has Anyone"), students often find it delicious for its contrapuntal deflation of a fantasy of knighthood so rarefied that it challenges any idealization of late medieval masculinity. This is not to say that they find the Tale of Melibee less boring in its sententious advice. But if we approach this tale with an eye to its relevance for Chaucerian masculinities, students are eager to read the narrative of Prudence as a meditation on gender and self-control. Indeed, students are here able to consider the gender implications of a cultivated form of passivity for masculinities more broadly. Perhaps tellingly, however, one of their persistent frustrations with Prudence's advice is her focus on submission. As an element of the stoicism that undergirds the tale's morality, she relentlessly recommends peace, no matter how seriously Melibee's enemies might have violated him or his family.[2] And though students easily understand the allegorical nature of Sophie's wounds and readily grasp the spiritual import of the humility Prudence recommends, most intently believe that Melibee's desire for vengeance is not only justified but serves as a sign of his empowered masculinity. Such claims productively open up a discussion of connections between certain forms of masculinity and violence: for an active, secular masculinity such as Melibee's, most students believe violence is warranted, since it is his responsibility to protect those others (even if they are allegorically and internally constituted) who reside within his personal domain.

With Prudence, Chaucer provides an opportunity for students to consider femininity's relational power over masculinity. Students who believe pilgrim Chaucer is initially feminized by his encounter with Harry Bailly are even more convinced by the end of Melibee. Besides the fact that Prudence seems to offer a paramount example of the ways that men are produced as submissive through the feminizing dominance of a woman, Harry Bailly's commentary at the tale's end seems to solidify the tale's emphasis on Prudence's shaping authority: "I hadde levere than a barel ale / That Goodelief, my wyf, hadde herd this tale! / For she nys no thyng of swich pacience / As was this Melibeus wyf Prudence" ("Rather than have a barel of ale / I wish that my wife Goodelief had heard this tale! / For she has nothing of such patience / As did Prudence, the Wife of Melibee"; lines 1893–96). Although Harry gives Prudence the patience that Melibee is supposed to end up with (thus collapsing her identity into her husband's character), Harry's response to the tale directs attention to his own wife's agency (Collette, "Heeding"). Harry recounts a litany of examples of his wife's unruliness, incidents involving verbal and physical affronts to his masculine power. He does not see Prudence's behavior, students agree, in the same way that he views his wife's conduct, even if he also recognizes Goodelief's power to influence his masculinity.

Since Harry's behavior is a product of his wife's goading, it becomes clear that masculine violence may not be a sign of control, and students must contemplate Prudence's claim that reacting to the provocations of his enemies only makes Melibee subject to their designs. Harry actually fears that Goodelief will drive him to violence, and thus to ruin: "I woot wel she wol do me slee som day / Som neighebor, and than go my way" ("I know full well that someday she will make me slay / Some neighbor, then go my way"; Mel 1917–18). Especially taken in relation to the failure that is Chaucer's Tale of Sir Thopas, which deliberately, if not ostentatiously, deflates a masculinity codified according to formulae of romance idealization, students agree that masculinities in *The Canterbury Tales* are far more complex than a series of portraits that distinguish different kinds of men. While Harry Bailly's complaints about Goodelief diminish his pretense of power, they also raise the possibility that masculine authority depends less on enacted violence and more on cultivated composure. Students certainly see the compensatory character of Harry Bailly's aggression, particularly as he attempts to recuperate his ideal of masculine control.

As a kind of reaction to his own exposure before the other pilgrims, Harry Bailly diverts attention from his marital impotence by looking to the Monk, whose appearance coincides with what David Wallace has rightly characterized as the "fantasy of a virile man" (*Chaucerian Polity* 309). Unlike Harry's confounding run-in with pilgrim Chaucer, the Monk seems immediately comprehensible in the terms of masculinity that Harry finds most appealing. According to Harry, who equates physical and cultural power, men cut from the same cloth as the Monk promise to redeem masculinity through their virile habits: "Haddestow as greet a leeve as thou hast myght / To parfourne al thy lust in engendrure, / Thou haddest bigeten ful many a creature" ("If you had as much liberty as you have might / To perform all thy desire in engendering, / You would have sired many a creature"; Mel 1946–48). Harry's fantasy of masculinity brings students back to the arts of portraiture, particularly as emphasized features reveal certain components of a constructed masculinity. What students frequently note about this characterization of the Monk, following as it does so closely on Harry's account of Goodelief's power, is its stark absence of the feminine. Our discussions of Harry's invested portraiture lead directly to the Monk's Tale itself, which formally contests the Host's idealization of a homosocial community built on the masculine capacity for violence.

Initially, at any rate, students are intrigued by the perfect symmetry of the Monk's narrative, especially its collection of diverse figures. With his mixture of heroes—biblical and heroic, ancient and contemporary, male and female—the Monk universalizes his definition of tragedy (Kelly 45–69). Indeed, nothing shows the structural regularity of medieval tragedy more clearly than the Monk's Tale. Yet as L. O. Aranye Fradenburg points out, bringing the "myghty" into narrative focus simply reveals their befallenness (*Sacrifice* 113–54). Privileging the suffering of lofty figures does not, as students might initially think, affirm their cultural power. Instead, it reveals the limits of such authority, linking greatness to temporal vicissitudes in an inescapable cycle of helpless display. In the Monk's series of fallen worthies, the changes wrought by time leave marks of destruction that are as easy to see as they are to predict. Even so, the Monk does not use his collection of recollected worthies to extol or recommend the power of foresight attributed to the virtue of Prudence in medieval representations. Instead, he unifies these disparate narratives using the ominous image of Fortune, who is relentlessly responsible for masculinity's incessant undoing. Moving from man to man, Fortune decimates each claim to masculine authority. Unlike Prudence, whose visibility is part of an idealized masculine consciousness, Fortune cannot be so easily subsumed. Indeed, it is her irreducible resistance to gender assimilation that makes her power so difficult to comprehend or counteract. Ally to Nero as well as Zenobia, Fortune makes no distinctions between those she befriends and those she betrays. Harry Bailly might like to imagine masculine greatness as impervious to feminine influence, but the Monk presents an even more frightening scenario, in which Fortune's power reaches beyond the differential particularities of gender.

The Knight's sudden interruption of the Monk, "That ye han seyd is right ynough, ywis" ("You've said quite enough, certainly"; MkT, line 2768), is both psychologically and historically revealing for Chaucerian masculinities in the classroom. As a consequence of the Knight's objection, students must contemplate the ways that different fictions implicate, even as they construct, various masculinities. I often ask students to discuss their responses to this moment: Are they, like the Host, grateful for the Knight's interruption? Are they, too, "bored" by this sequence? If so, and here I seek to take advantage of students' perpetual declarations of unconcern, I ask them what it means that their perspective might be different from the Knight's. What about the Monk's narrative, I ask, would arouse such feeling? Here we discuss the Knight's social relation to the figures featured in the Monk's catalog: while the Knight actually shares precious little with most of these worthies, students nevertheless understand that because he identifies with the figures featured in this series, the Knight does not want "To heeren of hire sodayn fal, allas!" ("To hear of their sudden fall, alas"; 2773).

A return to the Knight's General Prologue portrait is always effective at this juncture, for it recalls the somewhat incongruous detail of the Knight's composed temperament ("And of his port as meeke as is a mayde" ["And in deportment he was as meek as a maide"; line 69]). Such a trait might be necessary to manage the bloody martial encounters included in the Knight's history of battles, but what, I ask, would make such a measured character break the social protocols of tale telling to interrupt the Monk? After rereading the Knight's portrait, most students agree that his discomfort arises from a model of tragedy that ruins all manner of wealth, control, or respect that a man might achieve through his performance of masculinity. In other words, the Monk's leveling series suggests that there is no difference among masculinities: no matter how a man acts, Fortune's power will create and devastate greatness. For students with a strong belief in individualist notions of performative agency, the Monk's radical deflation of masculine power is preposterous. When it is read in the context of fragment 7, however, students are more likely to treat the failure of the Monk's Tale as another moment of Chaucerian levity regarding the differential fixity of gender. If anyone can occupy the position of masculine power privileged by Fortune, then its cultural power can be infinitely, albeit absurdly, extended.

Such is the comic logic I pursue with my students when we discuss the Nun's Priest's Tale, which remains a favorite among them, even when the focus of our inquiry is Chaucer's treatment of masculinities. Chaucer's story of cock and fox crystallizes a number of Chaucerian discourses, from the learned idiom of natural science to the comic parlance of household farce. Much of my discussion of gender representation in and around the tale follows the lead of Peter Travis, for I find his emphasis on Harry Bailly's queer admiration for the virile poetics of the Nun's Priest immensely instructive for students.[3] More broadly, Travis's exploration of the openness of the Nun's Priest's Tale, what he calls its "disseminal genius" (*Disseminal Chaucer*), obtains across fragment 7 and readies students for the careful consideration of masculinities in other portions of *The Canterbury Tales*. Pertelote's moral "wisdom" is a hilarious reflection on Melibee's Prudence in the same way that Chauntecleer's tragic fall is a delightful extension of the Monk's Fortune. Because students see the intertextual humor in Chaucer's construction of a cock's masculinity, the Nun's Priest's Tale enriches their readings of masculinities across these divergent stories.

What I would like to emphasize for teaching Chaucerian masculinities, then, is the valuable interconnectedness of those narratives—comic and serious—

that make up fragment 7. By moving from the General Prologue to these later tales, students get a better sense of the sustained diversity of masculinities in *The Canterbury Tales*, even while they tackle some of the most difficult narratives in Chaucer's frame collection. As students learn, the Monk's Tale is not a strange outlier from a more "congenial" poetic mode (Trigg), nor is the Melibee a stodgy holdover of "medieval" tastes in prose narrative (Foster, "Has Anyone"). While students might still come to see either tale as strange or both tales as stodgy, they do so in the light of a far more complex meditation on Chaucerian constructions of masculinity. Moral allegories authorize, just as tragic catalogs deflate, specific cultural fantasies, including those of gender. Rather than reduce masculinities in *The Canterbury Tales* to a restricted range of medieval types, students gain critical purchase on a greater variety of gender positions, including their own.

NOTES

[1] See also Pugh, Calabrese, and Marzec, as well as the introductory chapters of Crocker; Lees; and I. Davis.

[2] Strohm, "Allegory," articulates the traditional position, that the stoicism of this tale is Boethian. More recently, De Marco has argued that this tale's ethics are Ciceronian.

[3] Though I use Travis's *Disseminal Chaucer* as background for my teaching, I ask students to read his article "The Body of the Nun's Priest," since it offers a more compact reading of masculinities surrounding the Nun's Priest's Tale.

The Pardoner's "Old Man":
Postmodern Theory and the Premodern Text
Leonard Michael Koff

Because he does not assume a fundamental break between the medieval and the modern, Emmanuel Levinas can provide a valuable lexicon to help explain how Chaucer stands in his own historical moment and at the limen of his own values. A postmodern Levinas can reveal a medieval Chaucer for whom the themes of postmodernism are medieval themes as well. Barry Windeatt, for instance, has provided examples of Chaucer's "postmodern belatedness" in his essay "Postmodernism," although among themes not mentioned by Windeatt are assumptions about ethical behavior toward the other, who may, as an other, show us to ourselves. These assumptions present themselves in Chaucer as fictional projections of the engagements of mind that create ethical—and unethical—presence. Because we awaken to ourselves in the middle of existence—this is Levinas's vocabulary and Chaucer's assumption as an author—understanding how we exist with others makes ontological questions implicitly ethical ones; self-awareness in relation to the other is, for Levinas and for Chaucer the theorist and Chaucer the author, always ethical awareness.

Had Levinas read Chaucer, he would have found in him examples of literary art that put characters, as well as readers, in touch with their subjectivity, not merely in view of it. The best art for Levinas does not know what it seeks but rather lets characters and readers locate themselves in positions of exposure to what they know or presume to know (see Levinas, "Language" and *Entre Nous*; Bruns). Serious and comic by turns, Chaucer's poetry opens up rather than closes down ethical and social analysis; his poetry lets readers test their values through imagined cases, for he, like Levinas, works from inside the world. Literary critics have always found the refusal to leap immediately to speculative and ethical universals a tellingly Chaucerian virtue.

Because the old man in the Pardoner's Tale reveals the complexity of Chaucer's ethical analysis, he is central to any course that would explore what postmodernism can open up about Chaucer's relationship to his values. The Pardoner's old man shows that Chaucer can imagine those both in and not in the ethical coherence of the medieval world. The old man's condition of life—self-enclosed, withering, imagined as eternally alive in life, which is Chaucer imagining otherwise—throws into relief a world in which death exists (but not for the old man), where penance and rectification are efficacious (is the old man being punished by living eternally?), and where the self and its behavior can begin to be understood. The old man's anomalous state does not, however, let us see Chaucer's metaphysical discontent; Chaucer's imagining the old man does not reveal Chaucer's doubts about values or the nature of existence. Rather, the old man's presence in the Pardoner's Tale argues for Chaucer's interrogation of values in imagining for whom values exist.

In an undergraduate course on Chaucer that reads him with Levinas, I ask students to look at selections from Levinas's work that speak to the nature of ethical encounter: selections, for example, on its literary and public expression; selections on its value as interruption; selections on the nature of good and bad art—bad art is in reality the self seeing only the other as itself, blind to the necessity of being interrupted, where interruption puts the self, the economy of the "same," the self-totality, at risk—selections on the comforts of sameness and on ethics as the meaning of being; selections on kinds of transgressions toward God and toward humankind; selections on the expressions that one's obligation to the visible face of the other take; and selections on speech as metaphysical courtesy and the temptation to annihilate the other (see Levinas, *Existence*).

Chaucer does not have Levinas's vocabulary of the other, although he understands the other's place in revealing the lineaments of the medieval world. The old man knows, for example, where death is and directs the three rioters there: "up this croked wey . . . in that grove . . . under a tree" (PardT, lines 761–63). We never see death when the old man is presumably in death's grove, asking to die; we only *imagine* him as he wanders knocking on the earth, his "leeve mooder," to "leet me in" ("dear mother"; "let me in"; 731). Death for the old man is apparently not universal; death can send him back from "no death" to haunt the earth "lyk a restelees kaityf" ("like a restless captive"; 728), literally embodying the meaning of a world that does not connect old age and dying. Moreover, it is only after the rioters kill one another for the gold they find under death's tree that we understand that the death to which the old man directs the rioters is the death their cupidity causes. The old man sends the rioters to a parodic tree of knowledge whose fruit is their own desirous nature; he understands the rioters morally, though they are blind to themselves.

We should emphasize that the old man has not committed a transgression that thrusts him outside God's grace. This view of the old man misunderstands his heuristic function in the Pardoner's Tale. As a figure constructed by the terms that put him in confounding ways at the threshold of Chaucer's world, he points to that world; indeed, as a limen, he moves within it. The old man is a species of the ferryman, conducting us to the border between worlds so that we see first Chaucer's world more clearly and then our own, when we turn and look at both worlds. In this way, the old man opens up questions about the nature and ethical structure of existence. Death exists—the rioters cannot kill death, though they set out to do so—and death comes, literally and figuratively, in the Pardoner's Tale as a wage of sin. The old man is thus a figure of clarification and critique, not despair. Although he would exchange his "cheste" (of clothes, perhaps all his worldly goods) for "an heyre clowt to wrappe me" ("hair-cloth shroud to wrap myself in"; lines 734, 736), he is not afforded one. An atoned life—a reality in a medieval world and perhaps in our own—has no place in his, a world he carries everywhere, eliciting the terror that accompanies willful retreat from ethical choice.

In theorizing the consequences that sudden interruption creates, in bringing Levinas's lexicon of the other to bear on Chaucer, we come to understand that meeting the face of the other ruptures our sense of ethical comfort—for our own ethical good. Self-awareness grounded on the interruption of the "same" and on courtesy as an ethical response to the other, who has interrupted our sameness, is an idea of awakening central to Levinas and to Chaucer. Courtesy gives to the other his being in the world, his social place, signaling publicly that we would take in the other's effect on us. Being courteous, which is Levinas's first virtue and Chaucer's (Levinas provides the vocabulary that clarifies the way that acknowledging or not acknowledging that the other defines us ethically), demonstrates that we and the other exist (Levinas, "Toward the Other" 21). Moreover, being discourteous, which violates the otherness of the other, obliterating his place in the world, makes it possible for us to remain impervious to everyone. When the old man says to the three rioters, "Now, lordes, God yow see" ("may God protect you"; PardT, line 715), they refuse him as someone knowable; the proudest rioter speaks for the other two: "What, carl, with sory grace!" (717). Because for Levinas and for Chaucer we only experience clarifying, indeed revivifying moments—"first" moments in Levinas's vocabulary— when there is ethical encounter, the rioters' response to the old man illuminates their self-defining enclosure: they are morally dead even before they kill each other. Being alive for Levinas and Chaucer is beginning again, awakening to ourselves among others. For our own ontological good, for our own self-understanding, we should not refuse the always eternal other.

Chaucer and Levinas believe that we can never know ourselves as God does. Moreover, understanding who we are cannot be achieved on the harmonies, the impositions, of reason. Here is the place toward which classroom discussion ought to move, where Levinas's postmodern theory and the premodern text meet; that the aspiration of Western thought can take its mode of self and social analysis from above (purely from the unmediated) or purely from below (as recognition that we inhabit only a void) is an assumption Levinas and Chaucer refuse. Let me add that Levinas's arguments against the view that we live only in random contexts, voids we fill, ground Levinas's critique of postmodernisms like Alain Badiou's that, if brought to bear on Chaucer, only make him modern. Badiou's nonreligious postmodernism rests on set theory, seeing people in *situations* (Badiou's term for random contexts) that point to other random contexts. Badiou's arguments for reading only bring us closer to our own culturally bound universals, such as the notion that we live, know, and evaluate ourselves in contexts we create through bracketing (including and excluding) the elements of our apprehension. For Levinas, the contexts in which we find ourselves reveal transcendent openings: our being in the world rests in Being. This is also Chaucer's understanding of the relation between ontology and ethics.

In developing a course on Chaucer and the postmodern, I use, in addition to the Pardoner's old man, a range of other Canterbury tales. Among these are the Canon's Yeoman's description of alchemical hubris, which would rival God's creation; the mutually valorizing behavior of Romans and Christians in the Second Nun's Tale; the view in the Knight's Tale of identity, appropriation, and the ceremonial constructs that would rationalize behavior and the meaning of divine intervention; the Prioress's skewing of the idea of the other in her response to the Jew and her extension of community to pets; Muslim as well as British conversion to Catholicism in the Man of Law's Tale (conversion is appropriation of the other); the Hun at Europe's borders in the Squire's Tale; and the imaginary and the Arthurian other in the Wife of Bath's Tale, as well as the courtesies between the Friar and the Summoner and the ethical fallout of "quyting" groups in general. These tales and episodes within and between tales, read in the context of Levinas, ensure that when reading Chaucer we recognize Chaucer's strenuous engagement with social and ethical questions that still occupy us.

Designing the Undergraduate "Hybrid" Chaucer Course

Lorraine Kochanske Stock

A Rationale for Hybridizing Chaucer Courses

"Blended learning," the convergence of residential and online instruction, which is "the single-greatest unrecognized trend in higher education today," is predicted eventually to affect eighty to ninety percent of all college courses (Young). Such hybrid courses, in which students meet their instructors for only half of the usual face-to-face time in a bricks-and-mortar classroom, combine traditional pedagogy with instruction delivered through "technology-mediated learning." Most course content, student-faculty interaction, student-student interaction, assessments, and writing projects are delivered and experienced electronically through course management systems (CMS) such as *Blackboard*, *Moodle*, *Sakai*, or *Angel*. Social interactions are expressed in cyberspace through asynchronous message boards, synchronous chat rooms, and e-mail exchange. Such a computer-mediated learning environment takes advantage of available Internet resources—sound files, radio programs, video content, Web sites, and digital images—to supplement instructor-created electronic lectures, which are delivered as podcasts.

Why adopt blended learning? Burgeoning student enrollment, inadequate classroom space, escalating fuel costs, and campus parking-lot gridlock challenge university administrators to alleviate spatial congestion, curtail extra commuting, and accommodate the scheduling convenience of increasing numbers of nontraditional students who simultaneously attend college, raise families, and hold off-campus jobs. Advances in pedagogical software and CMSs, increased availability of personal electronic devices, and exponentially increasing Internet resources enable students to fulfill at least some coursework through hybrid or distance learning.

Supported by a modest technology grant, I redesigned my undergraduate Chaucer course as a hybrid. Now I would never teach Chaucer any other way. I offer practical advice about designing a Chaucer course that employs significant online content delivery, research activities, and writing projects. My suggestions also will enhance any traditional Chaucer course supported by a CMS.

The Nature of Blended Learning and Hybrid Courses

With reduced seat-time requirements, some students choose computer-mediated instruction, believing these courses will be easier. However, in well-designed online courses, students may spend more time on self-directed research and writing activities than they would in the traditional mode of passive lecture auditing and note taking. Blended learning courses require self-motivation and discipline beyond that expected in traditional classes. To compensate for this extra effort, students receive instruction or perform course activities away from campus anytime on home computers, at local public libraries, Wi-Fi-enhanced coffee shops, or their workplace after hours.

Increased convenience accompanies a commensurate sacrifice of the human social interaction expected by humanities students. Teaching a literature course online requires creating increased opportunities for this social aspect of the normal classroom experience. Designing and creating a course that employs blended learning requires a surprisingly large initial outlay of the instructor's time. Instructors adopting the hybrid format should begin planning and creating the electronic content at least a year before offering the course. For this initially substantial time investment, the instructor is rewarded with more free time in subsequent course offerings, when the already created materials require only minor adjustments and additions.

All online courses, whether delivered completely electronically or only partially so in a hybrid format, incur the challenge of keeping the student—physically distanced from his or her classmates and instructor—continually engaged with the course content as well as able to manage reading assignments, conduct outside research, and complete written projects on schedule. Without the impetus of meeting the instructor face-to-face twice or three times weekly—in which there are oral reminders of deadlines and clarifications about assignments—students postpone work required by online courses, spending more time on traditional courses. In a hybrid presentation of Chaucer's *Canterbury Tales*, maintaining continuous student engagement, ensuring completion of projects, and providing opportunities to master Middle English require incorporating extra structure in the course design.

The Chaucer Course as Pilgrimage: Mapping the Way

To provide structure, clearly organized course materials, and incentive to perform the required reading and writing activities in a timely way, I took my cue from the course's main text, *The Canterbury Tales*—a frame story about pilgrims participating in a storytelling contest. Organizing the course around the metaphor of pilgrimage, I designed the curriculum *as* a pilgrimage, tracing the students' journey from ignorance about Chaucer and medieval life to mastery of *The Canterbury Tales*, signaled by our mutual arrival, along with Chaucer's textual pilgrims, at Canterbury. For the CMS home page, I designed an interactive map of the London-to-Canterbury route that Chaucer's pilgrims followed. The students mirror the pilgrims' itinerary with their own journey toward mastery of Chaucer's poetry and aspects of medieval culture. For each week of the semester, I construct learning modules, or content units, corresponding to a fourteen-week division of Chaucer's *Canterbury Tales* and other course materials. These units are live-linked to towns placed along the London-to-Canterbury map. Students physically progress from London to Canterbury on the map and metaphorically mark progress toward completion of the course. Because Chaucer's narrator mentions fewer than fourteen towns, I selected other extant fourteenth-century destinations that pilgrims might have visited for "privee" breaks on the journey to Canterbury. My itinerary includes the expected stopping points of London, Southwark, Deptford, and so on, supplemented by London Bridge, Crayford, and Northfleet, making fourteen route locations. Clicking on each town on the map opens a guide to the module's contents—study questions about that week's assigned readings, links to electronic text files (some instructor created, others from established Chaucer-devoted Web sites) about Chaucerian literary genres, Middle English pronunciation, and links to URLs of relevant Web materials. The best of these include Harvard's *Geoffrey Chaucer Page* and the *Chaucer Metapage*.

Below the map, I created separate organizer pages containing URL links to a resource library of interactive materials such as relevant documentary radio programs archived on the Web; video clips of television documentaries and travel programs about the phenomenon of cross-cultural world pilgrimage; Middle English pronunciation sound files (see *Geoffrey Chaucer Page*); *Geoffrey Chaucer Hath a Blog* (Bryant) and Baba Brinkman's rap adaptations of select Canterbury tales. In evaluative feedback, the class consistently finds the map as organizing device effective for keeping them literally "on track" while covering the materials and for making them feel like actual pilgrims. This is excellent preparation for avatar writing assignments, in which they role-play as medieval pilgrims.

Because the heavy use of electronic content requires certain software (*QuickTime, RealPlayer*) to access the materials, I provide live links to sites where necessary software is freely downloadable. I dedicate a message board, the "General Forum," as a space where technological problems are reported and then addressed by technical staff and where any confusion about assignments or deadlines is articulated and answered. Once taught a few times, the most frequently asked questions can be stated and answered in a separate FAQ page.

Recuperating the Social Dimension

The missing social dimension of a hundred percent face-to-face course can be regained through online message boards or chat rooms in which the students post responses to the text and to one another. However, without the immediacy of hearing vocal intonation or seeing facial expressions and body language afforded by face-to-face contact, students are still unsure about which seldom-seen face is responsible for which expressed opinion, a detriment to true engagement. Moreover, not seeing the students twice a week literally prevents the instructor from connecting names to faces. To offset these byproducts of blended learning, I take digital photographs of all enrolled students on the first face-to-face class day and place these in a gallery of the CMS that is accessible to the entire class. Each photograph lists the owner's real name and the name of his or her avatar and displays the pilgrim badges earned as rewards for completing readings, writing projects, or other requirements. These virtual badges, scanned thumbnail icons of medieval pilgrim badges, both ensure the participants' continued engagement by rewarding them for completing tasks and keep the students competitively aware of what their cohort has accomplished, thus inspiring them to surpass their peers. The imposition of required weekly online quizzes, delivered by the CMS and performed on completion of a content module, also ensures that students keep literally on track, progressing through towns on the course map and completing that week's assigned material. This competitive aspect of the course dynamic mimics the contestive spirit between Chaucer's pilgrims in the storytelling contest, the course's subject. The same is true of the avatar assignment.

Becoming a Canterbury Pilgrim

After attending a workshop about employing "gaming" in pedagogical course design for a generation of students whose learning styles were affected by video games, computer games, and role-playing board games (see Lancaster), I became convinced that it was worth experimenting with such activities in my hybrid Chaucer course (see Gee; Aldrich; Prensky). Incorporating gaming into the writing projects' design, I ask each student to adopt a medieval pilgrim identity, whether one of Chaucer's textual pilgrims or added characters such as Margery Kempe, Julian of Norwich, King Richard II, John of Gaunt, Joan of Kent, an Arab or Muslim, and a Jew. The extra women compensate for the mere triad of female pilgrims among Chaucer's almost exclusively male cast. The Jew and Muslim, reflecting characters in certain tales, contribute a multicultural dimension to the experiment. All add richness to students' online interactions and variety to the written assignments produced in their avatars' "voices." These noncanonical additions also resonate with issues about the othering of women, Arabs, and Jews in medieval society, which can be explored when discussing the Man of Law's and Prioress's tales. Students research their avatars for the first several weeks within the text of Chaucer's *Canterbury Tales* (in the General Prologue portraits, the links, and the tales themselves), in books about medieval life and culture on reserve in the library, and in online resources. Having created self-designed personae, in whose voices they write, students contribute postings responding to a series of prompts. They upload these to a CMS message board accessible to all class members.

The first prompt is titled "Tell Me about Yourself." Assuming the identity of the historical Chaucer, I provide a first-person voiced model for their responses, conveying professional data about Chaucer's life as a civil servant; personal revelations about home, marriage, and family; and musings about his authorial avocation. The students are instructed to be creative but are warned that their five-hundred-word postings are evaluated according to how much and how well students convey what they have learned through their close reading of the text and their research about their avatar's character and profession. That is, the student impersonating the pilgrim Miller, for example, must reveal not only the professional duties and reputation of medieval millers but also the personal peccadilloes of Chaucer's Robyn. I encourage them to include in their discourse the language (where possible, in Middle English words) and tone appropriate to their character, whether foul or fair.

The invented avatars—Muslim, Jew, king, aristocrat, female mystic—must supply plausible rationales for why they have joined the usual suspects of this group of "sondry folk" making a *Christian* pilgrimage to Canterbury (GP, line 25). These creative responses have posited historically credible excuses for the presence of non-Christians or an anchoress on the pilgrimage. Because these postings are publicly available for all class members to read (and their next posting assignment requires that they read most, if not all, of their peers' postings), the students take special ownership of their course participation, and, like Chaucer's own pilgrims, they become competitive about the quality and content of their personal narratives. This ensures a caliber of writing seldom seen in traditional "term paper" assignments performed by previous nonhybrid Chaucer classes.

The next prompt is, "Respond to the first posting of another avatar in your avatar's voice"—scheduled several weeks after the first posting to allow the students time to read the postings and decide to whom and how to respond. This assignment has inspired lively interaction between the students in their role-playing, as lively as the "quyting" between Chaucer's original pilgrims in *The Canterbury Tales*' links. Postings are evaluated on the appropriateness of their avatar's way of addressing someone of a particular profession or social class, the information about both avatars with which they pack their messages, and the tone adopted in the discourse of their avatars' voices.

A third prompt requires that avatars undertake another virtual pilgrimage after exploring links to electronic materials about cross-cultural pilgrimage provided in the CMS resource library. These can include medieval Christian and non-Christian pilgrimages as well as modern pilgrimages to sites associated with popular culture icons (Elvis, the Beatles, Jim Morrison). This posting takes the form of a diary entry, a letter home to another pilgrim, or a blog entry like those on *Geoffrey Chaucer Hath a Blog*. The responses are fascinating and varied, drawing on almost endless permutations of medieval pilgrims and sites of transnational, transtemporal world pilgrimage. This assignment adds another multicultural dimension to the course, a dimension of which, I believe, Chaucer would approve, since it mirrors the othered religions and settings of various tales. The assignment permits forward time travel, a counterpart to the Knight's and Wife of Bath's tales, which travel backward temporally from Chaucer's fourteenth century.

The last prompt, in the semester's final week, is, "Choose the winning Canterbury tale in Harry Bailly's game, not from the Host's point of view, but in your avatar's judgment, and defend your selection." This prompt inspires myriad choices and defenses. By this time, students have finished *The Canterbury Tales* and are assessing the range of Dryden's "God's plenty" found in the fictional characters and the narrative moves of the pilgrim tellers. In a semester that has special focus on undergraduate research, students are required to contribute an article to a medieval magazine as though such a genre existed in the period. The article should be researched and written in the voice of their avatar. After they pitch two separate ideas from their avatar's point of view about subjects their avatar would be interested in or knowledgeable about, the magazine's editor (the instructor) gives the green light to the most feasible and researchable idea. The results are inventive, informed, and fun to grade: the Plowman writing about how to construct fieldstone walls, Richard II publishing a eulogy for Anne of Bohemia, the Physician writing a column about avoiding the Black Death. In all postings and magazine articles, rules of punctuation, spelling (except for Middle English words), and sentence structure are strictly observed and graded. The avatar role-playing postings and researched articles are hugely successful. Students take ownership of *The Canterbury Tales* and medieval English culture. Because they are so personally engaged with the writing projects, they earn grades usually at least one letter higher than for their traditional critical papers.

Special Challenges in Middle English Language Courses

The undergraduate Chaucer course is an intensive literature class about texts created in a culture located across an ocean and over six centuries removed from contemporary American students. The texts are written in a distant ancestor of modern English. Literary themes and genres are unfamiliar and exclusive to the period (fabliau, dream vision, beast fable, hagiography). Teaching temporally remote and geographically distant material in a regular face-to-face class is challenging enough, necessitating extensive show-and-tell of pictures, film clips, and music to render the Middle Ages less foreign. Much more challenging is the task of keeping students engaged when the material is presented through distance learning, which adds yet another layer of "distance" from the course content.

With half the usual face-to-face time, how does one cover a representative selection of Canterbury tales; Middle English pronunciation; specific medieval literary genres; cultural, religious, and political developments unique to Chaucer's time; conventions of medieval visual arts; the impetus to pilgrimage; and unique aspects of medieval Christianity? For every eighty-minute face-to-face class period, the hybrid instructor must invent electronic course content that substitutes for normal coverage in the second online eighty-minute class segment. This requires thinking creatively outside the box. Materials must be either available through links to other online sites or generated ex nihilo by the instructor, aided by technologically adept support staff.

Enhancing the Class "Handout" for Electronic Delivery

One seemingly obvious solution is to post electronic versions of the traditional paper handouts distributed in the face-to-face classroom, covering topics often supplemented by the instructor's impromptu minilectures. As Elliott Masie notes, in the face-to-face classroom, sparely outlined bullet points are clarified by the instructor's provision of context (an anecdote, an illustrative textual example) or questions raised by class members. Removed from human delivery and reception (often what learners best remember) and thus devoid of context, the content of such handouts can be meaningless when delivered in isolation online. For some learning styles, context trumps content (see Masie). When delivered in a *PowerPoint* presentation with interpolated and illustrative scanned images from medieval manuscripts, photos of medieval sites, and other visual enrichments, electronic handouts become context rich and interactive. Words and images can be effectively combined in the equivalent of an illustrated lecture created with Web-based page-editing software. I created such Web-page handouts about medieval pilgrimage costumes and customs, medieval gardens, and other relevant topics and stored them in the CMS resource library, the repository for all online course materials.

Enrichment through Aural Resources: Podcasts

Another way of adding the human dimension and all-important context to electronic handouts is to augment the *Word* document that constitutes the handout with recorded voice-over commentary by the instructor in the form of a podcast. Although it does not completely replicate the spontaneity of face-to-face discourse, a voice contributes a human dimension, allowing the instructor to emphasize with intonation what is important, thus providing the impromptu context that, Masie insists, is more memorable to certain learners (24). Sound provides human immediacy and missing context to otherwise dry, print-delivered, literally distant online instruction. A usefully portable and almost universal electronic vehicle for delivery of course material voiced by instructors or other experts is the personal electronic device, the most ubiquitous being Apple's iPod (see Levy). According to a survey of one hundred college campuses, the iPod is more popular among college students than beer ("Survey"). The device's portability permits students to listen to podcasts beyond the classroom, the library, or their personal computers. Used in the Chaucer course, podcasts can include content lectures, voice-overs supplementing visual images, voice-overs that accompany electronic textual segments of Chaucer's *Canterbury Tales* and provide pronunciation help or annotation of difficult Middle English terms, or verbal supplements to pictorially enhanced *PowerPoint* slide lectures. All these formats can be exported as movie files for seamless viewing or listening. When downloaded to personal electronic devices, audio podcasts permit students to listen to the materials repeatedly and anytime. For students for whom repetition is the most effective learning style, podcasts are more valuable than listening face-to-face to a live but immediately ephemeral lecture, notwithstanding accurate note taking.

I created two different types of podcast lectures. In one type, facing a webcam, I filmed myself talking to the computer screen, as if to a live class, about whatever topic was on the agenda of that week's module. I uploaded to the CMS the saved film clip of the video lecture as a compressed movie. The technical staff streamed the files and made them available as audio and video podcasts, which the students could listen to, watch on their computers, or download to their devices as sound or video files. Seeing their instructor's face, as if a talking head on a TV documentary, lends students immediacy and the human connection usually missing in online courses.

Another kind of podcast lecture is composed of a sequence of *PowerPoint* slides, each containing about ten lines of Middle English text centered on the slide with certain words or phrases color-highlighted and digital images illustrating the text chunk positioned marginally. In the Prioress's portrait, I highlighted *wimple* and inserted a marginal JPEG of that headdress. Over these illustrated-text slides I recorded commentary about the passage, referring to the highlighted, easily identifiable words or phrases. The voice-over permitted slow, exaggeratedly pronounced recitation of the Middle English verse. I discussed the artists' interpretations in the included visual images, whether manuscript illuminations of pilgrims or modern illustrations of *The Canterbury Tales*. Within the textual *PowerPoint* presentation, I also inserted video files of my face talking about the text or providing segue commentary between units. I exported all *PowerPoint* presentations as movies, producing a seamless, multimodal podcast about the selected passages.

My students respond enthusiastically to both types of podcasts: some prefer seeing my facial expressions while talking about the text; others like the combination of text, image, and voice-over. A mix of both styles of podcast serves various methods of learning. Voice-overs and pronunciation audio files bridge some of the distance in distance learning. They are attractive and useful tools that the instructor can gradually add to the hybrid course's Web site over time. Although they imprint the instructor's personal stamp on a set of otherwise impersonal online instructional materials, podcasts do take considerable time to produce.

Sound Files Available Online: Radio Programs

If time does not permit creating podcasts, there are abundant relevant sound files already available on the Web. Identify these by *Google* searching paired terms, such as "Peasants' Revolt" and either "radio program" or "podcast."[1] An excellent resource for sound files substantial enough to substitute for live-delivered lectures in a face-to-face class is the archive of Melvyn Bragg's BBC-4 radio program *In Our Time*, a weekly forty-five-minute discussion of various scientific, historical, literary, or cultural topics. Bragg, serving as the host, conducts a lively conversation with academic experts on that week's subject. Accompanying archived programs (available as "listen now" format, computer downloads, or podcasts) are transcripts of the discussions and a printable record that can be used for later consultation, which is a useful complement that accommodates various learning styles and disabilities. *In Our Time*'s archived topics include several appropriate for hybrid courses in *medieval* literature—programs about Merlin, the Holy Grail, Heloise and Abelard, Robin Hood, and others. Most useful for a blended Chaucer course is *In Our Time*'s "Chaucer," a conversation about Chaucer's life and career between Bragg and three distinguished Chaucerians: Ardis Butterfield, Carolyne Larrington, and Helen Cooper. This replicates having several eminent guest lecturers address your class. Unlike a live guest appearance, however, this virtual visit is permanent and infinitely repeatable.

Learning Middle English in a Hybrid Chaucer Course

To overcome the challenge of teaching the Middle English language in only half the usual class time, I require close reading exercises, using the online *Middle English Dictionary*, to convey that the meanings of words glossed by the textbook's editor are not necessarily the only meanings of that word in context.

Rather, they are an editorial interpretation of the text. Using the online *MED*, the students can explore the complex nuances of Chaucer's language from any computer connected to the Internet, thus bridging the distance endemic to the blended learning experience.

In the first weeks, students are taught how to use the online *MED* through a podcast composed of screen captures with voice-over, which leads them through the steps required to look up a word's denotations. Each week, they are assigned three Middle English words to search for in the *MED*, and at least one question on the weekly required quiz is tied to those words' denotations, thus ensuring that they consult the *MED* for weekly homework. This exercise leads directly to a midterm writing assignment, a one-thousand-word critical paper conducting a close reading of one of a group of important passages from the Knight's Tale and the Miller's Tale, using only the resources of the *MED* to substantiate the argument. Both the *MED* exercise and the close reading paper thoroughly immerse the students in Chaucer's language and provide a linked writing project that, along with the avatar postings, ensure internal cohesion in the assignments and desirable stability in a potentially chaotic distance-learning experience.

Final Thoughts

I believe that my students receive a richer experience about Chaucer's period and artistic productions than time would allow me to present in a hundred percent bricks-and-mortar classroom presentation. Since the students theoretically have heard my podcasts as their homework, the single weekly face-to-face meeting, reserved exclusively for discussion, has yielded the best classroom exchanges I've experienced in thirty-five years of teaching Chaucer. Both anecdotal and documented feedback from students suggest that they appreciate and use the myriad materials I create and constantly augment. They report watching videos or listening to podcasts at odd times, often in the middle of the night, when physical libraries are closed. Overall, I highly recommend undertaking this pedagogical pilgrimage. One caveat: allow sufficient time to develop the online content, research activities, and writing projects. The possibilities for expansion and enrichment of the course are as infinite as the Internet itself. The increasingly rapid changes in available technological tools multiply the options accessible to instructors for creating exciting interactive course content. The internal camera and microphone included in most computers now render podcast making almost child's play. These developments make possible increasingly successful experiences in teaching Chaucer in the hybrid format.

NOTE

[1] For sound files describing the causes and effects of the 1381 Peasants' Revolt, see "Voices."

Public Chaucer: Multimedia Approaches to Teaching Chaucer's Middle English Texts

Martha W. Driver

> So we ask of our new electronic tools: can you also help us to see and understand (in a Blakean sense) works of imagination, can you "advance our learning" of such works? And we ask ourselves: how might we manipulate these new tools to meet these special desires and requirements?
>
> (McGann 145–46)

Jerome McGann raised these questions in 2004, and we are still in the exciting process of answering them. This essay provides a brief overview of pedagogical approaches I use to teach Chaucer at Pace University in New York City, approaches that include filming, videoconferencing, and performance in the online virtual environment *Second Life*. Though it may seem counterintuitive, an expanded awareness of perceived audience, developed through multimedia approaches, inspires students to focus more intently on Chaucer's texts. Through the use of a variety of tools, students become deeply engaged with Chaucer and with medieval studies more generally.

For their final examination in spring 2006, students in my undergraduate Chaucer class were asked to prepare a favorite passage of more than eight lines from the short poems, *The Canterbury Tales*, or *Troilus and Criseyde*. They were to practice reading the passage aloud in Middle English and then, in a fifteen-minute presentation to the instructor, explain its meaning, its context, and why they chose it. Without telling the students beforehand, I hired a cameraman to film the examination. The filming of twenty students took about six hours to complete.

My main purpose in filming students reading Chaucer aloud was to emphasize the value of experiencing the text in Middle English, Chaucer's original medium, rather than relying on modern translations. At the beginning of the term, students were provided with basic guidelines on how to pronounce Middle English and were asked to consult several sections of the *Geoffrey Chaucer Page*, hosted by Harvard University, including "Chaucer's Language," "Middle English," and "Teach Yourself Chaucer." Students also listened to the recording of "Truth," which was the first poem read aloud in class. Students heard selected tapes from Brigham Young University's *Chaucer Studio* and watched clips, in modern and Middle English versions, from Jonathan Myerson's animated *Canterbury Tales*, made for the BBC in 1998. Students were encouraged to read aloud in class and also at home to better understand Chaucer's mastery of meter, verse forms, and sound as well as to develop basic comprehension and understand the etymology of modern words related to Middle English terms.

Subsequent classes have watched film clips of their predecessors. Through peer modeling, undergraduate students are encouraged to feel comfortable with reading Middle English aloud. In addition to showing, as I had hoped, that most of the Chaucer students had prepared sensitive interpretations that demonstrated their mastery of the meaning of Middle English (if not always its precise pronunciation), the filming experiment had several unexpected outcomes. Students tended to be very relaxed on camera and thoughtful in their responses to questions. The presence of a cameraman brought a third dimension into play, and students performed their best for the camera. (Could this be because students are members of the *YouTube* generation?) They were also revealing in a way they had not necessarily been in the classroom. A case in point was the student who chose to read the lines of the old man from the Pardoner's Tale and related them profoundly, simply, and sensitively to the death of her father, which she had not previously mentioned during the semester. While I have shown an hour or two of this film to subsequent Chaucer classes, a shorter clip is posted for student use on the *Blackboard* course management system and can also be accessed by anyone on *YouTube* (see *Students Reading Chaucer*).

The Chaucer film is one aspect of my ongoing interest in teaching medieval studies with multimedia, developed originally in 1996 with the inception of a course called *Beowulf* to *Lear*: Text, Image and Hypertext, in which freshmen and sophomore students studying Chaucer in a larger survey of medieval literature were encouraged to make Web sites incorporating their essays and to engage in *Blackboard* discussion and videoconferencing with students studying some of the same texts at other educational institutions (see Driver). Traditionally, students write for one person, the teacher, who is assumed to know more about the topic than the student; it is easy to understand why, in these conventional formal essays, students are not focused on guiding their readers and helping to interpret texts for them. In the *Beowulf* to *Lear* lab classes, students and teachers were the immediate audience, but when the student Web sites were posted on the Internet, the audience immediately and dramatically broadened. Because their work would be made available to the world, students were inspired to revise, edit, and expand their essays, and they also created some imaginative page designs to reflect their critical responses to the literature.

For several years, students in my classes met with students studying the same texts at Western Michigan University through videoconference and on *Blackboard*. The purpose of these exercises was to bring students into a larger learning community across institutions. In 2007, my *Beowulf* to *Lear* class met virtually and through videoconference with a class called Heroes: Text and Hypertext, taught by Carrie Griffin and Orla Murphy at University College, Cork, Ireland (UCC) (see *Heroes*). Students prepared for our three meetings (which included a discussion of the Wife of Bath's Tale) by studying the texts, directed in part by specific questions for consideration. Both classes posted on one *Blackboard* site to which all students had access.

This experiment worked very well because of the commitment and excellent preparation of my colleagues at UCC (and the outstanding technology staff at both institutions). One Pace student commented that videoconferencing enriched the learning experience because she heard new and "foreign" interpretations of the texts by her Irish peers. The Irish students tended to read the Wife of Bath as a not altogether attractive exhibitionist and renegade, while she was seen as a powerful widow and a sensitive storyteller by the American students (who had also read John Gower's analogue, "Sir Florent," and the anonymous "Wedding of Sir Gawain and Dame Ragnell"). The energy generated by preparation and performance in the videoconferences carried over to the standard classroom, and several students commented that our New York City class became closer and more focused as the discussions became more lively and competitive. Motivated by friendly rivalry, students in both groups became adept at quoting and arguing from the Middle English text. Further, students in both classes came to the realization that the concepts and texts discussed in one classroom may have a wider and sometimes a different meaning and relevance for another audience, depending on context. Again, careful study of Chaucer's original text was the key.

Chaucer's text was also central to a third recent experiment, undertaken by students at Pace: a pilgrimage through *Second Life*. *Second Life* is a virtual medium consisting of simulated environments (sims) in which avatars can participate in various activities; for the Chaucerian avatars, these included jousting, playacting, fencing, riding, and weaving, while some students also opted to attend Mass. (*Second Life* offers a range of churches and cathedrals in several denominations. Some sims, for example Renaissance Island, include the Mass in reenacting historical coronations and pageants. Students and their professor have attended mass in *Second Life*.) The students were charged with adopting a Canterbury pilgrim, reporting on that pilgrim to the class, and writing conventional essays and a research paper on related themes. They were asked further to develop their pilgrim as a *Second Life* avatar—to become their pilgrim, in effect—and to visit various *Second Life* medieval sites. As avatars, students were instructed to employ quotations from Chaucer and to discuss subjects appropriate to their characters. (The Miller and the Reeve were cautioned that their *Second Life* interactions had to remain PG-13!) Students participated in two plays at one of the four Globe Theaters in *Second Life*. The first performance of Shakespearean scenes drawn from Chaucer included other avatars in Thailand, England, Canada, and the United States, all onstage simultaneously.[1]

To create their avatars and tell their stories in *Second Life*, the students perused primary as well as secondary sources and also studied the illuminations in the Ellesmere manuscript and woodcuts illustrating *The Canterbury Tales* available online. They used Chaucer's text to find out how to shape details of their avatar's costume and personality. For the final class, students performed as their Canterbury pilgrims onstage at the *Second Life* Globe, not only for our class but for other onlookers. In this case again, the audience for student work was expanded, and students responded by reading Chaucer closely and carefully. One said, "[*Second Life*] provided me with the unique opportunity to visualize and contextualize the Franklin while constantly asking . . . what he would have done, all of which enriched my learning experience exponentially" (Ingenthron). Another remarked, "As I designed a female knight in a virtual environment, it was especially important to focus on textual evidence in order to create an avatar that stayed true to Chaucer's Knight while becoming an updated twenty-first century interpretation" (LeFebvre).

By emulating their peers on film and developing a sense of a larger audience through videoconferencing, *Blackboard* discussion, and performance in *Second Life*, students are encouraged to engage in the pleasure of reading Chaucer in Middle English. The public nature of these media, whether one is posting on *Blackboard* or talking across oceans, seems to advance learning, as McGann foresaw. But most important, though students are adept manipulators of technology, they also learn that many of the answers they seek are "in the book." The main emphasis remains on Chaucer's poetry as twenty-first-century students use new tools to experience anew the sweet delights of Chaucer's genius.

NOTE

[1] See Driver and Ray. The actors onstage with the students from outside the university were college professors, teachers, librarians, and, in one case, a trained theatrical actor.

Chaucer's Pilgrims in Cyberspace

Florence Newman

Chaucer's Canterbury pilgrims engage in one of the most common forms of medieval entertainment, telling tales. In this process of storytelling, they reveal something of their own personalities, backgrounds, and outlooks on life. Were the pilgrims of the General Prologue to be miraculously transported to the modern era, they would likely entertain one another and express themselves not only by storytelling but also by creating *Facebook* pages. This premise underlies a project that I assign in my upper-division undergraduate Chaucer course: students are asked to create a *Facebook*-style Web page for one of the pilgrims whose tales we will be reading for class. As with actual social networking sites, the pilgrims' personal pages branch out in various ways to connect to the online presence of other characters. The project evolves with the sequential unfolding of the tales as the pilgrims' prologues, tales, and epilogues add greater depth and complexity to the original portraits and as relationships emerge between characters and between tales. College-age students find the format familiar and get to exercise their creativity and sense of humor while developing their knowledge and understanding of the text. Because the generation of content is in their hands, students are motivated to continue the process of discovery for themselves.

While it is theoretically possible to construct individual and group sites on *Facebook*, we use our course *Blackboard/LearnOnline* site, which provides student pages, group pages, and a collective discussion board (the equivalent of a member's "wall" in *Facebook*), all under the instructor's control and without the privacy issues and other complications of actual social-networking sites. The three major components of the project are the pilgrims' home pages, group pages, and essays titled "A Reply to My Critics," which students post to the discussion board. The goals for the project are to demonstrate knowledge of critical studies of *The Canterbury Tales* and their historical and cultural contexts, as well as to encourage the students' connectivity and stimulate their imaginations. In addition to laying out the components of the project and the schedule for completing them, the assignment sheet indicates that I am counting on the class to come up with other ideas for fulfilling the learning goals, given that most students are more media savvy than I. The sheet also includes this note: "A certain amount of anachronism in the content of the pages may be inevitable (and fun), but your pilgrims should remain fourteenth-century characters and not modern ones." The project thus attempts to strike a balance between a Chaucerian spirit of playfulness and an academic attention to accuracy and verisimilitude.

Each pilgrim's basic page presents the information found in the General Prologue as the pilgrim himself or herself might present it under such headings as "Employment," "Interests and Activities," "Relationships," and

"Favorite Links." The first-person point of view offers a different approach to the portraits, which is particularly valuable for students who have previously studied the General Prologue. Students are encouraged to use the explanatory notes in our text, the *Riverside Chaucer*, and sources such as Laura Lambdin and Robert Lambdin's *Chaucer's Pilgrims* to elucidate details such as the Wife of Bath's gapped teeth and to place the pilgrim's profession or vocation in its medieval historical context. The picture for the profile sometimes is the Ellesmere illumination of that pilgrim or a photograph of the student in medieval costume. To show the possibilities of a personal page, I have devised a sample profile for the Host of the Tabard Inn, Harry Bailly, whose employment is, of course, in "the hospitality industry" (see the figure below). Students are required to have posted their basic profiles by the day that those pilgrims' portraits are due for discussion; the pages can be revised and developed, however, as we read more of *The Canterbury Tales*.

"Friending" takes place through groups, which can be easily assembled in *Blackboard*. At the request of students, the instructor can create, name, and assign group pages. The groups grow as affiliations among the pilgrims become apparent: the Pardoner joins the Monk and the Physician in "The Southwark

---

HARRY BAILLY

I am the proprietor of the legendary Tabard Inn, famed for its hospitality and its delicious Southwark ale. Our lodgings for weary travelers are commodious (only three to a bed!), and our cakes and meat pies are always the freshest. People often describe me as "jovial": I'm so eager to see that guests have a good time that sometimes I will take four or five days off work to accompany a party of pilgrims to Canterbury, even if it means risking the displeasure of that shrew Goodelief . . . er, I mean, Goodelief, my beloved wife.

http://www.godecookery.com/afeast/brew/brew012.html

Education and Work: Apprenticed at age *ten*; Innkeeper
Status: Married (alas!)
Activities and Interests: Games and contests, traveling, tales of *sentence* and *solas* (especially *solas*), return customers

---

Fig. Harry Bailly's Web profile

Investment Society," the Clerk congregates with the Prioress and the Parson in "The Thomas à Becket Fan Club," and "The Sins of the Tavern Book Club" forms after discussion of the Pardoner's Tale. The group pages have typically been the least active component of the pilgrim project, but members do post messages and create relevant links (e.g., a link on the "Thomas à Becket Fan Club" site to a translation of Edward Grim's account of the archbishop's death). Furthermore, the very conception of such groups involves interpreting the text (does the Franklin have a drinking problem or not?) and recognizing similarities and differences across the text (what forms of religious devotion are represented by the various pilgrims?). If speculations get out of hand, I can intervene to offer corrective or historicizing comments (e.g., the Franklin's morning "sop in wyn" would not have been an unusual breakfast for a wealthy individual in the fourteenth century [GP, line 334]).

The third portion of the project, "A Reply to My Critics," consists of a document that is written from the perspective of the pilgrim and summarizes two or three interpretive approaches to, or critical controversies regarding, the pilgrim's prologue and tale. It then offers a response to each (e.g., this critic is on the right track; this critic misunderstood me completely). The document serves the same purpose as a conventional critical survey but again with a slant both creative and "Chaucerian," in that the writer impersonates a fictional character who engages in an ongoing debate about the purpose and effect of literary art. For the summary of critical discussion, students consult the same reserve materials and databases that they would for a research paper, although the nature of the assignment favors general overviews like those found in the variorum editions of Chaucer's works. The document (500–750 words) is posted to a forum on the course discussion board, where other students can see and comment on it. Each "Reply" essay is due by the date the class is scheduled to read and discuss the pilgrim's prologue or tale, so the person who prepared the document can be called on to report what he or she learned about select scholarly interpretations. Perhaps because of the title of the piece, the response portion of the assignment often takes issue with standard approaches. For example, one student, speaking as the Summoner, vigorously attacks the line of criticism suggesting that his tale betrays his own anger and hypocrisy as much as it indicts that of Friar Thomas (J. Desmond). The student as Summoner singles out Charles A. Owen's claim that "the habit of exempla betrays the Summoner's anger as well as Chauntecleer's pedantic delight in the sound of his own voice" ("Morality" 231). He accuses such critics of unnecessary abstraction and a failure to attend to the literal meaning of the tale's antifraternalism, and he warns Owen by name to check his mail regularly, since a "Significavit" (order for imprisonment under canon law) may be arriving soon (GP 662). Despite its pugnacious tone, the "Summoner's" response brings together knowledge of the pilgrim's portrait, familiarity with critical opinion, and a thoughtful (if tongue-in-cheek) objection to viewing the tales more as reflections of their tellers than as narratives in their own right.

One obvious drawback of the assignment is the finite number of pilgrims with portraits in the General Prologue who also tell tales later: in other words, the project works best with a class of fewer than twenty students. The same pilgrim can be assigned to more than one student, however, and characters who have a tale but no General Prologue portrait, like the Nun's Priest or the Canon's Yeoman, could have a hypothetical profile constructed on the basis of their estates and occupations. The virtue of placing Chaucer's pilgrims in cyberspace is that the project can expand and contract depending on students' interests and the class size; the pilgrim pages and group pages could even be assigned on their own at the high school or junior high school level. Students become enthusiastically engaged by the creative aspect of the project at the same time that they are strengthening their critical skills and acquiring knowledge of Chaucer's most famous work. And as I witness a virtual community of twenty-first-century pilgrims emerging within the community of the classroom, I gain a greater appreciation of my students' ability to internalize and reinvent the Canterbury pilgrims in a modern medium.

Translating *The Canterbury Tales* into Contemporary Media

Timothy L. Stinson

In this essay, I describe an assignment that asks students to recast selections from *The Canterbury Tales* into genres and time periods familiar to them (for example, situational comedies, talk shows, news magazine programs) in order to help them understand the dramatic nature of the tales and to experience the processes of recomposition and reinterpretation integral to medieval authorship. The theatricality of many of the pilgrims in *The Canterbury Tales* is widely acknowledged, from the Pardoner's sermon to the Wife of Bath's self-presentation in her prologue. The narratives of many of the tales, meanwhile, are borrowed directly from the works of earlier poets and were often themselves reworked by Chaucer's followers. These medieval texts and acts of textual transmission have strong parallels in the recombinant nature of electronic texts and in the notion that anyone can copy, alter, edit, and retransmit a document—all of which most of our students experience daily. Many of these features also translate well to other media such as video and film.

Chaucer was very fond of moving stories from one environment to another and of combining multiple stories or genres in one work. This can be a difficult concept to demonstrate, however, when students are unfamiliar with the genres and narrative conventions in play. For example, telling students that the Nun's Priest's Tale is a fusion of beast fable and mock heroic tragedy interwoven with courtly romance conventions and encyclopedic traditions or that the Knight's Tale features an admixture of Boccaccian epic and Boethian philosophy has little clarifying effect on its own. Thus I prepare my students for the task of recasting these stories in new genres and settings by providing source texts that help them gain familiarity with how Chaucer reworked other writers.[1] These provide important context, allowing students to understand Chaucer's processes of composition and helping them decipher some of the many allusions and casual learned asides that populate his works. Studying how Chaucer reworked his sources also prepares students to become participants in the types of authorial activities commonly found in medieval literature, including redaction, synthesis, and transformation. As Mary Hamel has argued, "Few if any Middle English texts . . . were 'original' in the sense 'not derived from something else'; the expectation was that any Middle English work would be derivative to a greater or lesser degree" (204). Appropriating, splicing, altering, and adapting narratives are the very acts through which many of the tales were written, and they are activities at which our students can be admirably adept.

I ask students to participate in these authorial processes by working in groups to produce short skits or videos that translate tales of their choosing to new genres (many university libraries will lend video cameras). Student responses to this assignment frequently show an understanding of the medieval narrative, how it might be conveyed thoughtfully in contemporary genres, and the ways in which retelling a narrative emphasizes some aspects of sources while deemphasizing others, just as Chaucer did with his own. For example, in one class two groups chose to transform the Knight's Tale into popular television genres. The first placed the narrative within a talk show format, focusing on the interpersonal strife between Palamon and Arcite as well as the bewilderment of Emily. Each character was interviewed, and Theseus, the talk show host and moderator, attempted to negotiate the love triangle and explore the sincerity (or lack thereof) of each person's feelings. The second group, meanwhile, recast the story as an episode of the sitcom *The Office*, in which the cousins are first detained on charges of corporate espionage and then discover and quarrel over their mutual attraction to Emily. This reworking explored the ways in which the thematic concerns of epic or medieval romance tend to deflate when moved to other genres (just as Chaucer himself shows in the Nun's Priest's Tale) and drew upon the inherent humor that modern audiences often find in the conventions of courtly love. Each of these projects demonstrated an awareness of how the genre in which an author recasts a narrative alters the emphasis placed on certain aspects of that narrative.

The assignment also offers students an opportunity to explore and respond to the rich characterization found in *The Canterbury Tales*, as demonstrated when one group presented an elaborate mock documentary of the Wife of Bath as an episode of *E! True Hollywood Story*. She was reimagined as a small-town girl who used her wits and charm to marry a series of older Tinseltown executives. Although they die mysteriously, leaving the Wife increasingly wealthy and well connected, she is never convicted of wrongdoing and continues to gain experience and money while being the subject of gossip and intrigue. As with Chaucer's original character, the one created by the students is fully imagined; her traits are seen from a wide variety of perspectives, including that of the Wife herself; her former teachers, friends, and roommates; and a recent succession of young lovers with whom she has had violent public feuds.

This assignment encourages students to interact with the tales on numerous levels, as can be seen in the example of a group that adapted the Nun's Priest's Tale. The tale is a famously deft interweaving of diverse medieval genres and thematic foci. At the level of an animal fable that tells the story of a proud, amorous rooster who is tricked by—and in turn tricks—a sly fox, the story has an immediate appeal to students reading it for the first time. But there is much interspersed throughout this tale that is challenging and quite foreign. We have a fox who quotes Boethius, a discussion of the influence of the humors on health, references to medieval rhetoricians and grammarians, classical allusions, dream theory from the fifth-century philosopher Macrobius, and more. While the students' affections for the fable provide a good point of departure, instructors also have quite a bit of work to do to bridge the alterities that twenty-first-century readers encounter in this tale, including a host of scholarly allusions, a mash-up of overlapping genres, and a cornucopian display of literary techniques.

The group responded to this polyphony by recasting the tale as a *60 Minutes*–style news-magazine program. The subject of dreams and their problems and treatments thus became the subject of investigative journalism. Are dreams able to tell the future? Do they have physical causes? Do dreams hold a power that we can harness to help ourselves? The skit featured a nervous young man in the role of Chauntecleer, who could not sleep because of his nighttime dreams and daytime anxieties. An urban dweller, he is fearful of violent crimes and troubled by visions of being mugged on the street. His condition is worsened by a steady diet of violent television programming, junk food, and questionable self-help books. The part of Pertelote is transformed into a psychiatrist with an interest in alternative herbal therapies. The nervous young man's dreams prove prophetic when he is approached by a mugger (the fox) who first convinces him that they know each other from a party and then produces a handgun. But the situation is reversed when the protagonist alleges that the mugger has no pizzazz—he mugs with no style and handles his weapon ungracefully. Concerned over his image, the mugger hands over the weapon for some style pointers, and the tables are turned.

In this example, the students showed a clever understanding of the medieval work of fiction in their recasting of it. They were able to deliver conventions of programs like *60 Minutes* to a knowing and appreciative audience and to weave in other generic conventions as well: the exchange between mugger and would-be victim was more sitcom than news programming. They understood that today's expert on dreams would be a psychiatrist, and thus the narrator read bits of Freud in the voice-over, for certainly he has taken the place of Macrobius in our minds as a household name concerning the interpretation of dreams. And whereas Chauntecleer delivers a series of stories or vignettes related to dreams from Cicero, the Bible, and books on dream theory, the students rendered this as a series of narratives from more familiar sources, including a Lifetime movie, a self-help book, and the evening news. In producing these parallels, the students were engaged critically with the tale: How was it assembled and from what parts? How does it use the knowledge and experiences of its audience for both humor and instruction? What current texts, genres, and medical theories parallel those from Chaucer's day? As these students were able to demonstrate, this assignment provides a useful model for engaging with medieval texts, a new incentive for close reading that supplements traditional research and writing assignments, and a deeper understanding of both the dramatic nature of *The Canterbury Tales* and the ways in which medieval authors used their source texts.

NOTE

[1] Some student editions, such as the Norton, edited by Kolve and Olson, contain such source texts in appendixes. See also Correale and Hamel; R. Miller.

Digitizing Chaucerian Debate

Alex Mueller

In an attempt to enhance classroom discussion and improve student writing in my early British literature survey course, I tested the use of a blog. I selected the sparest template available, authorized only the basic functions of posting and commenting, and assigned the blog the (admittedly bland) title of *EngL 3003W*. Unlike stimulating blogs on medieval subjects such as *In the Middle* (Cohen et al.), my course blog became populated by uninspired postings, which elicited few comments that moved beyond superficialities such as "picturing them hanging in tubs made me laugh." I soon realized that I needed to establish a dialogic structure for the blog that would compel students to engage with one another—much as the pilgrims do in *The Canterbury Tales* in their efforts to "quit" each other through tale telling. Ultimately, I became convinced that this model of Chaucerian debate offered a stimulating means of engagement with literary texts across the early British literature curriculum.

To encourage classroom dialectic, I often turn to the "quitting" structure of *The Canterbury Tales*, within which pilgrims offer requitals of previous tales that range from exuberant acclamations to raucous attacks. Within these extremes lie productive forms of correction that emerge as subtle critiques, opposing arguments, and timely (or sometimes untimely) interruptions. The now well-known *Geoffrey Chaucer Hath a Blog* embodies this spirit of corrective debate (Bryant). The (until recently) anonymous author of this blog assumes the voice of Chaucer to "endyte" ("write") on topics ranging from the composition of *Troilus and Criseyde* to the death of Heath Ledger. Even the blog's subtitle, "Take That, Gower!," champions the blogosphere as a quitting space in which incisive commentary is de rigueur. When I first encountered this blog, I suspected that its imaginative role playing and Chaucerian requital could provide a model of interaction for students, which could intensify and enrich students' discussions of difficult texts. Perhaps if I had my students impersonate literary characters, they could fully immerse themselves in their roles and quit each other through the voices of their characters.[1]

As a result, I revised my course blog and assigned it a more combative title, *Quitting Your Classmates*.[2] I also selected a more medieval-looking template for the site, which fostered the impression that students were modern-day Adam Scriveyns inscribing their author's thoughts on a hypertextual manuscript. The blog remained basic in its functioning—still no images or video clips—because I was primarily concerned with students' written dialogues. To replicate Chaucerian correction, I had students respond to each other on the blog through an avatar assigned to them during the first week of the course, which demanded that they assume the personalities, perspectives, and sometimes even the language of characters in their postings and comments. Since the course surveys both medieval and early modern literature, the avatars ranged from Beowulf to Milton's Satan. To ensure active and informed dialogues, students were required to read their characters' texts during the first week of class and contribute postings and comments periodically throughout the semester. As they wrote from their characters' points of view, students debated issues relevant to assigned texts and their characters' historical and literary moments. For example, a reader of the blog could witness an exchange in which Spenser's Sir Guyon and Chaucer's Miller discuss the merits of Queen Elizabeth's identity as a virgin queen and her claim to have a "heart and stomach of a king" (326). It soon became clear that Chaucerian quitting was a heuristic that could integrate the seemingly disparate texts of the early British literature curriculum while also illuminating the distinctions between them. The students began to see themselves as embarking on a pilgrimage with unlikely literary companions such as Grendel, Julian of Norwich, Bertilak's Lady, and Prospero.

In addition to provocative postings and debates, such as Margery Kempe's "If Only I Could Write," students happily grappled in textual combat and hatched subplots within and between texts as the course proceeded. One notable example was Satan's acquisition of Marie de France's Lanval as a knight of his retinue, an alliance that Lanval regretted once he read *Paradise Lost*. He reproached Satan in a post that inspired the following versified response from Chaucer's Miller:

> You ask why does this Lucifer go on
> With plot to take up arms against high God.
> Although he's not as strong and fit to fence
> This Satan dude has got some eloquence.
> I've never heard of such an argument
> That God above is quite a cruel tyrant.
> Now Satan's got me leaning on his side.
> Perhaps I'll send him whiskey for the ride.
> How boring and oppressive it would be
> If none did question rules and appointees.
> I'm glad this Satan's going on his way
> Though soon he'll find himself with hell to pay.

These heroic couplets are striking in the way they showcase the Miller's interruptive irreverence and confront Miltonic politics, a rhetorical feat that would have been difficult to achieve in standard classroom dialogue. Lanval's default on his demonic bond provoked Satan to follow the Miller's response with some quitting of his own:

> Dear Lanval, why all the animosity? You were happy to accept my generosity, with a wife and riches that the heavens would envy. Yet now you question and doubt when the time draws near, could this be perhaps due to some hidden fears? If God could destroy my powerful empire, why were we left alive to plot and conspire? . . . If He could destroy us, don't

you think he would? . . . If you wish to scorn us and take the enemy's side, you must return to me your riches and your bride. . . .

Miller, my good man, I would love to sit and have a drink, so you can tell me exactly what a cuckold thinks.

In rhyming prose Satan denounces Lanval's disloyalty, interrogates Milton's theology, and even establishes a new alliance with the Miller. This interaction was not the exception to the rule. In almost every case, the students embraced the identities of their avatars and produced dialogues that demonstrated close and nuanced readings of course texts and their developing proficiency in social and literary argument.

The guise of the avatar and the asynchronous nature of blogging—an important quality for my students at an urban commuter campus—afforded students safe identities and discursive modes to explore and disagree about answers to difficult questions regarding human sexuality, gender roles, and theological debates that pervade early British literature. One of the most vexed topics, unsurprisingly, was the role of women, which invited a number of passionate perspectives and surprising revelations. In the post "Don't Anger Grendel's Mom," Beowulf complains that he has been forced to grapple with an inferior foe:

Why is this? We would not expect Guenevere to take up the gauntlet and slay Mordred for the wrongs he dealt to Pendragon. . . . Why was I forced to slay a female, a mother, a woman, and not a more powerful father?

In the mock "Speech to the Troops at Tilbury," Queen Elizabeth takes up "the gauntlet" and responds with characteristic intestinal fortitude:

Although you have showed great courage in a time of crisis and dissolved the anathema plaguing the Danes, I found your remarks . . . to be ignorant and contemptuous. Let me remind you that God hath made me His instrument and the defender of my humble people . . . I have the heart, stomach, and soul of a king, a king of England with royal blood. . . . Think not that I distrust your heroic intentions; perhaps, your articulation could have been better sharpened had you some time to spare with Roger Ascham.

Identifying Beowulf as an illiterate misogynist, Queen Elizabeth offers a scathing correction that could not have come from the mouth of Wealhtheow. These pairings of unlikely rivals opened up new avenues of inquiry across literary time and space, which encouraged students to juxtapose competing viewpoints and realize the metacritical potential of these texts.

Furthermore, these debates did not remain hermetically sealed within the blogosphere. As a result of this online prewriting, classroom discussions were enriched and student papers proved to be more argumentative. To cap the course, students had an opportunity to "out" themselves in a final seminar assignment that required that they revise one of the texts on the syllabus from their avatar's point of view and share their revision and reflection on this experience with their classmates. While many students expressed their initial frustration with the difficulty of assuming a voice other than their own, they recognized and appreciated the opportunities literary impersonations provide for academic debate.

I believe that such a blog format suits what has been called the "contestive spirit" of *The Canterbury Tales* and provides an imaginative and dialogic structure for a survey course that is often connected superficially and linearly through chronology alone (Fein, Raybin, and Braeger; Knapp). By anchoring the course in Chaucerian conflict, the course texts become subject to the volatility of quitting, an inherently dramatic reading practice. As Seth Lerer puts it,

> The drama of quitting illustrates what happens when an unintended reader gets ahold of literature. Texts always escape their makers, and no protestations of will or claims to specific intention or interpretation can control how everyone will take a tale. . . . The social function of literature—the meaning of specific stories, the communal uses of the written word, the political implications of utterances—rests with us.
> (*Yale Companion* 282–83)

As the "unintended" readers of Chaucer and the rest of the early British literature curriculum, the blog avatars authorize imaginative readings and produce new texts on a pilgrimage in cyberspace.

NOTES

[1] As it turns out, I am not the only one to have this idea. See Fitzgibbons for a clever "cross-voiced" assignment that also asks students to write as Chaucerian characters.
[2] See http://blog.lib.umn.edu/muel0274/quite/; see also the more recent version at http://quittingyourclassmates.wordpress.com/.

Signature Pedagogies in Chaucer Studies

Susan Yager

In an influential 2005 essay, the educational theorist Lee S. Shulman used the term "signature pedagogies" to refer to "types of teaching that organize the fundamental ways future practitioners are educated for their professions." For example, according to Shulman, the first year of legal education in the United States is "dominated by the case dialogue method of teaching," while clinical medical training is distinctive for "the phenomenon of bedside teaching, in which a senior physician or a resident leads a group of novices" through daily rounds (52). Each of these methods helps initiates think and act like members of their respective fields. Signature pedagogies matter, according to Shulman, because they "implicitly define what counts as knowledge in a field and how things become known. They define how knowledge is analyzed, criticized, accepted, or discarded" (54).

Although Shulman's comments focused particularly on training for the professions as traditionally defined—law, medicine, and the like—many educators in the liberal arts have been quick to adapt his ideas about signature pedagogies. In history, for example, Lendol Calder has suggested the practice of "uncoverage" as a signature pedagogy, while, as can be seen in two collections, *Exploring Signature Pedagogies* (Gurung et al.) and *Exploring More Signature Pedagogies* (Chick, Haynie, and Gurung), teachers in fields from music to mathematics have made efforts to articulate field-specific pedagogical practices. In general, a field is likely to develop signature pedagogies to the degree that its expected learning outcomes (e.g., skill in arguing or ability to measure blood pressure) are both specific and broadly accepted. By contrast, the more wide-open or loosely organized a field, the more difficult it is to define a truly signature pedagogy, and literary study is currently such a field. Practices that are common among teachers of literature, such as assigning individually written papers, are found across the spectrum of liberal arts disciplines. Other classroom activities, such as close reading, lecture, and discussion, are also very widely shared. There are many ways to become liberally educated; it's difficult, therefore, to isolate a practice that is peculiar to literary study beyond the broad categories of reading, interpretation, and research.

That being the case, Chaucer studies has no signature pedagogy to compare with those in legal and medical education, certainly not if, as Shulman put it, signature pedagogies are "forms of instruction that leap to mind" when we think about a field (52). The variety of approaches and methods in the present volume, as well as its 1980 predecessor and other collections on teaching Chaucer, suggests that few specific practices are common among all Chaucerians. The Squire's declaration "[a]s many heddes, as manye wittes ther been" ("as many opinions as heads"; line 203) applies to Chaucer studies as a whole: we lecture, we encourage discussion, we use technology, we (used to) abhor technology. Indeed, as regards pedagogy, Chaucerians teach according to their varied research interests. This tendency is easiest to see in retrospect: in the first edition of this volume, Robert M. Jordan's pedagogy is rhetorical and structural, E. Talbot Donaldson's broadly humane (qtd. in Gibaldi, "Materials" 7–8, 13–14), D. W. Robertson's historical ("Intellectual"), Susan Schibanoff's feminist ("Crooked Rib"). This variety of approaches is also on display in both Tison Pugh and Angela Jane Weisl's *Approaches to Teaching Chaucer's* Troilus and Criseyde *and the Shorter Poems* and Gail Ashton and Louise Sylvester's *Teaching Chaucer*, as well as the issue of *Exemplaria* from 1996 featuring the section "Teaching Chaucer in the Nineties: A Symposium," edited by Christine Rose. There is much to be said for such diversity—each practitioner plays to his or her strengths—but little that allows us to say, *this* is what Chaucerians do.

Seen another way, however, this very multiplicity of approaches can help us begin to identify what Shulman calls the "deep structure" of a signature pedagogy. As Shulman puts it, beyond their "surface structure," or "concrete, operational acts of teaching and learning" (54), signature pedagogies also reveal a "set of assumptions about how best to impart a certain body of knowledge and know-how" as well as a set of beliefs about what matters in a discipline (55). By examining current practice, as well as the trends in teaching Chaucer that have been articulated over the past generation, we can articulate optimal ways to reach our students, blending individual preferences with a "set of assumptions" we hold in common.

Certainly one assumption shared by the contributors to this volume and to other publications on Chaucer and teaching is that, no matter the state of the humanities at any time, Chaucer remains worth learning about, both intrinsically and as part of a sophisticated reader's training. A second common notion is that the material must be conveyed or shared by experts who take their job most seriously. I think it is fair to say that an ethical, personal connection exists between Chaucerians and their field and between teachers of Chaucer and their students; we are, at least, united in the notion that we should "gladly teche" (GP, line 308). For example, in 1980 Florence Ridley described the "duty and happiness" of Chaucer teachers in helping students achieve a "sudden electric shock of recognition" (xv), while Thomas J. Garbáty defined "our job" as to "lovingly and wisely" teach Chaucer, a job in which "we dare not fail" (47). A generation later, Pugh and Weisl found a "common thread" in "the belief that an invested and concerned teacher can overcome any challenge in teaching Chaucer's literature," a challenge whose "rewards are endless" (26).

A second assumption, one that has clearly emerged over the past generation, is that the Chaucer instructor should be an intermediary when necessary, a partner when possible. In contrast to the formal lecturers of past generations, such as George Lyman Kittredge and even Donald Howard ("Idea" 59), participants in this volume are eager to employ techniques that actively engage students in studying Chaucer. In *Teaching Chaucer*, both Fiona Tolhurst (61) and Gail Ashton (106) assert this point clearly, as do Myra Seaman (97) and Emma Lipton (in this volume). Jane Chance's contribution here, emphasizing the necessity of melding teaching and research, also demonstrates the movement from teacher-centered to student-focused teaching in Chaucer studies. Other common threads that emerge from the publications on the teaching of Chaucer include immediacy, complexity, and the intellectual milieu. These elements not only underlie the variety of approaches to Chaucer in the classroom but also influence which aspects of Chaucer's work receive critical and scholarly attention.

Despite disagreements in print and in practice concerning which tales should be taught, or even whether and how to use modernizations, I think Chaucerians share a desire to have students encounter Chaucer as immediately as they can — that is, in the original dialect if possible and using not only the eye but also ear, voice, and even body. For example, William Quinn's discussion in this volume on Chaucer's fluid and complex verse stresses that we need to "look and listen still." The long-standing arguments about how heavily to edit, punctuate, and annotate Chaucer also point to this concern. Diverse opinions on these matters stem, I think, not from conflicting ideas about the value of experiencing Chaucer but from disagreements about the degree of immediacy that is possible for modern readers. Jill Mann's lightly edited *Canterbury Tales* glosses "words and phrases with which modern readers may need immediate help" (Mann, "Editor's Note" xi); Michael Murphy's modern-spelling versions could scarcely be more different from Mann's, yet they too are designed to make Chaucer "more reader-friendly to students and general readers" ("Introduction"). To help the reader toward comprehension remains a common goal.

In Ashton and Sylvester's collection, Peggy A. Knapp gives voice to the value of teaching Chaucerian complexity: "The intellectual pleasures and profits involved in a Chaucer course are inextricably entwined," she says, because "you can't learn from Chaucer's work without having fun, and you can't have fun without exploring the complexities of Chaucer's representation of felt life in late medieval England" (17). This exploration of complexity has been performed in classrooms of many theoretical stripes; thirty years ago, Ridley praised the "intentional ambiguity" that "teases, inveigles the reader into the creative process" (xii), and in this volume the essays of Holly Crocker, Roger Ladd, and Becky McLaughlin continue to explore the social, narrative, and thematic complexities of Chaucer. Further evidence of complexity as a touchstone of Chaucer pedagogy are the two editions, half a century apart, of Chaucer's sources and analogues (Bryan and Dempster; Correale and Hamel), works such as Barry Windeatt's edition of *Troilus and Criseyde*, and the long life of Kittredge's ideas about Chaucer and the dramatic and Chaucer on marriage (*Chaucer* and "Chaucer's Discussion"). The last of these, as Lipton points out in these pages, remains a classroom landmark after nearly a century.

Chaucerians have long placed great value on teaching the poet in the context of Chaucer's intellectual and historical milieu and the broader picture of medieval literature. For example, in the first edition of this volume, Emerson Brown insisted that "students know specific texts and lore if they are not to miss important aspects of Chaucer's art" (65). This value can be seen even in quite early aids to teaching. An 1899 booklet on the General Prologue, for example, begins with Chaucer's biography and a section on his "literary development" (ix), including important sources and influences. Its editor, Frank Jewett Mather, was no naïf; he warns that dating Chaucer's works rests "only upon inference" and calls the division of Chaucer's works into French, Italian, and English periods an "obvious exaggeration" (ix, xxii). Mather relied on these elements not as hard and fast facts but as heuristics for teaching. Similar heuristics for understanding Chaucer—biographies, outlines of Chaucer's chief artistic and intellectual models, and major events and trends of the fourteenth century—can be found in editions, critical work, and teaching aids throughout the twentieth century. The tradition of examining Chaucer in the light of critical and cultural context is carried on in the present volume through the contributions of Patricia Clare Ingham and Kathryn L. Lynch.

According to Shulman, signature pedagogies may change with circumstances, although the underlying assumptions may not. For example, fewer and shorter hospital stays have affected the kinds of training conducted in health fields. In Chaucer studies, developments in digital scholarship have ushered in major changes in pedagogy, though the underlying impetus of deeper learning remains. Students can learn about medieval history, Middle English, and especially visual aspects of medieval culture much more efficiently in the digital environment, and easily available digital facsimiles and editions give students a less mediated experience of the medieval manuscript than was the case a generation ago. If anything is truly dead in Chaucer studies, it is Howard's railing against "audiovisuals": "Time is wasted with the mechanics of the thing.

The teacher must sacrifice some remnant of dignity groveling for switches and plugs" ("Idea" 59). The enormous amount of innovation, even in the last decade, in teaching Chaucer digitally is on display in the last section of this volume, "*The Canterbury Tales* in the Digital Age."

Chaucerians are unlikely ever to agree on a single best way of teaching Chaucer. Underlying Chaucer scholars' multiform practices, though, is a common drive to share their expertise and their love of the field with English majors, nonmajors, and the general reader. The classroom is becoming more virtual, the atmosphere more egalitarian, and theoretical approaches more numerous, but the "joy," in Chance's words, of teaching is a constant. What then might be our signature pedagogy, the practice at the heart of Chaucer studies? Perhaps it is our constant drive to make Chaucer new, to create again the "sudden electric shock of recognition" of a poet and thinker who provides such a heady combination of enjoyment and learning.

NOTES ON CONTRIBUTORS

Peter G. Beidler is the Lucy G. Moses Distinguished Professor of English, emeritus, at Lehigh University. He has written and edited many articles and more than twenty books, including *The Wife of Bath, Masculinities in Chaucer, Chaucer's Canterbury Comedies,* and *A Student Guide to Chaucer's Middle English.* In 1983 he was named National Professor of the Year by CASE (Council for Advancement and Support of Education) and the Carnegie Foundation.

Bethany Blankenship is an associate professor of English at the University of Montana Western. Her writing on pedagogy can be found in the *Washington English Journal,* the *Montana English Journal,* and *Academic Exchange Extra.*

Michael Calabrese, professor of English, California State University, Los Angeles, has authored numerous publications on medieval literature, including *Chaucer's Ovidian Arts of Love,* "Chaucer's Dorigen and the Female Voices of the *Decameron,*" and "Being a Man in *Troilus and Criseyde* and *Piers Plowman.*" He is on the editorial board of the *Piers Plowman Electronic Archive.*

Jane Chance, Andrew W. Mellon Distinguished Professor Emerita of English at Rice University, has published twenty-two books and over a hundred articles and reviews. Among them are *The Mythographic Chaucer, Woman as Hero in Old English Literature, The Literary Subversions of Medieval Women,* and *Medieval Mythography,* for which she has now completed the third volume. She received a doctor of letters from Purdue University in May 2013. Her article on Christine de Pizan's Isis/Io appeared in *Modern Philology* in 2013.

Howell Chickering, G. Armour Craig Professor of Language and Literature at Amherst College, is the author of numerous books and essays on Old and Middle English, including *Beowulf: A Dual-Language Edition,* "Unpunctuating Chaucer," and "Comic Meter and Rhyme in the Miller's Tale."

Andrew Cole is an associate professor of English at Princeton University. He is the author and editor of such works as *The Birth of Theory; Literature and Heresy in the Age of Chaucer;* and *The Legitimacy of the Middle Ages: On the Unwritten History of Theory.*

Donna Crawford teaches literature and writing in the Department of Languages and Literature at Virginia State University. She has published several articles on the Middle English verse romances and on fourteenth-century alliterative poems.

Kara Crawford teaches secondary school in San Diego, California. She began this project while studying at Yale thanks to a grant from the National Endowment for the Humanities. She continues to include medieval literature in the secondary-level curriculum and attends academic conferences to enhance her knowledge in the field.

Holly Crocker is an associate professor of English at the University of South Carolina. Her articles have appeared in the *Chaucer Review, Exemplaria, Medieval Feminist Forum, Shakespeare Quarterly, Studies in the Age of Chaucer, SEL, 1500–1900,* and a number of edited collections. She is also the author of *Chaucer's Visions of Manhood* and editor of *Comic Provocations*. She is currently completing a book titled "The Reformation of Feminine Virtue from Chaucer to Shakespeare."

Bryan P. Davis, professor of English and director of Institutional Effectiveness and Planning at Georgia Southwestern State University, has published on the transactions between fourteenth- and fifteenth-century manuscript and literary culture, including "The Rationale for a Copy of a Text: Constructing the Exemplar for British Library Additional MS 10574," "The Prophecies of Piers Plowman in Cambridge University Library MS Gg.4.31," and "Beating the Bounds Between Church and State: Official Documents in the Literary Imagination."

Martha W. Driver is distinguished professor of English and women's and gender studies at Pace University. A cofounder of the Early Book Society for the study of manuscripts and printing history, she has authored and edited twenty-one books and journals, including *The Image in Print: Book Illustration in Late Medieval England* and the *Journal of the Early Book Society*. She is a coeditor of the Texts and Transitions book series published by Brepols.

Robert Epstein is an associate professor of English at Fairfield University. His articles and essays have appeared in *Studies in the Age of Chaucer*, the *Journal of Medieval and Early Modern Studies*, *A Companion to Gower*, and other publications, and he is coeditor of *Sacred and Profane in Chaucer and Medieval English Literature: Essays for John V. Fleming*.

Frank Grady is professor of English at the University of Missouri, St. Louis, where he teaches courses in medieval literature, literary theory, and film. He has written widely on Chaucer and his contemporaries and is a former editor of *Studies in the Age of Chaucer*.

Patricia Clare Ingham is an associate professor of English at Indiana University, Bloomington. Her research and teaching focus on Chaucer and medieval romance, drawing on psychoanalytic, postcolonial, gender, and cultural theory. She is the author of *Sovereign Fantasies: Arthurian Romance and the Making of Britain*, coeditor of *Postcolonial Moves: Medieval through Modern*, and coeditor of the journal *Exemplaria*.

Alexander L. Kaufman is an associate professor of English at Auburn University, Montgomery. His research and teaching focus on fifteenth-century literature, historical literature and the chronicle tradition, medieval outlaws, and Arthuriana. He is the author of *The Historical Literature of the Jack Cade Rebellion* and is the editor of *British Outlaws of Literature and History: Essays on Medieval and Early Modern Figures from Robin Hood to Twm Shon Catty*. He edits, with Lesley A. Coote, Ashgate's series Outlaws in Literature, History, and Culture.

Leonard Michael Koff, an associate of the UCLA Center for Medieval and Renaissance Studies, has written *Chaucer and the Art of Storytelling* and published essays on medieval literature, Ricardian literary connections, the Italian trecento, and medievalism. He is a contributor to the MLA's *Approaches to Teaching the Poetry of John Gower* and coeditor of a volume in the Brill Presenting the Past series, called *Mobs*.

Roger A. Ladd, associate professor of English and theater at the University of North Carolina, Pembroke, is the author of *Antimercantilism in Late Medieval English Literature*. He is also the director of the Graduate Program in English Education.

Jacob Lewis is currently a lecturer at the University of Arkansas, Fayetteville. He has given numerous papers on medieval English literature, especially Middle English romance, and is presently working on "Tools for Tomorrow: The Utopian Function in Middle English Literature, 1350–1420."

Emma Lipton is an associate professor at the University of Missouri, Columbia, and formerly the book review editor of *Studies in the Age of Chaucer*. She is the author of *Affections of the Mind: The Politics of Sacramental Marriage in Late Medieval English Literature* and is currently working on a book titled "Performing Justice: Law and Theology in the York Plays."

Kathryn L. Lynch, Bates/Hart Professor of English at Wellesley College, has written widely on dreams, cultural geography, and food in medieval literature. The editor of the Norton Critical Edition of Chaucer's dream visions, she has published in such journals as the *Chaucer Review*, *Studies in the Age of Chaucer*, *Speculum*, and *Exemplaria*. She is also the author of two book-length studies, *The High Medieval Dream Vision: Poetry, Philosophy, and Literary Form* and *Chaucer's Philosophical Visions*.

Becky McLaughlin is associate professor of English at the University of South Alabama, where she teaches film, gender studies, and critical theory. She has written numerous articles on literature and film using a Lacanian framework. Her book, *Everyday Theory: A Contemporary Reader*, which she edited with Bob Coleman, is a practical guide to literary theory.

Robert J. Meyer-Lee is associate professor of English at Indiana University, South Bend. He is the author of *Poets and Power from Chaucer to Wyatt* and articles on Chaucer, manuscript studies, and fifteenth-century poetry.

Alex Mueller, assistant professor of English at the University of Massachusetts, Boston, is the author of *Translating Troy: Provincial Politics in Alliterative Romance* and various articles on pedagogy and medieval literature. His current project, "Veni, Vidi, Wiki: A Prehistory of Digital Textuality," is an investigation of how premodern pedagogical modes, such as classroom disputation and manuscript commentary, inform online writing environments, such as blogs and wikis.

Florence Newman, professor emerita of English at Towson University, has delivered numerous conference papers and written various articles on the *Gawain* poet and Chaucer ("'Christ Maketh to Man,' Stanza Four: A Case for Interpolation," "*Sir Gawain* and the Semiotics of Truth") and on Medieval women writers ("Violence and Virginity in Hrotsvit's Dramas," "Strong Voice(s) of Hrotsvit: Male and Female Dialogue").

Tison Pugh is professor of English at the University of Central Florida. He is the author of *Queering Medieval Genres* and *Sexuality and Its Queer Discontents in Middle English Literature* and editor of *Approaches to Teaching Chaucer's* Troilus and Criseyde *and the Shorter Poems* (with Angela Jane Weisl) and of *Men and Masculinities in Chaucer's* Troilus and Criseyde (with Marcia Smith Marzec).

William Quinn is a professor of English at the University of Arkansas, Fayetteville, and the director of the Medieval and Renaissance Studies Program. His publications include *Chaucer's Rehersynges*, *Chaucer's Dream Visions and Short Poems*, and recent articles on William Dunbar, *The Kingis Quair*, and *The Parliament of Fowls*.

Larry Scanlon is an associate professor of English at Rutgers University. He has authored a number of books and essays on medieval literature, including *Narrative, Authority, and Power: The Medieval Exemplum and the Chaucerian Tradition*. He is currently completing a study of medieval sexuality tentatively entitled "At Sodom's Gate: The Sin against Nature and Later Middle English Poetry."

Nicole Nolan Sidhu is associate professor of English at East Carolina University. Her publications include "'To Late for to Crie': Fabliau Politics in Chaucer's Reeve's Tale," and "Weeping for the Virtuous Wife: Laymen, Affective Piety, and Chaucer's Griselda." She is currently completing a book on obscene comic discourse, entitled "Indecent Exposure: Gender, Society and Obscene Comedy in Middle English Literature."

Deborah M. Sinnreich-Levi is an associate professor of English and communications at Stevens Institute of Technology, where she is the advisement coordinator for the College of Arts and Letters and the director of academic writing programs. She has published extensively on the fourteenth-century poet Eustache Deschamps.

Timothy L. Stinson is an assistant professor of English at North Carolina State University whose essays have appeared in journals including *Speculum*, the *Yearbook of Langland Studies*, and *Papers of the Bibliographic Society of America*. He is the editor of *The Siege of Jerusalem Electronic Archive*, codirector of *The Piers Plowman Electronic Archive*, and codirector of the Medieval Electronic Scholarly Alliance.

Lorraine Kochanske Stock, associate professor of English at the University of Houston, served as the president of the South Eastern Medieval Association and for five years was elected to the MLA's executive committee Middle English Language and Literature, Excluding Chaucer. She is completing a book titled "The Medieval Wild Man: Primitivism and Civilization in Medieval Culture." In 2008, she received the University of Houston Teaching Excellence Award for Innovative Use of Technology in Teaching for the creation of a hybrid online Chaucer course.

Jamie Taylor is assistant professor of English at Bryn Mawr College, where she teaches courses on medieval literature, literary theory, and legal culture. She is currently finishing a book-length study of representations of testimony and witnessing in late medieval English literature.

Peter W. Travis is the Henry Winkley Professor of Anglo-Saxon and English Language and Literature at Dartmouth College. He is the author of two books, *Dramatic Design in the Chester Cycle* and *Disseminal Chaucer: Rereading the Nun's Priest's Tale*, and the winner of the 2009 Warren Brooks Award for outstanding literary criticism. He teaches courses in the Icelandic sagas, Chaucer, medieval literature, critical theory, and a women and gender studies course entitled the Masculine Mystique.

David Wallace is Judith Rodin Professor of English at the University of Pennsylvania. The author and editor of more than sixty books and articles, one of his major studies of

Chaucer is *Chaucerian Polity: Absolutist Lineages and Associational Forms in England and Italy*. He served as president of the New Chaucer Society from 2004 to 2006.

Michelle R. Warren is a professor of comparative literature at Dartmouth College. She is the author of *History on the Edge: Excalibur and the Borders of Britain, 1100–1300* and *Creole Medievalism: Colonial France and Joseph Bédier's Middle Ages* and coeditor of *Postcolonial Moves: Medieval through Modern* and *Arts of Calculation: Quantifying Thought in Early Modern Europe*.

Tara Williams is associate professor of English at Oregon State University and author of *Inventing Womanhood: Gender and Language in Later Middle English Writing*. Her work on late medieval literature and culture has appeared in *Studies in the Age of Chaucer*, *Modern Philology*, *Chaucer Review*, *New Medieval Literatures*, and *Exemplaria*; she has also published on pedagogical issues in *Pedagogy* and *Profession*. Her current project examines fourteenth-century representations of marvels.

Susan Yager is an associate professor in English and the faculty director of the honors program at Iowa State University. Her research interests include the poetry of Geoffrey Chaucer, Chaucer translation and performance, and the intersection of pedagogy and medieval studies. She is the coeditor of *Interpretation and Performance: Essays for Alan Gaylord*, and her work has appeared in *Chaucer Review*, *Journal of English and Germanic Philology*, and *Philological Quarterly*.

SURVEY RESPONDENTS

Peter G. Beidler, *Lehigh University*
Craig E. Bertolet, *Auburn University*
Bethany Blankenship, *University of Montana Western*
Gina Brandolino, *Indiana University, Bloomington*
J. Justin Brent, *Presbyterian College*
Jennifer N. Brown, *University of Hartford*
Lynne Dickson Bruckner, *Chatham University*
Mark Bradshaw Busbee, *Florida Gulf Coast University*
Michael Calabrese, *California State University, Los Angeles*
Siobhain Bly Calkin, *Carleton University*
Mary Carruthers, *New York University*
Annalisa Castaldo, *Widener University*
Jane Chance, *Rice University*
Christine F. Cooper-Rompato, *Utah State University*
Donna Crawford, *Virginia State University*
Holly Crocker, *University of South Carolina*
Bryan P. Davis, *Georgia Southwestern State University*
Martha W. Driver, *Pace University*
Bonnie Duncan, *Millersville University*
Geoffrey B. Elliott, *University of Louisiana, Lafayette*
Robert Epstein, *Fairfield University*
LuAnn Fallahi, *Parkway North High School, MO*
John Fyler, *Tufts University*
Bruce Gilchrist, *Université Laval*
Susan Blair Green, *Mary Baldwin College*
David Hale, *State University of New York, College at Brockport*
Robert W. Haynes, *Texas A&M International*
Cara Hersh, *University of Portland*
Julia Bolton Holloway, *University of Colorado, Boulder*
Patricia Clare Ingham, *Indiana University, Bloomington*
Alexander L. Kaufman, *Auburn University, Montgomery*
Lauren Kiefer, *State University of New York, College at Plattsburgh*
Peggy A. Knapp, *Carnegie Mellon University*
Leonard Michael Koff, *University of California, Los Angeles*
Miriamne Ara Krummel, *University of Dayton*
Roger A. Ladd, *University of North Carolina, Pembroke*
Lisa Lampert-Weissig, *University of California, San Diego*
Jacob Lewis, *University of Arkansas, Fayetteville*
Thomas Liszka, *Penn State University, Altoona*
Kathryn L. Lynch, *Wellesley College*
James McNelis, *Wilmington College*
Edward E. Mehok, *Notre Dame College*
Alex Mueller, *University of Massachusetts, Boston*

Michael Murphy, *Brooklyn College, City University of New York*
Florence Newman, *Towson University*
Meriem Pages, *Keene State College*
Todd Preston, *Lycoming College*
Tison Pugh, *University of Central Florida*
William Quinn, *University of Arkansas, Fayetteville*
E. C. Ronquist, *Concordia University*
Ameer Sohrawardy, *Rutgers University*
Glenn A. Steinberg, *College of New Jersey*
Theodore L. Steinberg, *State University of New York, Fredonia*
Timothy L. Stinson, *Johns Hopkins University*
Lorraine Kochanske Stock, *University of Houston*
Jamie Taylor, *Bryn Mawr College*
Peter W. Travis, *Dartmouth College*
Michael Twomey, *Ithaca College*
Amy Vines, *University of North Carolina, Greensboro*
Lewis Walker, *University of North Carolina, Wilmington*
David Wallace, *University of Pennsylvania*
Martha S. Waller, *Butler University*
Patricia H. Ward, *College of Charleston*
J. A. White, *Morgan State University*
Tara Williams, *Oregon State University*

WORKS CITED

Works by Chaucer

Complete Works

Benson, Larry D., ed. *The Riverside Chaucer*. 3rd ed. Boston: Houghton, 1987. Print.

Fisher, John, ed. *The Complete Poetry and Prose of Geoffrey Chaucer*. New York: Henry Holt, 1977. Print.

Robinson, F. N., ed. *Poetical Works of Chaucer*. Rev. ed. Boston: Houghton, 1957. Print.

Skeat, W. W., ed. *The Complete Works of Geoffrey Chaucer*. 7 vols. Oxford: Clarendon, 1894–97. Print.

Editions of The Canterbury Tales

Benson, Larry D., ed. The Canterbury Tales: *Complete*. Boston: Houghton, 2000. Print. Riverside ed.

Boening, Robert, and Andrew Taylor, eds. *The Canterbury Tales*. 2nd ed. Peterborough: Broadview, 2013. Print.

———, eds. The Canterbury Tales: *A Selection*. 2009. Peterborough: Broadview, 2013. Print.

Cawley, A. C., ed. *The Canterbury Tales*. London: Dent, 1995. Print.

———, ed. *The Canterbury Tales*. London: Everyman's Lib., 1992. Print.

Fisher, John A., and Mark Allen, eds. *The Canterbury Tales*. Boston: Thomson, 2006. Print.

Howard, Donald, ed. The Canterbury Tales: *A Selection*. New York: Signet, 2005. Print.

Kolve, V. A., and Glending Olson, eds. The Canterbury Tales: *Fifteen Tales and the General Prologue*. 1989. New York: Norton, 2005. Print. Norton Critical Ed.

Mann, Jill, ed. *The Canterbury Tales*. New York: Penguin, 2005. Print.

Murphy, Michael, ed. *Canterbury Marriage Tales*. Brooklyn: Conor, 2000. Print.

Translations of The Canterbury Tales

Coghill, Nevill, trans. *The Canterbury Tales*. 1977. London: Penguin, 2003. Print.

Ecker, Ronald L., and Eugene Joseph Crook, trans. *The Canterbury Tales*. Palatka: Hodge, 1993. Print.

Fisher, Sheila, trans. *The Selected* Canterbury Tales. New York: Norton, 2011. Print.

Glaser, Joseph, trans. The Canterbury Tales *in Modern Verse*. Indianapolis: Hackett, 2005. Print.

Hieatt, A. Kent, and Constance Hieatt, trans. and eds. *The Canterbury Tales*. New York: Bantam, 1981. Print.

Hill, Frank Ernest, trans. *The Canterbury Tales*. Illus. Edward Burne-Jones and William Morris. Edison: Chartwell, 2007. Print.

———, trans. The Canterbury Tales: *Done into Modern Verse by Frank Ernest Hill*. Illus. Arthur Szyk. New York: Heritage, 1946. Print.

Hopper, Vincent F., trans. *Chaucer's* Canterbury Tales *(Selected): An Interlinear Translation*. 1948. Rev. ed. Andrew Galloway. Hauppauge: Barron, 2012. Print.

Nicholson, J. U., trans. *The Canterbury Tales*. Mineola: Dover, 2004. Print.

Raffel, Burton, trans. *The Canterbury Tales*. 2008. New York: Mod. Lib., 2009. Print.

———. The Canterbury Tales: *A New Unabridged Translation*. N.p.: BBC Audiobooks, 2008. CD.

Tuttle, Peter, trans. *The Canterbury Tales*. New York: Barnes, 2006. Print.

Wright, David, trans. *The Canterbury Tales*. 2008. Introd. and notes by Christopher Cannon. Oxford: Oxford UP, 2011. Print.

———, trans. *The Canterbury Tales*. 1985. Oxford: Oxford UP, 1998. Print.

Facsimile Editions of The Canterbury Tales

Parkes, Malcolm, and Richard Beadle, eds. *Cambridge Library MS GG.4.27*. 3 vols. Norman: Pilgrim, 1981. Print.

Ruggiers, Paul G., ed. The Canterbury Tales: *A Facsimile and Transcription of the Hengwrt Manuscript, with Variants from the Ellesmere Manuscript*. Norman: U of Oklahoma P, 1979. Print.

Woodward, Daniel, and Martin Stevens, eds. The Canterbury Tales: *The New Ellesmere Chaucer Monochromatic Facsimile*. San Marino: Huntington Lib. P, 1997. Print.

Other Works

Windeatt, Barry A., ed. *Chaucer's* Troilus and Criseyde: *A New Edition of Chaucer's* The Book of Troilus. New York: Longman, 1984. Print.

Primary and Critical Works

Aers, David. *Chaucer*. Brighton: Harvester, 1986. Print.

Akbari, Suzanne. *Seeing through the Veil: Optical Theory and Medieval Allegory*. Toronto: U of Toronto P, 2004. Print.

Albertano of Brescia. *Liber consolationes et consilii*. N.p., n.d. Web. 1 Aug. 2013. <http://freespace.virgin.net/angus.graham/Lib-Cons.htm>.

Aldrich, Clark. "Simulations and the Future of Learning: An Innovative (and Perhaps Revolutionary) Approach to E-learning." San Francisco: Pfeiffer, 2004. Print.

Amtower, Laurel, and Jacqueline Vanhoutte. *A Companion to Chaucer and His Contemporaries: Texts and Contexts*. Peterborough: Broadview, 2009. Print.

Anderson, David. *Before the Knight's Tale*. Philadelphia: U of Pennsylvania P, 1988. Print.

Andrew, Malcolm. *The Palgrave Literary Dictionary of Chaucer*. New York: Palgrave, 2006. Print.

Antrobus, Dave, et al., dirs. *The Canterbury Tales*. BBC, 1998–2000. DVD.

Arthurian Romances, MS 229. Beinecke Rare Book and Manuscript Library. Yale U Lib., 2013. Web. 26 June 2013.

Ashton, Gail. "Creating Learning Communities in Chaucer Studies: Process and Profit." Ashton and Sylvester 105–19.

Ashton, Gail, and Louise Sylvester, eds. *Teaching Chaucer*. New York: Palgrave, 2007. Print.

Astell, Ann. *Chaucer and the Universe of Learning*. Ithaca: Cornell UP, 1996. Print.

Badiou, Alain. *Ethics: An Essay on the Understanding of Evil*. Trans. Peter Hallward. London: Verso, 2002. Print.

Baird, Lorrayne Y. *A Bibliography of Chaucer, 1964–1973*. Boston: Hall, 1977. Print.

Baird-Lange, Lorrayne Y. *A Bibliography of Chaucer, 1974–1985*. Hamden: Shoe String, 1988. Print.

Baldwin, Ralph. *The Unity of* The Canterbury Tales. Copenhagen: Rosenkilde, 1955. Print. Anglistica 5.

Barlow, Gania. "A Thrifty Tale: Narrative, Authority, and the Competing Values of the 'Man of Law's Tale.'" *Chaucer Review* 44.4 (2010): 397–420. Print.

Barrington, Candace. *American Chaucers*. New York: Palgrave, 2007. Print.

Baswell, Christopher. *Virgil in Medieval England: Figuring the* Aeneid *from the Twelfth Century to Chaucer*. Cambridge: Cambridge UP, 1995. Print.

Baswell, Christopher, and Anne Howland Schotter, eds. *The Longman Anthology of British Literature: The Middle Ages*. 4th ed. Vol. 1A. New York: Longman, 2010. Print, Web.

Beard, Colin, and John Wilson. *Experiential Learning: A Best Practice Handbook for Educators and Trainers*. London: Kogan, 2006. Print.

Beck, James P. "Predrafting: On Having Students Write before We Teach Them How." *Journal of Teaching Writing* 5.1 (1986): 71–76. Print.

Beck, William S. The Draper's Dictionary: *A Manual of Textile Fabrics, Their History and Applications*. London, 1882. Print.

Beidler, Peter G. "Chaucer's Wife of Bath's 'Foot-Mantel' and Her 'Hipes Large.'" *Chaucer Review* 34.4 (2000): 388–97. Print.

———. "Low-Tech Chaucer: An Experimental Iambic Pentameter Creative Project." *Exercise Exchange* 46 (2000): 16–20. Print.

————, ed. *Masculinities in Chaucer: Approaches to Maleness in* The Canterbury Tales *and* Troilus and Criseyde. Rochester: Brewer, 1998. Print.

————. *A Student Guide to Chaucer's Middle English.* Seattle: Coffeetown, 2011. Print.

————, ed. *The Wife of Bath: Geoffrey Chaucer.* Boston: Bedford, 1996. Print.

Bendiner, Kenneth. *The Art of Ford Madox Brown.* University Park: Penn State UP, 1998. Print.

Bennett, Judith. *Women in the Medieval English Countryside: Brigstock before the Plague.* London: Oxford UP, 1987. Print.

Benson, C. David. *Chaucer's Drama of Style: Poetic Variety and Contrast in* The Canterbury Tales. Chapel Hill: U of North Carolina P, 1986. Print.

Benson, Larry D. *A Glossarial Concordance to the Riverside Chaucer.* 2 vols. Hamden: Garland, 1993. Print.

————. "The Yeoman." Chaucer [ed. Benson, *Riverside Chaucer*] 802–03.

Benson, Larry D., and Theodore M. Andersson, eds. *The Literary Context of Chaucer's Fabliaux: Texts and Translations.* Indianapolis: Bobbs-Merrill, 1971. Print.

Bergvall, Caroline. *Meddle English: New and Selected Texts.* Callicoon: Nightboat, 2011. Print.

"Beset." *Oxford English Dictionary.* 2nd ed. 2009. Print.

Besserman, Lawrence. *Chaucer and the Bible.* New York: Garland, 1988. Print.

————. *Chaucer's Biblical Poetics.* Norman: U of Oklahoma P, 1998. Print.

The Bible. Trans. of *Latin Vulgate Bible.* DRBO, n.d. Web. 30 July 2010. <http://www .drbo.org>. Douay-Rheims vers.

Biddick, Kathleen. "Coming out of Exile: Dante on the Orient Express." Cohen, *Postcolonial Middle Ages* 35–52.

————. *The Shock of Medievalism.* New York: Duke UP, 1998. Print.

————. *The Typological Imaginary: Circumcision, Technology, and History.* Philadelphia: U of Pennsylvania P, 2003. Print.

"Bisetten." *Middle English Dictionary.* U of Michigan, 2001. Web. 7 Jan. 2014.

Bishop, Kathleen A., ed. *The Canterbury Tales Revisited: Twenty-First-Century Interpretations.* Newcastle: Cambridge Scholars, 2008. Print.

Bisson, Lillian. *Chaucer and the Late Medieval World.* New York: St. Martin's, 1998. Print.

Black, Henry Campbell. *Black's Law Dictionary.* Ed. Bryan A. Garner. 9th ed. St. Paul: West, 2009. Print.

Black, Joseph, ed. *The Broadview Anthology of British Literature: The Medieval Period.* 2nd ed. Vol. 1. Peterborough: Broadview, 2009. Print.

Black, Maggie. *The Medieval Cookbook.* New York: Thames, 1992. Print.

Blake, N. F., ed. *The Cambridge History of the English Language, 1066–1476.* Vol. 2. Cambridge: Cambridge UP, 1992. Print.

————. *The Textual Tradition of* The Canterbury Tales. London: Arnold, 1985. Print.

Blamires, Alcuin. *Chaucer, Ethics, and Gender.* Oxford: Oxford UP, 2006. Print.

————, ed. *Woman Defamed and Woman Defended.* Oxford: Clarendon, 1992. Print.

Boccaccio, Giovani. *The Decameron*. Trans. John Florio. London: Isaac Jaggard, 1620. Print.

———. "From the Decameron, Tenth Day, Tenth Tale." Chaucer [ed. Kolve and Olson] 399–406.

Boitani, Piero, ed. *Chaucer and the Italian Trecento*. 1983. 2nd ed. Cambridge: Cambridge UP, 2013. Print.

Boitani, Piero, and Jill Mann, eds. *The Cambridge Companion to Chaucer*. 2nd ed. Cambridge: Cambridge UP, 2002. Print.

"Boke of Penance." *Cursor Mundi: Complete Set*. Ed. Richard Morris. London: Early English Text Soc., 1995. Print. EETS 68.

Boswell, Jackson Campbell, and Sylvia Wallace Holton. *Chaucer's Fame in England: STC Chauceriana, 1475–1640*. New York: MLA, 2004. Print.

Bothwell, James, P. J. P. Goldberg, and W. M. Ormrod, eds. *The Problem of Labour in Fourteenth-Century England*. Woodbridge: York Medieval, 2000. Print.

Bowden, Betsy. *Chaucer Aloud: The Varieties of Textual Interpretation*. Philadelphia: U of Pennsylvania P, 1987. Print.

Bowden, Muriel. *A Commentary on the General Prologue to* The Canterbury Tales. New York: Macmillan, 1948. Print.

Bowers, Bege K., and Mark Allen. *Annotated Chaucer Bibliography, 1986–1996*. Notre Dame: U of Notre Dame P, 2002. Print.

Bowers, John. "Chaucer after Smithfield: From Postcolonial Author to Imperialist Writer." Cohen, *Postcolonial Middle Ages* 53–66.

———. *Chaucer and Langland: The Antagonistic Tradition*. Notre Dame: U of Notre Dame P, 2007. Print.

Bragg, Melvyn. *In Our Time*. BBC, 2013. Web. 19 Apr. 2013. <http://www.bbc.co.uk/radio4/history/inourtime/index.shtml>.

Braud, Brandi E. "The Wife of Bath: 'Deef' as More Than a Hearing Problem." 2007. TS. Paper submitted for English 316: Geoffrey Chaucer, Rice U.

Brewer, Derek. *Chaucer*. London: Longman, 1973. Print.

———. *Chaucer: The Critical Heritage*. 2 vols. London: Routledge, 1978. Print.

Brinkman, Baba. *The Rap Canterbury Tales*. N.p., n.d. Web. 1 Apr. 2010. <http://www.babasword.com/>.

Brosnahan, Leger. "The Riverside Chaucer." Rev. of *The Riverside Chaucer*, ed. Larry D. Benson. *Speculum* 63.3 (1988): 641–45. Print.

Brown, Emerson, Jr. "Diverse Folk Diversely They Teach." Gibaldi, *Approaches* 63–75.

Brown, Peter, ed. *A Companion to Chaucer*. Oxford: Blackwell, 2002. Print. Blackwell Companions to Lit. and Culture.

Bruns, Gerald L. "The Concepts of Art and Poetry in Emmanuel Levinas's Writing." *The Cambridge Companion to Levinas*. Ed. Simon Critchley and Robert Bernasconi. Cambridge: Cambridge UP, 2002. 206–33. Print.

Bryan, W. F., and Germaine Dempster, eds. *Sources and Analogues of Chaucer's Canterbury Tales*. Chicago: U of Chicago P, 1941. Print.

Bryant, Brantley. *Geoffrey Chaucer Hath a Blog: Medieval Studies and New Media*. New York: Palgrave, 2010. Print.

Burger, Glenn. *Chaucer's Queer Nation*. Minneapolis: U of Minnesota P, 2003. Print.

Burnley, David. *A Guide to Chaucer's Language*. Norman: U of Oklahoma P, 1983. Print.

Butterfield, Ardis. "Chaucerian Vernaculars." *Studies in the Age of Chaucer* 31 (2009): 25–51. Print.

———. *The Familiar Enemy: Chaucer, Language, and Nation in the Hundred Years War*. New York: Oxford UP, 2009. Print.

Cahill, Thomas. *How the Irish Saved Civilization*. New York: Anchor, 1996. Print.

Caie, Graham D. "Innocent III's *De Miseria* as a Gloss on the 'Man of Law's Tale.'" *Neuphilologische Mitteilungen* 100.2 (1999): 175–85. Print.

Calabrese, Michael. *Chaucer's Ovidian Arts of Love*. Gainesville: UP of Florida, 1994. Print.

Calder, Lendol. "Uncoverage: Toward a Signature Pedagogy for the History Survey." *Journal of American History* 92.4 (2006): 1358–69. Print.

Calin, William. *The French Tradition and the Literature of Medieval England*. Toronto: U of Toronto P, 1994. Print.

Camille, Michael. *Image on the Edge: The Margins of Medieval Art*. London: Reaktion, 1992. Print.

Cannon, Christopher. "The Lives of Geoffrey Chaucer." Lerer, *Yale Companion* 31–54.

———. *The Making of Chaucer's English: A Study of Words*. Cambridge: Cambridge UP, 1998. Print.

———. *Middle English Literature: A Cultural History*. Malden: Polity, 2008. Print.

The Canterbury Tales *Project*. U of Birmingham, n.d. Web. 2 Sept. 2011. <http://www.canterburytalesproject.org/>.

Cantor, Norman. *In the Wake of the Plague: The Black Death and the World It Made*. New York: Free, 2001. Print.

Carlson, David. *Chaucer's Jobs*. New York: Palgrave, 2004. Print.

"Caroline Bergvall." *PennSound*. U of Pennsylvania, 2009. Web. 19 Apr. 2013.

Catholic Encyclopedia. Kevin Knight, 2009. Web. 19 Apr. 2013. <http://www.newadvent.org/cathen/>.

"Chaucer." *In Our Time*. BBC, 9 Feb. 2006. Web. 13 July 2013. <http://www.bbc.co.uk/programmes/p003hycq>.

"Chaucer and the Future of Language Study." *Studies in the Age of Chaucer* 24 (2002): 299–354.

Chaucer Bibliography Online. Ed. Mark Allen. N.p., n.d. Web. 2 Sept. 2011. <http://uchaucer.utsa.edu>.

Chaucer Concordance. E-Chaucer: Chaucer in the Twenty-First Century. U of Maine, Machias, 2007. Web. 5 June 2013.

Chaucer Metapage. Ed. Joseph Wittig. U of North Carolina, n.d. Web. 2 Sept. 2011. <http://www.unc.edu/depts/chaucer/index.html>.

Chaucer Review: An Indexed Bibliography. Ed. Peter G. Beidler and Martha A. Kalnin. Northwest U, 2002. Web. 2 Sept. 2011. <http://library.northwestu.edu/chaucer/>.

The Chaucer Studio. Australian and New Zealand Assn. for Medieval and Renaissance Studies, n.d. Web. 2 Sept. 2011. <http://creativeworks.byu.edu/chaucer/>.

Chazan, Robert. *The Jews of Medieval Western Christendom, 1000–1500*. Cambridge: Cambridge UP, 2006. Print.

———. *Medieval Stereotypes and Modern Anti-Semitism*. Berkeley: U of California P, 1997. Print.

Chestre, Thomas. "Sir Launfal." *Middle English Breton Lays*. Ed. Anne Laskaya and Eve Salisbury. Kalamazoo: Medieval Inst., 1995. *TEAMS Middle English Texts Series*. Web. 6 Jan. 2014.

Chick, Nancy L., Aeron Haynie, and Regan A. R. Gurung, eds. *Exploring More Signature Pedagogies: Approaches to Teaching Disciplinary Habits of Mind*. Sterling: Stylus, 2012. Print.

Cohen, Jeffrey Jerome. "Diminishing Masculinity in Chaucer's Tale of Sir Thopas." Beidler, *Masculinities* 143–56.

———. "The Flow of Blood in Medieval Norwich." *Speculum* 79.1 (2004): 26–65. Print.

———. "Introduction: Mid-colonial." Cohen, *Postcolonial Middle Ages* 1–18.

———. *Medieval Identity Machines*. Minneapolis: U of Minnesota P, 2003. Print.

———, ed. *The Postcolonial Middle Ages*. New York: Palgrave, 2000. Print.

Cohen, Jeffrey Jerome, and Bonnie Wheeler. "Becoming and Unbecoming." Cohen and Wheeler, *Becoming* vii–xx.

———, eds. *Becoming Male in the Middle Ages*. New York: Garland, 1997. Print.

Cohen, Jeffrey Jerome, et al. *In the Middle*. N.p., n.d. Web. 19 Apr. 2013.<http://www.inthemedievalmiddle.com/>.

Cole, Andrew. *Literature and Heresy in the Age of Chaucer*. Cambridge: Cambridge UP, 2008. Print.

Collette, Carolyn P. "Heeding the Counsel of Prudence: A Context for the *Melibee*." *Chaucer Review* 29.4 (1995): 416–29. Print.

———. *Performing Polity: Women and Agency in the Anglo-French Tradition, 1385–1620*. Turnhout: Brepols, 2006. Print.

———. *Species, Phantasms, and Images: Vision and Medieval Psychology in* The Canterbury Tales. Ann Arbor: U of Michigan P, 2001. Print.

Collette, Carolyn P., and Harold Garrett-Goodyear, eds. *The Later Middle Ages: A Sourcebook*. Basingstoke: Palgrave, 2011. Print.

Cook, William R., and Ronald B. Herzman. *The Medieval World View: An Introduction*. New York: Oxford UP, 1983. Print.

Cooper, Helen. *The Oxford Guides to Chaucer:* The Canterbury Tales. 2nd ed. Oxford: Oxford UP, 1996. Print.

———. *The Oxford Guides to Chaucer:* The Canterbury Tales. Oxford: Oxford UP, 1989. Print.

———. *The Structure of* The Canterbury Tales. Athens: U of Georgia P, 1983. Print.

Copeland, Rita. *Pedagogy, Intellectuals, and Dissent in the Later Middle Ages: Lollardy and the Ideas of Learning*. New York: Cambridge UP, 2001. Print.

Correale, Robert M., and Mary Hamel, eds. *Sources and Analogues of* The Canterbury Tales. 2 vols. Woodbridge: Brewer, 2002–05. Print.

Coulton, G. G. *Chaucer and His England*. 5th ed. London: Methuen, 1930. Print.

Cox, Catherine S. *Gender and Language in Chaucer*. Gainesville: UP of Florida, 1997. Print.

"The Crane." Dubin 483–91.

Crane, John Kenny. "An Honest Debtor? A Note on Chaucer's Merchant, Line A276." *English Language Notes* 4 (1966): 81–85. Print.

Crane, Susan. *Gender and Romance in Chaucer's* Canterbury Tales. Princeton: Princeton UP, 1994. Print.

Crawford, William R. *Bibliography of Chaucer, 1954–63*. Seattle: U of Washington P, 1967. Print.

The Criyng and the Soun. Ed. Alan Baragona. Virginia Military Inst., n.d. Web. 2 Sept. 2011. <www.vmi.edu/english/audio/audio_index.html>.

Crocker, Holly A. *Chaucer's Visions of Manhood*. New York: Palgrave, 2007. Print.

Crow, Martin M., and Virgina E. Leland. "Chaucer's Life." Chaucer [ed. Benson, *Riverside Chaucer*] xv–xxvi.

Crow, Martin M., and Clair C. Olson, eds. *Chaucer Life Records*. Austin: U of Texas P, 1966. Print.

Dane, Joseph. *Who Is Buried in Chaucer's Tomb? Studies in the Reception of Chaucer's Book*. East Lansing: Michigan State UP, 1998. Print.

Davidson, Alan. *The Penguin Companion to Food*. New York: Penguin, 2002. Print.

Davis, Isabel. *Writing Masculinity in the Later Middle Ages*. Cambridge: Cambridge UP, 2007. Print.

Davis, Norman. *A Chaucer Glossary*. Oxford: Clarendon, 1979. Print.

D'Avray, D. L., and M. Tausche. "Medieval Marriage Sermons in the Ad Status Collections of the Central Middle Ages." *Archive d'histoire doctrinale et littéraire du moyen âge* 47 (1980): 71–119. Print.

"Deaf." Def. 2. *Oxford English Dictionary*. 2nd ed. 1989. Print.

Decameron Web. Brown U, 2010. Web. 9 Apr. 2014. <http://www.brown.edu/Departments/Italian_Studies/dweb/texts/florio/day06.php>.

Delany, Sheila, ed. *Chaucer and the Jews: Sources, Contexts, Meanings*. New York: Routledge, 2002. Print.

———. "Chaucer's Prioress, the Jews and the Muslims." *Medieval Encounters* 5 (1999): 199–213. Print.

De Marco, Patricia. "Violence, Law and Ciceronian Ethics in Chaucer's *Tale of Melibee*." *Studies in the Age of Chaucer* 30 (2008): 125–69. Print.

Desmond, John. "A Reply to My Critics." *LearnOnline*. Towson U, 2009. Web. 15 Dec. 2009.

Desmond, Marilynn. *Ovid's Art and the Wife of Bath: The Ethics of Erotic Violence*. Ithaca: Cornell UP, 2006. Print.

Despres, Denise L. "Cultic Anti-Judaism and Chaucer's Litel Clergeon." *Modern Philology* 91 (1994): 413–27.

Digital Scriptorium. Columbia U, n.d. Web. 2 Sept. 2011. <http://www.scriptorium.columbia.edu/>.

Dinshaw, Carolyn. *Chaucer's Sexual Poetics*. Madison: U of Wisconsin P, 1989. Print.

Donaldson, E. Talbot. *Speaking of Chaucer*. New York: Norton, 1970. Print.

Dover, K. J. *Greek Homosexuality*. New York: Random, 1980. Print.

Doyle, A. I., and M. B. Parkes. "A Paleographical Introduction." Chaucer [ed. Ruggiers] xix–xlix.

"The Dreaming Damsel." Trans. Ned Dubin. *Nicole Sidhu's Chaucer Class*. N.p., n.d. Web. 19 July 2013. <http://myweb.ecu.edu/sidhun/La%20Damoisele%20qui%20songoit.pdf>.

Driver, Martha Westcott. "Medieval Literature and Multimedia: The Pleasures and Perils of Internet Pedagogy." *Teaching Language and Literature Online*. Ed. Ian Lancashire. New York: MLA, 2009. 243–53. Print. Options for Teaching 26.

Driver, Martha W., and Sid Ray, eds. *Shakespeare and the Middle Ages*. Jefferson: McFarland, 2009. Print.

Drogin, Marc. *Medieval Calligraphy: Its History and Technique*. New York: Dover, 1989. Print.

Dubin, Ned, trans. *The Fabliaux*. New York: Liveright, 2013. Print.

Duffy, Eamon. *The Stripping of the Altars*. New Haven: Yale UP, 1992. Print.

Dundes, Alan, ed. *The Blood Libel Legend: A Casebook in Anti-Semitic Folklore*. Madison: U of Wisconsin P, 1991. Print.

Dyer, Christopher. *Making a Living in the Middle Ages: The People of Britain, 850–1520*. New Haven: Yale UP, 2002. Print.

———. *Standards of Living in the Later Middle Ages: Social Change in England, c. 1200–1520*. Cambridge: Cambridge UP, 1989. Print.

Early English Aloud and Alive: The Language of Beowulf, Chaucer, and Shakespeare. Films for the Humanities and Social Sciences, 1991. DVD, videocassette.

Early Manuscripts at Oxford University. Ed. Matthew J. Dovey, Katherine Ferguson, and Emma Leeson. Oxford U, n.d. Web. 2 Sept. 2011. <http://image.ox.ac.uk/>.

Edler, Florence. *Glossary of Mediaeval Terms of Business: Italian Series, 1200–1600*. Cambridge: Mediaeval Acad. of Amer., 1934. Print.

Edmondson, George. *The Neighboring Text: Chaucer, Boccaccio, Henryson*. Notre Dame: U of Notre Dame P, 2011. Print.

Edson, E., and E. Savage-Smith. *Medieval Views of the Cosmos: Picturing the Universe in the Christian and Islamic Middle Ages*. Oxford: Bodleian, 2004. Print.

Edwards, Robert R. *Chaucer and Boccaccio*. New York: Palgrave, 2002. Print.

Elizabeth I. "Queen Elizabeth's Armada Speech to the Troops at Tilbury, August 9, 1588." *Elizabeth I: Collected Works*. Ed. Leah S. Marcus, Janel Mueller, and Mary Beth Rose. Chicago: U of Chicago P, 2000. 325–26. Print.

Ellis, Steve, ed. *Chaucer: An Oxford Guide*. Oxford: Oxford UP, 2005. Print.

———. *Chaucer at Large: The Poet in the Modern Imagination*. Minneapolis: U of Minnesota P, 2000. Print.

———, ed. *Chaucer: The Canterbury Tales*. New York: Longman, 1998. Print.

Epstein, Robert, and William Robins, eds. *Sacred and Profane in Chaucer and Late Medieval Literature: Essays in Honour of John V. Fleming*. Toronto: U of Toronto P, 2010. Print.

Essential Chaucer Bibliography. Ed. Mark Allen and John H. Fisher. N.p., n.d. Web. 2 Sept. 2011. <http://colfa.utsa.edu/chaucer>.

"Fat." *Middle English Dictionary.* U of Michigan, 2001. Web. 7 Jan. 2014.

Fein, Susanna Greer, David Raybin, and Peter C. Braeger, eds. *Rebels and Rivals: The Contestive Spirit in* The Canterbury Tales. Kalamazoo: Medieval Inst., 1991. Print.

Fink, Bruce. *A Clinical Introduction to Lacanian Psychoanalysis: Theory and Technique.* Cambridge: Harvard UP, 1997. Print.

———. *The Lacanian Subject: Between Language and Jouissance.* Princeton: Princeton UP, 1997. Print.

Finn, Patrick J. *Literacy with an Attitude.* 2nd ed. Albany: State U of New York P, 2009. Print.

Fish, Stanley E. "Interpreting the Variorum." *Critical Inquiry* 2.3 (1976): 465–85. Print.

Fitzgibbons, Moira. "'Cross-Voiced' Assignments and the Critical 'I.'" Ashton and Sylvester 65–80.

Forrest, Robert L., Jr. "Human Transaction in the Marchant's Prologue." 1981. TS. Paper submitted for English 323: Geoffrey Chaucer, Rice U.

Foster, Edward E., and David H. Carey. *Chaucer's Church: A Dictionary of Religious Terms in Chaucer.* Aldershot: Ashgate, 2002. Print.

———. "Has Anyone Here Read Melibee?" *Chaucer Review* 34.4 (2000): 398–409. Print.

Fradenburg, L. O. Aranye. "Criticism, Anti-Semitism and the Prioress' Tale." *Exemplaria* 1 (1989): 69–115. Print.

———. *Sacrifice Your Love: Psychoanalysis, Historicism, Chaucer.* Minneapolis: U of Minnesota P, 2002. Print.

Freedman, Paul. *Out of the East: Spices and the Medieval Imagination.* New Haven: Yale UP, 2009. Print.

Freire, Paolo. *Pedagogy of the Oppressed.* 1970. Trans. Myra Bergman Ramos. New York: Continuum, 2000. Print.

"From the *Sarum Missal.*" R. Miller 374–84.

Furnivall, Frederick James. *A Temporary Preface to the Six-Text Edition of Chaucer's* Canterbury Tales. London: Trübner, 1868. Print. Chaucer Soc. Pubs. Ser. 3.

Fyler, John. *Chaucer and Ovid.* New Haven: Yale UP, 1979. Print.

———. *Language and the Declining World in Chaucer, Dante, and Jean de Meun.* Cambridge: Cambridge UP, 2007. Print.

Galloway, Andrew. "Marriage Sermons, Polemical Sermons and the Wife of Bath's Prologue: A Generic Excursus." *Studies in the Age of Chaucer* 14 (1992): 3–30. Print.

———. *Medieval Literature and Culture.* New York: Continuum, 2006. Print.

Ganim, John M. *Chaucerian Theatricality.* Princeton: Princeton UP, 1990. Print.

———. "Cosmopolitan Chaucer; or, The Uses of Local Culture." *Studies in the Age of Chaucer* 31 (2009): 3–21. Print.

———. "Native Studies: Orientalism and Medievalism." Cohen, *Postcolonial Middle Ages* 123–34.

Garbáty, Thomas J. "And Gladly Teche the Tales of Caunterbury." Gibaldi, *Approaches* 46–56.

Gasman, Marybeth, et al., eds. *Unearthing Promise and Potential: Our Nation's Historically Black Colleges and Universities.* Spec. issue of *ASHE Higher Education Report* 35.5 (2010). *Academic Search Complete.* Web. 21 May 2010.

Gaylord, Alan, ed. *Essays on the Art of Chaucer's Verse.* New York: Routledge, 2001. Print.

———. "Scanning the Prosodists: An Essay in Metacriticism." Gaylord, *Essays* 79–130.

Gee, James Paul. *What Video Games Have to Teach Us about Learning and Literacy.* New York: Palgrave, 2004. Print.

"Geoffrey Chaucer." *Luminarium.* Aniina Jokinen, 1997–2012. Web. 23 Dec. 2013. <http://www.luminarium.org/medlit/garden.htm>.

Geoffrey Chaucer Online: The Electronic Canterbury Tales. Ed. Dan Kline. N.p., 8 Dec. 2008. Web. 2 Sept. 2011. <http://www.kankedort.net/>.

Geoffreychaucer.org. Ed. David Wilson-Okamura. N.p., n.d. Web. 2 Sept. 2011. <http://geoffreychaucer.org/>.

Geoffrey Chaucer Page. Ed. Larry D. Benson. Harvard U, n.d. Web. 2 Sept. 2011. <http://www.courses.fas.harvard.edu/~chaucer/>.

Geoffrey Chaucer: The Canterbury Tales. Films for the Humanities and Social Sciences, 1998. DVD, videocassette.

Geoffrey Chaucer: The Canterbury Tales: *The Classic Text: Traditions and Interpretations.* U of Wisconsin, Milwaukee, 6 Mar. 2013. Web. 2 Sept. 2011. <http://www4.uwm.edu/libraries/special/exhibits/clastext/clspg073.cfm>.

Gibaldi, Joseph, ed. *Approaches to Teaching Chaucer's* Canterbury Tales. New York: MLA, 1980. Print.

———. "Materials." Gibaldi, *Approaches* 3–28.

Ginsberg, Warren. *Chaucer's Italian Tradition.* Ann Arbor: U of Michigan P, 2002. Print.

Gleick, James. "Keeping It Real: Why, in an Age of Free Information, Would Anyone Pay Millions for a Document?" *New York Times Magazine* 6 Jan. 2008: 13. Print.

Goldie, Matthew Boyd. *Middle English Literature: A Historical Sourcebook.* Malden: Blackwell, 2003. Print.

"Gombert and the Two Clerks." Benson and Andersson 88–99.

Goodmann, Thomas A. "On Literacy." *Exemplaria* 8.2 (1996): 459–72. Print.

The Good Wife's Guide: A Medieval Household Book. Trans. Gina L. Greco and Christine M. Rose. Ithaca: Cornell UP, 2009. Print. Trans. of *Le ménagier de Paris.*

Graff, Gerald. *Professing Literature: An Institutional History.* Chicago: U of Chicago P, 1987. Print.

Gray, Douglas. *Later Medieval English Literature.* Oxford: Oxford UP, 2008. Print.

————, ed. *Oxford Companion to Chaucer*. Oxford: Oxford UP, 2003. Print.

Green, Dennis H. *Women Readers in the Middle Ages*. Cambridge: Cambridge UP, 2007. Print.

Green, Richard Firth. "The Pardoner's Pants (and Why They Matter)." *Studies in the Age of Chaucer* 15 (1993): 131–45. Print.

Greenblatt, Stephen, gen. ed. *The Norton Anthology of English Literature: The Major Authors*. 9th ed. New York: Norton, 2013. Print.

————. *The Norton Anthology of English Literature: The Middle Ages through the Restoration and Eighteenth Century*. New York: Norton, 2012. Print.

Griffith, Dudley David. *Bibliography of Chaucer, 1908–1953*. Seattle: U of Washington P, 1955. Print.

Grossinger, Christina. *The World Upside Down: English Misericords*. Turnhout: Miller, 1997. Print.

Gurung, Regan A. R., et al. *Exploring Signature Pedagogies: Approaches to Teaching Disciplinary Habits of Mind*. Sterling: Stylus, 2009. Print.

Gust, Geoffrey W. *Constructing Chaucer: Author and Autofiction in the Critical Tradition*. New York: Palgrave, 2009. Print.

Hahn, Thomas, ed. *Race and Ethnicity in the Middle Ages*. Spec. issue of *Journal of Medieval and Early Modern Studies* 31.1 (2001): 1–173. Print.

Hall, Donald. *Queer Theories*. Basingstoke: Palgrave, 2003. Print.

Halperin, David. *St. Foucault: Towards a Gay Hagiography*. New York: Oxford UP, 1997. Print.

Hamel, Mary. "The Use of Sources in Editing Middle English Texts." *A Guide to Editing Middle English*. Ed. Vincent P. McCarren and Douglas Moffat. Ann Arbor: U of Michigan P, 1998. 203–16. Print.

Hammond, Eleanor Prescott. *Chaucer: A Bibliographical Manual*. New York: Macmillan, 1908. Print.

Hammond, Peter. *Food and Feast in Medieval England*. Rev ed. Phoenix Mill: Sutton, 2005. Print.

Hanawalt, Barbara. *Chaucer's England: Literature in Historical Context*. Minneapolis: U of Minnesota P, 1992. Print.

Hansen, Elaine Tuttle. *Chaucer and the Fictions of Gender*. Berkeley: U of California P, 1992. Print.

Hawkins, Sherman. "Chaucer's Prioress and the Sacrifice of Praise." *Journal of English and Germanic Philology* 63 (1964): 599–624. Print.

Heffernan, Carol F. "Mercantilism and Faith in the Eastern Mediterranean: Chaucer's *Man of Law's Tale*, Boccaccio's *Decameron* 5, 2, and Gower's 'Tale of Constance.'" *The Orient in Chaucer and Medieval Romance*. Cambridge: Brewer, 2003. 23–44. Print.

Helmholz, R. H. *Marriage Litigation in Medieval England*. London: Cambridge UP, 1974. Print.

Heng, Geraldine. "Jews, Saracens, 'Black Men,' Tartars: England in a World of Racial Difference." *A Companion to Medieval English Literature and Culture, c. 1350–1500*. Ed. Peter Brown. Malden: Blackwell, 2007. 247–69. Print.

Henisch, Bridget. *The Medieval Cook*. Woodbridge: Boydell, 2009. Print.

Heroes: Text and Hypertext. U College, Cork, n.d. Web. May 2010. <http://heroespage .wordpress.com/our-classes-with-new-york/>.

Hieatt, Constance, Brenda Hosington, and Sharon Butler. *Pleyn Delit: Medieval Cookery for Modern Cooks*. 2nd ed. Toronto: U of Toronto P, 1996. Print.

Hill, John M. *Chaucerian Belief: The Poetics of Reverence and Delight*. New Haven: Yale UP, 1991. Print.

Hines, John. *The Fabliaux in English*. London: Longman, 1993. Print.

Hodges, Laura F. *Chaucer and Clothing: Clerical and Academic Costume in the General Prologue to* The Canterbury Tales. Cambridge: Brewer, 2005. Print. Chaucer Studies 34.

———. *Chaucer and Costume: The Secular Pilgrims in the General Prologue*. Cambridge: Brewer, 2000. Print. Chaucer Studies 26.

———. Message to Jane Chance. 13 Mar. 2010. E-mail.

Hoffeld, Jeffrey. "Adam's Two Wives." *Metropolitan Museum of Art Bulletin* 26.10 (1968): 430–40. Print.

Holloway, Julia Bolton. "Medieval Pilgrimage." Gibaldi, *Approaches* 143–48.

Holsinger, Bruce. *Music, Body, and Desire in Medieval Culture: Hildegard of Bingen to Chaucer*. Stanford: Stanford UP, 2001. Print.

"Hopeland." S.v. *Middle English Dictionary*. U of Michigan, 2001. Web. 7 Jan. 2014.

Horobin, Simon. *Chaucer's Language*. New York: Palgrave, 2007. Print.

Howard, Donald. *Chaucer and the Medieval World*. London: Weidenfeld, 1987. Print.

———. *Chaucer: His Life, His Work, His World*. New York: Dutton, 1987. Print.

———. "The Idea of a Chaucer Course." Gibaldi, *Approaches* 57–62.

———. *The Idea of* The Canterbury Tales. Berkeley: U of California P, 1976. Print.

Hugh of Saint Victor. *On the Sacraments of the Christian Faith*. Trans. Roy J. Deferrari. Cambridge: Medieval Acad. of Amer., 1951. Print.

"Humour, humor." *Oxford English Dictionary*. 2nd ed. 1989. Print.

Huppé, Bernard. *Fruyt and Chaf: Studies in Chaucer's Allegories*. Princeton: Princeton UP, 1963. Print.

Huscroft, Richard. *Expulsion: England's Jewish Solution*. Stroud: Tempus, 2006. Print.

Ingenthron, Blair. "Chaucer in Virtual Reality." 2010. TS. Pace U.

Ingham, Patricia Clare. "Pastoral Histories: Conquest, Utopia, and the Wife of Bath's Tale." *Texas Studies in Literature and Language* 44.1 (2002): 34–46. Print.

Ingham, Patricia Clare, and Michelle Warren, eds. *Postcolonial Moves: Medieval through Modern*. New York: Palgrave, 2003. Print.

Internet Medieval Sourcebook. Ed. Paul Halsall. Fordham U, 4 Nov. 2011. Web. 2 Sept. 2011. <http://www.fordham.edu/halsall/sbook.html>.

"An Introduction to Illuminated Manuscripts." *Catalogue of Illuminated Manuscripts*. British Lib., n.d. Web. 26 June 2013.

Jacobs, Kathryn. "The Marriage Contract of the Franklin's Tale: The Remaking of Society." *Chaucer Review* 20 (1985): 132–43. Print.

Jeffrey, David Lyle, ed. *Chaucer and Scriptural Tradition*. Ottawa: U of Ottawa P, 1984. Print.

Jerome. "Saint Jerome: From 'The Epistle against Jovinian.'" R. Miller 415–36.

———. "St Jerome, from 'Against Jovinian.'" Chaucer [ed. Kolve and Olson] 359–73.

Jones, Ernest. *The Life and Work of Sigmund Freud*. Vol. 2. New York: Basic, 1955. Print.

Jones, Malcolm. *The Secret Middle Ages: Discovering the Real Medieval World*. Westport: Praeger, 2003. Print.

Jordan, Robert M. "A Rhetorical and Structural Emphasis." Gibaldi, *Approaches* 81–88.

"Jupon." *Middle English Dictionary*. U of Michigan, 2001. Web. 7 Jan. 2014.

Kaske, Robert E. *Medieval Christian Literary Imagery: A Guide to Interpretation*. Toronto: U of Toronto P, 1988. Print.

———. "The Summoner's Garleek, Oynons, and Eek Lekes." *MLN* 74 (1959): 481–84. Print.

Keen, Maurice. *English Society in the Later Middle Ages, 1348–1500*. London: Penguin, 1990. Print.

Kelly, Henry Ansgar. *Chaucerian Tragedy*. Cambridge: Brewer, 1997. Print.

Kendrick, Laura. *Chaucerian Play: Comedy and Control in* The Canterbury Tales. Berkeley: U of California P, 1988. Print.

Kerby-Fulton, Kathryn, and Maidie Hilmo. *The Medieval Professional Reader at Work: Evidence from the Manuscripts of Chaucer, Langland, Kempe, and Gower*. Victoria: U of Victoria P, 2001. Print.

King-Aribisala, Karen. *Kicking Tongues*. Portsmouth: Heinemann, 1998. Print.

Kittredge, George Lyman. *Chaucer and His Poetry*. Cambridge: Harvard UP, 1915. Print.

———. "Chaucer's Discussion of Marriage." *Modern Philology* 9 (1911–12): 435–67. Print.

———. "The Marriage Group." 1912. Chaucer [ed. Kolve and Olson] 539–46.

Klassen, Norman. *Chaucer on Love, Knowledge, and Sight*. Cambridge: Brewer, 1995. Print.

Knapp, Peggy. *Chaucer and the Social Contest*. New York: Routledge, 1990. Print.

———. "Chaucer for Fun and Profit." Ashton and Sylvester 17–29.

———. *Chaucerian Aesthetics*. New York: Palgrave, 2008. Print.

Knight, Stephen. *Geoffrey Chaucer*. Oxford: Blackwell, 1986. Print.

"The Knight Who Could Make Cunts Talk." Dubin 143–77.

Koff, Leonard Michael. *Chaucer and the Art of Storytelling*. Berkeley: U of California P, 1988. Print.

Koff, Leonard Michael, and Brenda Deen Schildgen, eds. The Decameron *and* The Canterbury Tales: *New Essays on an Old Question*. Madison: Fairleigh Dickinson UP, 2000. Print.

Kökeritz, Helge. *A Guide to Chaucer's Pronunciation*. Toronto: U of Toronto P, 1961. Print.

Kolve, V. A. *Chaucer and the Imagery of Narrative: The First Five Canterbury Tales.* Stanford: Stanford UP, 1984. Print.

———. *Telling Images: Chaucer and the Imagery of Narrative II.* Stanford: Stanford UP, 2009. Print.

Kolve, V. A., and Glending Olson. "Chaucer's Language." Chaucer [ed. Kolve and Olson] xv–xix.

Kruger, Steven F. "Claiming the Pardoner: Toward a Gay Reading of Chaucer's Pardoner's Tale." *Exemplaria* 6.1 (1994): 115–39. Rpt. in *The Critical Tradition: Classic Texts and Contemporary Trends.* Ed. David Richter. 3rd. ed. New York: Bedford, 2007. 1692–1706. Print.

———. "Fetishism, 1927, 1614, 1461." Cohen, *Postcolonial Middle Ages* 193–208.

———. "A Series of Linked Assignments for the Undergraduate Course on Chaucer's *Canterbury Tales.*" Ashton and Sylvester 30–45.

Krummel, Miriamne Ara. "Globalizing Jewish Communities: Mapping a Jewish Geography in Fragment VII of *The Canterbury Tales.*" *Texas Studies in Language and Literature* 50 (2008): 121–42. Print.

———. "The Semitisms of Middle English Literature." *Literature Compass.* Wiley, 15 Dec. 2005. Web. 15 Apr. 2013. <http://dx.doi.org/10.1111/j.1741-4113.2004.00025.x>.

Kytle, Ray. "Prewriting by Analysis." *College Composition and Communication* 21.5 (1970): 380–85. Print.

Labyrinth: Resources for Medieval Studies. Ed. Deborah Everhart and Martin Irvine. Georgetown U, n.d. Web. 2 Sept. 2011. <http://labyrinth.georgetown.edu/>.

Lacan, Jaques. *The Four Fundamental Concepts of Psycho-analysis.* Ed. Jacques-Alain Miller. Trans. Alan Sheridan. New York: Norton, 1977. Print.

Lambdin, Laura C., and Robert T. Lambdin, eds. *Chaucer's Pilgrims: An Historical Guide to the Pilgrims in* The Canterbury Tales. Westport: Greenwood, 1996. Print.

Lampert, Lisa. *Gender and Jewish Difference from Paul to Shakespeare.* Philadelphia: U of Pennsylvania P, 2004. Print.

Lancaster, Lynne. *When Generations Collide: Who They Are, Why They Clash, How to Solve the Generational Puzzle at Work.* New York: Harper, 2002. Print.

Laskaya, Anne. *Chaucer's Approach to Gender in* The Canterbury Tales. Cambridge: Brewer, 1995. Print.

Lavezzo, Kathy. "Beyond Rome: Mapping Gender and Justice in *The Man of Law's Tale.*" *Studies in the Age of Chaucer* 24 (2002): 149–80. Print.

Lawrence, D. H. "Final Version (1923)." *Studies in Classic American Literature.* Ed. Ezra Greenspan, Lindeth Vasey, and John Worthen. Cambridge: Cambridge UP, 2003. 7–162. Print.

Lawton, David. *Chaucer's Narrators.* Cambridge: Brewer, 1985. Print.

Lees, Clare, ed. *Medieval Masculinities: Regarding Men in the Middle Ages.* Minneapolis: U of Minnesota P, 1994. Print.

LeFebvre, Nichole. "Chaucer in a Virtual Environment." 2010. TS. Pace U.

Leicester, H. Marshall, Jr. *The Disenchanted Self: Representing the Subject in* The Canterbury Tales. Berkeley: U of California P, 1990. Print.

―――. "Structure as Deconstruction: 'Chaucer and Estates Satire' in the General Prologue; or, Reading Chaucer as a Prologue to the History of Disenchantment." *Exemplaria* 2.1 (1990): 241–61. Print.

Lerer, Seth. *Chaucer and His Readers: Imagining the Author in Late Medieval England*. Princeton: Princeton UP, 1994. Print.

―――, ed. *The Yale Companion to Chaucer*. New Haven: Yale UP, 2006. Print.

Levinas, Emmanuel. *Collected Philosophical Papers*. Trans. Alphonso Lingis. Dordrecht: Martinus, 1987. Print.

―――. *Entre-Nous: On Thinking-of-the-Other*. Trans. Michael B. Smith and Barbara Harshav. New York: Columbia UP, 1998. Print.

―――. *Existence and Existents*. Trans. Alphonso Lingis. The Hague: Martinus, 1972. Print.

―――. "Language and Proximity." Levinas, *Collected Philosophical Papers* 109–26.

―――. "Toward the Other." *Nine Talmudic Readings*. Bloomington: Indiana UP, 2003. 12–29. Print.

Levy, Steven. *The Perfect Thing: How the iPod Shuffles Commerce, Culture, and Coolness*. New York: Simon, 2006. Print.

Lewis, C. S. *The Discarded Image: An Introduction to Medieval and Renaissance Literature*. Cambridge: Cambridge UP, 1964. Print.

Leyerle, John. *Chaucer: A Bibliographical Introduction*. Toronto: U of Toronto P, 1986. Print.

Librarius. Ed. Sinan Kökbugur. Librarius, n.d. Web. 2 Sept. 2011. <http://www.librarius.com/cantales.htm>.

Light, Richard J. *Making the Most of College: Students Speak Their Minds*. Cambridge: Harvard UP, 2001. Print.

Lindahl, Carl. *Earnest Games: Folkloric Patterns in* The Canterbury Tales. Bloomington: Indiana UP, 1987. Print.

Lipton, Emma. *Affections of the Mind: The Politics of Sacramental Marriage in Late Medieval English Literature*. Notre Dame: U of Notre Dame P, 2007. Print.

Lochrie, Karma. *Heterosyncrasies: Female Sexuality When Normal Wasn't*. Minneapolis: U of Minnesota P, 2005. Print.

Loomba, Ania, and Jonathan Burton, eds. *Race in Early Modern England: A Documentary Companion*. New York: Palgrave, 2007. Print.

Lorris, Guillaume de, and Jean de Meun. *Roman de la Rose*. Ed. Daniel Poirion. Paris: Garnier, 1974. Print.

Louens, Renaud de. *Livre de Mellibee et Prudence*. Correale and Hamel 331–408.

Luminarium. Ed. Anniina Jokinen. N.p., n.d. Web. 2 Sept. 2011. <http://www.luminarium.org/medlit/chaucer.htm>.

Lynch, Kathryn L., ed. *Chaucer's Cultural Geography: Basic Readings in Chaucer and His Time*. New York: Routledge, 2002. Print.

―――. "East Meets West in Chaucer's Squire's and Franklin's Tales." *Speculum* 70.3 (1995): 530–51. Print.

————. "The Pardoner's Digestion: Eating Images in *The Canterbury Tales*." *Speaking Images: Essays in Honor of V. A. Kolve*. Ed. R. F. Yeager and Charlotte Morse. Asheville: Pegasus, 2001. 393–409. Print.

————. "Storytelling, Exchange, and Constancy: East and West in Chaucer's *Man of Law's Tale*." *Chaucer Review* 33.4 (1999): 409–22. Print.

MacDonald, Nicola, ed. *Medieval Obscenities*. Woodbridge: York Medieval, 2006. Print.

Machan, Tim William. *Textual Criticism and Middle English Texts*. Charlottesville: UP of Virginia, 1994. Print.

"The Making of a Medieval Book." *The J. Paul Getty Museum*. J. Paul Getty Trust, n.d. Web. 26 June 2013.

Manly, John M., and Edith Rickert, eds. *The Text of* The Canterbury Tales*: Studied on the Basis of All Known Manuscripts*. 8 vols. Chicago: U of Chicago P, 1940. Print.

Mann, Jill. *Chaucer and Medieval Estates Satire: The Literature of Social Classes and the General Prologue of* The Canterbury Tales. Cambridge: Cambridge UP, 1973. Print.

————. "Editor's Note." Chaucer [ed. Mann] xi.

————. *Feminizing Chaucer*. Rochester: Brewer, 2002. Print.

————. *Geoffrey Chaucer*. Atlantic Highlands: Humanities, 1991. Print. Feminist Readings Ser.

Masie, Elliott. "The Blended Learning Imperative." *The Handbook of Blended Learning: Global Perspectives, Local Designs*. Ed. Curtis J. Bonk and Charles R. Graham. San Francisco: Pfeiffer, 2006. 22–26. Print.

Mather, Frank Jewett. *The Prologue from Chaucer's* Canterbury Tales. Boston: Houghton Mifflin, 1899. Riverside Lit. Ser.

McGann, Jerome. "Visible and Invisible Books: Hermetic Images in N-Dimensional Space." *The Future of the Page*. Ed. Peter Stoicheff and Andrew Taylor. Toronto: U of Toronto P, 2004. 143–158. Print.

McSheffrey, Shannon, ed. *Love and Marriage in Late Medieval London*. Kalamazoo: Medieval Inst., 1995. Print. TEAMS Documents of Practice Ser.

Le menagier de Paris. Chaucer [ed. Kolve and Olson] 420–21.

METRO: Middle English Teaching Resources Online. Harvard U, n.d. Web. 2 Sept. 2011. <http://metro.fas.harvard.edu/icb/icb.do>.

Meyer-Lee, Robert J. "Fragments IV and V of *The Canterbury Tales* Do Not Exist." *Chaucer Review* 45.1 (2010): 1–31. Print.

Middle English Compendium. Ed. Frances McSparran. U of Michigan, 22 Feb. 2006. Web. 2 Sept. 2011. <http://quod.lib.umich.edu/m/mec/>.

Miller, Mark. *Philosophical Chaucer: Love, Sex, and Agency in* The Canterbury Tales. Cambridge: Cambridge UP, 2004. Print.

Miller, Robert P., ed. *Chaucer: Sources and Backgrounds*. New York: Oxford UP, 1977. Print.

"The Miller and the Two Clerks." Benson and Andersson 100–15.

Minnis, Alastair J. *Fallible Authors: Chaucer's Pardoner and Wife of Bath*. Philadelphia: U of Pennsylvania P, 2008. Print.

Mitchell, J. Allan. *Ethics and Exemplary Narrative in Chaucer and Gower*. Cambridge: Brewer, 2004. Print.

Mooney, Linne R. "Chaucer's Scribe." *Speculum* 81.1 (2006): 97–138. Print.

Moore, David Chioni. "Is the Post- in Postcolonial the Post- in Post-Soviet? Notes toward a Global Postcolonial Critique." *PMLA* 116.1 (2001): 111–28. Print.

Morrison, Susan Signe. *Excrement in the Late Middle Ages: Sacred Filth and Chaucer's Fecopoetics*. New York: Palgrave, 2008. Print.

Mullaney, Samantha. "The Language of Costume in the Ellesmere Portraits." *Trivium* 31 (1999): 33–57. Print.

Mundil, Robin. *England's Jewish Solution: Experiment and Expulsion, 1262–1290*. Cambridge: Cambridge UP, 1998. Print.

Murphy, Michael. "Introduction." The Canterbury Tales: *A Reader-Friendly Version of the General Prologue and Sixteen Tales Put into Modern Spelling*. Ed. Murphy. *Webcore*. Brooklyn Coll., City U of New York, n.d. Web. 21 Jan. 2014.

Muscatine, Charles. *Chaucer and the French Tradition: A Study in Style and Meaning*. Berkeley: U of California P, 1957. Print.

———. "'What Amounteth Al This Wit?': Chaucer and Scholarship." *Medieval Literature, Style, and Culture: Essays by Charles Muscatine*. Columbia: U of South Carolina P, 1999. 48–55. Print.

Myers, A. R. *London in the Age of Chaucer*. Norman: U of Oklahoma P, 1972. Print.

Myerson, Jonathan. *The Canterbury Tales*. BBC, 1998. Film.

Myles, Robert. *Chaucerian Realism*. Woodbridge: Brewer, 1994. Print.

The Name of the Rose. Dir. Jean-Jacques Annaud. Perf. Sean Connery and F. Murray Abraham. 1986. Warner Home Video, 2004. DVD.

"NCTE/IRA Standards for the English Language Arts." *NCTE*. Natl. Council of Teachers of English, 1998–2013. Web. 22 Dec. 2013.

NCTE Principles of Adolescent Literacy Reform: A Policy Research Brief. *NCTE*. Natl. Council of Teachers of English, 2006. Web. 24 Sept. 2009.

Nelson, Marilyn. *Cachoeira Tales and Other Poems*. Baton Rouge: Louisiana State UP, 2005. Print.

Neuse, Richard. *Chaucer's Dante: Allegory and Epic Theatre in* The Canterbury Tales. Berkeley: U of California P, 1991. Print.

New Chaucer Society. Washington U, 2 Sept. 2011. Web. 19 Apr. 2013. <http://newchaucersociety.org>.

Ní Dhomhnaill, Nuala. "Why I Chose to Write in Irish: The Corpse That Sits up and Talks Back." *The New York Times*. New York Times, 8 Jan. 1995. Web. 6 July 2010.

Nolan, Barbara. *Chaucer and the Tradition of the Roman Antique*. Cambridge: Cambridge UP, 1992. Print.

————. "Chaucer's Tales of Transcendence: Rhyme Royal and Christian Prayer in *The Canterbury Tales*." *Chaucer's Religious Tales*. Ed. C. David Benson and Elizabeth Robertson. Cambridge: Brewer, 1990. 21–38. Print.

Nolan, Maura. "'Acquiteth Yow Now': Textual Contradiction and Legal Discourse in the 'Man of Law's Introduction.'" *The Letter of the Law: Legal Practice and Literary Production in Medieval England*. Ed. Emily Steiner and Candace Barrington. New York: Cornell UP, 2002. 136–54. Print.

North, John. *Chaucer's Universe*. Oxford: Oxford UP, 1990. Print.

Olson, Linda, and Kathryn Kerby-Fulton, eds. *Voices in Dialogue: Reading Women in the Middle Ages*. Notre Dame: U of Notre Dame P, 2005. Print.

Olson, Paul. The Canterbury Tales *and the Good Society*. Princeton: Princeton UP, 1986. Print.

Online Medieval and Classical Library. Ed. Roy Tennant. N.p., n.d. Web. 19 Apr. 2013. <http://omacl.org/>.

ORB: On-line Reference Book for Medieval Studies. Ed. Kathryn Talarico. N.p., 2003. Web. 19 Apr. 2013. <http://www.the-orb.net/index.html>.

Orr, Patricia R. "'Fat' and Chaucer's Monk." 1984. TS. Paper submitted for English 523: The Graduate Chaucer Trailer Course, Rice U.

Osborn, Marijane. *Time and the Astrolabe in* The Canterbury Tales. Norman: U of Oklahoma P, 2002. Print.

Owen, Charles A. *The Manuscripts of* The Canterbury Tales. Cambridge: Brewer, 1991. Print.

————. "Morality as a Comic Motif in *The Canterbury Tales*." *College English* 16.4 (1955): 226–32. Print.

Parkes, M. B. "The Planning and Construction of the Ellesmere Manuscript." Stevens and Woodward 41–48.

Patterson, Lee. *Chaucer and the Subject of History*. Madison: U of Wisconsin P, 1991. Print.

————. "Chaucer's Pardoner on the Couch: Psyche and Clio in Medieval Literary Studies." *Speculum* 76.3 (2001): 638–80. Print.

————. "'Experience Woot It Well It Is Noght So': Marriage and the Pursuit of Happiness in the Wife of Bath's Prologue and Tale." Beidler, *Wife of Bath* 133–54.

————. *Geoffrey Chaucer's* The Canterbury Tales: *A Casebook*. New York: Oxford UP, 2007. Print.

————. "'The Living Witnesses of Our Redemption': Martyrdom and Imitation in Chaucer's *Prioress's Tale*." *Journal of Medieval and Early Modern Studies* 31 (2001): 507–60. Print.

————. *Temporal Circumstances: Form and History in* The Canterbury Tales. New York: Palgrave, 2006. Print.

————. "'What Man Artow?': Authorial Self-Definition in the *Tale of Sir Thopas* and the *Tale of Melibee*." *Studies in the Age of Chaucer* 13 (1991): 117–75. Print.

Payne, F. Anne. *Chaucer and Menippean Satire*. Madison: U of Wisconsin P, 1981. Print.

232   WORKS CITED

Pearsall, Derek. *The Canterbury Tales*. London: Allen, 1985. Print.

———, ed. *Chaucer to Spenser: An Anthology of Writings in English, 1375–1575*. Malden: Blackwell, 1998. Print.

———. *The Life of Geoffrey Chaucer: A Critical Biography*. 1992. Oxford: Wiley, 1998. Print.

———. "Pre-empting Closure in *The Canterbury Tales*: Old Endings, New Beginnings." *Essays on Ricardian Literature: In Honour of J. A. Burrow*. Ed. A. J. Minnis, Charlotte C. Morse, and Thorlac Turville-Petre. Oxford: Clarendon, 1997. 23–38. Print.

Petrarch [Francesco Petrarca]. "Francis Petrarch: From *Letters of Old Age*, XVII, 3, 'To Giovanni Boccaccio.'" R. Miller 136–52.

———. "The Story of Griselda." Chaucer [ed. Kolve and Olson] 407–16.

———. "Two Letters to Boccaccio." Chaucer [ed. Kolve and Olson] 417–19.

Phillips, Helen, ed. *Chaucer and Religion*. Cambridge: Brewer, 2010. Print.

———. *An Introduction to* The Canterbury Tales: *Reading, Fiction, Context*. London: Palgrave, 2000. Print.

"The Pilgrimage to Canterbury, 1806–7." *Tate*. Tate, n.d. Web. 23 Dec. 2013. <http://www.tate.org.uk/art/artworks/stothard-the-pilgrimage-to-canterbury-n01163>.

Pollock, Frederick, and Frederic William Maitland. *The History of English Law before the Time of Edward I*. 2nd ed. 2 vols. Cambridge: Cambridge UP, 1968. Print.

Pope, Rob. *How to Study Chaucer*. 2nd ed. New York: Palgrave, 2000. Print.

Prendergast, Thomas. *Chaucer's Dead Body: From Corpse to Corpus*. New York: Routledge, 2003. Print.

Prendergast, Thomas, and Barbara Kline, eds. *Rewriting Chaucer: Culture, Authority, and the Idea of the Authentic Text, 1400–1602*. Columbus: Ohio State UP, 1999. Print.

Prensky, Mark. *Digital Game-Based Learning*. New York: McGraw, 2001. Print.

A Prologue to Chaucer. By Velma B. Richmond. Prod. U of California, Berkeley. Films for the Humanities and Social Sciences, 1986. DVD, videocassette.

Pugh, Tison. *Queering Medieval Genres*. New York: Palgrave, 2004. Print.

———. *Sexuality and Its Queer Discontents in Middle English Literature*. New York: Palgrave, 2008. Print.

Pugh, Tison, Michael Calabrese, and Marcia Smith Marzec. "Introduction: The Myths of Masculinity in Chaucer's *Troilus and Criseyde*." Pugh and Marzec 1–8.

Pugh, Tison, and Marcia Marzec, eds. *Men and Masculinities in Chaucer's* Troilus and Criseyde. Cambridge: Brewer, 2008. Print.

Pugh, Tison, and Angela Jane Weisl, eds. *Approaches to Teaching Chaucer's* Troilus and Criseyde *and the Shorter Poems*. New York: MLA, 2007. Print.

———. "Introduction: A Survey of Pedagogical Approaches to *Troilus and Criseyde* and the Shorter Poems." Pugh and Weisl, *Approaches* 23–26.

Reed, Teresa P. "Shadows of the Law: Chaucer's 'Man of Law's Tale,' Exemplarity and Narrativity." *Mediaevalia: An Interdisciplinary Journal of Medieval Studies Worldwide* 21.2 (1997): 231–48. Print.

Rhodes, Jim. *Poetry Does Theology: Chaucer, Grosseteste, and the Pearl-Poet*. Notre Dame: U of Notre Dame P, 2001. Print.

Richter, David, ed. *The Critical Tradition: Classic Texts and Contemporary Trends*. 3rd ed. New York: Bedford, 2007. Print.

Ridley, Florence. "Introduction: The Challenge of Teaching *The Canterbury Tales*." Gibaldi, *Approaches* xi–xvi.

Robertson, D. W., Jr. *Chaucer's London*. New York: Wiley, 1968. Print.

———. "The Intellectual, Artistic, and Historical Context." Gibaldi, *Approaches* 129–35.

———. *A Preface to Chaucer: Studies in Medieval Perspectives*. Princeton: Princeton UP, 1962. Print.

Robertson, Elizabeth. "Aspects of Female Piety in the *Prioress's Tale*." *Chaucer's Religious Tales*. Ed. C. David Benson and Elizabeth Robertson. Cambridge: Brewer, 1990. 145–60. Print.

"Robin Hood and the Monk." *Robin Hood and Other Outlaw Tales*. Ed. Stephen Knight and Thomas Ohlgren. Kalamazoo: Medieval Inst., 1997. *TEAMS Middle English Texts Series*. Web. 26 June 2013.

"Robin Hood and the Potter." *Robin Hood and Other Outlaw Tales*. Ed. Stephen Knight and Thomas Ohlgren. Kalamazoo: Medieval Inst., 1997. *TEAMS Middle English Texts Series*. Web. 26 June 2013.

Rogers, Shannon L. *All Things Chaucer: An Encyclopedia of Chaucer's World*. 2 vols. Westport: Greenwood, 2007. Print.

Rohman, D. Gordon. "Pre-writing: The Stage of Discovery in the Writing Process." *Teaching Writing: Landmarks and Horizons*. Ed. Christina Russell McDonald and Robert L. McDonald. Carbondale: Southern Illinois UP, 2002. 7–16. Print.

Roman de la Rose. Fifteenth century. MS Douce 195, f. 118. Bodleian Lib., Oxford.

Root, Robert K. "The Text of *The Canterbury Tales*." *Studies in Philology* 38.1 (1941): 1–13. Print.

Rose, Christine. "Teaching Chaucer in the Nineties: A Symposium." *Exemplaria* 8.2 (1996): 443–551. Print.

Rosenblum, Joseph, with William K. Finley. "Chaucer Gentrified: The Nexus of Art and Politics in the Ellesmere Miniatures." *Chaucer Review* 38.2 (2003): 140–57. Print.

Ross, Thomas W. "An Approach to Teaching Chaucer's Language." Gibaldi, *Approaches* 105–09.

Rossignol, Rosalyn. *Chaucer A to Z: The Essential Reference to His Life and Works*. New York: Facts on File, 1999. Print.

———. *Critical Companion to Chaucer: A Literary Reference to His Life and Work*. New York: Facts on File, 2007. Print.

"Royal MS 18.D.II." *Digitised Manuscripts*. British Lib. Board, n.d. Web. 23 Dec. 2013. <http://www.bl.uk/manuscripts/FullDisplay.aspx?ref=royal_ms_18_d_ii_f148r>. Folio 148r.

Rubin, Miri. *Gentile Tales: The Narrative Assault on Late Medieval Jews*. Philadelphia: U of Pennsylvania P, 2004. Print.

Rudd, Gillian. *The Complete Critical Guide to Geoffrey Chaucer*. New York: Routledge, 2001. Print.

Russell, J. Stephen. *Chaucer and the Trivium: The Mindsong of* The Canterbury Tales. Gainesville: UP of Florida, 1998. Print.

"Saint Martin's Four Wishes." Dubin 885–95.

Salvatori, Mariolina Rizzi, and Patricia Donahue. *The Elements (and Pleasures) of Difficulty*. New York: Pearson, 2005. Print.

The Sarum Missal in English. Trans. Frederick E. Warren. London: De La More, 1911. Print.

Scala, Elizabeth. *Absent Narratives, Manuscript Textuality, and Literary Structure in Late Medieval England*. New York: Palgrave, 2002. Print.

Scala, Elizabeth, and Sylvia Federico, eds. *The Post-historical Middle Ages*. New York: Palgrave, 2009. Print.

Scanlon, Larry, ed. *The Cambridge Companion to Medieval English Literature, 1100–1500*. Cambridge: Cambridge UP, 2009. Print.

Schibanoff, Susan. "Crooked Rib: Women in Medieval Literature." Gibaldi, *Approaches* 121–28.

———. "Orientalism, Antifeminism, Heresy, and Chaucer's *Man of Law's Tale*." *Exemplaria* 8 (1996): 59–96. Print.

Schildgen, Brenda D. *Pagans, Tartars, Moslems, and Jews in Chaucer's* Canterbury Tales. Gainesville: UP of Florida, 2001. Print.

Schultz, James. *Courtly Love, the Love of Courtliness, and the History of Sexuality*. Chicago: U of Chicago P, 2006. Print.

Schulz, Herbert. *The Ellesmere Manuscript of Chaucer's* Canterbury Tales. San Marino: Huntington Lib., 1999. Print.

Scott, A. F. *Who's Who in Chaucer*. London: Elm Tree, 1974. Print.

Scott, Kathleen L. "An Hours and Psalter by Two Ellesmere Illuminators." Stevens and Woodward 87–119.

Scully, Terence. *The Art of Cookery in the Middle Ages*. Woodbridge: Boydell, 1995. Print.

Seaman, Myra. "Teaching Chaucer's Postmodern Dream Visions." Pugh and Weisl, *Approaches* 97–100.

Sedgwick, Eve Kosofsky. *Between Men: English Literature and Male Homosocial Desire*. New York: Columbia UP, 1985. Print.

Seymour, M. C. *A Catalogue of Chaucer Manuscripts: The Canterbury Tales*. Vol. 2. Aldershot: Scolar, 1997. Print.

Shepherd, Margaret. *Calligraphy Alphabets Made Easy*. New York: Perigee Trade, 1986. Print.

———. *Learn Calligraphy: The Complete Book of Lettering and Design*. New York: Broadway, 2001. Print.

Shoaf, R. Allen. *Chaucer's Body: The Anxiety of Circulation in* The Canterbury Tales. Gainesville: UP of Florida, 2001. Print.

Shulman, Lee S. "Signature Pedagogies in the Professions." *Daedalus* 134.3 (2005): 52–59. Print.

Sidhu, Nicole. "'To Late for to Crie': Female Desire, Fabliau Politics and Classical Legend in Chaucer's Reeve's Tale." *Exemplaria* 21 (2009): 3–23. Print.

Simpson, James, ed. *1350–1547: Reform and Cultural Revolution*. Vol. 2 of *The Oxford English Literary History*. Oxford: Oxford UP, 2007. Print.

Skeat, W. W. *The Evolution of* The Canterbury Tales. London: Kegan, 1907. Print. Chaucer Society Pubs. Second Ser. 38.

Spearing, A. C. *Medieval Autographies: The "I" of the Text*. Notre Dame: U of Notre Dame P, 2012. Print.

———. "Narrative Voice: The Case of Chaucer's 'Man of Law's Tale.'" *New Literary History* 32.3 (2001): 715–46. Print.

———. *Textual Subjectivity: The Encoding of Subjectivity in Medieval Narratives and Lyrics*. Oxford: Oxford UP, 2005. Print.

Spencer, Colin. *Homosexuality in History*. New York: Harcourt, 1995. Print.

Spurgeon, Caroline F. E. *Five Hundred Years of Chaucer Criticism and Allusion, 1357–1900*. 1925. 3 vols. New York: Russell, 1960. Print.

Staley, Lynn. *Languages of Power in the Age of Richard II*. University Park: Penn State UP, 2005. Print.

Stanbury, Sarah. *The Visual Object of Desire in Late Medieval England*. Philadelphia: U of Pennsylvania P, 2008. Print.

Stein, Robert M. *Reality Fictions: Romance, History, and Governmental Authority, 1025–1180*. Notre Dame: U of Notre Dame P, 2006. Print.

Stevens, Martin, and Daniel Woodward, eds. *The Ellesmere Chaucer: Essays in Interpretation*. San Marino: Huntington Lib., 1997. Print.

Stevenson, Barbara. "'In Forme of Speche Is Chaunge': Introducing Students to Chaucer's Middle English." Pugh and Weisl, *Approaches* 144–48.

Stevenson, Kenneth. *Nuptial Blessing: A Study of Christian Marriage Rites*. New York: Oxford UP, 1983. Print.

Strohm, Paul. "The Allegory of the *Tale of Melibee*." *Chaucer Review* 2.1 (1967): 32–42. Print.

———, ed. *Middle English*. Oxford: Oxford UP, 2007. Print.

———. *Social Chaucer*. Cambridge: Harvard UP, 1989. Print.

Students Reading Chaucer. 2008. *YouTube*. YouTube, 21 May 2010. Web. 18 July 2013. <http://www.youtube.com/watch?v=d3y_NbgqRZQ>.

Sturges, Robert. *Chaucer's Pardoner and Gender Theory: Bodies of Discourse*. New York: St. Martin's, 2000. Print.

"Survey: iPods More Popular Than Beer." *Washington Post*. Washington Post, 7 June 2006. Web. 19 Apr. 2013.

Sylvester, Louise. "Teaching the Language of Chaucer." Ashton and Sylvester 81–95.

Tapscott, Don. *Growing Up Digital: The Rise of the Net Generation*. New York: McGraw, 1998. Print.

Taylor, Karla. *Chaucer Reads the* Divine Comedy. Stanford: Stanford UP, 1989. Print.

Theophrastes. "From 'The Golden Book on Marriage.'" Chaucer [ed. Kolve and Olson] 357–59.

Thompson, Stith. *Motif-Index of Folk-Literature: A Classification of Narrative Elements in Folktales, Ballads, Myths, Fables, Mediaeval Romances, Exempla, Fabliaux, Jest-Books, and Local Legends*. Bloomington: Indiana UP, 1956. Print.

Thomson, George. *The Illuminated Lettering Kit*. San Francisco: Chronicle, 2004. Print.

Tolhurst, Fiona. "Why We Should Teach—and Our Students Perform—*The Legend of Good Women*." Ashton and Sylvester 46–64.

Trapp, J. B., Douglas Gray, and Julia Boffey, eds. *Medieval English Literature*. New York: Oxford UP, 2002. Print. Vol. 1 of *The Oxford Anthology of English Literature*.

Travis, Peter W. "The Body of the Nun's Priest; or, Chaucer's Disseminal Genius." *Reading Medieval Culture: Essays on Medieval Literature and Culture in Honor of Robert W. Hanning*. Ed. Robert M. Stein and Sandra Pierson Prior. Notre Dame: U of Notre Dame P, 2005. 231–47. Print.

———. "Deconstructing Chaucer's Retraction." *Exemplaria* 3 (1991): 135–58. Print.

———. *Disseminal Chaucer: Rereading the Nun's Priest's Tale*. Notre Dame: U of Notre Dame P, 2010. Print.

Treasures in Full: Caxton's Chaucer. British Lib., n.d. Web. 2 Sept. 2011. <http://www.bl.uk/treasures/caxton/homepage.html>.

Trigg, Stephanie. *Congenial Souls: Reading Chaucer from Medieval to Postmodern*. Minneapolis: U of Minnesota P, 2002. Print.

Utley, Francis Lee. "Five Genres in the *Clerk's Tale*." *Chaucer Review* 6.3 (1971–72): 198–228. Print.

"Voices of the Powerless." *BBC Radio 4*. BBC, 1 Aug. 2002. Web. 19 Apr. 2013. <http://www.bbc.co.uk/radio4/history/voices/voices_revolt.shtml>.

Wallace, David. *Chaucer and the Early Writings of Boccaccio*. Woodbridge: Brewer, 1985. Print.

———. *Chaucerian Polity: Absolutist Lineages and Associational Forms in England and Italy*. Stanford: Stanford UP, 1997. Print.

Warren, Michelle R. "Introduction: Relating Philology, Practicing Humanism." *PMLA* 125.2 (2010): 283–88. Print.

———. "Post-philology." *Postcolonial Moves: Medieval through Modern*. Ingham and Warren 19–45.

Weir, Anthony, and James Jerman. *Images of Lust: Sexual Carvings in Medieval Churches*. London: Batsford, 1986. Print.

Whitson, Carolyn E. "The Not-So-Distant Mirror: Teaching Medieval Studies in the Working-Class Classroom." *Women's Studies Quarterly* 26 (1998): 42–55. Print.

Wimsatt, James. "One Relation of Rhyme to Reason." *The Verbal Icon: Studies in the Meaning of Poetry*. Ed. Wimsatt. Lexington: U of Kentucky P, 1954. 153–66. Print.

Windeatt, Barry A. "Postmodernism." *Chaucer: An Oxford Guide*. Ed. Steve Ellis. Oxford: Oxford UP, 2005. 400–15. Print.

Wogan-Browne, Jocelyn, et al. *Language and Culture in Medieval Britain: The French of England, c. 1100–c. 1500*. York: York Medieval, 2009. Print.

Wolfthal, Diane. *Images of Rape: The "Heroic" Tradition and Its Alternatives*. Cambridge: Cambridge UP, 1999. Print.

Wood, Chauncey. "The Sources of Chaucer's Summoner's 'Garleek, Onyons, and Eke Lekes.'" *Chaucer Review* 5.3 (1971): 240–44. Print.

The World of Chaucer: Medieval Books and Manuscripts. Comp. Julie Gardham. U of Glasgow Lib., n.d. 2 Sept. 2011. <http://special.lib.gla.ac.uk/exhibns/chaucer/index.html>.

Yeager, R. F., ed. *Chaucer and Gower: Difference, Mutuality, Exchange*. Victoria: U of Victoria, 1991. Print.

"Yēman." *Middle English Dictionary*. U of Michigan, 2001. Web. 4 Dec. 2013.

Young, J. R. "'Hybrid' Teaching Seeks to End the Divide between Traditional and On-line Instruction." *Chronicle of Higher Education* 22 Mar. 2002: A33. Print.

Zieman, Katherine. "The Auctor Speaks: Ricardian Poetics and the Framing of *The Canterbury Tales*." *Answerable Style: The Idea of the Literary in Medieval England*. Ed. Frank Grady and Andrew Galloway. Columbus: Ohio State UP, 2013. 75–94. Print.

Žižek, Slavoj, and John Milbank. *The Monstrosity of Christ: Paradox or Dialectic?* Ed. Creston Davis. Cambridge: MIT P, 2009. Print.

Zoolander. Dir. Ben Stiller. Paramount, 2001. Film.

INDEX

Modern Language Association of America
Approaches to Teaching World Literature
To purchase MLA publications, visit www.mla.org/bookstore.

Achebe's Things Fall Apart. Ed. Bernth Lindfors. 1991.
Arthurian Tradition. Ed. Maureen Fries and Jeanie Watson. 1992.
Atwood's The Handmaid's Tale *and Other Works.* Ed. Sharon R. Wilson, Thomas B. Friedman, and Shannon Hengen. 1996.
Austen's Emma. Ed. Marcia McClintock Folsom. 2004.
Austen's Pride and Prejudice. Ed. Marcia McClintock Folsom. 1993.
Balzac's Old Goriot. Ed. Michal Peled Ginsburg. 2000.
Baudelaire's Flowers of Evil. Ed. Laurence M. Porter. 2000.
Beckett's Waiting for Godot. Ed. June Schlueter and Enoch Brater. 1991.
Behn's Oroonoko. Ed. Cynthia Richards and Mary Ann O'Donnell. 2014.
Beowulf. Ed. Jess B. Bessinger, Jr., and Robert F. Yeager. 1984.
Blake's Songs of Innocence and of Experience. Ed. Robert F. Gleckner and Mark L. Greenberg. 1989.
Boccaccio's Decameron. Ed. James H. McGregor. 2000.
British Women Poets of the Romantic Period. Ed. Stephen C. Behrendt and Harriet Kramer Linkin. 1997.
Charlotte Brontë's Jane Eyre. Ed. Diane Long Hoeveler and Beth Lau. 1993.
Emily Brontë's Wuthering Heights. Ed. Sue Lonoff and Terri A. Hasseler. 2006.
Byron's Poetry. Ed. Frederick W. Shilstone. 1991.
Works of Italo Calvino. Ed. Franco Ricci. 2013.
Camus's The Plague. Ed. Steven G. Kellman. 1985.
Writings of Bartolomé de Las Casas. Ed. Santa Arias and Eyda M. Merediz. 2008.
Cather's My Ántonia. Ed. Susan J. Rosowski. 1989.
Cervantes' Don Quixote. Ed. Richard Bjornson. 1984.
Chaucer's Canterbury Tales. First edition Ed. Joseph Gibaldi. 1980.
Chaucer's Canterbury Tales. Second edition. Ed. Peter W. Travis and Frank Grady. 2014.
Chaucer's Troilus and Criseyde *and the Shorter Poems.* Ed. Tison Pugh and Angela Jane Weisl. 2006.
Chopin's The Awakening. Ed. Bernard Koloski. 1988.
Coetzee's Disgrace *and Other Works.* Ed. Laura Wright, Jane Poyner, and Elleke Boehmer. 2014.
Coleridge's Poetry and Prose. Ed. Richard E. Matlak. 1991.
Collodi's Pinocchio *and Its Adaptations.* Ed. Michael Sherberg. 2006.
Conrad's "Heart of Darkness" *and* "The Secret Sharer." Ed. Hunt Hawkins and Brian W. Shaffer. 2002.
Dante's Divine Comedy. Ed. Carole Slade. 1982.

Defoe's Robinson Crusoe. Ed. Maximillian E. Novak and Carl Fisher. 2005.
DeLillo's White Noise. Ed. Tim Engles and John N. Duvall. 2006.
Dickens's Bleak House. Ed. John O. Jordan and Gordon Bigelow. 2009.
Dickens's David Copperfield. Ed. Richard J. Dunn. 1984.
Dickinson's Poetry. Ed. Robin Riley Fast and Christine Mack Gordon. 1989.
Narrative of the Life of Frederick Douglass. Ed. James C. Hall. 1999.
Works of John Dryden. Ed. Jayne Lewis and Lisa Zunshine. 2013.
Duras's Ourika. Ed. Mary Ellen Birkett and Christopher Rivers. 2009.
Early Modern Spanish Drama. Ed. Laura R. Bass and Margaret R. Greer. 2006.
Eliot's Middlemarch. Ed. Kathleen Blake. 1990.
Eliot's Poetry and Plays. Ed. Jewel Spears Brooker. 1988.
Shorter Elizabethan Poetry. Ed. Patrick Cheney and Anne Lake Prescott. 2000.
Ellison's Invisible Man. Ed. Susan Resneck Parr and Pancho Savery. 1989.
English Renaissance Drama. Ed. Karen Bamford and Alexander Leggatt. 2002.
Works of Louise Erdrich. Ed. Gregg Sarris, Connie A. Jacobs, and
    James R. Giles. 2004.
Dramas of Euripides. Ed. Robin Mitchell-Boyask. 2002.
Faulkner's As I Lay Dying. Ed. Patrick O'Donnell and Lynda Zwinger. 2011.
Faulkner's The Sound and the Fury. Ed. Stephen Hahn and Arthur F. Kinney. 1996.
Fitzgerald's The Great Gatsby. Ed. Jackson R. Bryer and Nancy P. VanArsdale. 2009.
Flaubert's Madame Bovary. Ed. Laurence M. Porter and Eugene F. Gray. 1995.
García Márquez's One Hundred Years of Solitude. Ed. María Elena de Valdés and
    Mario J. Valdés. 1990.
Gilman's "The Yellow Wall-Paper" and Herland. Ed. Denise D. Knight and
    Cynthia J. Davis. 2003.
Goethe's Faust. Ed. Douglas J. McMillan. 1987.
Gothic Fiction: The British and American Traditions. Ed. Diane Long Hoeveler
    and Tamar Heller. 2003.
Poetry of John Gower. Ed. R. F. Yeager and Brian W. Gastle. 2011.
Grass's The Tin Drum. Ed. Monika Shafi. 2008.
H.D.'s Poetry and Prose. Ed. Annette Debo and Lara Vetter. 2011.
Hebrew Bible as Literature in Translation. Ed. Barry N. Olshen and
    Yael S. Feldman. 1989.
Homer's Iliad *and* Odyssey. Ed. Kostas Myrsiades. 1987.
Hurston's Their Eyes Were Watching God *and Other Works.* Ed. John Lowe. 2009.
Ibsen's A Doll House. Ed. Yvonne Shafer. 1985.
Henry James's Daisy Miller *and* The Turn of the Screw. Ed. Kimberly C. Reed and
    Peter G. Beidler. 2005.
Works of Samuel Johnson. Ed. David R. Anderson and Gwin J. Kolb. 1993.
Joyce's Ulysses. Ed. Kathleen McCormick and Erwin R. Steinberg. 1993.
Works of Sor Juana Inés de la Cruz. Ed. Emilie L. Bergmann and Stacey Schlau. 2007.
Kafka's Short Fiction. Ed. Richard T. Gray. 1995.

Keats's Poetry. Ed. Walter H. Evert and Jack W. Rhodes. 1991.
Kingston's The Woman Warrior. Ed. Shirley Geok-lin Lim. 1991.
Lafayette's The Princess of Clèves. Ed. Faith E. Beasley and
    Katharine Ann Jensen. 1998.
Works of D. H. Lawrence. Ed. M. Elizabeth Sargent and Garry Watson. 2001.
Lazarillo de Tormes *and the Picaresque Tradition*. Ed. Anne J. Cruz. 2009.
Lessing's The Golden Notebook. Ed. Carey Kaplan and Ellen Cronan Rose. 1989.
Works of Naguib Mahfouz. Ed. Waïl S. Hassan and Susan Muaddi Darraj. 2011.
Mann's Death in Venice *and Other Short Fiction*. Ed. Jeffrey B. Berlin. 1992.
Marguerite de Navarre's Heptameron. Ed. Colette H. Winn. 2007.
Works of Carmen Martín Gaite. Ed. Joan L. Brown. 2013.
Medieval English Drama. Ed. Richard K. Emmerson. 1990.
Melville's Moby-Dick. Ed. Martin Bickman. 1985.
Metaphysical Poets. Ed. Sidney Gottlieb. 1990.
Miller's Death of a Salesman. Ed. Matthew C. Roudané. 1995.
Milton's Paradise Lost. First edition. Ed. Galbraith M. Crump. 1986.
Milton's Paradise Lost. Second edition. Ed. Peter C. Herman. 2012.
Milton's Shorter Poetry and Prose. Ed. Peter C. Herman. 2007.
Molière's Tartuffe *and Other Plays*. Ed. James F. Gaines and
    Michael S. Koppisch. 1995.
Momaday's The Way to Rainy Mountain. Ed. Kenneth M. Roemer. 1988.
Montaigne's Essays. Ed. Patrick Henry. 1994.
Novels of Toni Morrison. Ed. Nellie Y. McKay and Kathryn Earle. 1997.
Murasaki Shikibu's The Tale of Genji. Ed. Edward Kamens. 1993.
Nabokov's Lolita. Ed. Zoran Kuzmanovich and Galya Diment. 2008.
Works of Ngũgĩ wa Thiong'o. Ed. Oliver Lovesey. 2012.
Works of Tim O'Brien. Ed. Alex Vernon and Catherine Calloway. 2010.
Works of Ovid and the Ovidian Tradition. Ed. Barbara Weiden Boyd and
    Cora Fox. 2010.
Petrarch's Canzoniere *and the Petrarchan Tradition*. Ed. Christopher Kleinhenz
    and Andrea Dini. 2014.
Poe's Prose and Poetry. Ed. Jeffrey Andrew Weinstock and Tony Magistrale. 2008.
Pope's Poetry. Ed. Wallace Jackson and R. Paul Yoder. 1993.
Proust's Fiction and Criticism. Ed. Elyane Dezon-Jones and
    Inge Crosman Wimmers. 2003.
Puig's Kiss of the Spider Woman. Ed. Daniel Balderston and Francine Masiello. 2007.
Pynchon's The Crying of Lot 49 *and Other Works*. Ed. Thomas H. Schaub. 2008.
Works of François Rabelais. Ed. Todd W. Reeser and Floyd Gray. 2011.
Novels of Samuel Richardson. Ed. Lisa Zunshine and Jocelyn Harris. 2006.
Rousseau's Confessions *and* Reveries of the Solitary Walker. Ed. John C. O'Neal
    and Ourida Mostefai. 2003.
Scott's Waverley Novels. Ed. Evan Gottlieb and Ian Duncan. 2009.

Shakespeare's Hamlet. Ed. Bernice W. Kliman. 2001.

Shakespeare's King Lear. Ed. Robert H. Ray. 1986.

Shakespeare's Othello. Ed. Peter Erickson and Maurice Hunt. 2005.

Shakespeare's Romeo and Juliet. Ed. Maurice Hunt. 2000.

Shakespeare's The Taming of the Shrew. Ed. Margaret Dupuis and
Grace Tiffany. 2013.

Shakespeare's The Tempest *and Other Late Romances*. Ed. Maurice Hunt. 1992.

Shelley's Frankenstein. Ed. Stephen C. Behrendt. 1990.

Shelley's Poetry. Ed. Spencer Hall. 1990.

Sir Gawain and the Green Knight. Ed. Miriam Youngerman Miller and
Jane Chance. 1986.

Song of Roland. Ed. William W. Kibler and Leslie Zarker Morgan. 2006.

Spenser's Faerie Queene. Ed. David Lee Miller and Alexander Dunlop. 1994.

Stendhal's The Red and the Black. Ed. Dean de la Motte and Stirling Haig. 1999.

Sterne's Tristram Shandy. Ed. Melvyn New. 1989.

Works of Robert Louis Stevenson. Ed. Caroline McCracken-Flesher. 2013.

The Story of the Stone (Dream of the Red Chamber). Ed. Andrew Schonebaum
and Tina Lu. 2012.

Stowe's Uncle Tom's Cabin. Ed. Elizabeth Ammons and Susan Belasco. 2000.

Swift's Gulliver's Travels. Ed. Edward J. Rielly. 1988.

Teresa of Ávila and the Spanish Mystics. Ed. Alison Weber. 2009.

Thoreau's Walden *and Other Works*. Ed. Richard J. Schneider. 1996.

Tolstoy's Anna Karenina. Ed. Liza Knapp and Amy Mandelker. 2003.

Vergil's Aeneid. Ed. William S. Anderson and Lorina N. Quartarone. 2002.

Voltaire's Candide. Ed. Renée Waldinger. 1987.

Whitman's Leaves of Grass. Ed. Donald D. Kummings. 1990.

Wiesel's Night. Ed. Alan Rosen. 2007.

Works of Oscar Wilde. Ed. Philip E. Smith II. 2008.

Woolf's Mrs. Dalloway. Ed. Eileen Barrett and Ruth O. Saxton. 2009.

Woolf's To the Lighthouse. Ed. Beth Rigel Daugherty and Mary Beth Pringle. 2001.

Wordsworth's Poetry. Ed. Spencer Hall, with Jonathan Ramsey. 1986.

Wright's Native Son. Ed. James A. Miller. 1997.